THE SILENT REAPING

THE SILENT REAPING

L. R. POWELL

ISBN: 979-8-88685-060-3 (Paperback)
ISBN: 979-8-88785-061-0 (Hardcover)

Library of Congress Control Number: 2026940011

Any references to historical events, real people, or real places are used fictitiously. Names, characters, and places are products of the author's imagination.

Book design by Allison Chernutan.
Edited by Patterson Hood.
Map design by Natalie Davis.

Printed in the United States of America.

First printing edition 2026.

emily@fracturedmirrorpublishing.com
Fractured Mirror Publishing
Knoxville, Tennessee

www.fracturedmirrorpublishing.com

For Kody,
who would take a blood spike to the
shoulder for all of his girls, without
hesitation, and be proud to wear the scar

The
Three Great Nations
N
W E
S
Vardos
Northern Lupos Pass
Thlena River
Lake Lupos
Central Valley
Sigova
Maraleon
The Lupos Mountains

edorra
The
rozen Plains
he Jade Mountains
Norden Lake
Balmorea
Far East River
Eastern Wastelands
Ravenhold
he Vast Plains
Fullbrim River

CONTENT ADVISORY

Please be aware that *The Silent Reaping* is an adult, romantic fantasy and is intended for readers age 18 and older. The following can be expected within the story:

Language
PTSD and panic attacks
Kidnapping
Violence and gore (descriptive battle scenes, light torture, violent attacks/fights)
Death
Explicit sex scenes
Magic involving blood

NEED A REFRESHER?

Scan the QR code for a recap of *The Violet Mage* before jumping into *The Silent Reaping*!

PRONUNCIATION GUIDE

Aegis — EE-jiss
Balmorea — Bal-more-ee-uh
Gaius — Guy-uss
Maraleon — Mahra-ley-OWN *(country name)*
Marelian — Mah-RELL-ee-un *(someone from Maraleon)*
Nedorra — Neh-door-uh
Pyotr — P-yoh-ter
Raygon — Ray-gahn
Vilicus — Vill-ih-cuss *(singular)*
Vilici — Vill-ee-chee *(plural)*

Chapter One

ARIA'S WORDS TAUNTED OPHELIA'S MIND:

"They're coming, Elia…The Reapers. They're a branch of the Acolytes of Vindicta, and they are coming…for you."

As soon as the last word fell from her lips, Aria went limp in Ophelia's arms, causing panic to stiffen her hold. Someone said something, but Ophelia missed it as she frantically scanned her sister's face.

"Ari?! Aria!"

Alphonse moved in, scooping Aria up in his arms and bounding out of the Hall. Ophelia scrambled to her feet and followed after him, her steps faltering at the amount of blood now staining her dress and coating her arms and hands.

"How did she get here? Who did she come with?" Alphonse barked.

"She came to the castle on horseback with a mage from the Temple. He said she came through Balmorea's mirror and would not accept medical care, insisting she needed to see you and Princess Ophelia immediately," Gaius explained, holding his robes up to keep pace with Alphonse.

"Did no one come through with her?" Ophelia asked. "Surely, the mages at the Temple could have seen through the mirror whether she was alone or not. What of her *husband*?"

Sigova had welcomed winter in the days since the end of the battle in the valley, but Ophelia did not feel the bite of its cold air as it seeped into the castle. Anger heated her blood and sent it racing through her veins as she watched Aria's hair sway limply in front of her with each of Alphonse's steps. Elliot's hand fell to the small of her back, and Ophelia released a shuddering breath. She met his gaze as they walked, rage furrowing his brow as well.

"We will find answers once she is well enough to tell us herself," Gaius insisted. "Our first priority is seeing to her injuries."

Injuries that shouldn't exist. Injuries that never should have occurred. Her family had left Aria in Balmorea's hands, one of Maraleon's most precious gifts, and *this* is how they saw to her care?

Aria's blood cooled on her skin, lighting the anger in Ophelia's veins anew. She clenched her hands into fists.

"How could they do this to her?" she whispered, her mind rejecting what reality presented at her feet.

Elliot's hand smoothed slow circles along her back. "One thing at a time, as Gaius said," he replied, his touch belying the fury she heard in his tone.

Gaius called for Lyla as the group charged through the door of his study. Lyla immediately flew through the curtain in the corner of the room, worry painted across her brow at

Gaius' tone. Her eyes widened when they fell on Aria, limp in Alphonse's arms.

"Wha—?"

"We need water to clean her wounds," Gaius commanded as Elliot and George cleared the exam table of the jars and bottles scattered across its surface, sending them crashing to the floor.

"Wounds?" Lyla gasped. She grabbed one of the water pails next to the hearth and set it over the fire to heat. Alphonse placed Aria on the exam table as Lyla muttered some words Ophelia didn't quite understand. The fire in the hearth roared. *Right. Fire and wind are Lyla's strongest abilities.*

Ophelia drew her attention back to her sister and rushed to stand next to her father.

"We need to lay her on her stomach," Gaius said, the wrinkles in his forehead deepening. "It appears the worst of her injuries are on her back."

Ophelia's jaw clenched at the whimper that escaped Aria's lips as Alphonse and Gaius rolled Aria onto her stomach. Aria's eyes began to flutter open, and a cry worked itself from her throat as consciousness saturated her senses.

"Shh, Aria. We're here," Ophelia said gently, kneeling before her sister's face. "Gaius will fix you right up, just like he did when I got hurt. Remember? The boar?" Aria nodded, tears running down her cheeks. Her eyes snapped shut, and she screeched as Gaius and Alphonse peeled her cloak off her back. Ophelia brushed away the tears from Aria's face, stroking her hair down the back of her head as Aria's cries morphed into sobs.

Lyla gasped as she brought the pail of water to Gaius' side, and Alphonse inhaled sharply through his nose before passing the blood-soaked cloak to George. Behind her, Nell muffled a cry of shock, and a muttered curse fell from Elliot's lips. It had Ophelia's eyes snapping up to Gaius and her father, bleak expressions hardening both of their brows. She stood up to gain a clearer view, and her heart seized in her chest.

The dress at Aria's back had been cut down the middle, splayed open to reveal the swollen stripes covering her back, weeping her blood. The flare of anger that overcame her at the sight of Aria's back sent her heart thrashing in her chest. This was cruel and barbaric. There's no way Aria did something that deserved such a punishment. *How did this happen?*

Her breaths grew ragged, and her body trembled with the effort of holding in her fury. The scent of amber hit her senses the moment before sturdy hands settled gently on her shoulders and squeezed—a small gesture of silent comfort.

Aria released another cry as the cool air of the study licked at her open wounds. Ophelia's head shot down to her sister, but Alphonse knelt in front of her before Ophelia had the chance.

His voice was low and soothing. He stroked her hair and uttered something to calm her, but Ophelia didn't hear it. Her singular focus was on the bloody lacerations spanning her sister's back.

George, Lyla, and Nell shuffled chaotically around the study, grabbing clean cloths and salves, as Gaius barked orders. Aria's cries grew stronger.

Her face crumpled. "Oh, Ari," Ophelia whispered, her eyes tracing over the swollen lines cutting across her sister's back. Six? Seven lashes? Ophelia couldn't be sure. Some crossed. Some were thicker than others. Some laid wide, exposing parts of her flesh that were never meant to feel the cold winter air or the warm rays of the sun. Rage had Ophelia's hands itching with the need to peel away what remained of the blood-soaked dress from her sister's back, to remove every trace of what her sister went through.

The coppery tang of blood hit her nose, and she froze, the images of mangled men scattered across a field of bloody mud flashed through her mind. Shouts of agony ringing in her ears causing her vision to narrow—

"Ophelia, the wine."

Her head jerked up to find Elliot handing her a goblet filled almost to the brim. Had he been trying to speak to her?

"Give her the wine."

Ophelia nodded sharply and took the goblet of Gaius's tonic-laced wine before kneeling next to her father. "Drink, Ari. It'll help with the pain."

Aria's breathing fell from her lips in uneven pants, but she nodded. Alphonse helped roll her onto her side as Ophelia slowly lifted the goblet to her mouth. Aria did not hesitate, taking deep gulps as soon as the wine spilled against her lips.

Ophelia looked up to see Lyla, Nell, George, and Elliot around the table preparing the linens to clean Aria's wounds. Gaius glanced at Aria as he mixed some sort of salve. "It's a good sign that she's awake," he said gently, Ophelia realizing he was speaking to reassure her.

She nodded. "I will help heal her."

"Your heart is not steady, child—"

"I will help heal her," Ophelia repeated firmly as Aria finished off the wine.

Gaius lowered his gaze to her. "Then you best begin calming your heart. I feel your soul churning in anger. You will not be able to visualize—"

"I can do it," she insisted, jumping to her feet. Her anger did churn. It threatened to burst from her chest and exact the retribution she desired for her sister, but it would not inhibit her. "I healed Mira's melted flesh as her pain permeated *my* body. I connected with the minds of thousands of men on a furious battlefield and *spoke* to them as Pyotr's memories surged through my mind. Yes, my anger *will* run wild in my veins, but it will *not* stop me from healing her." Ophelia's lip trembled as her nails dug into the side of the wooden table.

A pair of hands came to rest on her shoulders again. The warmth of his body at her back and the scent of amber drifting past her were a comfort to her frantic heart. Her grip on the table loosened.

"She will be all right," Elliot gently assured her. "We have her now. She is safe."

Safe.

She was supposed to be *safe* in Balmorea.

Elliot's hands slid up and down Ophelia's arms until her breathing slowed. She closed her eyes and leaned back against his chest, the thrashing of his heart telling her that he was fighting the rage within himself as well. Ophelia narrowed her focus to Elliot's soothing presence to still her flailing heart as Lyla cleaned Aria's wounds. Nell followed behind, gently patting her skin dry, as Gaius spread the salve over her injuries.

Ophelia glanced at her sister's face. Aria winced with each swipe and pat along her back, but she did not cry out. Her eyelids drooped as Alphonse's fingers moved in soothing strokes over her hair; the wine tonic was working.

Bless Gaius and his wine.

"Her wounds had begun healing. It seems traveling reopened them," Lyla noted, discarding the soiled linen.

"Her wounds aren't too deep either," Gaius said as he finished spreading the salve over Aria's lashes. He glanced up at Ophelia. "Not nearly as deep as your wound was. This should not take long."

"I will do it," Ophelia said.

"My child, now might not be the best time for practice—"

"Enough, Gaius," Ophelia snapped and raised her hands to hover above Aria's back. She inhaled deeply, feeling Elliot take his place behind her, as she closed her eyes and held the image of Aria's back firmly in her mind.

She pictured the swelling receding, the broken red flesh returning to a healthy pink. She imagined the flayed skin neatly, slowly, knitting back together, fusing into a sheet of smooth porcelain. Ophelia slowly spread her hands above Aria's back as purple mist floated down from her hands, heat pulsing from her palms to Aria's wounds. Ophelia opened her eyes, holding her hands steady as the last of the mist floated down to cover her sister's back. She released her breath and looked down as the last, and largest, of the lashes in the middle of Aria's back resealed. Her shoulders relaxed, and she sank back against Elliot.

"Well done, Elia," he whispered, pressing a kiss to her temple as he wrapped her in his arms.

Ophelia held her eyes on Aria as Gaius smoothed his hand over the thick pink scars lining her back.

"That was a marvel, my dear," Gaius breathed as he and Lyla leaned over Aria to examine her back. Gaius lifted his head and smiled. "You did it, and without uttering so much as one incantation."

Ophelia lifted her eyes from her sister. "You already knew I don't need to incant spells."

"Knowing without seeing is much different from knowing *and* seeing," Gaius replied as he gently prodded Aria's back with his fingers. "Some of your magic lingers in her skin. I expect it is still working, perhaps to heal the remaining scarred tissue."

Confusion scrunched Ophelia's brow. "So, the scars will heal, then? But I still have scars from when you healed me."

Gaius smirked. "Yes, but I am not a Vilicus. Did you visualize her as healed with scars?"

Ophelia shook her head. "Then there is no reason to believe these scars will linger."

Ophelia pursed her lips and cast a glance at her sister. She was asleep. Ophelia hoped Gaius' words were true. Aria didn't deserve these scars, and she should not have to live with the reminders of whatever had caused them.

Alphonse rose to his feet. "We should move her to her chambers."

"I suppose we will have to wait until she wakes to find out what happened," Ophelia said. A wave of angry heat washed down her spine.

"Could you read her heart, Ophelia?" Alphonse asked.

Unease simmered in Ophelia's stomach, and a cold sweat dotted the back of her neck. Her heart thrummed, and her lungs seemed to twist and tighten in her chest the more she considered the idea. Ophelia rolled her shoulders back and swallowed. "The mere thought of sifting through her thoughts without her permission feels...*wrong*. I feel it... even considering it turns my stomach sour."

Alphonse knit his brows together, and he nodded as he ran his hand over Aria's hair.

"Her ladies didn't come with her," Ophelia noted. "Lady Nell and I will help bathe and change her. I'll stay with her tonight, too. I don't want her to wake up alone."

"I'm sure Charlotte will want to come stay with her as well," Alphonse said. "I'll send word to Gregor then have dinner sent up to her chambers for when you are finished changing her." He scooped Aria in his arms again and strode towards the door. Ophelia moved to follow him, but Elliot took her hand and pulled her back.

"Are you all right?" he asked, his concern heavy in his eyes as if she had been the one flayed open on the exam table.

She nodded, worrying the inside of her lip with her teeth. "I didn't use too much magic to heal her. Actually, I think I used more to heal Mira in the valley."

He cupped her face with a hand, shaking his head. "That's not what I meant. I can see you're physically fine, but has your heart settled?" His thumb stroked over her cheek, and she sighed.

"I think so." She nodded. "For now, at least."

He pulled her to his chest, and she buried her nose into his neck, relaxing for the first time since Aria burst through the doors of the Great Hall. She had never felt anger so consuming, never knew she was even capable of harboring such fury. She had felt the magic within her pooling and whirling in response to it, ready to strike at her word. Elliot had been the one to pull her back, centering her, anchoring her.

"Thank you," she said, enclosing her arms around his waist. "I fear I almost lost myself."

"Nonsense," he replied, placing a kiss on the top of her head. "I will always find you."

Aria woke up as Alphonse set her down on her bed, groggy from the wine. Soon after, Charlotte arrived and froze at the sight of Aria covered in dried blood and grime. Her hand flew to her mouth to muffle a sob before she launched herself across the room to her sister's side.

The fear had left Aria's eyes, but the sadness held firm, seeming to stake its claim on the joy her gaze once held and binding her completely in its grief. She didn't speak a word the entire time Charlotte, Ophelia, and Nell cleaned her up and helped her into a clean shift. She didn't move to reassure them of her wellbeing. She made no small talk, made no mention of her life in Balmorea.

Ophelia didn't push her. Aria had been through enough without also having to endure an interrogation from her younger sister, but the unanswered questions never ceased their gnawing in her mind. Aria always chose her words carefully, weighing the importance of each one before she spoke. She would talk when she was ready. But the silence, the absence of the cheerful chime in her voice that sweetened the air of any room she occupied, settled on Ophelia's chest like a stone.

Ophelia was relieved to see Aria nibble on some bread as Charlotte brushed out her hair. She took a few spoonfuls of soup, too, before getting up and heading to bed.

"I'll stay with her tonight," Ophelia said to Charlotte as Nell tidied up their dinner dishes.

Charlotte frowned but nodded. "I'll inform Gregor and the king of her condition then come back in the morning."

Ophelia nodded, then Charlotte leaned down and pressed a kiss to Aria's temple, whispering something to her that Ophelia couldn't quite hear. Once she left, Ophelia climbed into the bed and opened her arms to her sister. Aria silently accepted the invitation and curled up against her. A few heartbeats passed, and Aria's breathing slowed, but Ophelia remained awake, watching over her sister for a few moments more until she, too, succumbed to the exhausting events of the evening and fell asleep.

Ophelia woke the next morning to the cool rays of winter sun peering in through Aria's curtains. Movement beyond her sister caught her eye, and she gently slid her arms from beneath Aria and sat up, finding Nell setting a tea kettle over the fire in the hearth. Ophelia yawned and laid back into the pillows, shifting her attention back to her sister just as Aria's eyes fluttered open. Sadness steeped in ocean blue sleepiness greeted her.

Ophelia gave her sister a moment to adjust to her surroundings, to realize she wasn't dreaming and the reality of all she had endured was, in fact, real. A sad smile tugged at Ophelia's lips, and she took Aria's hand. "Morning, Ari."

Aria took a deep breath and cleared her throat. "Morning," she whispered.

"How are you feeling?"

Aria sighed. "About as good as I can, given my circumstances." Confusion wrinkled her brow, and she shot up, rolling her shoulders and reaching for her back. "How did this—My back—it's, it's—"

Ophelia sat up. "It's healed, Ari. Just rest."

"But how…?" She trailed off, frowning as if working to recall what happened the previous day.

"Gaius and I healed you," Ophelia responded. "The real question is: Why did we need to heal you at all?" Ophelia stroked the back of her sister's hand with her thumb. "Ari, what happened?"

Aria released a shuddering breath, her eyes filling with tears. "I don't know where to begin. So much has happened in so little time."

Ophelia took both of her sister's hands into hers, holding her gaze. "It has, and it pains me that you bore all of this alone."

"I wasn't alone," Aria said.

"Of course," she replied. "Your ladies, I'm sure, have been vital for you, and—"

"And Marius," Aria cut in, her voice cracking with emotion.

"Marius?" Anger rose in Ophelia at the mention of the man who was meant to protect her sister, to love her.

Aria met Ophelia's eyes, tears trailing down her cheeks. "He is very dear to me."

"*Dear* to you?" Ophelia scoffed. "Look what he did to you!"

"He didn't do this—"

"He sure as shit didn't stop it!"

"Do not speak of what you do not know, Ophelia," Aria said coolly.

Ophelia trembled with anger. Balmorea had marred her

sister's body. Had it also marred her mind? Distorted how she viewed reality?

"Then help me understand. How could one who allows such awful things to happen to you be so dear to you?"

Aria closed her eyes and swallowed. "He's—It's." She gave a tired sigh. "There's so much to it. I don't know where to begin. One thing would seem so small and singular, unrelated to anything else, until more was uncovered, and I suddenly found myself the bearer of secrets no one lives to repeat."

"You knew too much," Ophelia said.

Aria wiped her cheeks. "I'm not sure if the king knows how much Marius and I uncovered. The whipping was…a different matter, but at this point, I'm not sure I can truly say it was unrelated to anything else."

Whipped.

Ophelia's jaw clenched. "*Why* were you whipped? Where was Marius?"

"Raygon wanted information," Aria said, frowning. "At least, that's what we think based on his ramblings. After he returned from Maraleon, he was furious. He said something about you being a Vilicus and accused me of withholding information to destabilize Balmorea."

Ophelia closed her eyes and squeezed her sister's hands. She knew it had been too good to be true. That Raygon's eagerness to make amends with his neighboring countries had been nothing more than embellishments and feigned enthusiasm used to throw off suspicion.

Guilt dug its claws into Ophelia's lungs. Raygon had chosen to lash out at Aria simply because she was connected to Ophelia, making excuses to harm her because it would result in the least amount of consequences for him. Aria was the first person to be stung by the change in Ophelia's status to Vilicus, and the thought sent her heart plummeting to her stomach. Who else would suffer because of her power and purpose?

"I'm so sorry, Ari." Ophelia paused, the unanswered question burning on her tongue. "But what of *Marius* in all of this?"

"He never abandoned me," she replied, her face crumbling with emotion. "We didn't know what the king was planning upon his return. It all happened so fast. When Marius tried to intervene, he—Raygon hurt him. I'm not quite sure what all he did, but we were separated, and when Marius was finally able to come to me…" Aria swallowed, "he was in better shape than me, but only just. He came to me as soon as he could, but the damage had already been done." She gestured toward her back.

Ophelia leaned her forehead to her sister's. "I'm so sorry, Ari."

They both released a sigh as Nell placed a tea tray on the bedside table. Aria snatched a slice of bread off of it, bit into it, and sighed again. "My mind and my heart ache, but there's so much I have to tell you. Ophelia, you really are in danger."

Ophelia frowned. "Not right now. You should rest."

"I can't just lay here and mourn what happened; I'll go mad! Those involved will not pause to allow me to rest, either." Aria dropped back into the pillows and took a deep breath as she nibbled on her morsel of bread.

An idea lifted Ophelia's brows. "Aria, would you share your memories with me?"

Aria knit her brows together. "That was what I intended to do."

"No, no. Will you *show* them to me? Would you allow me to read your heart?"

"Raygon spouted something about heart reading. It is one of your Vilicus abilities, yes?" Ophelia nodded. "What do I need to do?"

"Only remember. Whatever it is you want me to see, bring it to the forefront of your mind and I will see it," Ophelia explained.

Aria released a deep breath then nodded to indicate she was ready.

Ophelia raised her hand, pressed her palm to Aria's forehead, and was sent into the whirlwind of her sister's memories.

CHAPTER TWO

OPHELIA'S STOMACH DROPPED AS SHE FELL through the nothingness. She lost all sense of up and down, but it was quicker this time, less chaotic than she had come to be familiar with. She landed smoothly and was able to reorient herself more quickly than before.

She found herself in a fine cushioned seat at the head of a large dining hall. She peered out over the crowd of guests and spotted her own red hair sitting next to her father at a table to the right in front of a wall of sweeping stained glass windows. Her eyes drifted across the room, eyeing the scarlet and gold banners that hung along the sandstone walls. This was not the Great Hall in Maraleon. This was Aria's wedding.

Her lady, Collette, drew her attention, asking if she would like more wine or food. Aria was waving her off, assuring her that she was fine for the moment, when a light caress tickled the back of her right hand. Glancing away from the festivities, she found Marius's eyes on her, and her breath hitched.

"I find myself continually surprised by how different your voice sounds when you speak Leonese," Marius said with a smirk, the words pouring from his tongue in silky Balmorean. He brushed his fingers along hers, gently twining them together. Aria reciprocated, her skin warming under his touch, and she gave him a shy smile.

"Is that so, Your Serene—?"

"Marius," he cut in, his gentle urgency sending Aria's heart fluttering. "Just Marius, remember? And, yes. It is." His eyes met hers, the warm brown glowing into a shade of copper that made her melt.

She swallowed but didn't back down, and Ophelia was surprised by her sister's bravery. Aria had always been easily embarrassed and modest with her affection. "How so, Marius?"

A flash of desire darkened his eyes, and he paused for a moment, seeming to drink in the way his name sounded on her lips. "Your voice is airier, brighter," he finally said. "Balmorean suits your tongue well, but the sweetness in your tone when you speak Leonese…" He smirked, taking a sip from his goblet. "No sound has ever made my blood rush so."

Aria's heart flailed, and she released a nervous laugh. "A— Are you saying you prefer me to speak my native tongue instead of the language of you and your people?"

"They are your people now, too, but I'd only prefer it when we are alone. Perhaps it is greedy of me; I do not relish the thought of other men enjoying the sweet lilt of your voice as I do when you speak your native tongue." He leaned toward her. "I should like to keep that for myself."

Ophelia felt Aria's cheeks burn. Did Aria *truly* want her seeing this memory?

Aria's heart thrashed in her chest as Marius's words and all they suggested whipped over her. She was nervous and excited, caught between the modesty that had been engrained into her all her life and the thrill that kissing Marius promised.

An unfamiliar boldness overtook her, and she held his eyes. Her tongue flicked across her lips, and Marius's heated gaze tracked the movement. "Then I will be happy to oblige you whenever you desire such an indulgence, Marius," she said in smooth Leonese.

He met her reply with a wicked grin.

The memory faded as soon as his lips descended on hers then reformed into a library.

Aria sat in a lounge chair by a window, warm sunlight fanning through the glass, brightly illuminating the page she was reading. The stone hearth off to her left was alight with a small fire which warmed her toes.

Aria closed the novel in her lap and stood, winding her way through the aisles in search of the right shelf to replace her book and retrieve another. As she turned around another corner, her eyes landed on a small figure wearing the familiar brown robes of the Acolytes of Vindicta. She had learned of the small order of priests in her "princess lessons," as Ophelia called them, but had never been in such close proximity to one since arriving in Balmorea.

It was not uncommon for the presence of the Acolytes to be felt in the castle; Sowers, the priests of the higher rank of the Acolytes, frequented the castle, some being top advisors to the king. They were easy to spot, always scuttling behind the king and his retinue, the silver chain worn around their waist clinking in time with their steps.

But the priest before Aria wore no adornment. *He must be a Spade*, she thought, a priest of the lower rank, making his presence in the library all the more curious—Spades were not permitted to leave the Temple of Stone in Ravenhold proper.

The robes were unmistakable; the person standing before her was most assuredly a Spade, and if he was trying to disguise his identity by simply donning his hood, he would be sorely disappointed to find Aria knew otherwise.

Her eyes traveled over the figure on the opposite end of the aisle. He was short and not broad-shouldered. His hands were pale and delicate, *which would probably explain why he was sent to work in the king's library instead of temple duties like the other Spades*, Aria thought, *assuming he's* supposed *to be here.*

Presently, he was replacing books on the shelf, and he did not seem to notice her as she approached. As he reached up, the sleeve of his robes fell, revealing a leather vambrace on his forearm.

Aria's eyebrows rose in surprise. *A priest in battle armor?*

Before the thought weaved into completion in her mind, her eyes snagged on his wrist—on the imprint of a scythe in red ink that was peeking out from under his vambrace.

Tattoos and battle armor. What sort of priest *was* this?

Aria's eyes shifted to the shelf before the priest, wondering what literature would tempt him to risk a journey from the Temple of Stone. She began to scan the titles but was unable to read many of them. Most of the titles were in languages she had never studied before, held together by bindings so worn she feared they would crumble to dust under her scrutiny. But, of the titles she could read, it seemed most were academic works. She chanced a step towards the priest as her casual gaze slid from the shelves back to where he stood. "I did not think Spades were permitted to leave the Temple of Stone," she said.

The priest started, and whipped his head towards her, the hood of his robes slightly falling back.

Or rather, the hood of *her* robes.

It was an instant. Aria would have doubted it had she not seen for herself. A woman wore the priest's robes, but what shocked her more was the woman's appearance. Her skin was pale, almost gray, sunken in at her cheeks. Her eyes held no color; bottomless black irises glanced at her before snapping the hood back over her face.

"Oh, excuse me. I mistook you for a priest because of your robes. My apologies," Aria sputtered out.

The woman didn't address Aria's comment and swiftly turned on her heel, bolting toward the opposite end of the aisle with a grace Aria did not think a simple priest could possess. A breath later, she disappeared around the shelf.

Aria stood, curious, in the aisle as the scene faded, taking Ophelia to another memory.

When her surroundings reshaped, Ophelia found herself in what appeared to be Aria's bedchamber.

Aria was lying in the bed wearing a thin shift, and the warm, solid length of Marius's body was pressing against her. Ophelia immediately flushed as she oriented herself, realizing Marius was holding her sister in their bed as they conversed. Aria fiddled with the ties of his shirt, and Marius traced slow circles on her shoulders with his fingers. It was a peaceful and intimate moment—another memory Ophelia felt she was intruding on. As the unease simmered in Ophelia's stomach, Marius's fingers on Aria's shoulder stilled.

"One of my Shadows reported back to me just this morning about the person you encountered in the library the other day."

"Oh?" Aria sat up next to him. "And what did they find?"

His brow sank. "It's much more serious than I expected."

"How so?"

"My Shadow was killed this evening, mere hours after meeting with me."

Aria gasped. "Do we know by whom?"

The furrow in his brow deepened. "My father's men."

Aria's mouth dropped. "How can you be sure?"

"The paths my Shadows take often intersect. He was seen being hauled away by a man known to serve my father in Ravenhold's underbelly, and his body was placed somewhere it was sure to be found—a reminder and a warning to those who ask too many questions too close to the Crown."

Raygon was known even throughout the Three Great Nations for his lack of tolerance and cruel methods, but killing a man for asking questions? "Surely your father would not need to kill someone who knows about women parading around the palace disguised as priests."

Marius scrubbed his face with his hand. "They aren't just any women. They are called Reapers. They are the highest ranked members of the Acolytes of Vindicta, and they report directly to my father."

Aria's brow wrinkled. "I still don't understand why knowing this warrants a death sentence."

"Because no one knows about them. They are another of the *many* secrets my father keeps from me." Bitterness edged into his voice, the reminder that his father didn't trust him with decisions or information of state affairs regarding Balmorea's well-being still a fresh wound, though inflicted years ago.

"Why would he keep them secret? Is it so shameful to have women serve in the priesthood?"

"It's not that. Well…for the most part," Marius replied. "It is because they are assassins."

The air left Aria's lungs.

"Assassins," she repeated. "What was an assassin doing in the library?" Her heart stuttered at the memory of the Reaper's vambrace coming into view when she replaced the book on the shelf. *What else must be concealed under those robes?*

And she walked *right* up and tried to start a friendly conversation with—with an *assassin*. Aria paled at the thought.

"I don't know. Did you check to see which books the Reaper returned?"

Aria smirked. "I might have." She scooted off the bed and padded to a chest across the room, returning with three books in her arms. "All three are on magic, I think," she said, plopping back on the bed at Marius's side. "I didn't know the Acolytes used magic."

Marius squinted as he flipped through the first book. "They don't."

Aria's eyebrows rose, and she propped herself up on an elbow to face him. "Perhaps it is for study, then. They worship Pyotr, so perhaps they study how his magic helps to make the land flourish? To be honest, I could not understand much of what the text said."

Marius hummed. "It is written in an archaic dialect of Balmorean. Our language and writing have evolved since this time, but many of the texts I had to read as a boy were written as such."

Aria watched as his eyes skimmed across the lines of the page, noting every twitch of concentration—how he raised a single eyebrow as he read, how he nibbled the inside of his lip when considering something. A smirk tilted the side of his mouth as his eyes slowly rose from the page to meet her stare.

"See something you like?" he asked playfully, and her cheeks heated.

She sank her teeth into her bottom lip to hold in a nervous laugh, and Marius's eyes tracked the movement, his pupils dilating as they narrowed in on her lips.

"Maybe," she replied coyly before nodding to the book. "What does it say?"

He chuckled and sat up straight, turning the book to show her the different runes and their interpretations. "Putting the runes together in different patterns is what creates spells. This is Pathgar's philosophy." His brow furrowed. "I didn't realize we even had tomes of Pathgar's in Ravenhold."

Aria raised her eyes from the book. "Were they all lost?"

"Burned, from what my teachers told me. Pathgar's philosophy deals in Blood Magic, and Blood Magic was outlawed by the Order of Mages centuries ago." Marius's brow sank further. "All three of these are about Blood Magic."

Word of Blood Magic had never been uttered in Maraleon. Ophelia's confusion and curiosity matched that of her sister's, and as if Aria knew Ophelia was present in her memory, she asked the question that sat on Ophelia's tongue. "Why was Blood Magic outlawed?"

Marius sat back and opened his arm invitingly, and Aria eagerly obliged by sliding into his embrace. "Admittedly, since it is outlawed and its teachings forbidden, I don't know all that much." His fingers began their methodical circles on Aria's shoulder as he spoke. "Blood Magic functions by deriving power from the lifeforce held in one's blood. Animal blood can be useful, but it's short-lived. It is human blood that holds the most power."

Aria's eyebrows rose. "Drawing power from another's lifeforce."

"Exactly. It awards the caster immense power, but at great cost. Many lives were lost to the casting of magic through Pathgar's philosophy, both casters and their conduits alike." His brow drew together, his fingers pausing from their circles on her shoulder. "The prolonged use and exposure to Blood Magic could also explain the appearance of the Reaper in the library. You said her skin was pale, almost gray?" Aria nodded. "It's a...a *dirty* kind of magic, giving great power but distorting and twisting all that it touches. There are many reasons it was outlawed."

A flash of panic sliced through Aria's chest. "We should not have these books in our chambers." She shot up and began collecting them, shuffling across the room to return them to her chest as if the king's men would bust down their door any moment to label them as traitors.

Marius chuckled. "We will be fine. Return them discreetly tomorrow, and that should be the end of it."

The easy smile on his face as he lazed in their bed eased

her anxiety. She returned to the bed slowly, letting her eyes rove over and admire him until another thought sprung forth in her mind. "Are we in danger for knowing this now? About the Reapers and their...unique subjects of study? Your Shadow lost his life gaining this knowledge."

Marius shook his head as Aria climbed back into his arms. "I don't believe so. They are called my Shadows for a reason. Any investigation my father has launched to look into my people has always led him to their faceless leader. A man, whose identity remains unknown, referred to as *The Wraith*." Marius tossed her a smirk before sighing and leaning his head against the backboard. "The mystery behind the Reapers deepens though. Along with their, as you said, *unique* subjects of study, and their particular duties and loyalty to my father, the rank of Reaper is only bestowed upon women. There are no men ranked Reaper."

Aria frowned. This didn't make sense. In almost every aspect of life in Balmorea, from the vendors on the streets to the servants in the castle, women are not held in high esteem. Deemed weaker in mind and body, as Mira is portrayed against Pyotr in the Balmorean lore Aria had read, women are appointed to no prominent positions anywhere in society and have almost no impact on the world they live in. Wives of the nobility hold no more weight in societal affairs than the favor they curry with their husbands, should they hold any favor with them at all. It is even frowned upon to see women running their own booths in the market without a husband, father, or some other male family member in her company. Raygon elevating a group of skilled women to the highest rank given to the Acolytes of Vindicta sat in stark contrast to the beliefs perpetuated throughout his kingdom.

The only thing about it that made sense to Aria was that he kept them secret—because what *shame* it would bring the throne of Balmorea if the nation knew its covert affairs were handled entirely by *women*. Aria scoffed at the thought.

"I suppose it makes sense why they would wear their hoods, then, when no other priests do. But surely, they don't believe their identities are so easily hidden."

Marius shrugged. "If they dabble in Blood Magic, they could have any number of abilities at their disposal. Veiling their appearance with magic among them."

"For all except the one in the library, that is." Aria smirked. "She had no disguise over her appearance, *and* I snuck up on her. Hardly the skill and senses one would expect from a member of the highly trained, deadly assassins of the king."

"Perhaps she was having an off day."

"Or she has not yet mastered Blood Magic, which would explain why she was borrowing the books," Aria replied then sighed, leaning her head against Marius's chest and wrapping her arms around his waist. The steady cadence of his heart bestowed a comfort over her she'd never known she needed before him, but her brow still knit together as she considered their conversation. Tilting her head back to look into his face, she said, "It seems out of character for your father to employ women in such a fashion, though."

"I don't disagree with you," Marius replied with a shrug. "I suppose my father believes no one would ever suspect a lowly woman of the treacherous deeds he has them commit." An impish smirk slid across his face. "What woman would be able to out-match a man?"

His smile sent a flush to Aria's cheeks and pulled a giggle from her belly. "Well, they certainly outwitted you. You didn't even notice them around the castle before I mentioned anything."

"You've got me there, *gien veela,*" he said with an amused chuckle.

Gien veela. My light.

The endearment sent warmth blooming through her chest.

"I must say, though," he went on, "I have been most pleasantly distracted as of late, and can hardly be blamed for such shortcomings."

"Oh, my. Neglecting your duties already, Your Serene Highness? We've been married less than a month, and already, I fear the country will fall into ruin before we know it," Aria replied.

He smiled, sparing a glance to her lips before smoothing a hand over her hip. "The whole of our world could burn, and I would not raise a care or concern if you were content in my arms."

The blooming warmth in her chest burst. A grin tugged the sides of her mouth as her hand smoothed over his chest. "Well, that doesn't bode well for the rest of the country because I find myself most content."

"Then my duties will continue to find themselves neglected."

Another giggle fluttered from her lips as he leaned in and kissed her, and Ophelia was sent from the memory.

CHAPTER THREE

THE WHIRLWIND SENT OPHELIA INTO ARIA'S NEXT memory, alone in what must be her and Marius's bedchamber. Aria was sitting on the edge of the bed, and bright light poured through the window. Aria's heart pounded in her ears, her stomach bubbling with nerves. A moment later, Marius appeared in the doorway, and Aria shot to her feet, stomach flipping. A smile tugged at his lips as he shut the door.

"Have you been waiting for me?" he asked, striding towards her, dropping a kiss to her cheek. "I received word that my father will be returning this afternoon around lunch. Hopefully, he'll be bearing good news despite the precarious situation he created."

Precarious, indeed. Marius had cursed when his father's council and the commander of Balmorea's forces returned without the king, explaining Raygon was being held in Sigova for launching an unwarranted attack against two ally nations—acts that added to the number of casualties already incurred in Pyotr's attack on the valley's military defensive. Marius had immediately begun working with the council on drafting a proposal to negotiate his father's release.

Then, there was the matter of Ophelia's involvement in the situation. The Violet Mage is what the commander said the men had started calling her. She had stopped Pyotr and ended the battle between the three nations in the same night. The last the commander had heard before being forced from Maraleon, Ophelia had not recovered from the battle and remained unconscious. That was three days ago.

"They must have come to a resolution," Aria said.

"It appears so," he replied, taking off his jacket and draping it over the back of a chair.

Silence hung between them, and Aria shuffled uncomfortably on her feet, wanting to speak but unable to find the words to say. Marius narrowed his eyes and walked towards her, sliding his hands around her waist.

"Is everything all right, *gien veela?*"

She nodded again. "Wonderful, actually." A phrase, no doubt, contradictory to the expression painted across her face.

He cocked his head to the side, and she took his hands, guiding him to sit next to her on the bed. Aria took a deep breath, her mind skipping from thought to thought like a pebble across the surface of a lake, but all of her thoughts centered in one place, and it made Ophelia's heart clench.

"It's been a little over a month since we've married," Aria started. Marius smiled and squeezed her hands. "And, well, you see…" She swallowed. "I've been growing ill the past few mornings."

Marius's brows knit together. "Do you need me to send for Master Cliva, then?"

Aria shook her head. "No, no. Well, maybe. It's just—I—I've…"

He raised his hand to cup her cheek. "Aria," he said softly. "What's wrong?"

Her gaze clung to his, and she swallowed again. "I—I've not had my courses."

The pinch in his eyebrows did not relax. "Then you *are* unwell. Has your time in Balmorea been so distressing as to suppress your courses? Is it your sister? I know you are concerned about her after the news from the valley. Or do you suspect someone is poisoning your food perhaps?" He gave a sharp shake of his head. "No, our hounds are too highly trained, and all your food is tasted before it is brought before you."

Aria huffed out a laugh, her lips bending into a small smile. "Marius, do you truly not understand what this means?"

He paused and met her gaze, confusion etched on his brow.

"Marius, I…I think I'm with child."

She held her breath. There was no reason for her to think he would be displeased or angry. Uncertainty pounded through her veins, regardless. She wasn't sure she was ready to be a mother. She knew so little of caring for a baby, of raising a child—an *heir*.

Her life in Balmorea with Marius, and the love that had grown between them was still so new. In many ways, they still knew each other so little. Would the addition of a child into their lives uproot the budding happiness they'd eked out for themselves? Earth and Sea—what if Marius didn't want a child so soon?

Marius's face softened and a weight lifted from her chest. "Pregnant?" he repeated, eyebrows arching.

She nodded. "I think it's still rather early yet. It has been a little over a week since I should have bled, and I only started to feel ill a few days ago."

He framed her face in both of his palms, his smile so broad she feared it might split his cheeks. "We're...we're going to have a baby?"

She met his smile with her own and nodded. "I think so."

He let out a sharp exhale as he stroked his thumbs across her cheeks. "This is *wonderful*, Aria."

Every fear in her heart shattered to pieces.

Wonderful. She repeated to herself. *He's happy. He's happy we're having a baby.*

She placed her hands over his, and excited laughter took the place of words they couldn't find to express the joy flooding their hearts. Marius leaned in and met her lips with his. He kissed her gently, sweetly, every movement of his lips a gift of thanks, an act of reverence.

He pulled away, placing his forehead to hers. "We can place a bassinette right here next to your side of the bed, near the window. But wait..." He stood up and began to pace, eyes bright with wonder. "When will the baby be born? Late summer? Fall? The window might be too cold. We will have to have blankets made."

Aria laughed and stood, striding towards him and wrapping her arms around his waist, laying her head against his chest. He wrapped her in his arms and pressed his lips to the top of her head.

"Thank you," he whispered.

Aria pulled her head back to look into his face. "Is it not

a wife's highest honor to bear children for her husband?" she asked with a playful smile.

His expression softened. "No. It is a husband's blessing to be given a wife. And that is what you are to me, *gien veela;* my light, my blessing." He slid a hand from her back, pressing his palm to her stomach. "But it is *a husband's* honor to be gifted a child by his wife." His smile widened. "I did not know it was possible for one to feel such happiness."

Aria didn't either.

Her eyes welled with tears, and her voice cracked with emotion. "I'm happy, too." She pushed up on her toes and met his lips with hers as the memory faded.

Ophelia stood before Raygon in Aria's memory. Marius stood next to her sister, tightly clutching her hand as the king paced behind his desk in a room that appeared to be the king's study. His assistant and priest stood behind them in the shadows.

"You knew what she was," Raygon said gravely, holding his gaze to the ground as he paced, "before I let you into my home. You knew she was a mage, and you said *nothing.*" Raygon's head whipped to Aria.

Aria swallowed. "You mean my sister, Your Majesty?"

"Don't play dense! Of course, your sister!" Raygon bellowed. Marius tugged her closer. "She fancies herself the *Vilicus of Mankind.* One on equal grounds with Pyotr." He scoffed.

Aria's brows drew together. "I have not heard her called *Vilicus* before. We only just learned Ophelia had magic before I came to Balmorea."

"Ah, then allow me to explain," Raygon cut in with derision. "Apparently mankind has a Vilicus, a steward of its own, just as the land and sea have. And your dear sister is mankind's steward."

A scoff echoed from the shadows behind them.

Aria glanced at Marius then returned her gaze to Raygon, confusion painted across her face. "I don't understand. The prophecy only stated she was meant to stop Pyotr—"

"You knew of the prophecy as well, then?! So much Alphonse has kept secret from the rest of the world."

"We didn't know of the prophecy until recently, either. I can assure you: you are not the only one my father has kept secrets from."

Raygon leaned over his desk, narrowing his eyes. "Of course."

"And even if that weren't the case," Marius cut in, "why would her sister's propensity to use magic be something of such great importance to Balmorea?"

Anger flashed in Raygon's black eyes as they cut to Marius. "Because of the nature of her magic." Raygon straightened then returned to his pacing. "You knew she had great magic but did not warn me before I left."

Marius stepped in front of Aria. "What was there to warn you of? Maraleon didn't contact us as an enemy but to form an alliance, one that had already been established through my marriage to the crown princess. There was no reason to believe King Alphonse sought any ill will with Balmorea. Do you truly think he is trying to destabilize our court?"

"No," Raygon said coolly. "But his youngest daughter might be."

"This is madness," Marius seethed. "Why would she want such a thing?"

Raygon rounded his desk, his eyes transfixed on Aria. "What does she know? When she speaks of restoring balance to the Earth, what does she mean?"

Aria's eyes darted between Marius and Raygon. "Balance? I—I don't know. She only ever mentioned being chosen to stop Pyotr. I've never heard her refer to herself as a Vilicus or heard her talk of restoring balance to anything."

Raygon's eyes bored into her as though trying to measure the fabric of her soul before saying, "Protecting her will not serve you."

"You threaten my wife?!" Marius shouted before the back of Raygon's hand cracked against his temple, sending him stumbling to the side. Raygon gripped Aria's arm, and terror lanced through her bones.

"You're lying."

"I'm not! I swear to you!" Aria cried as Marius shoved himself back between them.

"What is this, Father? What happened after the battle that distorts your thoughts so?"

"Distorts my thoughts?" Raygon cocked his head at his son, releasing Aria's arm. "You were not there, Marius. You did not see the feat the princess performed on the battlefield, nor the display of her power later when the three kings reconvened! She claims to have *shared* the thoughts and feelings of Pyotr with us, but none were true!"

A grunt of agreement came from the shadows.

"She must have manipulated the Steward of the Land, seemingly to stop the fighting, but I suspect there is more she hasn't revealed. With power like hers and with the influence of the Vilici, one can only wonder at her intentions when she speaks of 'restoring balance.'" His eyes narrowed back on Aria. "But since someone already knew much more than she led us to believe, I have a feeling we will get our answers soon enough."

Aria's eyes grew wide as she clutched Marius's arm. "I have told you all I know, Your Majesty. My sister only intended to save mankind. She had no other motivation. To be honest, had Ophelia been able, she would have forfeited this responsibility in favor of a nice day's ride in the wood or a hunting expedition. She has no desire to…to do whatever it is you think she schemes to do!"

Anger flared Raygon's nostrils, but Marius pushed a hand against his father's chest. "That is *enough*, Father. You have had a trying few days, and you need rest. You are not thinking clearly."

Raygon slapped away Marius's hand and glared into his eyes. "My mind is clear as glass." Glancing to the shadows Raygon nodded then began walking towards a door at the back of his study.

Two hands grasped Aria's arms and dragged her toward the door after Raygon.

"Don't fucking touch her!" Marius's fist swung, finding its mark against the cheek of the king's assistant. The man fell to the ground, and Aria jerked herself free of the priest, flying into Marius's arms. "You go too far!"

Raygon was suddenly before them, Marius's wrists clutched in his hand, and raised above his head. "Now, now, Marius. No need for violence," Raygon tsked as two small, hooded figures appeared and re-claimed Aria's arms, pulling her away. "I'm only going to ask her a few questions—"

"You son of a bitch!" Marius shouted as his knee plunged into his father's stomach. Raygon doubled over with a grunt, releasing his son's hands. Marius darted after Aria, but Raygon clutched the hair at the back of his son's head and jerked him back, placing a knife to his throat. Marius inhaled sharply. "You wouldn't. I'm your only heir."

Raygon chuckled and nodded to Aria. "I need not worry about an heir now that your wife is with child."

Marius and Aria froze, and Raygon's brows rose in feigned surprise. "Oh, no! Was I not supposed to know yet?" His expression dropped. "I suggest you rethink your course of action, my son, if you wish to see the birth of your child."

"Stop, Marius!" Aria whimpered. She had never felt more pathetic, more useless, than at that moment. "Don't—I will be all right."

"See, there?" Raygon crooned. "No need to fuss."

"Why are you taking her below?" Marius spat as Raygon lowered the knife, tossing free his son's scalp. "It is no place for a princess, especially not my *wife* who is with child!"

The two hooded figures continued to draw Aria into the doorway, their grips firm but their hands small. Looking down, Aria caught the edge of a scythe tattoo peeking from the wrist of one of the hooded figures. Panic flooded her chest.

Reapers.

Her face crumpled as she looked back towards Marius. He stepped towards her as if to follow when the king's assistant moved behind him, bringing the butt of a dagger to the back of his head. Aria screamed as Marius fell to the floor, and the memory faded.

When her surroundings cleared, Ophelia saw Aria standing in the middle of a cell, her arms stretched above her, chained to the ceiling. Aria frantically looked around to gain her bearings. It was almost completely dark in the cell, save for a bit of light that peeked through a small, barred window near the top of the wall. It was cold and damp, and Aria could only make out Raygon and the two hooded figures from before. One stood beside Raygon while the other grabbed a long cord of some kind and stepped behind her. Aria's eyes darted across the cell a second time—Marius wasn't there. She swallowed the dread that clogged her throat. "Where is Marius?"

"Indisposed at this time," Raygon replied.

Aria's jaw tightened. "Is he all ri—"

"You needn't worry about the crown prince," he interjected, annoyance lacing his tone.

The crown prince. Not *my son* or *your husband* or even *Marius.* Aria knew that Marius and his father were not close, but she had not expected him to speak of him so coldly.

She shuffled on her feet, the chains constraining her movements and the shackles digging painfully into her skin. "Is this entirely necessary, Your Majesty?"

"I'm afraid so," Raygon sighed regretfully, and she grimaced at his false remorse. "I tried speaking with you plainly, but you would not be forthcoming with me—"

"Because I do not have the knowledge that you seek—!"

A bright flash of pain blinded her as a fist connected with her temple. She stumbled to the side, the only thing keeping her from hitting the ground being the chains anchoring her in place. Her head throbbed as pain reverberated through her skull. She blinked, willing her eyes to refocus.

Raygon stood stone-faced, hands clasped in front of him as one of the hooded figures returned to his side. "You may be my son's wife, but that does not give you the authority to speak to me in such a manner." He stepped towards her, leaning forward, his foul breath puffing into her face. "You will do well to remember that."

Aria huffed in frustration, pain still blurring her vision. "Yes, Your Majesty."

"Good. Now then," he said, straightening. "Let's not make this harder than it needs to be and start with something simple, shall we?" Raygon spun on his heel and meandered across the cell.

Aria braced herself. She was a Balmorean princess now, loyal to the throne of Balmorea, to her husband and to his father, but she was determined not to endanger the lives of her family simply because this man felt he had been tricked. She took a deep breath when Raygon asked, "What elements does your sister wield?"

"Why do you want to know about Ophelia?"

Raygon paused where he stood. A moment later, the crack of a whip split the air, and fiery pain lit across Aria's back. A hiss tore from her lips.

Raygon peered over his shoulder. "What elements does your sister wield?"

"Perhaps if you explain the reasoning behind your questions I can—"

Another crack and a burst of pain. She grunted at the discomfort; the layers of her dress dampened the whips strikes but did not block them entirely.

Raygon nodded to the hooded figure next to him, and the figure stepped behind her, ripping the fabric at the back of her dress. A rush of cold air hit her exposed back.

Raygon placed a finger under her chin and lifted her eyes to his. "I only need your information, dear. No clarification is needed."

"You're going to hurt her." Aria's lip quivered despite herself.

"I will defend what is mine, Aria," he said, dropping her chin and stepping backward. "If your sister threatens that, I will do what I must." He nodded again, and the whip met her bare back like a tongue of fire. It flared then pulsed into a smoldering burn that never receded. Her scream seemed to shake the bars of her cell, morphing into heaving cries. "Answer my question, Aria: What elements does your sister wield?"

Aria ground her jaw against the pain at her back, slowing her breathing to compose herself. "I don't know."

Crack.

Aria's scream rasped her throat, tears welling in her eyes in its wake.

What does he want? Why does he want to know about Ophelia? The questions swirled in her mind, solidifying her resolution: she had to protect her sister—

The memory of Marius's hand sliding to her stomach, his eyes flashing with awe and happiness played before her eyes, and her resolve crumbled.

Sadness, bitterness, and regret completely overshadowed the happiness that burst from her soul only hours before. Aria squeezed her eyes shut and inhaled a shaky breath. "I've only ever seen her use wind."

CHAPTER FOUR

OPHELIA AWOKE TO A CRACK AND THE FIERY burn of slicing skin clawing across her back. She cried out in hopeless agony, still in the cell, still in Aria's memory.

Five days. How much longer will he keep me here? The thought echoed in Aria's mind.

Oh, Ari. Ophelia's heart lurched. *Five days of this?*

"You said she only need look at an object, and it does as she commands," Raygon said, slowly drifting through the rays of the afternoon sunlight that peeked through the barred window. "Is that correct?"

The whip cracked again when she didn't answer, and a scream launched from her throat. "Yes," she sobbed. *As I told you before* was left unsaid, but it rose to her tongue, itching to be uttered. Three days ago, she might have dared the quip.

But not today.

Not with the endless pain searing her back, distorting time and words. She couldn't waste her energy on another scream or sob or the heaving it would take to regain a sliver of composure. She had to remain guarded to ensure she didn't say anything that would further endanger Ophelia… and she needed to take as much information from this cell with her as she could. For that, she needed her wits about her, and another lash might steal what little she had left.

"And you say her power's strength is with wind, correct?" Raygon asked, brows furrowed as he paced calmly in front of her, hands clasped behind his back.

The chains that suspended her wrists dug into her skin. The hard stone of the cell scraped at the knuckles of her bloodied toes. A breeze from the window nipped at the open wounds at her back, and she gasped in a gulp of air that morphed into a series of hopeless whimpers. "I only ever saw her use wind at the castle. I don't know if she uses other elements," she said, her shoulders straining to support her body as she heaved for air, her body's strength failing to support her.

Aria's mind clung to the memory of Ophelia playing in the wind, to any ounce of happiness it could find as Raygon began to rattle off his dizzying slew of thoughts and conclusions. Aria remembered watching Ophelia through her bedchamber window as she stood among a whirlwind of leaves in the castle courtyard, welcoming the escape from the reality she had lived in this cell. She closed her eyes and could almost feel the warm cup of tea in her hand as her forehead pressed against the cool glass of her window. The soft furs under her feet warmed her toes as a wide smile spread across her cheeks. What a wonder it had been to see her sister wielding magic.

Another crack tore open the empty space of her cell. Another scream shot into the air.

"Don't make me continue to repeat myself," Raygon said sharply as he continued his methodic pacing across her cell. "My patience grows thin, as does your usefulness."

Dread flooded Aria's chest. *I'm going to die here.*

She swallowed back her anguish at the thought. "Apologies, Your Majesty. Please ask me again. I missed your question."

I'm going to die here.

He's going to let me die.

He's going to kill me.

Tears spilled from her eyes, burning the cut on her cheek.

He leaned down and peered into her eyes. Annoyance painted his brow. "If wind is her affinity, how does she read another person's thoughts and memories? Unless I am mistaken, wind cannot do such things."

Aria's brows scrunched together. "I was unaware she had this ability. Sh—she never spoke to me about it. I only know of her energy manipulation."

"Then it is more likely she cannot do such things and was simply lying," a female voice commented from the shadows beyond her cell. Aria's ears perked up, though her expression remained solemn—this was the first time either of the Reapers had spoken. Either a misstep on their part, or they did not see it as a matter of consequence that Aria knew the person standing next to Raygon was a woman.

Raygon gave an exasperated exhale and stood. "A conclusion I would agree with had I not encountered this power myself." Raygon stalked toward the voice and crossed his arms. "I felt no wind when she placed her palm to my forehead."

"And wind does not penetrate that which is not in the physical plane. Wind cannot touch one's mind," the woman replied.

"Bringing us back to this ability to visualize." Raygon turned to face Aria. "She just *thinks*, and what she pictures *happens*?"

Aria nodded, her head sinking into a weak bob.

Another crack, another slice of pain, another scream followed by a rattle of chains.

Raygon clutched the hair at the top of Aria's head and yanked it back, forcing her to meet his gaze. "You will *speak* when your king asks you a question."

Aria's vision dotted with flashes of light. She squeezed her eyes shut. "Yes, Your Majesty," she whimpered.

"What spells does she incant? Whose philosophy does she follow?"

Aria shook her head. "I've never heard her say any spells or charms. She just pictures what she wants, and it happens."

Raygon scoffed as he released her hair.

"The possibilities of what she could do are endless if this is the case," another woman's voice said from behind her.

Aria scoffed internally. Apparently, Raygon preferred to let the women dirty their hands for him.

"We also can't confirm what she does or does not know of the Aegis," the woman near Raygon said. "Every day, it weakens."

There it was again. That word.

Aegis.

Yesterday's lashings had been dedicated to determining what Ophelia knew of the mysterious *Aegis*, though Aria never learned what it was or why it was of such great importance to the king.

Aria hung her head and sank against the chains. Her shoulders burned for relief, but she pushed back the pain as best she could, steeling her senses to listen—something Raygon evidently did not expect her to do, given how freely his tongue flew in his dungeon.

Aria tried to ignore the dread pooling in her stomach with each new revelation Raygon carelessly dropped; there was no way Raygon planned to release her after revealing, what she surmised were, some of his closest kept secrets. If she let her mind linger too long on such thoughts, though, the despair would consume her.

"In the past year," the woman continued, drawing Aria's attention back to the conversation between the Reaper and the king, "more and more sacrifices have become necessary to sustain it." The assassin's brown robes whispered across the dirty cell floor as she stepped into the dim light, her hood up to hide her ashen face and black irises.

Raygon nodded. "This can go no further. We can't risk it. Send word to Trella. She is to act immediately." Raygon stepped out of the cell followed by the Reaper with the whip. The metal bars clanged loudly as the door slammed shut and the light of a warding spell flashed. "No traces of Balmorea are to be left on her death."

Aria sucked in a quiet gasp, and her head flew up as she watched Raygon and his two reapers exit the dungeon.

Silence, soft and delicate, floated over her cell, and Aria stood still, giving herself over to the peace that it offered as daylight began to wane. The sun's warm rays jutted through the small window of her cell, and she shut her eyes against the light. She hung her head, taking a deep breath to steady her thoughts. Pain lanced through her body as her lungs filled with air, and her head grew hazy. Exhaustion and despair washed over her as she strained to remember all that was said between the king and his assassins.

No traces of Balmorea are to be left on her death.

A weak sob escaped her throat when her mind finally connected the pieces of Raygon's cryptic words. He'd meant Ophelia. The past five days had all been about Ophelia. But why? She was no threat. Why didn't he see that?

And Raygon had just given the order for her murder.

Anguish scoured the inside of her chest. Aria was going to die in a cell in the bowels of the Black Keep, hundreds of miles away, unable to do anything about the threat to her sister's life. This couldn't be happening. He couldn't do this—

"Aria." Marius's soft voice drifted across her cell.

Marius? She frowned down at the stone at her feet, and her heart ached. She missed her husband. Where was he? Why hadn't he come for her? Had Raygon hurt him too?

She choked on a sob at the thought, and tears slid down her cheeks.

"*Gien veela,*" Marius's voice said, breaking at the end. "Look at me."

Marius…

Her head shot up, and as soon as her eyes met his, she came apart. "Marius," she sobbed.

His hands clenched around the bars of the cell, worry painting his brow. "I'm here, *gien veela*. We're getting you out of this terrible place."

A spark flashed near her cell door, and it swung wide on its hinges. Marius shot across the cell, a limp to his gait, and a dark figure followed behind him. Once he reached her,

Marius took her face in his hands, smoothing away the tears streaming down her cheeks with his thumbs. Something coarse rasped across her cheek, and she realized it was from the linen wrapped around Marius's palms.

Now that he was close enough, she was able to fully take him in, and her heart cracked. Bruises mottled his cheeks and jaw, and his eyes were bloodshot and heavy with exhaustion. She counted two small gashes on his face that were scabbing over, a swollen split in his lower lip, and another through his left brow, which had been stitched up.

Before she could ask him what had happened, he asked, "Are you bleeding, Aria?" His throat worked on a swallow. "Have you…bled?"

Silence hovered between them before she understood what he was asking. She shook her head.

"No. The only blood that has spilled from me comes from my back and no more." He released a breath of relief and pulled her to his chest, mumbling words of thanks into her hair.

The figure that entered with him suddenly appeared at Aria's side and grabbed the shackles at her wrists. He was a young man, about Marius's age, who wore a plain brown robe with no adornment. Panic clawed up her throat.

"You brought an Acolyte with you?" she cried before the man released two more quick bursts of light, and Aria sank into Marius's arms. A flash of pain scored down her back and a hiss of pain fell from her lips.

Marius cursed, gingerly lowering her to her knees and carefully keeping his hands from her back. Despite the pain, Aria finally felt like she could breathe now that he was near.

"Sandro isn't an Acolyte," Marius reassured her. "He's a mage from the temple, here to help."

Aria didn't have the energy to protest. She nodded and leaned into her husband, resting her forehead to his shoulders and taking in his warmth and the comfort of having him near. She took in a deep breath, then another, before her mind flew back to what the king had just revealed. Her head snapped up. "Raygon's sending Reapers after Ophelia, Marius."

Marius tensed, his brows dropping into a frown. "Are you certain?"

She nodded. "He doesn't understand her power and is afraid she knows of something called an Aegis. He told the Reaper with him to contact someone named Trella and to tell her that 'she is to act immediately' and that 'no traces of Balmorea were to be left on her death.'"

Marius cursed under his breath before he dropped his forehead to hers. "I'm so sorry, Aria." Pain laced his words.

He pulled back and looked at Sandro. "We need to mend her back."

"We don't have time to heal her right now," Sandro gritted out. "It's a miracle they haven't discovered us yet as it is."

"I said mend, not heal," Marius snapped. "She is in too much pain and will be unable to move quickly like this."

Sandro huffed then stepped behind her. He began muttering an incantation, and a flare of heat washed over her back. Aria's hands bunched in the fabric of Marius's shirt, and she bit back the scream that rose in her chest. She dropped her forehead to his shoulder, and he gently grasped her arms, smoothing his palms up and down her biceps.

"Where were you?" she gritted out, trying to pull her mind from the agonizing burn crawling across her skin.

His hands at her arms flexed, and she felt the ire rolling off him. "The king was displeased with my *defiance* in his study before he took you and saw to it that I was chained and disciplined in a similar fashion to this, though not nearly as cruel." He dropped his lips to the top of her head, his voice tightening with regret. "I'm so sorry, *gien veela*. I'm so fucking sorry."

"There," Sandro said. "Her wounds are closed and some of the inflammation has decreased, so she should be able to move more easily."

"Thank you," Aria breathed as Marius pulled out a cloak from his satchel and wrapped it around her shoulders. The fabric of the cloak felt scratchy across her sensitive skin, but it was bearable.

He raised a hand to her cheek. "We need to move quickly. We're getting you to safety. Do you think you can walk?" Marius asked.

Aria nodded, pulling on his shoulders to help herself stand. "Where are we going? Is there another way other than the passage to the king's study?"

"Yes, but it's guarded. Sandro incapacitated the guards for the time being, but we don't have long before they wake. We must hurry, and we must be quiet."

Aria nodded and followed behind the two men through a dark, narrow passage lit only by the flame hovering in Sandro's hand. Aria gave no thought to where they were going and did not try to map the way in her mind. They seemed to weave through doorway after doorway before finally emerging into a circular chamber lit by a tall, narrow window above a singular, wooden door. Two men in scarlet uniforms lay on their backs on either side of the passage they emerged from, swords in hand.

"Did they see you?" Aria asked. "Are you in danger now for helping me?"

Sandro placed a hand on the door and closed his eyes, mumbling another incantation.

"No," Marius replied. "Sandro did his work before I entered. No one saw me, or him, for that matter." A flash of light from Sandro's hand, and the massive iron padlock clunked to the stone floor. He lifted the handle and pulled open the door.

Aria released her breath at the sight of the grassy field, washed orange in the rays of the sunset. But she had no time to admire it. Marius guided her down the short set of stairs and helped her onto his horse before mounting behind her. Sandro unhitched him from the post and handed Marius the reins.

"Thank you, Sandro," Marius said. "I will never forget this."

Sandro placed his palm to his chest and bowed. "It was an honor, Your Serene Highness. Now, go quickly. Morgan is expecting you at the Temple."

"Thank you, again, Sandro," Aria said before Marius prodded his horse into a gallop. They stayed off the paths, hugging the tree line in the hope of going unnoticed in the shadow of the trees' canopies. Marius wrapped his arm tightly around Aria's waist as they rode, pressing her to his chest. She bit her cheek at the pain that radiated down her back at the contact, letting her head fall back against his shoulder in a silent plea.

"Almost there," he said, pressing a kiss to her temple.

"Where are we going?"

"To the Order's temple at the edge of the city. See? There, just ahead."

Confusion furrowed her brow. *Why are we going to the temple?* The lashes on her back slowly began to throb, and the cloak on her back steadily grew damp. She clenched her jaw and kept her eyes on the temple ahead of them. *Almost there.*

Marius slowed the horse as they approached a massive yet plain stone structure. The stone walls were tall, the points of four towers being all that was visible from within.

Marius dismounted quickly then helped Aria down. She winced as he lowered her from the horse, both of their gazes falling to the front of his shirt.

It was covered in blood. *Her* blood.

Concern laced his brow. "Come, we must hurry. You need a healer." He took her hand and led her to a nearby wooden door set inside the wall leading into one of the towers.

Marius rapped on the door and said something in Balmorean that Aria didn't understand, dizziness and exhaustion claiming her clarity of mind. A tall, old man with wispy, white hair wearing pale gray robes answered the door a moment later.

"You're late," the old man, who she assumed was Morgan, said.

Marius's jaw ticked. "The king spent more time with Her Serene Highness than anticipated," he replied, helping Aria through the door. "Is everything prepared?"

"Yes," the old man said as he led them down a set of stairs leading below ground into a wide, stone chamber lit on all four walls by torches. Black tapestries with strange, gold symbols hung on each wall between the torches, framing a massive mirror at the back of the chamber. A red rug swept across the floor, bringing relief to Aria's aching feet.

Marius never let go of her hand as they walked across the chamber towards the mirror. He and the old man exchanged a few words that Aria did not strain to understand—her mind was too tired to translate, her body too stiff with pain to fight the pull of her husband's hand.

When they finally arrived at the mirror, Aria realized that what was before her was actually two mirrors fastened next to each other, but their reflections did not appear in either upon their approach. Instead, the image of a man in similar gray robes stood in the mirror to the right. His eyes grew wide when they landed on Aria, and he shifted uncomfortably on his feet.

"What is this?" Aria asked, interrupting whatever conversation the old man and Marius were having. "What's going on?"

Morgan and Marius exchanged a look before the old man nodded. He placed his palm to his heart and bowed then backed away.

Marius turned to Aria and motioned to the mirrors. "These mirrors work as passageways between the Three Great Nations. The Order's temples in Sigova and Vardos have them as well. This is also how the temples communicate with each other. You step through the mirror on the left to enter Nedorra. You step through the mirror on the right to enter Maraleon." He turned to her and raised his hand to cup her face. "I'm sending you back to Sigova."

Panic flared in her chest. "What?"

"I have to keep you safe." Pain etched a line between his brows as his other hand lowered protectively to her belly. "I have to keep *both* of you safe. I will not let him unleash any more of his wretchedness on you." He pulled her face into his chest, dropping his lips to the top of her head. "I'm—I'm so sorry, Aria. This never should have happened."

Aria's hands twisted in the front of his shirt as she choked down the sob clogging her throat. "But what about you?" She pulled back to look at him. Anger and heartache warred in Marius's deep brown eyes—eyes that were normally filled with warmth and playfulness when they looked upon her—and her heart cracked further. She raised a hand and gingerly brushed her fingers over the split in his brow. "Will he not continue to unleash his wretchedness on you, too?"

This couldn't be happening. Mere days ago, they'd shared in the greatest joy of their lives together. Their future was bright and exciting and so full of promise. How did they get here? Bitter tears spilled down her cheeks.

"Come with me," she pleaded.

He dropped his forehead to hers, curling his hands around her biceps. "I can't." His voice was strained with emotion, and he gently pulled her closer, hands flexing with what felt like the need to wrap her in his arms. "The king will know I helped you if we both disappear. We have laid a trail leading north to make it seem like you are fleeing to the mining villages. It will buy you time. You are safer if I am not by your side."

"But *you* are not safe as long as you sleep under the same roof as that man. Nor will I be any safer in Sigova; he already has Reapers in Maraleon, Marius. Who knows how many?" Her voice faltered. "He is already planning to use them to kill Ophelia. Who's to say I won't be next?"

Marius shook his head. "You pose no danger to him or Balmorea."

"On the contrary, I know a great deal of information he would likely not want falling into my father's lap."

"He does not know all that we have discovered, and I doubt he suspects you were in good enough condition to listen to his blathering in your cell."

"And if he does decide I am a loose end to be tied up? Sigova is no safer than Ravenhold."

"You know the signs," he insisted, sliding his hands up to her wrists, and her grip on his shirt loosened. "The scythe tattoo, the ashen skin, the black irises—"

"And what of you?" she asked again, her chest clenching and causing her breaths to stutter. "If he truly thinks he has secured his line through our child, he no longer has a need for you."

"He won't risk it. Not with you gone." Marius paused, squeezing her wrists as he seemed to choose his next words carefully. "It is still early yet, and not all pregnancies are assured to…endure to delivery. He knows this. And with you, and our baby, out of reach, he will not dispose of me so easily. I can handle the king, *gien veela*. You need not worry," he said as his thumbs smoothed across the inside of her wrists.

"But you shouldn't have to handle him alone." Her lip quivered as she clutched his shirt tighter, pulling him flush against her. "Don't send me away."

He closed his eyes and swallowed. "I cannot keep you safe here. I have already failed in that. I will never fail you again. I can't—" he gasped in a breath, "I can't lose you."

"And I can't lose you." She met his eyes with determination. "Either you come, or I stay. I will not be apart from you."

He dropped his forehead to hers. "You must, Aria. You will be under your father's protection where you can receive healing and be safe. And there is also Ophelia to consider."

He pulled back to meet her gaze. "We are the only ones who know what the king plans, and if she truly is this Vilicus of Mankind, more than just *her* life is at risk."

He lowered a hand to her stomach, and Aria's face crumpled again. She rested her forehead against his chest, his heart beating a staccato beneath. Ophelia felt the turmoil wrestling within Aria against her sister's better judgment—she didn't want to leave Marius, regardless of whether their knowledge could save Ophelia and the rest of the world or not, and a brief wave of shame washed over her.

But the baby.

Aria's heart twisted.

Ophelia didn't blame her sister for her feelings. Had their roles been reversed, and Elliot had been in Marius's position, Ophelia wasn't sure she would have responded any differently. But Aria had always been too selfless to give into such flippant thoughts. She straightened as much as her injuries would allow and swallowed a bitter sob. "This will not be the last time I ever see you."

He took her face in his hands again. "No, it will not."

"Swear it to me, Marius."

He leaned down and captured her lips. "You are the greatest good that has ever happened to me, Aria. If I could have found another way to keep you safe *and* by my side, that is where we would be right now." His gaze pierced hers, punctuating his next words. "This I vow to you: I will handle the king, I will make Balmorea safe for our family, and I will bring you home."

Home.

Balmorea was Aria's home now. *Marius* was her home.

"I will bring you *both* home, *gien veela*. I swear it."

"Marius—"

His lips came down on hers again. He kissed her with the abandon of a man who didn't know what the future held, desperate to atone for the shortcomings Aria never held against him. He gently drew her closer, as if to promise he would prove himself worthy of her, not realizing that, to her, he already had. She opened for him, tasting him one last time, drinking in all he would give her, and her heart shattered.

Marius.

A tear rolled down her cheek. Then another.

Sweet Marius.

His lips slowed, and he pulled away. His thumb stroked her cheek then followed the line of her jaw to her chin, tilting her head up and connecting his eyes with hers.

"I love you, Aria."

The breath was sucked from her lungs.

A hand suddenly gripped her arm and tugged, pulling her backwards through a hollow plane. She floated through darkness. There was no warmth or chill. No breeze fluttered through her skirts or her hair. She was simply suspended— cradled in stillness.

Her feet landed on solid stone. The whisper of robes came from behind her, and two hands steadied her shoulders. When she looked up, Marius was still there, watching through the mirror with clenched fists to ensure she made it through safely.

She parted her lips to say his name, but he was already gone.

CHAPTER FIVE

OPHELIA WASN'T SURE HOW MUCH TIME HAD passed before she pulled herself from Aria's shoulder, before the tears and the pain finally ebbed enough that she could form a coherent thought, take in a full breath.

Ophelia took Aria's hands in her own, frowning as her mind raced and sifted through the memories her sister shared with her, when her thoughts settled on one thing—

"You—you're having a baby, Ari," she said. A sharp gasp came from where Nell stood by the hearth. Tightness wound itself around the wonder rising in Ophelia's chest followed by a flash of rage. Raygon *knew* she was pregnant and still chained and whipped her.

Aria nodded in confirmation, sadness gripping her faint smile.

"You have not bled, Ari. The baby is safe. *That* is something," Ophelia said.

Aria's brows knit together, her face straining to hold in

her pain, fighting to hold up the dam of her emotions and not collapse under their weight. She pressed her palm to her stomach. "It *is* something, but what of Marius? What of our future? The baby's future?" she asked, losing her hold on her composure with each burning question. "Nothing is certain—how can a child be kept safe amid such danger? Raygon is poison. I *cannot* raise my child within the same walls as him."

"That is why Marius sent you here," Ophelia cut in, squeezing her hands. "He knew this was the best place for you—where you would be welcomed and protected and properly cared for."

Aria shook her head, tears spilling from her eyes. "What if—" she sucked in a sob, "what if Raygon discovers Marius helped me escape and kills him? Or what if he sends his Reapers to come for me—it was wishful thinking for Marius to assume the king would not seek my death simply because I'm out of reach and with child." Her head shot up, eyes wide. "Earth and Sea, Ophelia! He's sent Reapers after *you*." A sob tore from her throat. "None of us are safe."

Ophelia swallowed. "As terrifying as it is to know someone seeks to end my life, you must remember: our kingdom is formidable in its own right. We are protected here. *Safe*." She wrapped an arm around Aria and pulled her close. Aria laid her head on Ophelia's shoulder.

"I don't feel safe anywhere," Aria whispered, and Ophelia squeezed her eyes shut. The despair that hung in those words…Ophelia had never heard such sorrow in her sister's voice.

"We will keep you safe, Ari. *I* will be safe. But we need to tell Papa all of this, and we need to have Miss Lyla examine you," Ophelia replied, lifting the tone of her voice as much as she could. "We need to make sure you and the baby are well looked after."

Aria nodded and sniffed, wiping her nose before leaning back into the pillows, nibbling at the smashed piece of bread in her hand.

Ophelia looked to Nell to have her fetch Lyla and to send word for her father. Nell nodded before turning for the door, schooling her expression against the tears turning her eyes glassy, but a knock came to the door before she could leave.

"It's the king, ma'am," Nell announced. "He wants to check on Her Highness."

Aria nodded as she sat up in the bed.

Nell opened the door wide, and Alphonse entered, his eyes skating across the room before landing on his daughters sitting together in Aria's bed, both of their eyes still puffy from the flood of Aria's memories. Alphonse's face softened as he rounded the bed and took Aria into his arms.

"How are you feeling, my dear?" he asked, holding Aria tight against his chest.

"Better than yesterday."

He pulled back. "I'm very relieved to hear that. Does your back cause you any pain?"

"No. Ophelia did well," she replied with a small smile.

"Good." Alphonse nodded with brows drawn together. "As much as I know it pains you to remember, you must tell me what happened to you."

"Of course," Aria replied with a sniff. She and Ophelia then began recounting Aria's memories, giving as much information as Aria could remember about Raygon's interrogations, the Reapers, and Raygon's assassination plans. Ophelia's heart caught in her throat when Aria shared with Alphonse that she was pregnant. It should have been another happy moment. It was news that should have brought joy and excitement to the room. Alphonse should be shouting from the tallest tower of the castle that he was going to be a grandfather, but the news, though still happy, came with a heaviness that bore heartache upon those it was shared with.

Ophelia's anger flared again—this was another moment stolen from them by Raygon.

Alphonse took Aria's face in his palms, leveling gentle, yet determined eyes, to hers. "We will make this right." Aria nodded, another tear falling down her cheek. "And we cannot let word slip that we suspect an assassination attempt. It will cause chaos and make preventing such an act all the more difficult."

"I'm sure Aria's dramatic arrival has been the talk of the servants' wing," Ophelia said. "What do you plan to do about the gossip?"

Alphonse nodded. "Gregor and I discussed this last night. We'll say Aria was travelling to Sigova for your wedding when her caravan was attacked. She alone escaped into the city, and we have not received word from the rest of her party."

"And the prince?" Ophelia asked. "Will people not wonder what happened to Aria's husband? A renowned warrior among his father's forces?"

"Even the strongest of fighters can be caught off guard," Aria said, staring off with glassy eyes. Her jaw ticked as she took a deep breath in through her nose. "We don't have to say we suspect he's dead, just missing. That should be enough to stave off any prying gossip."

Ophelia squeezed Aria's hand, and Aria squeezed hers in return. Things shouldn't be this way. They should be chattering about Ophelia's wedding, trading secrets, and giggling over the advice Aria said she would bring her sister for her wedding night. They should be thinking of baby names and wondering what color eyes Aria's child will have.

Instead, they are devising cover stories and huddling in their chambers for safety.

More stolen moments.

A knock came to the door, and Nell answered to find Lyla on the other side, coming to check on Aria's back before the day got started. Nell allowed her in, and she made her way over to Aria. Ophelia's heart sank—Aria would have to share, for a third time, the heart-wrenching good news. Without her husband. Without the certainty that the goodness a new baby promised awaited her in the future.

Ophelia left Aria with Lyla and took a moment to speak with her father before he left Aria's chambers. "What of Lord Barnham in all of this?"

"What about him?"

"Will he still be permitted to visit? Perhaps you could allow him to remain armed while in the castle for an added layer of protection for me. You know he is a capable warrior." Perhaps she was being selfish to ask this so soon after Aria's return and the implications brought with it, but the thought that someone in the city, perhaps even in the castle, was ordered to carry out her death only strengthened her need to have Elliot close. "Or perhaps we could allow him to stay in one of the guest chambers until the wedding…"

Alphonse grunted in dissent.

"I know what you're thinking, Papa, but he makes me feel…safe. And I know I'm safe here with you, I just, he—"

Alphonse's eyes softened a fraction. "You love him. I understand." A small smile tugged at the corner of his mouth. "He will still be permitted to visit, and I will allow him to remain armed while he's in the castle, but he need not stay in one of our guest chambers. Earth and Sea know I don't need any other unsightly characters sneaking around the corridors in the middle of the night trying to gain access into your chambers."

Ophelia huffed out a laugh as Alphonse smirked back at her and stepped into the corridor.

Elliot stood in Alphonse's study with George and Prince Gregor, waiting for the king. A tense silence hung heavy in the room. Gregor stood with a drink in front of one of the large windows looking down into the courtyard while Elliot and George stood on the periphery of the room. Elliot felt his gaze go distant as his memory sifted through the events of the previous day. Everything had happened so quickly, then Ophelia was sequestered off with her sister, and he hadn't been able to see her before leaving. Sleep came to him in short bursts, his worry for Ophelia and Aria pulling his mind into a near constant spin.

But he knew whatever answers they were going to receive once Alphonse arrived would likely not be comforting, and he did his best to brace himself for the worst.

Alphonse shoved through the door to his study, Lucias close behind him, the sound causing Gregor, Elliot, and George to start where they stood before quickly bowing.

"Father, how is she?" Gregor asked, striding across the study towards the king. Elliot and George quickly fell in line behind him. A thousand questions rushed to Elliot's tongue, and he had to clench his jaw to keep from voicing them out of turn.

Alphonse sighed as he dropped into the chair behind his desk. "As well as can be expected," he said, Elliot noting how the king's grip on the arms of his chair tightened. "The situation is more complicated than anticipated."

"How so?" Gregor asked as he sat in one of the chairs opposite Alphonse's desk, leaning over to rest his forearms on top of his knees.

"Raygon's words of restoration between the Three Great Nations after the conflict in the valley were lies." Lucias handed Alphonse a glass of whiskey from which the king took a long swig. "The revelation of Ophelia as the Vilicus of Man sat so poorly with him that, upon his return to Balmorea, he tortured Aria for information. And when she could give him nothing he considered of value, he left her for dead in the dungeons, all the while knowing she was with child."

Stunned silence held its grip on the three men's throats, Alphonse's blunt report hitting them like a slap in the face. Elliot shifted on his feet as he wiped a hand over his mouth, his mind fighting to wrap itself around Alphonse's words.

Alphonse knocked back the remainder of his whiskey and slammed his glass onto his desk. "There's more."

Of course, there is, Elliot thought, clenching his fists in time with his jaw. He felt George bristle beside him.

Alphonse raised his eyes to meet Elliot's. "Raygon has sent assassins after Ophelia."

The air left Elliot's lungs, and he felt the color drain from his face. "Assassins?" The word came out breathy, and his heart jumped as it passed his lips.

Alphonse nodded.

"Fuck," Gregor said.

"And since we consider this a viable threat," Alphonse continued, "we will need to discuss some sort of plan to vet out any traitors who might be among the castle staff in hopes of intercepting an assassin before they make their move."

Elliot's stomach bottomed out. How was Ophelia taking this? Finding her sister so gravely injured was bad enough, but to then learn of a plot to take her life on top of the weighty burden she already carried from her new role as mankind's Vilicus? He needed to see her.

"Lord George and I are at your disposal, Your Majesty," Elliot said.

Alphonse raised his eyes back to Elliot and nodded. "Good. You will be needed."

CHAPTER SIX

OPHELIA REMAINED IN ARIA'S CHAMBERS THE REST of the day. Conversation lightened as the day went on, shifting to topics about how Aria was adjusting to life in Balmorea and the time she had spent with Marius. Ophelia also told her sister of her and Elliot's time together and explained the events that took place before and after Pyotr's return. Having experienced it all was one thing, but explaining it was quite another. Ophelia hadn't realized how fantastic it all sounded until the words spilled from her lips, but Aria listened unfazed.

The two of them fell asleep that night laying on their pillows, reminiscing over old memories in the castle.

Ophelia suddenly found herself standing in the Central Valley.

The sun was high, spilling its light from a cloudless sky. Lush greensward and a mix of bright flowers stretched across the meadow to the foot of the mountains. A light breeze lifted her hair and fluttered the skirts of her dress.

"Ophelia," a familiar voice called from behind her. She turned to find Pyotr, standing with his arms crossed over his chest about five yards away, apparently too impatient for her to gain her bearings before alerting her to his presence.

His ash-gray hair was pulled to the nape of his neck, a few stray strands fluttering into his face, and his cinnamon-brown eyes bore into her. The tension in his jaw told her this was not a friendly visit.

"Pyotr," she replied with a slight bow of her head. "I didn't think I would see you for some time. To what do I owe the pleasure of your company?"

"You told me you would not turn away from the atrocities mankind commits," he said, forehead creasing. "Are you doing so now, or do you truly not sense it?"

Ophelia frowned. "I'm ignoring nothing. Is there something I should be aware of?"

Pyotr relaxed his shoulders, dropping his arms to his sides, and let out a sigh. "There is something far in the east that I must show you," he said.

"What is it?"

"It's difficult to explain." He held out his hand to her. As soon as she took it, their surroundings faded then brightened, pulling forth a different location. They stood with their backs to the bank of a wide river, a forest skirting both sides.

Pyotr stepped into the wood, and Ophelia followed.

"What wood is this?" Ophelia asked. Tall, beech trees with their bright green leaves stretched all around her, seeming to rake the sky from where she stood. Leaves and twigs crunched beneath their feet as they walked, and a cool breeze wound around them. With the flow of the river behind her and the sight before her, the place felt peaceful, untouched by man and animal alike.

This was how Pyotr longed for the world to be.

"This is the wood farthest to the east in the land you call Balmorea," Pyotr replied, keeping his eyes ahead of him.

Ophelia froze. "We are almost to the Eastern Wastelands?"

Not much was known about the Wastelands or why nothing thrives there, but the tales of the wild beasts that inhabit the wastelands held firm in Ophelia's mind; winged beasts with white fur, long, sharp claws and teeth, who use their bottomless black eyes to hypnotize their victims into becoming their next meal. "It's not safe here."

Pyotr's lips quirked upwards. "We're in your dream, Ophelia. I am merely showing you what I've seen. Ease your mind. There is nothing more sinister out here than what I am to show you."

Knowing Pyotr was connected to her thoughts, Ophelia flushed with embarrassment at being placated like a frightened child in the dark, but his comment stirred her curiosity. "Truly? There aren't any monsters out here?"

A smile softened the tension in his jaw. "Truly. No unnatural creatures dwell here. Nor is there a Wasteland."

Ophelia balked at his statement. "You're kidding. Every map I have ever seen of the Three Great Nations shows the Eastern Wastelands stretching from the south-eastern coast of Balmorea to the north-eastern coast of Nedorra. There are no people there. It's all dried land that can yield no crop and scorching skies that give no rain. There is no life east of the Far East River—"

"And yet here we are, east of the Far East River."

Ophelia's head darted from right to left, looking for evidence he was mistaken.

"Trust me, Ophelia. I will explain everything when we arrive."

Ophelia nodded and warily continued.

She wasn't certain as to the distance they traveled, nor the time it took them to reach their destination, but she could feel they were getting close. An uneasiness began to churn in her chest, spreading to quake her stomach. With each step, her heart raced faster, her legs grew heavy, and a cold sweat broke out along her brow. Every instinct in her body told her to turn and run, that continuing forward would only result in death.

"Pyotr, what's happening?" she panted, pressing a palm to her chest as her lungs burned to keep pace with her flailing heart.

"So, you feel it now," Pyotr said.

"Feel *what* exactly?"

He turned to face her. "Fight the dread that coils in your belly. You are not in imminent danger. The repulsion is part of the pestilence that hovers over these lands."

"Pestilence?"

"It's just up ahead."

After another hundred yards the trees dispersed and before them, stretching from the forest floor up as far up as Ophelia's eyes could reach, spanned some sort of barrier. The repulsion in Ophelia's stomach exploded. Her vision fractured and pain seared her mind. Her hand flew to her temples as her knees hit the ground. Her heart flailed, and her breath came out in ragged pants. Panic flared to life, consuming her like a wildfire.

Flee.

Run.

Escape.

"P—Pyotr, I can't stay here."

Pyotr knelt before her, placing his hands on her shoulders. "Focus on your breathing. Imagine your lungs filling with air, hold in your breath, then imagine it spilling out before you."

Ophelia's pounding heartbeat filled her ears. She dug her fingers into the soil and fought the overwhelming panic, inhaling deeply, then she held her breath.

One...two...three.

She exhaled. Opening her eyes, she watched as her breath parted the leaves from the ground below her.

"Good. Again."

Inhale. Hold. Exhale.

With each subsequent breath, the fog in her mind subsided. The electric energy that frenzied her heart waned. The churning unease remained, but her panic had ebbed.

Inhale. Hold. Exhale.

Ophelia lifted her head and took in the sight before her.

The barrier was a murky gray that seemed to flow and shimmer like a curtain in the wind, or was it playing off the sunlight? There was no sound. No chirping birds, no flutter of leaves. The area was stagnant, filled with trees and foliage and eerie silence.

Ophelia stood and stepped forward, raising her hand to touch the barrier when Pyotr caught her wrist.

"You cannot touch this...*thing*. It was made to repel and destroy anything that draws too close." He dropped her wrist and picked up a fallen tree branch, tossing it at the barrier. A grinding, crunching sound resounded from where the branch collided into the barrier, then the branch was simply gone. There was no shadow through the murky, translucent wall to reveal the branch had passed though. No ash floated to the ground. No crumbles of bark. There was no trace of it.

Ophelia's eyes widened. "What is this? Why is this here?"

"It is a barrier of some sort, erected with vile magic," he spat. "I can taste it on my tongue, feel it buzzing in my veins." He grimaced then leveled his eyes to hers. "Can you hear it?"

"Hear it?"

"Close your eyes," he instructed. "Listen."

Ophelia did as he said and opened her mind to the barrier. Just as she had in the valley, she visualized connecting with the barrier, stretching her senses towards it. A shock shot up her arm, up her neck, and burst in her mind.

Screams.

Cries.

Pleas for mercy.

From men and women, young and old.

Ophelia covered her ears, desperate to dampen the cacophony of voices. She stepped back and felt her foot splash into a puddle. She looked down—

Blood.

She had stepped in blood. The puddle swelled around her feet, flowing in thousands of tiny streams from the barrier. She gasped, and her eyes flew open. Pyotr stood before her, his hands steadying her shoulders.

"Those voices…hundreds, *thousands* of people. Is that what you hear?" Pyotr's jaw clenched, and he nodded. "Are they trapped? Are they imprisoned inside the barrier for some reason? Have you been able to breach it, Pyotr? Do you know what is on the other side?"

Pyotr dropped his hands, shaking his head. "I cannot breach this barrier. It was made with magic outside my realm, otherwise, I assure you, it would no longer be here."

"Outside your realm?"

"This was made by the magic of man."

"Are you certain? Has Mira tried?" she asked, already knowing the answer.

"Yes, on both accounts."

Ophelia sighed then began to pace along the foot of the barrier, observing it, examining it. *Who did this? Why is this here?* Her thoughts ran rampant as she tried to riddle it all out.

"I saw blood," Ophelia said, "with the screams. Blood flowed from the barrier and covered the ground I stood on." Her eyes climbed up the expanse of the barrier, squinting into the sky. "I don't think we heard the screams of the living, Pyotr."

"I don't think so either." His voice was quiet. Silence coiled around them at the edge of the wood. Questions hung in the air as they considered this malign barrier raised with magic and blood.

It functions by deriving power from the lifeforce held in one's blood, Marius's words from Aria's memory echoed in her mind, and she gasped.

"It's Blood Magic."

"*Blood Magic?*" Pyotr repeated, a grimace plastered across his face. "Such a horrid thing exists?"

The memory of Aria's discussion with Marius flooded her mind. "I—I don't know much. I know it was made illegal by the Order of Mages hundreds of years ago, but a small, hidden faction of religious zealots who work for the king of Balmorea study it. My sister's husband called it a dirty magic because it requires the lifeforce in one's blood to cast. Many casters use the blood of others instead of their own."

Pyotr's nostrils flared. "When I thought mankind could be no worse." Just then, the barrier pulsed, a wave of magic rippling across its surface and disappearing into the air. Pyotr's brow sunk into a frown. "It has been doing this as well."

"It's…*losing* magic?"

"Weakening, perhaps?"

She paused, her teeth playing on the inside of her cheek. "How long do you think this barrier has been here? I can't imagine this much Blood Magic being used goes unnoticed."

"It went beyond *your* notice."

"But I live a considerable distance from here. Where did you first notice it?"

His eyebrows knit together. "I was quite close."

Ophelia nodded. "The Reapers of Balmorea studying Blood Magic and this barrier being present at their border cannot be a coincidence." She whipped around to face Pyotr. "Thank you for bringing this to my attention. Is there anything else I need to know?"

Pyotr shook his head. "I know nothing more than what we have discovered here. If I learn anything new, I will inform you."

"Thank you, Pyotr. I'll do what I can to fix this," she said, meeting his eyes. He nodded, and the scene around them faded to darkness.

CHAPTER SEVEN

NELL LEANED BACK AGAINST THE WALL OF THE corridor across from the castle's kitchens and waited for a kitchen maid to finish preparing Aria and Ophelia's morning tea. The corridor was too quiet, too vacant. It gave too much space in Nell's mind for her thoughts and memories from the past day to run wild.

The hour was too early for most to begin their day— even for her, normally. But after the events of the past two days, despite her bone deep exhaustion, sleep never came for Nell, and she found herself sliding out of bed before the sun.

It all felt like a fever dream—too horrible to be true, yet too real to deny.

Nell had seen Aria's back when she collapsed in the Great Hall and how Ophelia had healed her. She'd seen the two sisters the morning after Aria arrived—had watched every emotion under the sun play across Ophelia's face as she relived Aria's memories. And she'd listened afterward, with dread sinking in her stomach like a stone, as each new revelation came to light. *Reapers. Assassinations. A baby. Torture.*

She let her head fall back against the cold stone, closing her eyes against the pressure building behind them and swallowing down the emotion rising in her throat. One errant tear rolled down her cheek as a familiar, haughty voice echoed from down the corridor.

"Lady Nell? What a lovely surprise this fine morning."

Nell's eyes flew open, embarrassment bursting in her chest before she quickly brushed her fingers under her eyes to wipe away any tear stains. Her eyes landed on George as he swaggered toward her, the smile that charmed countless women into his bed spread wide across his wicked lips.

And yet, her traitorous heart still flipped in her chest. *It's just part of his game*, she reminded herself.

Nell had known of George and his perpetual dalliances, and as such, had appreciated his pretty face and knee-weakening smiles from a distance whenever their paths crossed. But once Ophelia and Elliot began spending more time together, and George's attention shifted and began to settle on her in more than simple passing glances, she set her defenses in place.

The fact was, George was dangerous, and Nell liked dangerous things entirely too much.

Every time he shined his light on her, she felt just how easily she'd give too much of herself to him. She knew he would ensnare her and that she'd happily allow herself to be entangled in him—her heart all too eager for the free fall that being with him promised.

And she knew that when he eventually tired of her and moved on to the next woman, there would be no soft landing from that free fall. She would crash to the ground and shatter to pieces, left to sift through the broken shards, and hope there would be something of herself left.

That's why, when Nell turned to face him and her eyes locked with the mischief dancing in his emerald irises, her armor locked in place, and she set a bored expression on her face. "Lovely? I'd have to agree. But a surprise it most certainly is not."

He stopped in front of her, crossing his arms over his chest, and peered down at her. She awaited the quip that, no doubt, was loaded on his tongue, but it never came. Instead, his grin faded, and a line formed between his brows. "You're crying," he said, dropping his arms, and the mirth in his green eyes shifted into concern.

His voice was achingly gentle, as though he were trying to be careful with her. As though she were the one who'd been tortured or had an assassin hunting her. Her brow bent at the sudden shift in his demeanor. It unsteadied her, made her anxious. She didn't know how to navigate an interaction with *this* George.

Was he *worried* for her?

Her heart did another traitorous flip.

Nell shook her head and dropped her gaze to the floor, crossing her arms over her stomach. "Much has happened," she sighed. "And even if I'm not the one in the direct line of fire, the events of the past two days have still taken their toll."

George chanced a small step forward, and his leather and cedarwood scent surrounded her. Heat bloomed in her cheeks.

"The king shared everything that happened with Lord Barnham and me. Or, at least, much of it, if not everything," he said gravely. "I don't doubt how heavily it all weighs on you as well."

She nodded, and his concern for her sent her stomach fluttering. Or was this part of his game too? Her eyes snagged on the sword strapped to George's hip before she could riddle it out, and the fluttering in her stomach turned sour. *That's right.* The king was allowing Elliot to arm himself while in the castle, so it made sense that the same allowance would be made for George.

She looked up to him, eager to focus her mind on something else. "What are you doing here so early? I didn't realize you functioned regularly before the sun rose."

A smirk slid across his face. "Oh, there are many things I'm apt to do before the sun rises."

Nell rolled her eyes, relief lightening her chest—she knew how to deal with flirty George. "I doubt any of those things have you wandering the corridors at this hour."

"You would be correct." His smirk slid into a lopsided smile that sent the butterflies now taking up residence in her stomach into flight once more. "I imagine I'm here for a similar reason as you. The king permitted Lord Barnham and me to stay for a night. I'm here for his lordship's morning tea."

"I see."

A maid opened the kitchen door, drawing Nell's attention. "That'll be the princesses' tea." She stepped toward the kitchen and took one of the trays of bread, cheese, and fruit extended to her. "I suppose I'll be seeing you," she said to George as she made her way down the corridor, the maid following behind her with another tray.

"You would be so lucky, Sweetheart," George called after her.

The nickname sent a flash of irritation through her, causing her to falter a step. She shook her head and ignored him as she continued toward Aria's chambers.

Ophelia woke to the soft morning light twining through the curtains hanging over the tall windows in Aria's chambers. She sat up to the sound of a crackling fire and the light clang of metal on a tray. Nell was already there.

"Good morning," Nell whispered as she removed the kettle from the spit over the fire. Ophelia yawned with a nod and leaned back into the pillows. She pressed the heels of her palms against her eyes, grasping at the fringes of her dream with Pyotr.

Danger east of the Far East River. A force that repels those who get too close. And a barrier cast with the blood of others. Of *thousands*.

Ophelia dropped her hands to her side. She would be making a visit to Master Gaius today.

A long sigh floated from the pillows next to her, and Ophelia felt Aria shift as she rolled to face her. Aria's eyes were still puffy from sleep, and she had a crease on her cheek from the way her pillow folded against her face. A smile tugged at Ophelia's mouth. "Morning."

"Morning," Aria replied with a yawn.

"Did you rest well?" Ophelia asked, rolling to face her sister.

Aria nodded. "A dreamless sleep from what I can remember."

"And how is your back?"

Aria sat up and rolled her shoulders, bent forward, and arched her back. She shook her head. "Not a twinge."

"Very good."

She must have seemed in a daze because Aria's eyes narrowed on her. "What's wrong?" she asked, leaning back into the pillows.

Ophelia met her gaze and raised her eyebrows. "Oh, nothing. Just a strange dream."

Nell glanced in her direction then continued making their tea. Aria's brow bent with concern. "More dreams?"

"Yes," Ophelia nodded. "Not a nightmare." She shifted her eyes to Nell. "Pyotr visited me. We will need to go speak with Master Gaius this morning."

Nell nodded in understanding as Aria took Ophelia's hand. Ophelia offered her a small smile in return. "I assure you, it was nothing like my other dreams of Pyotr. He was nice this time." Well, as nice as Pyotr *could* be, she supposed. "I hope not to be too long. I'll come back afterward."

"You don't have to spend your every moment with me, Elia. Your life doesn't need to stop just because mine has."

Ophelia's heart tightened at her words, and her brows knit together. "Your life hasn't stopped, Ari." She squeezed her sister's hand, desperate to find adequate words to bring her comfort, but what could she say? Could she really assure her sister that, though the future seemed uncertain right now, it didn't mean there was nothing good yet to come for her? She could name all the good things she saw coming in Aria's future, but in the wake of her sister's recent heartache, that felt too callous. Ophelia squeezed her sister's hand again, settling on, "Besides, time with you is never a waste." She pressed a kiss to the back of Aria's hand before shuffling from the bed and stepping behind the dressing screen to change.

Once dressed, Ophelia gave Aria a quick hug then stepped out of her chambers only to abruptly stop before colliding with the cold, metal plate covering the back of a royal guard. Ophelia's eyes travelled up the massive frame of the behemoth standing before her then swung to Nell. Nell grimaced.

"They've been here all night on the king's orders."

No less than six royal guards lined the door to Aria's chambers, and the stark reminder that someone was seeking to end her life curdled her stomach.

Ophelia nodded, swallowing down the reality that though the extra precautions were inconvenient, they were necessary.

She stepped between the wall of guards, three falling into step behind her and Nell, and headed toward Gaius' study.

Dim sunlight spilled through the windows of the corridor, casting long shadows along the cool, gray stone. The walk to Gaius' study wasn't far, but it seemed to drag on against the steady drum of three pairs of boots echoing off the stone walls. It was confining, and intrusive, and...unavoidable. But if this assassin wasn't discovered quickly, the suffocation of being constantly flanked by burly men in armor would end Ophelia before a blade ever threatened her.

Ophelia's hands balled into fists, and she drew in a deep breath as two figures rounded the corner before them.

Ophelia's heart lightened at the sight of Elliot. His chestnut brown hair fell loose just past his shoulders with a slight wave. It was longer than their first encounter all those months ago at the fall tournament, framing the stern expression set on his brow. George followed behind him, his sandy blond hair peeking over Elliot's shoulder a short distance behind him.

Both men were dressed casually this morning, wearing simple tunics with black pants and boots, leather belts slung around their waists to carry their swords—another reminder that she was in danger.

But instead of the dread she felt at finding six royal guards outside Aria's bed chambers, Ophelia knew Elliot brandished his sword not out of some sense of duty or demand, but because he loved her, and would do all he could to protect her.

As the two men drew closer to their small entourage, she saw the moment Elliot's eyes softened with recognition. A flush bloomed up her neck, and a smile spread across her lips.

She rushed forward, flinging her arms around his waist and burying her nose into his neck. Warmth and amber greeted her senses, and a sigh fell from her lips. "I missed you," she said as his arms slid around her back. She vaguely registered Nell and George quietly greeting each other off to the side.

Elliot hummed and dropped a kiss to the top of her head. "I missed you, too," he murmured into her hair. "I was worried about you."

Ophelia pulled back, meeting his gaze with a frown. "Worried? About me?"

He nodded as his hazel eyes met hers. "You were so angry and hurt when I left you. I knew whenever Aria shared what happened to her, it would only cause you more pain." He leaned his head down, resting his forehead against hers. "When you anguish, I anguish."

Her heart swelled at his words. She would never know what she did to deserve this man.

Ophelia closed her eyes and breathed him in before raising her chin to meet his eyes. "I'm all right," she said. "What happened to Aria *was* horrifying, but she's safe now and healed, and there are other things to worry about."

Elliot nodded. "Your father told us about the assassin."

"Ah, yes, *that*," she replied, pulling back farther. "There's something else now, though, too." Elliot's brow furrowed in confusion as Ophelia took his arm and continued their journey through the corridor. Nell and George slid in seamlessly behind them before the guards enveloped them once more. "Pyotr visited me in a dream last night, like the dreams I had before with Ezra. He brought something to my attention that I need help riddling out. We are on our way to Master Gaius right now."

Gaius' study door stood open when they arrived. The old mage sat behind his desk, round glasses balanced on his nose as he squinted at a mess of parchments.

There are always parchments, Ophelia thought as she entered the study, the familiar bite of healing herbs assaulting her senses all at once.

"Good morning, Master Gaius," Ophelia said loud enough to stretch across the space without mistake. The court mage raised his head, and his eyes widened in surprise.

"Good morning, Your Highness and…company," he said as he stood and made his way around his desk.

Ophelia followed Gaius' gaze to the guards as they stationed themselves at each window and entrance.

"It's the king's orders," Ophelia said as she, Gaius, and the rest of their party gathered in the seating area in front of the old mage's desk. "I don't know all that he has shared with you since Aria arrived."

Gaius nodded as they all took their seats. "He shared word of the assassin. Is that why you have come this morning?"

"No, actually," Ophelia replied. "Pyotr visited me in a dream last night. He showed me something disturbing, and I've come to you for help with understanding it."

Elliot smoothed a comforting hand along her back as she went on to explain the details of her dream, recounting how there were no dangerous creatures in the forest beyond the Far East River. She spoke of the eerie stillness of the wood and the sickening repulsion, then described the barrier itself.

"When I stretched my magic to connect with it, I heard thousands of screams. It was a chaotic storm of noise, yet I could make out each individual voice—young, old, man, woman, child. And I saw rivers of blood spilling from the barrier's edge. I think Blood Magic was used to cast it."

Elliot's hand on her back stilled. "*Blood Magic*?" he asked, his voice holding a severe edge.

Ophelia nodded, giving the same explanation Marius gave Aria in her sister's memory. "It's the practice of gaining power by pulling it from the life force of another through their blood, if I understood it correctly." Gaius gave her a grave nod in confirmation. "When Aria shared her memories with me about—about what happened to her in Balmorea, she showed me how she and Prince Marius discovered a secret branch of the Acolytes of Vindicta called Reapers. They are trained assassins who answer only to the king, and they study Blood Magic."

"That is quite the presumption, given Blood Magic has been outlawed for centuries," Gaius replied.

"I am aware," Ophelia said, shifting in her seat. "Even if we posit that Blood Magic was not used to cast it, how could such a barrier exist without anyone knowing?"

Gaius shook his head. "That I cannot answer," he said, narrowing his eyes. "But I imagine you are not seeking answers about this barrier out of mere curiosity."

Ophelia shook her head. "It's distorting the balance of the land, and neither Pytor's nor Mira's magic have any effect on it."

"I see," Gaius replied. "Then you're seeking a way to bring it down."

Ophelia nodded.

Gaius stood from his seat and began scanning the wall-length bookshelf behind his desk. "Well, there are instances in history that could give us insight as to how the caster erected this barrier."

Ophelia and Elliot stood and followed Gaius around his desk, Nell and George moving to stand in front of it.

"Other mages have cast barriers like this before?" Ophelia asked.

Gaius nodded as he pulled a thick tome from a shelf and rifled through its pages. "Normally, when magic is used to cast a spell so large, it must be cast through, and contained inside, a conduit."

Gaius placed the tome on his desk. The yellowed pages of ancient text depicted runic diagrams and images of what seemed to be historic events. "Several decades ago, an earthquake shook the sea off our southern coast, causing the waters to recede—a sure sign that when the waters returned, they would not stop at the beaches." Gaius slid his wrinkled finger to a fading image of a wave crashing against a wall of some sort. "A team of mages used earth magic to erect a wall, a Stoneward, at the border of the land to prevent the widespread devastation such a wave would bring." He flipped to the next page, revealing more runes and a drawing of what looked like a murky, glass stone. "An earth stone was needed to cast the vast spell and hold it in place. Once the water receded to its normal depth, the stone was destroyed, taking the wall with it."

"Then this blood barrier likely also has some sort of conduit," Elliot said.

"A blood stone?" Ophelia asked, the thought sending a shudder down her spine.

"I would imagine so," Gaius replied as he turned and replaced the tome on his shelf.

"How does one even go about creating a blood stone?" Ophelia asked, disgust sharpening her voice.

"That I don't know, otherwise I would be a blood mage," Gaius said simply as he sat at his desk. "But something tells me it requires substantial amounts of blood."

Something said in one of Aria's memories came to Ophelia's mind, and she felt herself pale. "One of the Reapers in Aria's memories with Raygon mentioned that since the event of the valley, more sacrifices have become necessary to sustain it. They were talking about an Aegis. Could this Aegis be this barrier?"

Gaius' eyebrows rose, and he released a sigh of resignation. "As a Stoneward is a barrier of earth, an Aegis is a barrier of blood." A collection of muffled curses sounded around the mage's desk.

"King Raygon is sacrificing people to cast a blood barrier? But why?" Elliot mused.

Ophelia's nostrils flared. "It has to come down," she said, anger edging her voice.

They all nodded in agreement.

"Then to bring down this barrier, we need to find and destroy the blood stone. Is that correct, Gaius?" Elliot asked.

Gaius nodded, opening his mouth to speak, but stopped himself.

Ophelia sighed. "I know that look. Out with it, Gaius."

The old mage gave an apologetic smile. "There is another way you can bring down the barrier, but I don't think you will like it."

"Go on," Ophelia prodded.

"If you…separate a mage, or mages, from the spell they cast, it will also be broken."

Ophelia's stomach dropped. "By separate you mean…if the caster is killed."

Gaius nodded. "If you kill the spell's caster, the spell dies with them."

CHAPTER EIGHT

DEATH. OF COURSE. THE ANSWER WAS DEATH.

Since learning of her role as Vilicus of Mankind and setting out on her journey to stop Pyotr, death had become a much more tangible presence in Ophelia's life than before. If it didn't follow her out in the open, it hid in the shadows, hovering behind her, seeping into every open crevice of her life: a gruesome inevitability. And she was afraid that, no matter how hard she tried, she would never be rid of it.

Raygon was killing people to feed this barrier. Protective anger flared in her chest. *He's destroying my realm—my people.*

Their group made its way through the corridors. Ophelia walked quietly beside Elliot as her mind fretted over all that was just uncovered while Nell and George followed after them.

Elliot brushed his fingers across the back of her hand, pulling her from her daze. When she met his gaze, worry was painted across his brow. She gave a faint smile.

"And here I was thinking all I'd have to do was saunter my way to Balmorea and 'poof' the barrier away with my magic," she said, trying to lighten the mood.

Not so much as an eyebrow twitched in amusement among her companions.

Ophelia sighed, her shoulders slumping. "I'll need to go to Balmorea,"

Elliot brought her fingers to his lips. "Not tomorrow."

"But soon. Who knows when more lives are going to be given to hold it in place?" Ophelia said, anxiety rising in her voice. "And where, among the Reapers, do we even begin to search for the caster? Or the stone?"

Elliot paused, gently turning Ophelia to face him. "Elia," he said, his voice low and soothing. "We don't have to figure it all out today." He raised his hand, brushing his thumb along her jaw. "Let's take the day to think and wrap our minds around everything then take it to your father in the morning to work out a plan."

Ophelia nodded, and Elliot pressed a kiss to her forehead.

The rest of the day seemed to pass in a blur. Her mind was muddled, moving chaotically between ideas too quickly, one thought unable to solidify before the next one emerged.

After dinner, as Elliot took tea with her in her chambers, exhaustion finally quieted her mind. As the evening grew later, Nell and George were dismissed with the assurance that Elliot would follow shortly behind them. Nell had narrowed her gaze at Ophelia but didn't protest, and neither had George—something Ophelia was grateful for. The day had worn heavy on her, and she just wanted the space to breathe and settle in a way that she only could when Elliot was with her. Her father would probably send someone to fetch him before long anyway.

The two sat on the floor before the hearth, Ophelia curled up between Elliot's legs. His arm lazily draped over her hip as his hand smoothed slow circles on her stomach, the glide of his fingers along the velvet of her dress, relaxing her.

"I'll need to go to Balmorea soon," Ophelia said, breaking their silence.

"*We* will go to Balmorea," Elliot said. "I will not allow my wife to travel across the continent on a dangerous journey without me again."

My wife.

Warmth bloomed through her, and she nuzzled her forehead into his neck, a small smile on her lips. She would be his wife in just under two weeks, yet it still felt too far away. "We still need to go soon, though. This must be dealt with quickly."

"Hm," Elliot considered. "Perhaps we can honeymoon in Balmorea, then, instead of at your family's estate on the coast."

Ophelia pursed her lips, and her heart sank as realization settled heavy in her chest. Their wedding was two weeks away, but people were *dying* for this barrier—each month, from what the Reaper in Aria's memory said. She swallowed. "Should I not act sooner to deal with the Aegis? People are dying."

Elliot's hand on her stomach stilled. "You want to leave before the wedding?" His voice was quiet and a bit surprised, but the slight edge of disappointment in his tone didn't escape her. She knew it wouldn't be a short trip, something he likely surmised as well, but could this matter truly wait?

Ophelia was opening her mouth to reply when a knock came to the door, the voice of one of the maids filtering through. Ophelia sighed then got up to let her in.

Adelaide curtsied then stepped inside, curtsying again as Elliot approached. Her head remained lowered, and she wrang her hands as she spoke. "His Majesty sent me with word for His Lordship as I was coming to collect Her Highness's tea dishes. He said that the time has come for you to return to Hargrave, My Lord," she said, voice quivering, before turning to the dishes on the table in Ophelia's room and stacking them onto the tray she'd carried in.

Elliot laughed quietly behind Ophelia, and she turned to watch as he slipped on his boots and strapped his sword belt around his waist. "I best be off, then."

Heaviness settled over Ophelia as Elliot's hand came to rest at her waist, and he pressed a kiss to her forehead. She didn't like leaving their conversation up in the air like this, but her father wasn't giving them much of a choice. As though reading her mind, he added, "We'll talk more about it in the morning."

She nodded, and he squeezed her waist before stepping out of her chambers and closing the door behind him.

Ophelia sighed then frowned as her mind wandered over the logistics of travelling to Balmorea. They needed to leave soon, but there's no way they'd be able to travel all the way to the far east, figure out how to bring down the Aegis, bring it down, then return before their wedding.

But waiting until after the wedding made her stomach knot. She couldn't simply push this issue to the back of her mind and do what she wanted, no matter how loudly her heart screamed for her to do so.

As her thoughts tangled, the air around her suddenly constricted, tightening her chest. Ophelia gasped, doubling over and falling to her knees.

There was no other way to describe it but repulsive. Where her magic was light and wispy, dancing rhythmically in time with her thoughts and the will of her heart, this magic sliced and clawed. It was dense and harsh, taking from and destroying whatever it touched. She felt it pooling and writhing angrily behind her to a haunting song of whispers.

She spun around, desperate to find the source of the vile feeling and eradicate it, to see Adelaide advancing on her with a blood red sword jutting from her palm.

It was then that everything clicked into place in her mind. This was Trella, the Reaper sent to kill her disguised as a chamber maid. Adelaide came into Ophelia's room each morning to scoop the ashes from her hearth and start the fire. She collected dishes after meals and redressed Ophelia's bed. The sheer number of opportunities this woman has had to take her life since she returned from Nedorra made her stomach turn. How many others like Trella were there roaming the castle, moving through the corridors, learning its ins and outs while the rest of them were none the wiser?

Bile burned the back of her throat at the thought, but she didn't have time to give it too much space in her mind before Trella lunged for her.

Ophelia jumped back as Trella's fully-formed blood sword swiped inches from her abdomen.

"Guards!" Ophelia shouted as she stumbled back into her bedside table, causing her daggers to clatter to the floor.

Trella was undeterred and arched her sword to bring down over Ophelia's head. Ophelia's instincts intervened, and Trella's sword froze mid-swing, the Reaper's eyes widening in disbelief.

Realization flickered through Ophelia as Trella struggled to pull her sword from the air. A new image formed in Ophelia's mind as she crouched down to retrieve her daggers, and when her hands closed around the cool, ivory handles, she tightened her grip, and Trella's sword shattered to pieces.

The Reaper gave a frustrated growl as Ophelia jumped to her feet, and her chamber door burst open. Guards poured into the room, armor clattering over the discordant shouts of several voices. Elliot's voice immediately drew Ophelia's attention, but before she could find him, Trella took her to the ground with a song of whispers on her tongue.

Ophelia's stomach curdled as Trella moved, straddling her then trapping her wrists over her head with one hand in a few quick moves. The whispers continued as the Reaper swept her free hand over the room, and a wall of fire flared in its path, separating Elliot and the guards from her and Ophelia.

"*Fuck*! Ophelia!" Elliot yelled.

Something warm and smooth like glass wrapped around Ophelia's wrist, and a wave of panic washed through her. "You don't have to do this," she said, desperate to end this before anyone was hurt. Death could not be the answer to every trouble mankind faced. "There's no need for such violence!"

Trella scoffed. "You insult the great Pyotr by placing yourself equal to him. You will die for the blasphemy you spew."

Frustration, fear, and anger swirled together in Ophelia's chest. "I haven't spoken any blasphemy—!"

"Lies!" Trella pressed her knee into Ophelia's chest. "Everything you say is lies!"

Movement beyond the flames drew Trella's attention, and what must have been several pails full of water collided with the flames because the hiss and heat of steam caused the wall of fire to sputter. A flash of hope burst within her when she spotted Elliot, sword in hand, poised to launch himself through the flames.

Trella's grip on her wrists tightened as she held up her palm toward the flames and spat a harsh spell of whispers. A moment later, a scarlet spike shot from her hand, and Elliot's cry of pain rang out.

"Elliot!" Ophelia screamed as she thrashed against Trella's hold. Her eyes shot back to the Reaper. "Stop this! Please!"

Trella's weight was too heavy on her chest, her foul breath skating across her face as she shouted something in angry Balmorean. And when Ophelia's lungs did not fill, her mind took her straight back to the pine thicket in Nedorra.

The coldness of snow seeped into Ophelia's shirt and pants. She couldn't breathe.

No, no, no, no—

"*No!*" The scream tore from her throat, purple mist releasing from her body in a wave. Trella was thrown across the room, causing her to crash into the wall where Ophelia's magic held her suspended a few feet off the ground.

Ophelia sucked in a deep inhale and sat up, her mind jumping between her chambers and the pine thicket. She stood, her trembling hands still bound and clutching her daggers. *The sound of jeering laughter reverberated in her mind.*

She stepped toward the wall, toward Trella, until she stood before her. The Reaper struggled against the hold of Ophelia's magic which had her pinned to the stone. Trella's eyes glanced at the flames, and they jumped higher. *Black flames engulfed a lifeless body.*

Ophelia gasped and plunged her daggers into Trella's chest.

The Reaper released a grunt, and her eyes grew wide. Ophelia's eyes met Trella's, peering into black pits of stolen life, and watched as the remaining life she held faded to nothing. Trella's body went limp, the flames snuffing out with the life of their caster, and when Ophelia released her daggers, Trella's body fell to the floor.

Ophelia's eyes widened as she took in the limp form at her feet. *A man lay face down in bloody snow.* A sob tore from Ophelia's throat as she stumbled backwards, blinking rapidly—desperately trying to clear the image from her mind.

She pried her gaze away from the body before her, looking down at her hands, and the remaining breath left her lungs. The spell that had bound her wrists was broken, now staining her skin. Blood soaked her wrists, her fingers, her palms. The coppery tang of another life thickened the air around her and clung to her skin like candle wax. She swiped at it, desperate to rid her hands of the death she could never seem to escape, but it only smeared, glazing her skin in red. She dropped to her knees.

I did it again.

I killed her.

Her vision tunneled, narrowing to the body lying on the floor.

I killed her.

She scrambled backward until her back hit something solid, her eyes fastened to Trella's body.

I killed her.

I killed her.

I killed her. I killed her. I killed her!

Another life. Another member of mankind. Gone, at her hand.

Ophelia saw nothing of her chambers. Nothing of its charred ground or the stains of blood that littered its floor and wall. She did not hear the pounding of hurried boots or the shouts of the guards. Her gaze went distant, her soul numbed.

"Ophelia."

Someone was calling her name.

"I'm here, Ophelia. I've got you."

Elliot's voice.

He was all right.

"Ophelia, look at me." His voice shook, his fingers closing around her jaw trembled. He pulled her face to his, and she met his wild hazel eyes. Blood was splattered across his cheeks and his tunic. His chest heaved.

She felt his arms folding around her as he tucked her body tight against him. "It's okay, Ophelia. I'm here. I've got you."

His words loosened something inside her, and her eyes filled with tears.

I killed her.

"I know. I'm so sorry," he said, anguish coating his words as his hold on her tightened. "I'm so sorry."

Ophelia sucked in her first deep breath, clutching the blood-soaked front of Elliot's tunic, then fell apart in his arms.

CHAPTER NINE

ABOUT HALF AN HOUR AFTER RETIRING FOR THE evening, the sound of shouts and pounding boots drew Nell from her chambers. Smoke wafted in the corridor from the direction of Ophelia's chambers. Her stomach dropped, and she bolted through the corridor with the flood of guards.

She rounded a corner and crashed into a sturdy chest, strong hands clamping around her waist.

"Nell!"

Her head snapped up, gaze colliding with light green eyes, void of their usual mirth, peering down at her with wild panic.

George's words came out in a rush. "I was just coming to get—"

"I heard all of the guards running," Nell interrupted, "then saw the smoke coming from Ophelia's chambers—"

"Ophelia's been attacked—"

Nell's heart seized, and her limbs went rigid. She heard

nothing after that, merely staring at George's moving lips but deciphering none of what he uttered.

Ophelia's been attacked. Ophelia's been attacked. Ophelia's been attacked rounded her mind in maddening circles.

And then she was moving.

Nell twisted out of his arms and darted for the princess's chambers.

A group of guards stood huddled just outside the entrance to the room. Thinking they were attempting to block anyone from entering, she elbowed her way through and was surprised at the lack of resistance she received from them.

Once she stepped inside the door, she understood why, standing as frozen as the guards behind her, heart in her throat.

The room was in ashen tatters. A thick, black burn mark split the space in half. Smoke and ash floated in the air, stinging her eyes. Nell sucked in a gasp when her eyes fell to the blood-stained wall and the lifeless body of a maid crumpled before it in a pool of blood.

And when her gaze finally landed on Ophelia, a muffled sob wrenched itself from her throat.

The princess's hands and dress were covered in blood. She laid crumpled and weeping in Elliot's lap, clinging to the front of his tunic, as though it were the only thing anchoring her to the present. Elliot clutched her to his chest, head ducked low, speaking gently into her ear, and the king knelt helplessly at their side, a host of emotions playing across his features all at once.

Nell was running again, eating up the distance in a few strides before collapsing to her knees before Elliot and Ophelia. Elliot, too, was covered in blood. A deep gash in his shoulder soaked his shirt red, and his skin was pale. Nell had no idea how he was still conscious after such blood loss.

"Ophelia," Nell whimpered, wanting to reach out and take her hand, embrace her, do *something*. There was so much blood. She must have been in pain. Nell clenched the fabric of her skirt in her hands as George lowered himself to the ground next to her. She wasn't sure how she knew it was him, the smell of burnt fabric and smoke too thick in the air for her to detect his usual leather and cedarwood scent. But with his warm presence beside her and his steady hand sliding up her back to rest between her shoulder blades, she simply knew.

"Has someone called for Gaius? Have her wounds been bound?" Nell sputtered, helplessness pushing her mind to seek out things she could do, to find problems that she could fix.

"The king has sent for Gaius, but the princess isn't wounded," George responded, his voice low. "We've gathered that none of it is her blood."

Nell sucked in a stuttered breath as her eyes raked over as much of Ophelia's person as she could. *That was a relief at least.* But it only raised more questions for her. "How did this happen?"

Nell's mind spun around every possibility, every scenario that could have led them here. "Was it the assassin? Where are they?" she asked, eyes frantically scanning their surroundings. "Have they been caught? Are they still at large?"

George's hand slid up to the nape of her neck and lightly squeezed. "No. The assassin has been killed."

Nell frowned as she looked at him. His eyes flicked to the dead body behind her, and Nell followed his gaze, taking in the scene more fully. Her eyes fell to the distinct daggers protruding from the maid's chest, and she felt the color drain from her face.

She looked back to George and sucked in another stuttered breath.

"That was the assassin?" she whispered, and George nodded.

Oh, Ophelia.

The king's eyes had followed theirs, and she saw something flash in them. His gaze went distant for a moment, then he blinked, and his vision seemed clear, as though he'd willed away his own shock. He pushed to his feet and began giving orders to the guards to begin cleaning up, to call for Gregor, to check on Aria, and to cover the *earth and sea's damned corpse.*

"How...?" Nell breathed, pulling her attention back to Ophelia.

"The assassin entered the princess's room disguised as a maid. She has apparently been working at the castle since the conflict in the valley and was familiar to castle staff. She came under the guise of cleaning up Her Highness and Lord Barnham's dishes from their tea and had word from the king that His Lordship was to leave for the evening," George explained. "Shortly after Lord Barnham left, the guards heard the princess call for help."

The flirty lilt his voice usually carried was noticeably gone, a gentler, sterner tone taking its place.

Nell turned to face him, his hand slipping down her back from her nape and smoothing slow circles between her shoulder blades. His light green eyes softened around the edges when she regarded him. It was achingly tender.

His touch, his gaze—meant to calm and soothe. Meant to ground her and reassure her.

And as each brush of his hand loosened something in her chest, she struggled to reconcile the George before her and the George she thought she knew. This was no time for his games, but something told her he wasn't playing one right now, that perhaps *this* was truly who George was— steady, gentle, strong—and he was being this way with *her*.

George's throat worked on a swallow before he continued, as though his next words were difficult to get out. "The guards breached the door, Lord Barnham with them. He said once they entered, the assassin separated them from the princess with a line of flames, and when that didn't work to keep him away, she launched a blood spike at him that impaled him, pinning him to the wall through his shoulder." George nodded toward Elliot's wound. "Half the guards worked to pull the spike from the wall to free him while the others brought in pails of water and beat at the flames with cloaks, but that only served to weaken the flames. Nothing would extinguish them. They couldn't see what was happening through the flames, but once the princess killed the assassin, the flames disappeared, and the spike in Lord Barnham's shoulder 'melted'—as the guards described it. That's when he was finally able to go to her, but the princess was…" he trailed off.

Nell's throat tightened as hot tears spilled down her cheeks, and she had to fist the skirt of her dress to hold in the sob that rose in her throat. She should have been here. Her paltry skills with a knife would have been something, anything, as long as Ophelia hadn't been made to face this alone.

Even as she said it to herself, it was edged in doubt. *What could you have done against an assassin? One of Raygon's mage-assassins, no less?*

Frustration and anguish lanced through her. Guilt and shame biting at their heels.

A large, calloused hand folded over hers, George's arm at her back pulling her into his side, and she felt herself lean into him—let herself lean into him, just this once.

None of them spoke for a long time, too stunned to determine what to do next, how to move forward, as Alphonse's shouted commands and the guards' shuffling boots sounded around them. Gaius and Lyla came at some point to see to the injured and examine the corpse. Ophelia's sobs had quieted by then, her gaze having gone distant.

Gaius's voice shook Nell from the haze hanging over them. "She needs to be taken to another room in the wing. Being here is not good for her mind."

"It has already been prepared," Prince Gregor said. Nell blinked, her brow bending. *When had the crown prince gotten here?* "The maids are drawing a bath for her as we speak." The stiff set to his shoulders and clipped tone told her he was not as collected as he was portraying himself to be. He gestured toward the door where Lucias was waiting. "Lord Lucias will guide you to where you need to go."

George jumped to his feet, holding out a hand to help Nell up as well. She took it and stood by his side, taking in, once again, the evidence of the horrors of the evening.

"Your Highness," George said with a bow. "Might I request accommodations for His Lordship as well? He also—"

"Already done," the prince cut him off. "Your usual chambers have been prepared."

George bowed his head. "Thank you, Your Highness."

Gregor swiveled his focus to Elliot and Ophelia, kneeling to level himself with his youngest sister. His entire demeanor changed; his sharp edges softened as he smoothed errant strands of her hair behind her ear. This was her big brother, not her crown prince.

"We need to get you out of here, Elia," Gregor said, his tone gentle. "We need to get you cleaned up and in a better place to get some rest."

She nodded slowly, not lifting her gaze to him. Not focusing on anything.

The next moment, he was gently pulling Ophelia from Elliot's arms, but Elliot tightened his grip on her in protest. "I will take her."

"Not with that shoulder, Barnham. Miss Lyla will be paying you a visit once you make it to your chambers," Gregor replied as he took his sister into his arms and stood.

Elliot was already pushing himself up, legs almost buckling under his own weight before George caught him. Elliot sucked in a hiss at the pain.

"Adrenaline's worn off," George commented, as he steadied Elliot and draped his uninjured arm over his shoulders. "You're probably feeling everything now."

"I need to go with her," Elliot said, his face scrunching with a wince.

"Not right now you don't," George said, shifting his gaze to meet Nell's. "Lady Nell will be taking care of the princess for now."

Nell started, coming back to herself after standing frozen in place with shock. "Y—yes," she managed with a quick nod before bolting after Gregor.

Ophelia was alive. The assassin was dead, she reminded herself. Ophelia wasn't hurt and she was safe…for now.

She shoved the thought down, the dread beginning to swirl in her stomach as Prince Gregor's back came into view. She took in a steadying breath and lifted her chin, wiping away the final dregs of tears from her cheeks as she followed him and Gaius into what she assumed would be Ophelia's temporary chambers.

As Gregor slowly lowered Ophelia into a nearby chair, Gaius began asking her questions about whether she was hurt or felt pain anywhere. Nell steeled herself against the burn at the back of her eyes. No amount of tears would change what Ophelia had gone through. No amount of tears would haul this new, raw burden from Ophelia's shoulders, or change the fact that Nell hadn't been there when her best friend—her damn near sister—had needed her, so she would waste no more time on them.

Steeling her resolve, she knelt next to Ophelia and took her hand as Gaius examined her.

George stood beside the chair where Elliot sat, arms crossed over his chest and jaw tight. Lyla cut away the material of his tunic and tossed it to the ground. George's eyes raked over his friend as the mage examined his wound.

"The spike you described must have been made entirely, or mostly, of blood. You said it 'melted' when Trella died?"

she asked, and Elliot nodded his head. "That must be the majority of the blood on your tunic, then. There's no possibility you'd be conscious, nonetheless able to stand, if it had all been yours."

George wiped a hand over his face. He should have been there. There was no reason for him to have been there, Lady Nell hadn't been there either, but his heart wouldn't see reason. He and Elliot always fought together, side by side, back-to-back. They moved seamlessly together and were a force among the king's fighters. If he had been there, perhaps things wouldn't have taken the horrifying turn that they had. Ophelia never should have had to raise a blade against Trella, never should have had to step anywhere near a fight to survive. The guilt gnawed at his nerves.

George noted how Elliot squeezed his eyes shut and forced in a deep, steadying breath. It sent a pang through George's chest. He knew Elliot was reliving his worst memories from the attack. Moments he'd probably forgotten had happened until the rush of adrenaline faded and the memories forced themselves to the front of his mind, hijacking any peace and calm he was trying to cling to. It always happened after a battle. There was no stopping it, only breathing through it, and fucking and drinking your way into distraction lest the memories taunt you into madness. It was a practice George likely took far too much comfort in, even after the fighting was over and everyone had returned home.

"Drink this, My Lord," Lyla said, shoving a flask into Elliot's empty hands. The mage was either oblivious to the signs of what Elliot was going through or simply doing what she could to pull Elliot from further descent into anguish. Either way, Elliot wasted no time uncorking the flask and knocking it back.

After a few minutes, the tension seemed to ebb from Elliot's shoulders, his hands finally unclenching, and George felt himself relax a fraction as well.

Lyla cleaned the entry and exit wounds in Elliot's shoulder then covered them in a salve before holding her palms over each and mumbling an incantation. Elliot's jaw rippled as his skin began to stretch and knit back together, but he remained perfectly still, whatever Lyla had given him likely rounding the sharpest edge of the healing process.

The gash in Elliot's shoulder was deep but sealed quickly; only a circle of pale, puckered skin was left to indicate any injury had ever marred his shoulder. "I will send a sleeping draught shortly, but I hope you will not wait for it before you try to get some rest," Lyla said.

Elliot nodded blankly. "Thank you, Miss Lyla," he said, his voice dull and tired. That seemed to be all the mage required, because she gathered her things and left promptly afterward.

George stuck his hand in the water of the bath Prince Gregor had the maids draw for Elliot earlier and winced, his gaze flicking to Elliot. "It's tepid at best. Shall I call—"

But Elliot was already shucking off his pants and stepping into the tub. George didn't protest—Earth and Sea knew they'd bathed in worse conditions, and he had no doubt that Elliot was anxious to remove all traces of the night from his person. So, when Elliot submerged himself in the water, Georged helped scrub the sweat and blood from his friend's skin.

The unexpected scent of smoke drifting from Elliot tugged George's thoughts back to Ophelia's chambers, but it was Nell's face that came to his mind—the memory of the two of them sitting helplessly in front of Elliot and Ophelia, the determined set to her brow despite the tears rolling down her cheeks— and a renewed sense of pride he had no business feeling bloomed in his chest. She'd been so strong and resolved, and it had surprised him, though it really shouldn't have.

He'd seen her like that before, when Ophelia had been injured by that boar all those months ago. At the time, he thought it must have been a fluke—the shock and adrenaline of the moment taking hold of her and pushing her to do what was needed to save her friend.

But she never wavered. She dove right into the fray. Her hands had been as covered in blood as his by the time it was all over, and not once had she recoiled from the brutal injury or fallen into a panic.

During his time in the king's forces, he'd seen the strongest of men cower and freeze at the sight of their bloodied brothers and friends, but not Nell. She'd been more a soldier on a fucking battlefield that day than a demure noble lady, and fuck if his respect for her hadn't grown because of it.

As he thought back, he wasn't sure if anyone had checked on her after that incident. He'd had a passing thought of doing so but hadn't wanted to make things difficult for Elliot by asking after a woman he wasn't connected to.

He wished he had.

Perhaps adrenaline and shock had played a part in her reactions that day in the wood, and even some in all that happened this evening. But lightning rarely ever strikes in the same place twice, and the moment she twisted out of his arms and bolted for Ophelia's chambers, he knew this was simply who she was.

George's mind slowly returned to the present as he rinsed the soap from Elliot's hair, noticing how his friend's stare had gone distant once again. "The only ones on which you should be casting blame are Raygon and his damn assassin. You are in no way culpable in any of this."

Elliot hummed in agreement before releasing a beleaguered sigh. "The mind accepts logic. But the heart and mind don't always see eye to eye."

George knew that all too well. "Then it is up to you to find a way to bring them into alignment, otherwise this guilt will drive you mad."

"I know," he replied, rubbing his eyes with the heels of his palms. "I'll feel better once I can be with her again."

"Of course," George said. "As soon as we are done here, I'll go see if she's ready for you."

Chapter Ten

Ophelia stared into the warm. pink-tinged water as Nell gently worked the shampoo through her hair. She'd never seen Ophelia so quiet, so shaken, before. There was no determined set to her brow or a sign that the wheels in her mind were spinning as she attempted to resolve an issue and move forward. She didn't chatter on about what had happened, giving Nell her usual moment by moment breakdown of events like she had after the tournament all those months ago. She simply sat in the bath, knees to her chest, face vacant of life once again.

Nell found herself unable to fill the empty space with chatter. What words could she possibly have that could ease the weight Ophelia bore? Trying to foster a conversation felt too irreverent—as though it wouldn't be cruel of her to expect Ophelia's mind to pry itself from the events of the evening and simply jump into an easy conversation.

So, she didn't disturb the silence, choosing only to break it if Ophelia did, or to ask her simple things like if she wanted tea or needed more blankets. The only thing Ophelia seemed hesitant about was lighting a fire.

She'd stared at the cold logs in the hearth warily, dozens of emotions flashing in her eyes before purple mist drifted into the air, and a fire roared to life. Ophelia's eyes had lifted to Nell's then, an unexpected determination rimming ice blue. "My fears will not rule my life. I will not let them."

Nell simply nodded in agreement.

Soon after, a knock came to the door, and Nell's heart leapt when she found George on the other side. He looked tired, as she was sure she did as well, but something in her chest eased at the sight of him. She quickly buried the feeling but didn't miss how his face seemed to soften when his eyes landed on her. Or maybe she'd imagined it.

"Lord George," she said by way of greeting.

"Lady Nell," he replied with a wan smile. "How is she?"

Nell glanced over her shoulder, finding Ophelia curled up in a chair in front of the hearth. "I think she's doing as well as can be expected," she replied, turning back to face him. "And Lord Barnham?"

George nodded. "The same, though he is anxious to see her."

"Of course. Bring him over."

A handful of minutes later, Elliot was rushing through the door, kneeling in front of Ophelia before the hearth. Nell heard him murmur something to her, and she lifted her head from her knees. Elliot took her face in his hands and rested his forehead against hers.

Nell suddenly felt like an intruder, propriety be damned. She gestured for her and George to leave, and George nodded, following her into the corridor.

Nell shut the door behind them then nodded to the guards as she and George walked away. Nell wanted to thank him for taking the lead in so many ways earlier, for his steadying presence, but the words wouldn't form on her lips. She opened her mouth then closed it, every word she wanted to say simply dying on her tongue. Heat rose to her cheeks as she floundered, unable to guide her thoughts from the jumbled mess in her mind to her mouth, when George spoke first.

"You were very brave tonight, Lady Nell," George said, and her forehead creased.

"I—what?" She stopped in her tracks and turned to face him, confusion threading through her tone.

"You were very brave tonight," he said again. "I'd scarcely told you Ophelia was in danger before you ran straight into the fray, not knowing what you would find."

As he said it, she felt the color drain from her face. "When you say it like that, it sounds more idiotic than brave."

George's lips twitched and he gave a small huff of laughter. "Some might argue that being brave requires a twinge of idiocy."

Nell rolled her eyes. "No one says that."

She began walking again, making her way toward her chambers, and George walked beside her, a small smile brightening his face.

"I do believe *I* just said it."

"Ah, so it *must* be fact, then, is that it?" she replied, unable to help a smile from spreading across her lips as well.

"Naturally."

His smile grew, mirroring hers, and she felt her heartbeat stutter at the sight. Warmth crept into her cheeks, and the tightness in her chest eased.

But as they neared her chamber door, and the reminder of what she'd just walked away from began to seep into the moment, guilt gnawed at her—Ophelia narrowly escaped death mere hours ago, and she was in the corridor doing... whatever *this* was.

Nell dropped her eyes to her hands. "Well, thank you. I didn't feel particularly brave. I felt rather useless, actually," she admitted. "But you truly were brave. You knew exactly what to do and where to go and what steps to take next..."

A warm finger slid under her chin and lifted her gaze. Light green, flecked with gold peered down at her. Some emotion she couldn't identify, bright and warm, softened his eyes, and she felt her heart's answering sigh.

"Don't do that," he told her.

She frowned. "Don't do what?"

"Speak of yourself as if you aren't the brightest star in the sky," he replied.

She sucked in a breath, suddenly realizing how close they were to each other. It always seemed to be like that with George. When he was near, she ended up swaying into him, unaware of the draw he had on her. Unable, and admittedly unwilling, to fight against the tug of his gravity.

His breath coasted across her cheek, and each of her senses flared to life. She felt the warmth of his body radiating through his shirt, the light brush of his thumb along her jaw stealing her breath.

"You were strong and determined. You stayed with Ophelia when looking away or leaving for somewhere safer would have been easier to bear." He slid his knuckle up her jaw, brushed his thumb along her cheek. "You stepped into the darkness with her and didn't flinch at what you found there. You sat in the darkness with her, and that takes bravery."

His voice was quiet, smaller than she'd ever heard from him before. His tone held a sense of awe, his gaze on her almost reverent.

Doubt in the honesty of his words crept in. Yet as she gazed back into his eyes, she couldn't bring herself to lock her armor in place. She found no deception or mischief hidden in his eyes. His usual shift into flirty charmer never came. He simply held her gaze and let the sincerity of his words hover in the space between them.

A whispered, "Oh," was all she could manage, so taken aback by his words that barely a breath remained in her lungs for a proper response. Were his words true? Did he truly see her in this light? Or was he simply adept at noting her insecurities so he could capitalize on them?

His throat worked on a swallow, and he dropped his hand, taking a step back from her. "It's late. You should get some rest."

Nell cleared her throat and nodded. "Yes. You, too."

He turned on his heel with a nod and made his way toward his chambers when Nell finally found her voice. "Lord George," she called to him.

He spun to face her, his expression so open it made her heart ache. "Thank you," she told him.

A small smile tugged up the side of his mouth, but no mischief shone in his eyes. Something akin to affection flashed across his face, or perhaps she imagined it. "Goodnight, Lady Nell," he said, before continuing down the corridor.

"Goodnight," she whispered to the empty corridor before entering her chambers, her mind and heart tangled in a muddled mess.

CHAPTER ELEVEN

Elliot rushed through the door, finding Ophelia staring blankly into the bright flames burning in the hearth. A vice clamped around his heart as he approached her, knowing the flames were pulling her mind back to the attack—knowing she was reliving those final moments over and over.

He knelt in front of her and gently spoke her name to pull her from the haunting memories. It seemed to be all she needed to shake her from her daze, because she lifted her head to meet his gaze, and his heart shattered anew at the emptiness in her eyes. He took her face in his hands and pressed their foreheads together. "I'm here, Elia," he whispered. "I'm here, and I will stay right by your side."

She didn't respond, but he felt the breath of her sigh brush across his lips, and it was answer enough. He pulled back and ran his hands over her arms and legs, checking for injuries. He remembered they'd said she hadn't suffered any physical injuries, but some instinct deep within him, born on some battlefield, drove him to search her anyway.

Ophelia's hands came up to cover his, stilling him.

"I'm all right."

His chest tightened, and he slid his hands from under hers to cup her face. "I'm so sorry, Elia."

She met his eyes, and a fraction of the sadness held in hers melted away.

"How is your shoulder?" she asked, sliding a tentative hand under his shirt toward the injury.

"Miss Lyla healed it," he replied. The warmth of her touch seeped into him, and he felt some of the tension drain from his muscles. Her fingers brushed over the scar, lingering over the mottled skin.

"Let me see it."

Elliot pulled his shirt over his head and tossed it over the back of the divan.

Ophelia turned him so the firelight illuminated his injury. She brushed her fingers across it several times, but he couldn't feel it through the numb scar tissue.

Purple mist danced between them as she continued brushing her fingers over his skin. The flesh at his shoulder tugged and rippled. He followed the path of her fingers, watching as the skin of his shoulder smoothed and sensation returned under her touch.

"Now there are no marks from this night on your skin," she said before leaning down to place a gentle kiss to where his scar had once been.

His heart ached, and he pressed a kiss into her hair. "I will never mind wearing the scars I receive while fighting to protect you."

Ophelia pulled back to meet his gaze, silver rimming her eyes, and shook her head. "I don't think I could bear it to see you hurt again because of me."

His thumb brushed under her eyes to sweep away a falling tear. "Elia—"

She shook her head and placed her fingers over his mouth to quiet him before pressing her forehead to his again. They both inhaled deeply and remained that way for several moments, grounding themselves in the other, letting the other's presence soothe and reassure that, despite the horrific events of the night, they both made it out alive.

"We should get some rest," he finally said before scooping her up and carrying her to the bed.

His eyes landed on the small bottle sitting on the table next to her bed, and he picked it up. "Did Master Gaius leave this?"

Ophelia nodded. "It's a sleeping draught."

Elliot uncorked and sniffed it, the scent immediately sending his memory back to the tent he shared with George when they were called to arms to fight for the king. It was a common draught circulated throughout the camp when the fighting was over—when the bone-deep exhaustion from forcing yourself to stay awake was always preferable to reliving the nightmare of the battlefield in your dreams. The draught helped whoever drank it to rest, heal, and, most importantly, sleep dreamlessly. Elliot's heart gave a painful tug. He hated that she needed it but was relieved such a concoction was available for her.

He handed it to her, and she took it from him, drinking it down with a grimace. He slid into the bed next to her as she set the bottle back on the table and wordlessly curled up in his arms. Moments later, her breathing deepened, telling him she'd fallen asleep.

But as Elliot laid there with Ophelia curled up in his embrace, his mind never quieted. It raced over everything he could remember from his past month in the castle. In the madness that had been preparing for Pyotr's return, had he overlooked something that might have otherwise caught his attention? This woman, this assassin, had lived and worked among them since Balmorea had arrived in Maraleon, and not once did suspicion rise around her. How could this have happened?

Elliot's mind launched itself back to the attack, and the memory of Ophelia curled up at the foot of her bed, covered in blood and horrified by what she'd done, twisted something in his chest.

Taking another life, no matter how justified, weighed heavily on one's soul. It hollowed something within you, the pain numbing you. Elliot had faced it many times before. But killing a stranger on a battlefield was very different from plunging a dagger into the heart of someone you knew, someone you trusted, who betrayed you.

But for Ophelia, it was more than a stain on her soul. As Vilicus of Mankind, the importance of human life had shifted for her. Mankind was precious —something she was meant to protect and guide. He knew she saw Trella's death as a failure to fulfill the purpose she was chosen for, no matter how justified.

Guilt and condemnation consumed him. She should never have been put in a position like this. He was supposed to protect her, and he failed. Everything that happened to her was his responsibility—if he had been faster or stronger or more aware, she could have been spared this. His mind coursed over the attack over and over, trying to identify which move, which attack, which choice he should have made differently to change the outcome of the night.

Ophelia's face after the attack, blank and void of emotion, dragged itself to the forefront of his mind. The way she had seemed to simply float in existence, not thinking, not caring…he'd never seen her so empty. His chest clenched at the memory, and he squeezed his eyes shut, forcing in a deep, steadying breath. There was nothing he could do now. Dwelling on what ifs would only drive him mad, but the aching in his chest saw no reason. Elliot pulled Ophelia closer against his chest and pressed kisses into her hair, letting the feel of her warmth and the scent of lavender pull his mind back to the present where she was alive and safe.

After what felt like several hours of being unable to find sleep, Elliot gently laid Ophelia next to him on the bed and slid from under the covers. He found his shirt on the divan and shrugged it on before a light knock came from the door and King Alphonse quietly stepped into the chambers.

Alphonse walked to the edge of the bed and combed over his sleeping daughter with his eyes. He looked tired. His clothes were neat, but his hair hung limp, his eyes sunken with exhaustion, and his beard was unkempt, as though he'd spent the entire evening running his hands through it and tugging at it.

"We've looked through the contracts for all recent hires, and nothing looks suspicious as of now. I find it difficult to believe, though, that Raygon would leave only one assassin in Sigova to spy and carry out his bidding," Alphonse said quietly.

"You think there could be a team of them within the castle?"

Anxiety flared in Elliot's chest at the thought.

"That's one theory," Alphonse replied, sitting in a chair near Ophelia's bed. "But an entire network of even the most trained spies would be difficult to manage so far from their base, don't you think? We also don't know how many Reapers Raygon has at his disposal. Could he have afforded to leave so many spies here and forgo protection and gathering intelligence at home?"

Elliot wiped a hand down his face and sighed. "What are our next steps, then?"

Alphonse paused, holding his gaze on Ophelia, and Elliot's eyes followed. She seemed to be resting peacefully, free of any burden or pain. She didn't toss and turn, she didn't mumble, and a frown never creased her brow. She simply laid there in quiet sleep. It was the work of the potion, of course—a cruel trick on those who cared most for her to make it seem as though she would move on quickly from this, that her heart wouldn't be forever marred by such horrors. Elliot could tell by Alphonse's pained expression that he understood as much.

"Tonight, we rest. And most of tomorrow, I imagine. As difficult as it may be to follow such a command, Barnham, you need to rest as well. We will both need our wits about us to help her," he nodded to Ophelia, "and determine how to move forward." Alphonse stood from his seat and reached into his pocket, pulling out a familiar small vial. "For you," he said, handing it to Elliot. "On behalf of Gaius."

Elliot took the bottle and nodded—another sleeping draught, for him. Alphonse clapped Elliot on the shoulder then turned and left the room.

Elliot stared at the bottle in his hands. He knew Alphonse was right, that he needed to rest, but the need to watch over Ophelia himself gnawed at his nerves.

Before he could decide otherwise, he unstopped the bottle and knocked back the bitter liquid. He laid next to Ophelia, pulled her into his arms and waited for sleep to claim him.

The next morning Elliot woke to a dim room, though some light shone through the sides and bottom of the curtained window. A few candles were lit—new candles. Lady Nell must have stopped in earlier.

Elliot's eyes scanned the room, looking for any abnormalities or dangers when, from his chest, Ophelia said, "No worries. I've already checked. This room is as safe and dull as they come."

Elliot turned his head to meet her eyes. A flicker of her usual light sparked behind her ice blue irises, and the knot in his chest loosened. He placed a kiss on her forehead and took a deep inhale of her scent. Lavender and warmth and the hints of the distinct scent of her filled his senses, and he hummed in contentment. "How are you this morning?" he asked, gently rubbing a hand along her spine.

She didn't answer for a long while. Her mind seemed to drift to some other place before returning to the present. She closed her eyes and swallowed. "When Lyla and I were traveling to the Norden Lake, we were attacked. Well, I was attacked. Lyla was at our little camp."

Elliot frowned but continued his slow caresses at her back. She was nervous, or maybe scared. He wasn't sure, but the shake in her voice told him this was not an easy story for her to tell, so he let her go on without burdening her with questions.

"It was twilight, and I was out in the wood hunting for dinner. By the time I knew something was wrong, it was too late. Three men ambushed me. They knocked me flat on my back. One man pressed his knee into my sternum so hard I couldn't breathe, which allowed the other two the ability to…explore."

Elliot's hand stilled on her back. His anger flared, threatening to burst through his chest. He clenched his jaw to stay his rage and leveled his voice. "Explore…?"

She nodded. "One was obsessed with my hair. The other was more interested in the contents of my pouch. He moved on to my waistband after that."

Elliot released a sharp exhale, his blood boiling. "Did they—?"

"—No. Lyla intervened before it escalated."

Elliot took another deep breath and forced himself to relax. He began to smooth his hand up and down her back again, the motion and physical connection steadying his temper. He ducked his chin and nuzzled his nose into her hair. "What happened after Lyla intervened?"

Ophelia took in a slow, shuddering breath then said, "We killed them. Lyla and I."

Elliot closed his eyes, the familiar vice clamping around his heart again, and he pulled her closer into him. "I'm so sorry," he whispered. What else was there to say? There were no encouraging words or platitudes that could remove the taint taking someone's life places on one's soul. He wasn't responsible for what happened, and even if he didn't mourn the loss of those men's lives, he bore Ophelia's pain with her all the same.

She paused then went on. "At one point during the attack last night, Trella had me pinned to the floor on my back and, suddenly, I was back in the pine thicket with those three men." Her voice quavered, and it sent the anger within him roaring to life. "I panicked, and my magic answered by throwing her across the room against the wall. Then everything kept pulling my mind back to that night—the flames, the blood..." her voice went distant, the memory, no doubt, playing before her eyes. "I don't even remember getting up and walking across the room to her. I just remember standing in front of her as my magic pinned her to the wall. She caused the fire to flare, and I...I just reacted." She shifted her head up to meet Elliot's gaze, and tears rimmed her eyes. He lifted his hand to her cheek, brushing his knuckles along her jaw—another reassuring touch to connect himself to her, to ground him against the rage and grief and sadness clamoring inside his chest.

She bore so much pain, and it killed him that he could lift *none* of it from her.

"I stabbed her," Ophelia continued. "I drove both of my daggers into her chest to the hilt then held her to the wall and watched her die." Her tears fell in earnest, and her face crumbled. "Her limp body fell to the floor in a widening pool of her own blood, and all I could see were those two men dead in the snow, feeling anew the horror from that night. But as I sat on the floor, staring across the room at Trella's body, I didn't feel sorrow or fear. I only felt relieved." She sucked in a deep breath that ended in a sob. "Who am I, Elliot? Why must death follow me like this?"

"Elia," he said, his voice soft and gentle. He wrapped both of his arms around her waist and pulled her flush against his chest, stroking her hair as she released her tears, her pain, her sadness. "Trella was trying to kill you. Nothing but her death would have stopped her." He pressed a kiss to the top of her head. "Relief at not being killed is not something to be ashamed of."

"I felt no remorse."

"And now? Can you honestly say you don't suffer from the guilt of her death?" He pulled himself back so they faced each other, side by side in the bed. "You were falling to panic after the attack. Adrenaline and instinct were what drove you. Your feelings in those moments were not steady, and they were *not* a reflection of your heart or who you truly are, Ophelia."

Another sob pried itself from her throat. "How can you be sure? I feel as though I'm becoming a monster."

Elliot took her hand in his and pressed a kiss to her fingers. "You aren't," he said with conviction, holding her hand to his chest. "Monsters never worry about whether or not they are becoming monsters. They never feel remorse and never take responsibility for what they've done." He squeezed her hand. "The fact that this weighs on you is proof enough that your heart has not gone cold."

She held his gaze. "I fear for what might become of me in the future."

Elliot pulled her closer, pressing his forehead to hers. "I'll be by your side, just as I am now. If you ever stray too far into the shadows, I will be here to pull you back into the sun."

Her eyes fell shut, warm tears falling down her cheeks. "You promise?" she whispered.

"Have no doubts, my love," he replied.

She nodded and buried her nose into his chest, and he engulfed her in his arms once more. Elliot's heart swelled with grief and love and protection, still in disbelief that any of this had happened to her—was happening to her. Happening to *them*.

A few minutes later, Elliot felt the steady rise and fall of her breathing and knew she'd fallen back asleep. He settled himself more comfortably, pulling the blankets up over Ophelia's shoulders, and joined her in sleep.

CHAPTER TWELVE

THE NEXT MORNING OPHELIA STOOD ON THE dais at the head of the Great Hall where she and Elliot were to stand as they committed their lives to each other. Her eyes brimmed with unshed tears as she watched the servants jostle about, taking down the finery that adorned the hall for her and Elliot's wedding. She squeezed Elliot's hand, watching as vase after enchanted vase of red camellias and white primroses were removed from atop the numerous pedestals scattered about the hall, as the snowberry garland was pulled from the windows and doorways, and the banners of both their families colors were taken off the walls.

"It has only been postponed, Ophelia. Your union has not been rejected all together," Alphonse said, Gregor, Aria, and Charlotte at his side. "But with the attack on your life and our uncertainty as to how many other Reapers there are among us, putting off the wedding is best for now."

"What's *best*..." she huffed, turning to face her father and brother. "Wouldn't holding a wedding make a show of strength and send the message that, despite the attempt on my life, we stand tall and proud without fear? Choosing to celebrate instead of cower?" Her anger hadn't risen so quickly within her since she was a girl, but the familiar feeling settled in her chest, causing her to tremble.

She felt a small, steadying hand rest atop one of her shoulders—Aria, helping to ground her and stay her rage. Ophelia reached up to clutch her sister's hand and released a long breath through her nose.

"That is a valid point," Gregor replied, "but until we can guarantee that the castle is safe, we can't rule out that another assassin wouldn't use the event as an opportunity to get close to you and make a second attempt on your life." His tone was soft, and remorse filled his eyes—the gentle big brother she saw so little of.

"This isn't a decision any of us wanted to make, Elia," Alphonse said gently. "But the situation is too volatile right now, especially as we work to keep word of the attack quiet."

Ophelia closed her eyes. They wouldn't change their minds. This decision, made by the king and crown prince—not her father and brother—would not be reversed.

Who knew how long before the safety of the castle could be confirmed? How long would she and Elliot have to wait?

Ophelia swallowed to hold in the sob fighting to break free from her chest. This couldn't be happening. Not this. Amid the darkness that shadowed the castle these past days, the wedding was her single ray of light shining through the clouds. It was the only thing she had to look forward to—a promise of happiness for her future despite so much pain. Could one single good thing not be afforded to them?

More stolen moments.

Anger flared again, veiled by her bitter sadness. "I didn't realize we were now allowing Balmorea to dictate our decisions."

"Ophelia," Aria gently chided.

She knew it wasn't a fair accusation to make, but her heart saw no reason.

Before her father or brother had a chance to admonish her for her comment, Ophelia turned on her heel and rushed out of the hall, putting as much distance between her and her family as possible.

She tore through the corridors without paying attention to where she was going or who might be following her. Her heart ached, and she needed to get away, to take a breath, to think.

This couldn't be happening.

First Raygon attempted to take her life. Now, without even trying, his choice reached further into her life, like a knife sinking deeper into a wound. And just as blood flows from the edges of a blade deep-seated in flesh, Ophelia bled greater sadness, greater pain.

She felt her life slipping through her fingers—every desire and hope she held for her future turning to ash in her palms and drifting away in the wind. No matter how hard she fought or how tight she closed her fists, she could hold on to nothing, change *nothing*. Every choice she made, every dream she dared hope for, was set against the whims of destiny. And the lack of agency she held, the lack of even the smallest influence over her own life, suffocated her.

The one thing, the one person, she did choose was Elliot, and now it felt as though he was slipping through her fingers as well.

After a set of stairs and several turns, Ophelia slowed her pace, realizing she'd inadvertently made her way back to the royal family wing. She stopped before the door of her temporary chambers, flanked on both sides by an obscene number of guards, and took a deep breath. In that moment, reality finally sank in and the pain seared her heart—she wouldn't be marrying Elliot next week, and the uncertainty as to whether she ever would shadowed her heart in further despair.

Ophelia released her breath, and the moment the last huff of air blew from between her lips, her sobs let loose.

She leaned her forehead against the door, then Elliot was suddenly behind her, wrapping his arms around her waist, pulling her tightly against his chest. "Elia," he whispered in her ear. His voice was so tender yet strained. She let her head fall back against his shoulder as she cried.

She felt him reach out and open the door with one hand then gently guide her into the chambers before closing the door and taking her back in his arms.

"It's not forever, Elia," he murmured, nuzzling into her neck. "Perhaps a spring wedding will be more pleasant than a wedding in late winter. The weather will be nicer, the wildflowers will be in bloom— a new beginning for Nature and for us." He was trying to soothe her, but the ache in his voice betrayed his words.

She took another deep breath, turning in his arms, and he kissed away the trail of tears on her cheek. "I don't want to wait."

"I know," he said. "Me neither."

"We shouldn't *have* to wait."

"We shouldn't," he agreed. "But we do." He pressed a kiss to her forehead, to her cheek, to her jaw, and she felt the tension begin to trickle away.

Elliot knew how this news would devastate her—she knew it made his heart ache as well— but he also knew how to comfort her, how to seek comfort in her. He knew how to show her that even if they wouldn't be able to declare in front of everyone they knew and loved that they had chosen each other, his choice was unchanged. She was his, and he was hers.

Ophelia slid her hands up his chest and let her eyes fall shut, focusing on his warm breath fluttering against her neck, on the soft press of his lips against her skin.

She felt in the trembling of his hands around her waist how it pained him to have to wait. In the tightness of his embrace, how greatly he needed to be near her. She felt how desperately he wanted her in the soft yet urgent kisses he trailed down the column of her neck. She slid her fingers into his hair, feeling how his breath stuttered, tickling her skin.

She needed him, and he needed her, too.

She pulled him away from her neck, and the moment their eyes connected, his mouth was on hers.

There was no soft build. No slow, seductive brushes of lips. Their kiss was wild and possessive. A riot of grabbing hands and thrashing tongues.

Elliot hooked his hands around her thighs and lifted her up, wrapping her legs around his waist. He pushed her into the nearest wall, and she smiled, humming her approval. It was easier to kiss him like this, easier to feel him.

And she felt all of him.

From the soft chestnut strands between her fingers, to his hot tongue sliding against hers. From his hands squeezing her ass to his desire pressed against her core—she felt him *everywhere*.

Ophelia moaned into his mouth, and he ground his hips against her, small flutters low in her stomach hinting at what was to come. She frantically tugged at his tunic, hands fumbling to pull it up and over his head, desperate to feel the warmth of his skin. He pulled back, chuckling at her unsuccessful efforts, and the sound rumbled through her, down to her toes. She shivered, and he nipped at her bottom lip before slowly sliding her down his body to set her on the floor.

His smile was wicked, her eagerness seeming to spur his desire, and a flush warmed her cheeks. He pulled his tunic over his head and tossed it to the ground, toeing off his boots as Ophelia kicked off her shoes. But before Elliot could pull Ophelia back into his arms, her hands and mouth were on his chest, pushing him back into the bed.

Elliot hummed as he slowly stepped backward, seeming to relish the feel of her mouth and tongue brushing along his skin.

His legs bumped into the foot of the bed, and Ophelia pushed him farther, forcing him to sit. She stood between his legs and let her eyes take in the muss of his hair, the slight part of his lips, the flush of his cheeks, the want hooding his eyes.

She slid her hands up his chest to wrap around his neck, and he raised his palms to rest on her hips, pulling her closer. "What do you want, Elia?" It was an offer, she realized.

A gesture in word for her to take the lead, to guide them however she pleased.

His lips lowered to the hollow of her throat as his hand slid up her stomach, his fingers finding the laces at the front of her dress and tugging them free. Ophelia closed her eyes and released a sigh. Her head spun, intoxicated by the feel of his lips and tongue brushing down to the swells of her breasts.

"As much as I love those beautiful sounds you make, I need to hear your words, Elia," he chided, going no further than pressing light kisses to her chest until she spoke.

She paused a moment longer before saying, "Lay on your back." Her voice was a silk she'd never heard before.

He lifted his head and met her eyes, heat flaring amidst his hazel irises. He gave her a crooked smirk before doing as she commanded and laying on the middle of the bed. She followed him, crawling up his body and straddling his hips. "Give me your hands," she said.

He did, and she laced her fingers with his, pressing their interlocked hands into the pillows above his head. She lowered her lips to his, kissing him, slow and decadent, dipping long, lazy strokes of her tongue into his mouth. She ground her hips against the bulge in his pants, and he let out a quiet groan into her mouth. Heat shot down her body, ripples of pleasure lighting up her core. She rolled into him again, and Elliot huffed out a breath, clenching his jaw.

He knew she needed this. When every decision had been taken from her, made for her about what she was to do or who she was to be, he gave her this tiny sliver of control. He gave her the power, let her guide them. He was giving her the freedom she yearned so deeply to reclaim.

He squeezed her hands. "Let me touch you," he said against her lips, the longing in his voice thrilling her.

"Not with your hands," she replied.

A smile crept up his lips. "Do you want my mouth on you, Elia?"

"Yes," she breathed.

He gently brushed his nose across hers. "Tell me where and how you want me."

"My breasts," she said, the first thought to crop up in her mind.

He deftly pulled his hands away from hers and ripped the top of her dress open, his tongue sliding over one nipple, his thumb teasing the other. She sucked in a gasp, and he did it again.

Ophelia closed her eyes and narrowed her focus to every place his mouth touched, on how he deftly changed the pressure of his tongue or lightly nipped at her with his teeth to shock her. He alternated light flicks with long strokes until finally closing his lips over her nipple and sucking. She released a high-pitched moan as a jolt of pleasure danced through her, hips jerking when he pinched the other.

Elliot suddenly stopped, and Ophelia whimpered at the loss of his mouth. "We must be quiet, Elia," he said, gaze flicking to the door. "There are eyes—and ears—everywhere, remember? Can you stay quiet for me?"

She nodded her agreement, and he nipped her bottom lip. "Words, Elia."

"Yes," she breathed, "I can be quiet."

His lips tipped up into a wicked smirk. "Good girl," he said before rewarding her with a swipe of his tongue over her nipple. She bit her lip, swallowing back a moan, and he hummed his satisfaction, the sensation against the sensitive peak sending pleasure skittering up her spine.

"Is this the only place you want my mouth?" he asked as he brushed his lips in light kisses along her breasts.

A stuttered breath flew from her as she shook her head. "No. No, it's not," she breathed.

"Then where should I kiss you next?" Another crooked smile tugged at the side of his mouth, and he dragged his teeth over his bottom lip. He locked his scorching gaze with hers and awaited her answer.

She sat up and pulled her dress over her head, tossing it to the floor and leaving her in only her shift. Elliot's eyes trailed from her face down her neck to her exposed breasts. His tongue darted out to wet his lips, and the motion sent liquid heat flooding her core with the memory of what he'd done to her with that tongue. She had her answer for him.

Elliot's eyes dilated as she drew the skirt of her shift up her thighs, exposing her center to him.

"Here," she said.

Surprise flickered through her as he clamped his hands around her hips and hauled her forward, pulling her down to his mouth. She'd expected him to push her to her back, not—

Oh.

She gasped at the first long drag of his tongue through her aching flesh, and he groaned at her taste, his hands roving up her thighs to her hips and back. He snaked his hands around to her ass and squeezed, holding her more firmly to his lips. Delicious pressure coiled deep in her stomach as his tongue moved against her, through her, within her. Her body grew languid with every kiss of his lips and more sensitive with each stroke of his tongue. Yet, as much as she knew that he was aware of where she ached for him, he carefully avoided it, teasing her.

Frustration launched her fingers into his hair to hold his head steady as she tilted her hips to angle herself against his tongue.

Yes. She fell forward on a moan, catching herself on the headboard, and Elliot clamped a hand over her mouth, stilling his tongue. Her eyes snapped open to meet his, dismay coursing through her as she leveled him with a glare.

He raised a brow, mirth lighting his hazel eyes as he pressed a kiss to her slick center. "Quiet, Elia, or I stop."

She huffed out a breath but nodded her agreement. She probably would have agreed to just about anything if he'd only put his mouth on her again.

He placed a kiss to her inner thigh then returned his lips to where she ached.

Her legs trembled as he worked her, and the sounds of his tongue lapping at her center heightened the pleasure pulsing through her. His palm muffled her breathy moans as her movements grew more frantic. She climbed higher and higher, and when he finally launched her over the edge, she clamped a hand over his and moaned into his palm as euphoria crashed through every limb of her body, into every fissure of her being.

Elliot held her to his tongue and eased her through the waves of her release, slowing to lazy licks and soft kisses as her body grew pliant. He moved to kiss the inside of her thighs, and his fingers lightly smoothed along the tops of her thigh as his other moved to cup her cheek.

"Good girl," he murmured into her skin, and a zing of satisfaction had her core clenching.

Once her heart finally slowed, she crawled backwards down his body, and dove for his lips. The taste of herself on his tongue sent a jolt of awareness through her.

"I love you," he said between kisses, "so much I can scarcely breathe." He brought his palms to her cheeks and stopped her, pressing his forehead to hers. "Listen to me. No matter how long we must wait, no matter what we must face, it's always you and me. What we have is boundless. There is nothing that could keep me from loving you."

Her lips were on his again, emotion trapping any response she could hope to give him in her throat. How could she ever explain to him the way he'd woven himself into the very fabric of her soul? How being with him felt like finding the one whose heart sang in harmony with her own? She'd never find words sufficient enough to express the fullness of her love for him. To describe the need for him that burned through her veins, the way she felt their hearts intertwine when they lost themselves in each other.

She pulled back. "I love you," she gasped, hoping her eyes, and her voice, and her touch could convey what her words simply couldn't.

Ophelia sat back and began unfastening the ties of his pants, tugging at the waistband. He lifted his hips, and she pulled his pants down his legs, immediately taking him in her hand when he sprang free.

A low, "*Fuck*," fell from his lips.

Bracing her other hand on his chest, she lined the head of him with her entrance and met his eyes. "It's you and me. Just like you said. Always," she said, then she sank onto him.

Elliot's head flew back, his mouth falling open on a silent moan at the same time Ophelia gasped, tensing as she braced her other hand on his chest at the unexpected fullness.

Elliot's head snapped forward, and he shot up onto his elbows. "Are you all right?" Concern bent his brow as his hand came up to her cheek.

She nodded, though she was sure uncertainty painted her face. "I think so," she said. "It's…different from before." She tried pushing down further and hissed at the discomfort.

Elliot pulled her closer, his nose brushing along her cheek. "Slowly," he murmured. "There's no rush." He slid his hand around her waist, gently trailing his fingers up and down her spine as he brushed his lips against hers, the tenderness relaxing the tension in her muscles. She sank farther and gasped again, Elliot releasing a sharp breath.

"Okay?" he asked.

She braced her hands on his shoulders, tentatively pushing herself up, then sinking back down. She tested the motion again and nodded, sliding her fingers into his hair and pulling his mouth to hers as she continued moving and adjusting to him.

Her pace gradually quickened, and soon she was trembling as the tension began to coil deep in her core again. She pushed Elliot back into the bed, following him with her mouth, rocking her hips into him. She kissed his lips, making her way down his jaw, his neck, down his chest.

But when she sat up atop him, she winced, not realizing how much deeper he'd gone with the shift in position. She braced her hands on his chest again, and Elliot's hands flew to her hips.

"Relax," he whispered, lightly smoothing his fingers up and down her sides. He gave her a moment, allowing her to take a breath before firming his grip on her hips and guiding her into a slow roll.

"*Oh*," she breathed, her eyes fluttering as a sharp breath flew from Elliot's lips.

Elliot's hands fell away from her, his fingers crumpling the bed linens as Ophelia rolled her hips around him, discovering what lit her from within and what made him weak. With each roll, with each shift of her hips, the most sensitive part of her pressed into Elliot's hips and shocks of pleasure jolted through her. But it wasn't enough, and as though he'd read her mind, Elliot gently took one of her hands from his chest and slowly brought it to his lips. He drew her middle finger into his mouth, and heat whipped through her as his tongue swirled around the tip.

Slowly, he pulled her slick finger from his mouth and guided it to where they were joined. When she rolled her hips again, and her finger pressed directly into her swollen bundle of nerves, pleasure burst through her, and a groan fell from her lips. *Perfect.*

Elliot's hand clamped over her mouth again, but there was no chiding in his eyes or his tone.

"*You* are perfect," he said with a quiet groan.

She must have said that out loud, but she was too lost to the pleasure to linger on it. This was perfect. He was perfect.

Given all the unexpected and unknowns they'd faced, and would continue to face, the one certainty she had, the one thing she would choose every time, was him.

Elliot's breathing grew ragged, the muscles of his torso clenching. "That's it, Elia. Ride me. Take what you need from me." His hands flew to her hips, his fingers biting into her flesh as he began to thrust up into her. She matched his moves with each roll of her hips, biting her lip to hold in her moans as another release began to crest. "You are so fucking beautiful—so undone and wild for me."

All she could manage was a whimper in reply. From without and within, she felt him—his body melding with hers, his heart tangling with hers, his words setting her alight.

Elliot slid a hand around Ophelia's neck and pulled her mouth down to his. His thrusts turned quick and sharp, his hand tightening in her hair as he groaned her name against her lips like a plea. His hand in her hair fell to her hip, and he clutched her as he gave his final few thrusts then released a deep moan into their kiss.

Ophelia pulled back and watched the shift in his expression as he too was undone for her, enthralled by the way he shattered before her in pleasure.

And as she watched him lose himself in her, falling deeper and deeper into bliss, she followed him, losing herself in him just as fully.

Chapter Thirteen

ELLIOT WOKE. WHAT FELT LIKE A FEW HOURS later, to the late afternoon light filtering through the drapes. Ophelia still slept, curled against his chest, but with the increased guard, and his history with Alphonse's many eyes in the castle, his anxiousness kept him from enjoying the moment, and he peeled himself from the bed to dress. Elliot didn't think Alphonse would make a spectacle of it, but the king's past dealings in matters such as these were not ones marked by understanding and graciousness.

As he buttoned his pants and pulled a tunic over his head, his eyes fell to Ophelia's sleeping form, and a longing so deep for the day when they could simply be together without the fear of any backlash from her father or his council hit him like a knife to the gut.

Aria and Lady Nell stopped by shortly after to check on Ophelia, but when they found her sleeping, they promptly left. Elliot assumed Nell and Aria relayed this to castle staff because no one disturbed them the rest of the day, and he was thankful for the reprieve.

Ophelia finally stirred as the afternoon light began to fade into the pinks and oranges of evening. Elliot loosened his grip as she sat up and stretched, giving him a lazy, tired smile. Her eyes were a bit puffy from sleep and her hair a bit wild, but her ice blue eyes were bright and alert.

Elliot reached a hand up and tucked her bright red strands behind her ear, tracing the line of her jaw back down to her chin. "How are you feeling?"

Her brows sank slightly. "Better, though my heart still aches."

Elliot hummed in agreement and dropped his hand to the curve of her waist, drawing lazy circles along her stomach with his thumb.

"What about you?" Ophelia asked, pressing a palm to his chest. "I know I'm not the only one who aches."

"My heart still aches as well." He ran his hand up and down her hip and thigh. "But I also find the sting has eased." He brushed his lips across her forehead. "You are my solace."

"As you are mine." She gave a small smile and nuzzled into the crook of his neck, palm brushing lightly across his chest.

They laid in comfortable silence for a long while, leaving the other to their thoughts but never alone. When baser needs finally urged them from the bed, Ophelia and Elliot peeled apart. Ophelia dressed while Elliot called for Nell and George to have dinner brought to the room then dismissed them for the rest of the evening.

As the maids cleared their dinner plates, Ophelia stood at the window, watching on as the sun made its descent. Elliot admired her silhouette outlined in the evening light for a moment before joining her, wrapping his arms around her waist and resting his cheek at her temple.

"I haven't stopped to watch the sun set in quite some time," Ophelia mused, leaning into Elliot's embrace.

"Life has kept us busy as of late," Elliot replied, pulling them into a gentle sway as they watched.

"It has, and not necessarily for the best." Ophelia turned in his arms and slid her hands around his neck, fingers free to run through his hair. "Since the wedding has been delayed, and since this matter with the Aegis is urgent, we should make good use of our time and go investigate it."

Elliot's eyebrows rose. "Go investigate the Aegis? In *Balmorea?*"

"I know it seems mad—"

"Because it *is* mad, Ophelia." Elliot pulled away, running a hand down his face as anxiety and anger bloomed in his chest in tandem. "Raygon tried to kill you from his throne far off in Ravenhold, and now you want to charge straight into the viper's nest?"

"It's not as if we are going to send a letter announcing our plans," she replied, crossing her arms over her chest. She frowned. "This is something I would have to do anyway, regardless of how the sovereign of another nation feels about me. We already talked about taking the trip after the wedding."

That was before he knew the threat on her life was so pressing. Before they knew there were enemies hiding among their ranks in the castle. Elliot shook his head. "No. It's too soon. There will be too many eyes watching you."

"The longer we wait, the greater the number of lives given to the Aegis grows. Innocent lives—people—lost in my domain," Ophelia said, chancing a step towards him, gentle concern lacing her tone.

"I will not see you sacrifice yourself for the honor of your cause," Elliot spat. Bitterness, hot and sharp, sunk its claws into his stomach. This was the first time he had ever resented her duty as Vilicus. She had been in danger before, but those times she was cautious, calculated. This felt like desperation, like flippancy. "You aren't thinking clearly. You're making these decisions through a lens of pain and fear."

Ophelia's eyes, at first soft and delicate, shifted severely. "I can't make objective decisions through pain and fear?" She sneered. "You mean like how I planned out the valley's entire defense for Pyotr's return the morning I learned I would soon have to face him? Or how I was able to heal Aria despite the tumult within me? How I was able to kill an assassin who attacked me by surprise before she killed me?" She closed the distance between them and glared up into Elliot's eyes, inches from his chest. "I am many things, Elliot Marxley, but I am not one who is controlled by her emotions."

Elliot's jaw ticked. This was too sudden, too soon. She escaped death by the length of a fingernail only two days ago. Could she not rest? Recover her mind?

There was also the fact that Balmorea would likely be looking for her to launch their next attempt on her life, and this idea of hers to travel right to Raygon's door would almost guarantee his success.

Elliot opened his mouth to speak, but Ophelia raised a hand to stop him. She paused a moment, seeming to rein in the anger reddening her cheeks, then continued. "Balmorea was the next issue on my list of things to deal with after the wedding. Since there is no more wedding, the next item on the list now takes precedence."

Elliot shook his head and cupped her face with his hands. "No. You take precedence, Ophelia. *You* do." He dropped his forehead to hers and closed his eyes. "All this danger, and you haven't even left the castle. What of travel through the wood? The Southern Pass? Ravenhold?"

"We could arrange travel through the mirrors."

He pulled away to peer down into her eyes. "I doubt the temple mages in Ravenhold would welcome the princess their king is trying to kill with open arms."

"They don't know he's trying to kill me."

"Perhaps, but they will absolutely not keep your arrival a secret from him. And the moment he learns you came through the mirrors, he will be after you." He held her eyes, pleading with her through his gaze to see reason, to focus on something else—anything else. He ran his thumb along the smattering of freckles across her cheek. "You have been given the responsibility of stewarding mankind, not dying for them."

She reared back. "Who says I will die?"

Elliot stepped back and shoved a hand through his hair. "You almost died two days ago, Ophelia, while I was there, armed and by your side! How many more successive brushes with death do you need to convince you to flee from danger instead of run toward it?"

"Are you denying that there is an urgent matter to be dealt with in eastern Balmorea involving my realm?"

"I'm not, but you won't be able to do anything about it if you're not rested and recovered. Give your heart time to heal," he pleaded. He would beg her if he had to. He'd promise her anything, everything, if she would rethink this.

Ophelia shook her head and began shuffling back and forth in front of the window. "I can't stay locked up here, Elliot. Always on edge, waiting for the next assassin to pick the lock to my door and poison my tea or make quick work of it and drive a dagger through my heart. I need to get away from this place before it is tainted for me entirely. I need to do something of value, of real purpose." Her eyes met his, ice blue irises pleading for her case as well. "I won't become a resting target for Raygon's assassins. Balmorea will be the last place he would expect me to flee to. Now is the perfect time."

Logically, it was a decent plan—moving within an enemy's blind spots. But every fiber of his being screamed: *Danger! Pain! Death!*

"And I wouldn't be going alone," Ophelia added, stopping to stand before him. "You said you would go with me."

"I will absolutely be going with you. It's just—I just…"

"I know," she said, taking his hands in hers. "We won't charge in blind. I have some ideas of how we can get into Balmorea without drawing attention to ourselves. Will you trust me? Will you help me?"

He wanted to say no. Wanted to keep her here in the castle, with vetted workers on high alert. Wanted her where she would be comfortable and provided for.

But he knew her determination and knew she would do this with or without his help. Going with her to protect her, though he now doubted himself like never before, was the only alternative to sending her into enemy territory alone.

Elliot's jaw ached from how hard he clenched his teeth, and a headache began to form at the front of his skull. The room was suddenly too small, too stifling. He was angry and afraid and anxious and needed to leave before he did or said something he would later regret.

"Fine," he said as he turned and headed for the door.

"Where are you going?" Ophelia asked, the sudden alarm in her voice sending an ache through his heart.

"I need to clear my mind," he said without turning to face her. He rolled his neck before stepping into his boots and opening the door, anger roiling in his chest.

His hands trembled as he walked, and he vaguely registered the steady stream of boots following closely behind him as his feet carried him forward, his mind running too wild to focus on any one thing.

Yes, every other time she'd run head first into danger, she'd always ended up all right. Her intellect and magic had proven to be greater strengths to her than they would have been for any other person in her same position, but this thought did nothing to ease the tension cramping his shoulders.

Because, yes, she's been all right before, but how much longer could he rely on fate to be on her side?

CHAPTER FOURTEEN

OPHELIA STARED AT THE DOOR AS ELLIOT disappeared behind it, her arms wrapped tightly around her torso. His eyes had never held such severity towards her before. His tone had never been so tight and sharp. She placed a palm against the frantic rhythm of her heart in her chest and sucked in a breath.

She must go east. He knew this wasn't a matter of her wants and desires, didn't he? That she was bound to steward and take care of mankind? Did he truly believe she was acting recklessly? Would he go with her but resent her the entire time?

She turned back to face the window as the sun made its final descent below the trees of the wood, and a sob broke free from her throat. Her vision grew blurry with tears again, and she did everything she could to swallow them back, fighting against the yawning emptiness threatening to engulf her.

No more tears, she admonished herself. Tears solved nothing; they offered no answers. She would waste no more time on tears.

Elliot had his own struggles to work through. Looking back, it probably wasn't wise to spring her plans to leave for Balmorea so soon, but she couldn't help it. She had to keep the wheels of her mind working or the space created from growing idle would only become consumed with grief and despair. She would be lost to the numbness that both terrified her and appealed to her, and that was not something she could give herself to when people far off were dying.

She took another steadying breath as a wave of exhaustion washed over her. She felt raw within, exposed, as though her heart had been left to the mercy of the midsummer sun. Her mind seemed to be cracking—too much was happening too quickly. How was she meant to handle it all?

Ophelia rubbed at the ache beneath her sternum and stripped down to her shift, laying her dress over the foot of the bed. A chill ran down her body when she noticed the fire in the hearth had burned to embers. She walked towards it, tugging a blanket from the back of one of the nearby chairs and draping it over her shoulders. She took in the embers, willing them to reignite, and the fire flared back to life. She sighed as the warmth seeped into her bones then sat in one of the chairs before the hearth, pulling her knees to her chin and wrapping the blanket around her legs.

She sat there, staring into the flames as her argument with Elliot hung in the air around her, a familiar hollowness yawning within her.

Mere hours ago, they had laid themselves bare before each other, giving and taking such comfort and love and pleasure. Yet now, it seemed that nearness was forgotten and tainted against the backdrop of a few words. Was their love truly so fragile? Was this the end of Elliot's patience with her?

A tear fell free from her, rolling down her cheek despite her determination to stay her tears, and in that moment, she had never felt so alone.

Elliot's fingers raked through his hair as he paced in the stables. It was the first place he thought to go, and once he started on his path, his course was set.

Reckless, dangerous, impulsive. That's what this idea of rushing to Balmorea was. Couldn't she see as much?

Every terrible outcome that could possibly happen to them as they traveled east crowded his mind as he attempted to plan their journey.

They couldn't travel in a royal carriage or even the carriages from Hargrave—they would be too conspicuous. Not only would it make their presence known once they arrived in Ravenhold, but worse, they would signal to the bandits populating the wood that they were wealthy and a good target for a raid.

They could bring a small group of trained men to help defend against an attack, but that would, again, draw attention to themselves.

Traveling just the two of them on horseback not only presented the same issue with bandits, but also took away the safety of numbers and made every creature in the wood an enemy to them as well.

Elliot was no weakling, and Ophelia with all her magic could hardly be called a liability, but using her magic would also attract unwanted attention. Magic wasn't uncommon, but a wealthy, single, female mage of marrying age living so close to Sigova who hadn't been swept up by an apprenticeship with the Order? Finding a herd of spotted unicorns grazing in the Central Valley would be more likely.

Then there was the matter of her appearance. Elliot was plain enough. Dressed down, one would never know he was the heir to a noble house of Maraleon. But Ophelia. She was the fiery princess known to the kingdom for her red hair, smart mouth, and sharp shooting. He wasn't sure dressing her down would do anything to hide who she was, and he dared not suggest she wear a wimple and veil again, unless he simply *wanted* a tongue lashing.

Dying her hair might work, but that only solved one of the rapidly multiplying problems in Elliot's mind. He didn't even hear when George announced his presence and entered the stable.

"My Lord?" George called, now three feet away from him. Elliot started.

He turned and heaved a sigh, giving George a curt nod before continuing to wear a path in the stable's dirt floor. It occurred to him at that moment that he hadn't even factored in George and Nell to his trip plans.

Elliot stopped his pacing and ran a hand down his face before glancing to the stable's entrance, remembering the guards posted outside and the reason why they were following him. Elliot nodded George toward a secluded section of the stables, the farthest stall from the guards, then turned to face him. "Ophelia wants to travel east," he said, his voice low. "To investigate the strange barrier Pyotr showed her."

George's eyebrows rose then sank into a frown. "She wants to travel to Balmorea?" he asked, matching Elliot's low tone. Elliot nodded, shoving a hand through his hair as he continued his pacing. "She was almost assassinated two days ago!" The words came out in a frantic whisper-shout.

The comment sent a fresh chill down Elliot's spine. He squeezed his eyes shut and clenched his fists. *She was* almost *assassinated.* Almost.

"I have reminded her of this," Elliot replied dryly. "She seems to think the recent attempt on her life by one of his own would be enough to make a trip to Balmorea a move Raygon wouldn't anticipate."

George ambled towards Elliot, stopping and leaning against the stable wall near his pacing friend. "And you disagree."

"Of course, I disagree!" Elliot threw his arms out. "Balmorea wants her *dead.* No doubt Raygon has his Reapers lurking about for any sign of her, plotting their next move. She should be avoiding the place at all costs, not traipsing through its doors!"

"I'm sure she wouldn't *traipse* in," George replied. "Skipping perhaps—"

"Now's not the time for your jokes, George," he snapped, his voice holding a severe note. Elliot rubbed at his sternum, the simmering restlessness in his chest would not ebb. It caused his limbs to shake and his heart to beat a staccato, the sensations making him want to crawl out of his own skin. He sat down roughly on a nearby hay bale and dropped his forehead in his palms. "I couldn't protect her here, in the most fortified place in all of Maraleon."

He let his doubt linger unsaid in the air as George took a seat next to him.

"We were all taken off guard, not just you, Elliot," George said. "We were out-maneuvered by people trained to be undetectable as they take out their marks."

"That doesn't make me feel any better, George."

"And what about Ophelia? How has this weighed on her?"

Elliot was silent. He knew she wasn't unaffected. The night she spent huddled in his arms, confessing her deepest fears and sorrows, drew itself to the forefront of his mind. "It weighs heavily on her."

"And yet she doesn't want to hide away. She seeks to face her next adversary head on, no doubt with you at her side. It surprises you that Ophelia's response to grief is action?"

No, Ophelia's response to her grief did not surprise him. It terrified him.

He was reminded of the night she first found out she was meant to save mankind in Gaius' study all those months ago. She was terrified, but she didn't bury herself in her fear. She never denied it, but she never let it hinder her either. It wasn't in her blood to think of self-preservation if it meant others might suffer for it.

That bleeding heart of hers will get her killed, the bitter voice in his mind spat.

He shook his head free of the thought. The great compassion Ophelia held for people she would never even know—her bleeding heart—was what drove her. It's what made her who she was.

And it's what drew him to her.

Ophelia wouldn't be the woman he loved without her bleeding heart, and no matter where it led her or how much pain it might cause him, he could never ask her to change.

This was the impasse he found himself staring down: follow Ophelia into danger unknown or do what he could to force her to act against herself in the name of unstable safety.

He grimaced at his own selfishness.

George's voice broke through Elliot's thoughts. "You said yourself that Raygon likely has Reapers looking for her. I'm sure they've heard the unease traveling throughout the castle and know the royal family is spooked." George placed his palm to his chest. "Were I one of these Reapers, I'd expect the princess to be shut away more tightly inside the castle. It wouldn't make sense for her to leave with potential danger lurking in the shadows."

"That's exactly my point—"

"No, that's exactly *my* point," George interrupted. "The danger is here, in Sigova, surrounding the castle. No one expects her to leave."

"There's no way to know what they think or expect."

"Think like a soldier, Elliot, not like a lover blinded by fear."

Elliot shot to his feet, fists clenched at his side as he continued treading a path in the stables. Of course, he was blinded by fear. Fear was all he saw. Flames consuming a room. Blood pooling on the floor. The eyes of the woman he loved still as night, staring into nothingness. The scent of death *everywhere*.

His heart began to race again, his panic flaring back to life. His hands flew to his hair and clenched as he sucked in breath.

In for five seconds, hold for five seconds, release for five seconds. Repeat.

Elliot stood in the middle of the stables, quietly fighting his internal panic as he came to terms with the reality of the situation.

George was right.

Ophelia was right.

And there would be no stopping her if she wanted to leave. Even if leaving him behind would shatter both of their hearts, Ophelia was too noble to let her heart sway her decision—something he knew well yet still accused her of the contrary.

Elliot felt George place a hand on his shoulder and Elliot dropped his hands to his sides. "You're right," Elliot said quietly. "But I've never been more terrified for anything in my life. It's my duty to stay by her side and protect her, but now, after this, I'm unsure whether I'm worthy of that honor anymore."

George scoffed, rounding Elliot to face him. "You are the only one placing this shame upon your own shoulders. Even the king doesn't blame you." George crossed his arms over his chest, narrowing his eyes on his friend. "Have you told her how you feel?"

Eyes lowered, Elliot clenched his jaw and shook his head.

"Then start there. Then give up this besotted martyr nonsense. You know you're going to Balmorea with her, so figure out a plan that will keep you both safe." George patted Elliot on the shoulder then led him towards the stable doors.

CHAPTER FIFTEEN

As Elliot made his way back from the stables, shame washed over him.

He had left her.

In the middle of her unease and fear, he left her alone to drown in her own thoughts. Thoughts that likely tilted toward the negative, as his did at the moment.

Walking away in anger was his father's knee-jerk reaction to adverse situations in their family. Elliot learned, as he grew older, that the duke never pursued making amends—*he* was never at fault. Instead, he waited for his wife to approach him, choosing not to speak with her or be in the same room as her until such time.

It infuriated Elliot to watch—the *childishness* of it. And yet, he had done the same to Ophelia. His chest tightened; the sudden longing to touch her and comfort her overwhelmed him.

Mind whipping frantically between remorse and fear and anxiousness, he didn't realize he'd already made it back to Ophelia's chambers until he stood square in front of her door, the scuff of guard boots echoing in the corridor around him.

His intention had been to walk slowly and calmly back to Ophelia's chambers. Control his breathing, organize his thoughts. But here he was, standing stiffly in the corridor, heart in his throat and nothing of value in his mind.

He still felt wound too tightly from their argument earlier, but he knew George was right. The situation wouldn't change, and he wouldn't all of a sudden feel better about her decision to sneak into Balmorea, so waiting for his heart to still before speaking with her would be useless—it would never happen.

No, he'd have to wade through the darkness and face her without knowing if or when there would be any light. Light was not a guarantee anymore.

Elliot wasn't sure how long he stood outside Ophelia's door surrounded by guards before finally plucking up the courage to enter. He opened the door, closing it gently behind him before toeing off his boots.

The room was dark, save for the glow of a fire burning low in the hearth. A chill still lingered in the air though, the stone beneath his bare feet icy.

He had taken a few steps into the room when his eyes fell on Ophelia curled up in a chair before the hearth. She was so still, he thought she might have fallen asleep. But once he reached her side, his heart shattered.

She sat in the chair with her arms wrapped around her legs. Her cheek rested on her knees and a blanket was draped across her shoulders, but she wasn't asleep. Her eyes were open, staring blankly into the flames, haunted and vacant.

His chest tightened, and he knelt before her. "Ophelia," he whispered, brushing a few wavy, red locks behind her ear, smoothing his thumb over her cheek stained in dried tears. He shut his eyes and set his jaw against his self-loathing. *Fucking idiot.*

He dropped his hands to her ankles and rested his forehead against her shins. "I'm so sorry. I never should have left you." He swallowed, gently smoothing his palms up and down her calves, choking on his own breath to find the right words to say to her.

He felt her hand run through the hair at the back of his head, and his chest loosened a fraction. He let out a long breath before lifting his eyes to hers. She met his gaze, sharper, brighter. She lifted her head from her knees but didn't pull her hand from his hair.

"I'm sorry I upset you," she said, barely above a whisper.

Elliot frowned, shaking his head. "You have nothing to apologize for."

A hint of a smile tilted up the side of her lips. "I realize I didn't bring up my plans in the most delicate of ways."

He straightened up on his knees to match her height and cupped her face between his palms, never dropping his eyes from her. "You shouldn't feel you have to tiptoe around me. You should be able to speak freely with me without fear of upsetting me."

She gently wrapped her fingers around his wrists. "But that is what we do with those we love—we take care with our words for the sake of their heart and feelings."

He shook his head. "It's not the same. You were simply telling me of your plans, not insulting me." He pressed his forehead to hers and took a deep breath, the faint traces of lavender on her skin soothing him. "Regardless of what it was, we should work through it together. It was wrong for me to have left you. I'm sorry."

She lowered her feet to the floor as she slid her fingers up his wrists and gently pulled his hands away from her cheeks. She folded her hands into his and held them to her chest. "You needed to clear your mind. I understand that."

His chest tightened. She was too kind. He didn't deserve this gentleness from her. He brought their hands to his mouth and pressed light kisses to her knuckles.

"Perhaps—"

"No," he interrupted, pressing another kiss to her fingers as the memory of his father snapping a book closed and leaving the drawing room the moment his mother stepped through the door came to mind. The way his mother steeled herself against the tears he knew she would shed later in private. His stomach roiled. "I never should have left you. Regardless of the circumstances." He set her hands down in her lap and sat back on his heels, resting his hands on her knees. "We are to be wed, Ophelia. Partners. Not master and subordinate." He hugged her calves and rested his forehead against her knees. "Can you forgive me?"

Ophelia ran her fingers through his hair again, and he sighed at her touch. "There is nothing to forgive."

He shook his head. "I have much to atone for."

"Elliot—"

He lifted his head to meet her gaze. "You needed me to stay by your side and help you move forward after one of the most terrifying days of your life—you needed me to help keep the darkness at bay—and I walked away from you." He sucked in a breath, pressure building behind his eyes as the guilt heaped itself on his back. "You needed me in that fight with Trella and I…I couldn't protect you. And when I finally got to you, it was too late. You were so hurt and lost, and I should have been there to spare you that pain. I have failed you greatly, Elia." His voice broke at the end.

"Elliot, stop," she replied softly, cupping his cheeks in her hands, forcing his gaze to hers. His heart shattered anew at the tenderness and concern her eyes held for him. "You're here with me now. Trella sprung her attack unexpectedly on all of us. Neither of us could have known to expect it. And even if we had, she was a mage. Have you ever fought against any mages before?"

Elliot shook his head. He hadn't, but that didn't matter. "I was too subdued and wasn't paying attention—"

Ophelia tilted her head, giving a faint smile. "We were both caught off guard."

"The whole point of me entering the castle armed was to protect you because we suspected you would be targeted here." He fisted the fabric of her shift. "And I failed."

Ophelia's gaze bore into his. Her concern shifted into gentle determination.

"You're right," she replied. "You are armed in this castle to defend the royal family, including myself, against those who would seek to harm us. But who is to protect my protectors?" Elliot shook his head and opened his mouth to speak, but she cut him off. "I have been given power unlike that of any other, and just as you vow to protect me with your sword, I vow to protect you with my magic." Her face fell slightly. "If this is the standard by which you are measuring your worth as a man, a husband, a partner, then I'd say I failed you as well." She ran a hand over his chest just below his shoulder where a wound from one of Trella's blood spikes had once been.

Elliot shook his head. "It isn't the same—"

"But it is, Elliot." She fisted the fabric of his tunic at his chest. "My heart stopped when Trella launched that spike at you." She sucked in a breath. "If I have all this unthinkably powerful magic and can't even protect the ones I love most with it, then I have failed as Ophelia, as your future wife, as a mage, and as mankind's Vilicus."

His hand engulfed hers at his chest. "No," he rasped, shaking his head. "Ophelia, it's not—you didn't—"

"Then don't speak of failing me simply because you were not the one to win the battle," she said through clenched teeth, her voice shaking as tears rimmed her eyes. "I love you, I am safe, and you are safe. That is all that matters."

Elliot nodded and released a sharp breath before pushing up on his knees and covering her lips with his. He kissed her desperately—a claim, a declaration. And she met him just as fully.

Fuck, he loved her, and he would spend the rest of his life telling her in a thousand different words, showing her in a thousand different ways. He'd spend the rest of his life trying to deserve her, and still, it wouldn't be enough.

He'd failed her, almost *lost* her, yet she didn't find him wanting in any way. She still deemed him worthy of loving her, and as that revelation washed over him, something settled within him, and the words he told her before resounded through his soul: *You are my solace.*

Chapter Sixteen

The next morning. George found himself with Ophelia, Elliot, and Nell in Ophelia's temporary chambers. The air around the hearth grew heavy with tension as Ophelia explained her and Elliot's plan to travel to Balmorea.

George was already aware of Ophelia's desire to travel to the Aegis, but this was the first time Nell was hearing it. Nell sat rigid in the chair next to him, anger tightening her jaw. Or was it fear?

Once Ophelia finished speaking, Nell inhaled deeply and took a sip of her tea.

"You've gone mad."

"I said as much," Elliot mumbled, and George snorted into his teacup. Ophelia shot Elliot a withering glare before shifting her attention back to Nell.

Ophelia and Elliot looked exhausted. Dark circles hung under both of their eyes, and neither of them had bothered to change into clothes for the day. George assumed it was from their fight last night, but if their proximity was any indication, they seemed to have made amends. Elliot was slouched next to Ophelia, one arm draped lazily along the back of the divan behind her, his fingers tracing lazy circles along her shoulder. And Ophelia leaned into him, wrapped in a blanket with her feet curled underneath her.

"I know how it sounds, but with the wedding postponed and the Aegis causing imbalance in the east, I can't simply sit and do nothing," Ophelia explained.

Nell pursed her lips as she set her empty teacup on the table before her. He could tell she wanted to protest, but even George, in the little amount of time he'd gotten to know Ophelia, knew well enough that arguing with the princess about something she'd made up her mind about would only be a waste of breath.

Nell sat back in her chair with a sigh and the movement sent her jasmine and honey scent floating in George's direction—a scent that would have brought him to his knees had he not already been seated. His eyes fell on her, and he silently took her in.

Unlike the rest of them, Nell didn't seem tired. Her golden-brown eyes were bright and alert, her appearance neat and tidy, as though she'd been up for hours getting things done while the rest of them had been lolling about in their laziness. The thought quirked his lips up to one side.

He hadn't seen her since the night of the attack, their duties in the aftermath keeping both of them busy and never allowing their paths to cross. He wanted to talk to her. The last time he'd seen her, she'd been so defeated. Her eyes had been filled with such sadness, and her voice had been so frail. The mere memory of it caused his chest to ache. Had anyone checked on her? Didn't they know the burdens she silently heaped upon herself? He hadn't, until their short conversation in the corridor before they'd parted ways, and the thought that she had been dealing with all of this alone made his stomach turn.

The urgency to make sure she was all right paced within him like a caged animal. He wanted to ask her how she felt. To know if she'd been sleeping well or if she'd been having nightmares. Had she given herself the time she needed for her heartache to settle or had she forced herself to limp through the past few days with a wounded heart because binding it would've been too painful?

His gaze traveled to Nell's profile, and his heart swelled as his eyes followed the slope of her nose to the slight pout of her lips. His eyes fell further, sliding down the swath of her copper hair draped over her shoulder, fixating on where it brushed against her neck. He clenched his fist to keep from reaching out and running his fingers through the strands. She was painfully beautiful and fierce, and he'd never wanted any other woman the way he wanted Nell—with the totality of his being. Everything within him called to her, drawn to her light like a sunflower to the sun.

Oh, shit.

His heart hammered in his chest. *This…was he—*

"We stayed up most of the night going through as many possibilities as we could think of for how to get into Balmorea unnoticed," Ophelia said, pulling George's attention back into the conversation. "We've determined that there are two issues that need to be resolved for that to happen. The first being how to travel to Balmorea in a group without being conspicuous."

"And the second?" George asked before taking a sip of his tea, a quick attempt to rejoin the conversation lest his silence draw some sort of suspicion towards him.

"Disguising Ophelia's appearance," Elliot answered.

Nell sighed. "You mean her hair," she said, crossing her arms over her chest. George did *not* notice how the motion pushed her tits together into perfect round swells above the neckline of her dress. He felt the blood rush to his dick, and he shifted in his seat, inwardly chiding himself.

"The amount of time we've spent finding ways to disguise that hair of yours," Nell grumbled, a playful edge to her tone.

George forced his eyes from Nell, setting his attention across the seating area to Elliot. "I may have an idea for your means of travel," he said. "My father has worked with a group of Balmorean merchants for many years. It's not uncommon for commoners to barter passage with them from time to time. They are currently in Sigova. I'm sure I could set something up for you two to travel with them into Balmorea."

Ophelia looked to Elliot then back to George. "That would be very helpful."

"As for your hair," Nell jumped in, a pensive set to her brow. "I'm sure I can find some way to dye it darker."

"What, like Aria?" Elliot asked.

Nell shrugged. "Maybe. I've heard about hair treatments in passing among the ladies at court. I'll just need to go into the lower town and do some looking around."

Ophelia nodded. "Very well, then. If you two would work on finding a solution for those issues, Elliot and I will work on plucking up the courage to speak with my father about all this."

Elliot's head fell to the back of the divan with a tired sigh, and Nell grimaced.

George stood from his chair. "I suppose we might as well get to it, then." Nell, Ophelia, and Elliot stood with him, and he turned to face Nell, playfully offering his arm with a teasing smile. "Shall I escort you into town then, Lady Nell?"

Nell turned back to Ophelia. "Is there any way you'll reconsider this?" she asked in a tone so forlorn it constricted something in his chest.

Ophelia shook her head. "I must do this." Elliot wrapped a protective hand around her waist and pressed a kiss into her hair, but Ophelia kept her eyes on Nell.

"Very well," Nell said, then she turned on her heel and brushed past him for the door, leaving George standing there with an outstretched elbow looking like an idiot. He dropped his arm to his side, sketched a quick bow to Ophelia then followed after her.

CHAPTER SEVENTEEN

NELL BLEW THROUGH THE CASTLE, ONLY STOPPING by the kitchen to borrow a bag to carry the supplies she would be purchasing in town. She knew George wouldn't be far behind her, but she didn't want to see him. Or rather, she didn't want him to see her in the pitiful state she was in at the moment.

The past few days, she'd been able to stay busy by looking after Aria. When Aria hadn't needed her, she went to assist Gaius and Lyla or helped in the kitchens. She couldn't stop moving. If she did, her thoughts would run wild, dipping to dark places from the night of the attack. If she'd been more cautious, if she'd been more observant, if she'd only stayed behind, or if she were stronger or cleverer, would she have noticed something sooner and given Ophelia more time to act?

What if the assassin had been successful? She would have died, and there's nothing you could have done to stop it because you're weak.

The possibilities drove her mad. They pulled her from sleep and riddled her waking thoughts. She *had* to keep busy, otherwise her uselessness from that night would stand plainly before her, mocking her, and she would break under its scrutiny.

And now there was this.

Ophelia wanted to go to Balmorea to investigate the Aegis. She wanted to find out more about it and try to find the blood stone to bring it down, which Nell completely understood, but it was too soon. Balmorea's eye would surely still be on them, and she wanted to run straight into the gaping maw of her enemy anyway, hiding under a different hair color and different clothes and calling herself safe.

And Nell could do nothing to stop her.

Her eyes had begun to burn when George's voice broke through her punishing thoughts.

"Slow down, Sweetheart! I promise the market will still be there if you arrive in twenty minutes instead of ten," he called to her, the patronizing lilt in his voice grating on her nerves. She was in no mood for this.

She stopped but didn't turn to face him, choosing to stay where she stood and wait for him to catch up to her. She clenched and unclenched her fists as she waited, already fighting her rising irritation at the carefree way he charged into her day like everything was completely fine and their two best friends weren't about to set out on a journey they may never return from.

A handful of seconds later, George appeared at her side slightly short of breath, his hair windswept and his usual playful smirk turning his lips up on one side. *How dare he look so good right now.*

"You really made me work for the honor of strolling to town in your presence," he said, and Nell rolled her eyes before continuing toward the lower town at her quick pace.

"You wound me with those daggers in your eyes, Sweetheart. This morning in Her Highness's chambers was the first time we've seen each other in two days." He pushed his bottom lip out into an overexaggerated pout. "It almost feels as though you aren't happy to see me after our time apart."

She clenched her teeth. *Their time apart?* Like they were a pair of besotted lovers who'd been unjustly wrenched apart? She rolled her eyes again. "I hardly noticed. Some of us have been busy doing things to be helpful."

George gave a mock gasp, placing a palm over his heart. "I have been *very* helpful. The king has had me assisting with his investigation into the castle staff. I've hardly had a free moment to breathe."

Nell's brow arched at that. Had they discovered anything? Were there other assassins working among the castle staff?

Nell bit her tongue to keep from asking. She knew George was trying to lure her into a conversation so he could continue to needle her, and she wouldn't have it. "You must be so honored," she said flatly.

"Very much so," he replied with a nod.

They walked in silence after that, Nell grateful for the reprieve though still very aware of his hovering presence. She practically felt his eyes burning into the side of her head, and her simmering irritation rose further.

A few minutes later, the gate to the lower town came into view, and George asked, "Where are you going for your errand for the princess?"

Another roll of her eyes. "To the market, obviously."

"I knew that, but where in the market? So I know where to meet you after I'm finished with my business."

She heaved a sigh. "I don't need a guard dog, George. Go take care of your business, and I'll take care of mine."

He leaned in conspiratorially, lowering his voice. "You mentioned coloring the princess's hair. I'm merely curious about where you're going to look into such things."

"Well, be curious up someone else's ass. I'm in no mood for your particular sort of trouble this morning."

A wicked gleam flashed in George's eyes. "Oh, to be allowed the chance to sate my curiosity up your—"

Nell saw red.

"—Is there no other woman whose skirts you can try to get into this morning? I have things to do," she snapped.

He cocked a brow, leaning down to be level with her eyes, amusement dancing among the light green of his irises. "Am I one of those things you must do? How long must I wait until you get to me?"

She clenched her teeth; *he was doing this on purpose.* Her irritation burned into hot rage, and she briefly considered reaching for the knife she now kept strapped to her thigh.

"You are impossible," she ground out before barreling toward the market.

He didn't stop her.

The last thing she heard before stepping through the gate was his peal of laughter, and, despite her anger, her stomach flipped at the sound. *Damn George and his fucking charms.*

She seethed as she made her way into the market until she realized the sadness that had nearly overtaken her moments before had dissipated. Annoyed frustration had replaced it, but she no longer felt as though she would be swallowed by her misery.

She stopped in her tracks, puzzled by the realization. George had behaved how he always did, flirty and untoward, but had he been trying to irritate her? That is, for more than simply finding her irritation amusing? Nell looked over her shoulder for George, knowing he likely wouldn't be there but still feeling startled by the disappointment that settled over her all the same.

She shoved it down and continued into the lower town, inwardly chiding herself. He'd shined his light on her, in that way she knew was meant to weaken her resolve, and it had worked. She longed for more time beneath his warm rays, just like she always did. But Nell was now coming to find that time spent outside of George's light was colder than it used to be, and the understanding of what that meant terrified her.

Around midday, Nell had everything she needed. She thanked the herbalist, who had patiently worked with her to find exactly what would be needed to color Ophelia's hair, then left the apothecary.

Despite her earlier melancholy, then her annoyed frustration thanks to George, she left the apothecary in a lighter mood. She'd set out to complete a task, and she'd done so quickly and efficiently.

Nell supposed it was the sense of purpose and accomplishment that had settled her nerves. Stay busy, keep the mind occupied, and it won't have the space to suffocate you with the reminder of all the ways you've failed your best friend and all the things out of your control. It had worked after Ophelia had been attacked by that boar. Then again, when she'd left for Nedorra and the threat of Pyotr's return had loomed over them. Busy was good. Busy meant there were things she could do to be useful.

As she made her way back toward the castle, a familiar figure stepped out of a clothier's shop just up the road. She stopped and watched as George shook the hand of a tall, blond man, his usual charming smile set in place. As the blond man returned inside the shop George faced the street and let his eyes rove over the different stalls and people milling around. He seemed to be taking everything in when his eyes landed on her, and his lopsided grin spread across his lips. Her heart stuttered in her chest as he made his way in her direction. Had he been looking for her?

She shook the thought from her mind as she continued on her way, tucking the written directions the herbalist had given her into her knapsack. George tracked the motion and raised a brow.

"Did you find what you were looking for?" he asked.

"I did," she said, then nodded to the small sack he now carried. "It seems like you've come away with a bounty as well."

He shrugged as they began to make their way toward the castle gate. "It's not much—just some tunics to replace a few that were damaged recently," he replied, a hint of unease flickered in his eyes, and Nell realized he was referring to Elliot's clothes that were ruined in Ophelia's attack.

She felt the blood drain from her face. "I see."

"Ah, but…wait—" George said, stopping in his tracks and rummaging through his bag. A few moments later, he pulled something from within in triumph. "Found it," he said with a wide smile. He slung the bag under his arm, pinning it to his side, and began untying a string that held a cheese cloth around a small item.

"The clothier hadn't opened yet when I arrived, so I popped into the bakery to kill some time." He held his hand out to her, offering her the contents from within the cloth wrapping. Nell blinked in surprise.

It was a stack of cookies.

Nell's lips curled up as she nicked a golden-brown cookie from atop the small stack. "What are you, a child? You went to the bakery first thing in the morning, and instead of getting something sensible like bread, you bought cookies?"

Mischief lit his eyes. "Yes, I did."

She chuckled before taking a bite into it. A mixture of tart sweetness burst on her tongue, and her eyes flew to George, surprise fluttering through her. "You got lemon cookies?"

"Yes," he said, then he seemed to backpedal. "Well, these weren't the only ones I got, but I ate the other ones already." He patted his stomach with his hand as if providing evidence for his claim, and Nell chuckled.

"I didn't realize you liked lemon cookies. I thought I was the only person in all of Maraleon who favored them." She huffed a bewildered laugh before taking another bite of her cookie and continuing their walk toward the castle.

George fell into step beside her, a small smile turning up his lips. "I don't particularly care for them, but I know you do, and when I got to the bakery this morning, Mrs. Bentley had just taken a batch out of the oven. The whole shop smelled of lemon buttercream, and it reminded me of you, so I grabbed a half dozen to give to you later."

Warmth spread through her chest. "These are for me?"

"Yes," he said, sheepishly scratching the back of his neck with his free hand. "I was actually worried these might not hold up by the time I was able to get them to you, so it was lucky running into you on the way back to the castle."

It was Nell's turn to stop in her tracks. She stared up at him and took a moment to search his eyes. His light green irises held a ring of gold around the pupil, the gold like a beam of sunlight cutting through a spring meadow.

She always marveled at how bright and expressive his eyes were—at how she could always tell what he was feeling by simply looking into his eyes. Every emotion flashed within the light green and gold in their own distinct dance. It's how she could tell that he was nervous right now.

Wait…nervous?

He must have seen the confusion painted across her brow because he went on to answer her silent question.

"No one ever touches the lemon cookies on the tea tray except you," he said. "And you never take any of the other cookies, only the lemon ones. Which is really a shame because the vanilla crème cookies are clearly the superior option."

He'd been paying attention to her during all those tea times? Enough to discover her favorite cookie? Lemon cookies weren't a usual preference to take with tea, so her choice probably just stood out to him and that's why he remembered it. That made much more sense. But the butterflies in her stomach had no use for logic or reason and fluttered to life all the same. The warmth blooming in her chest crept up her neck, and she couldn't keep the smile from tugging at the side of her mouth.

She narrowed her eyes, hoping the shift was quick enough to hide the effect he was having on her.

"Trying to get back into my good graces after being such an ass this morning, are we, Lord George?"

He chuckled, the sound smooth and decadent, and something tightened low in Nell's stomach.

"I behaved in no such way," George replied, mirth shining in his eyes before softening into something gentler. "You were just so upset this morning. I didn't think the cookies would take away all the worries plaguing your mind, but I did think they might brighten your day a bit?" His voice turned up at the end, his earlier nervousness seeping into his tone.

Her heart kicked in her chest as she tried to process what he was saying to her. At the implications his words held. She dropped her eyes to the five remaining cookies stacked perfectly in his hand and carefully reached for them from his upturned palm. Her fingers brushed his skin, and a shiver ran down her spine, the contact momentarily distracting her. Her hand jerked, and the cookies tumbled over.

George quickly brought his other hand up to keep the cookies from falling to the ground, his warm hand encompassing Nell's to steady her hold, and her stomach bottomed out. A nervous laugh fluttered from her lips.

"Earth and Sea, sorry about that," she said, willing steadiness into her voice, feeling her cheeks grow hot as she frantically tried to wrap the cookies back up into the cheesecloth without making a greater fool of herself. "They did—I mean, thank you. For the cookies. That was kind of you." She kept her eyes on the cookies as she tied the string.

She saw George shift on his feet in her periphery before he cleared his throat. "Not at all, Lady Nell," he replied.

Desire sparked in her core at the way her name fell from his tongue, and she wondered if that had been his aim all along.

George didn't do sweet things like this. He never usually needed to, his charm and wit doing the heavy lifting for him to lure women into his bed. And yet, Nell had resisted his charms time and time again. So, was this simply a new strategy in the same game?

Her stomach knotted at the thought. But when she searched his eyes for a hint of his intentions, she didn't find the haughty pride or playful mischief she was expecting. His eyes were soft, and perhaps a bit hesitant, as they gazed back at her. Mixed among the sea of green and gold, she found warmth and affection, and the gentleness his eyes held had her sucking in a sharp breath.

She quickly tucked the cookies into her bag and turned to continue up the path toward the castle, and George fell in step beside her once again.

As they walked, Nell tried to puzzle out everything that had happened between her and George since they'd both left the castle that morning—no, since she first met him all those months ago. But the more she thought about and tried to reconcile what she knew of the man walking beside her and what she'd come to know of him, the more she realized her perception of George may not have been entirely accurate—a mosaic of a person with missing tiles.

When they finally arrived at the castle and went their separate ways to prepare for the evening, Nell felt the carefully placed armor around her heart begin to chip and fall away. She was finding that she no longer wanted to don it when she was with George. It was heavy and stifling, and having to hold it in place was beginning to wear on her. She briefly thought that this could have been what George had been trying to do all along—to chink and damage her defenses into uselessness. But as Nell walked into her chambers and dropped off her items, George's gentle chiding of her from the night of Ophelia's attack echoed in her mind.

Don't do that.

Don't do what?

Speak of yourself as though you are not the brightest star in the sky.

She sighed and fell back onto her bed as the memory faded from her mind, groaning internally when she realized her heart was easing closer and closer to that forbidden ledge, and longing ever deeper for the freefall it promised.

CHAPTER EIGHTEEN

Three days later, just before dawn, Ophelia waited behind the castle for Elliot to meet her so they could set out on their journey to Balmorea. Alphonse, Gregor, Charlotte, Aria, and Nell waited with her to see her off, but none of them spoke to each other, the heaviness of dread choking the air around them.

A chill breeze blew by, kicking up the scent of stale, dead grass from the henna Nell had used to darken Ophelia's hair, and Ophelia grimaced. Nell assured her the smell and color would fade over the next few weeks, but Ophelia wasn't sure she'd be able to bear it that long. There wasn't enough lavender in all the meadows of Maraleon to ward off the fetid odor, and in quiet moments, she began weighing the merits of soldiering through the smell or simply shearing her hair altogether.

Discomfort aside, dying her hair achieved its purpose. The color was so dark that, coupled with pulling the hood of her cloak over her head, and her very dressed-down wardrobe, she was unrecognizable. Nothing about her appearance would draw anyone's attention. Even Aria hadn't realized who she was the first time she'd seen her sister with brown hair.

That same day, George had secured Ophelia and Elliot passage to Balmorea with a group of merchants returning to Ravenhold for spring. A small fee was charged for the two of them to travel with the merchants to cover the purchase of feed for their horses and the cost of the mercenaries hired to accompany the group as they traveled. The arrangement had everything Elliot and Alphonse had required in order to feel better about the two of them traveling east: safety in numbers, trained fighters, and discretion.

It had been Ophelia's idea, though, to have her and Elliot travel to Balmorea under the guise of being a newlywed couple honeymooning in warm Ravenhold before traveling north to the Jade Mountains where she would handpick the jade stone that would be set into her wedding ring.

The steady sound of hoof beats pulled Ophelia's attention forward where she found Elliot, illuminated by the torch that Alphonse carried, trotting toward them, George following behind him. Something in her chest loosened, and she exhaled a sigh of relief.

"What a sendoff party we have here," Elliot said as he dismounted, bowing to the king before locking eyes with Ophelia and smiling. His two dimples were still visible through the scruff he'd begun to grow along his jaw to help disguise his appearance, and Ophelia couldn't help the flush that ran up her neck at the sight of him.

Ophelia stepped into Elliot's embrace, and he dropped a kiss to the crown of her head. "Good morning," she whispered.

"Good morning," he replied into her hair. "I missed you."

"I missed you, too," she murmured into his shoulder.

"It hasn't even been twelve hours since you last saw each other," Nell teased at the same time George groaned an exasperated, "Earth and Sea." A smile spread across Ophelia's lips, and she all but heard Nell's eye roll. Elliot pulled back, a small smile on his lips too.

"Are we ready, then?" he asked as he stepped towards her saddle bags. Light conversation drifted from where her family was gathered, and she nodded in reply.

Elliot ran one last cursory look over her saddle bags anyway. "Bedroll, bow, scabbard, arrows, clothes. Ah, good," he remarked, smiling as he pulled one of her boar tusk daggers from where it was sheathed in her bow scabbard. "You brought them."

She nodded again. "Can never be too prepared, right?"

She'd felt almost sick when she'd taken the daggers in hand and packed them, but she knew from experience that it would be better to have the extra weapons than not.

He must have seen the apprehension on her face because he stepped towards her and placed a kiss on her forehead. She welcomed the small act of comfort, closing her eyes and inhaling him deeply, grounding herself against the rising panic from the memories those daggers held.

"I know," he whispered, and the tension clamping her muscles eased a bit. Elliot of all people understood her and the turmoil within her that seemed to simmer and never die down. And as such, he expertly shifted the subject.

"Did you pack enough food?"

Ophelia opened her eyes and turned to one of her saddle bags.

"Dried fruit, jerky, hardtack, cheese, nuts, wine," she listed off as she rummaged through the bag. "I imagine we'll be able to hunt small game on the road to eat as well."

Elliot nodded as his brows bent over his eyes, and he pulled the sides of her thick, fur-lined cloak tighter around her shoulders.

She pressed her index finger between his brows to smooth out his frown. "I suppose it's time for us to head off, then," she said, turning to face Nell and the others.

"It appears so," Alphonse replied, his tone grave.

Alphonse had been livid when Ophelia and Elliot had shared their plans for traveling to the Aegis three days prior. He'd outright refused to let her go, threatening to lock her within the castle and prevent any and all staff from providing her any supplies or means of travel.

In the end, the threat of Pyotr unleashing his wrath upon mankind again should Ophelia do nothing to bring down the Aegis caused Alphonse to relent.

Ophelia gave her father a small smile before Nell, Aria, and Charlotte stepped forward to embrace her.

"Please stay safe," Nell said, her voice not holding the same confidence it did the last time she'd bid her farewell like this—when Ophelia hadn't had a target on her back and no one had attempted to kill her.

Ophelia pulled back. "I will. It's a long journey, but I'm hoping we will be back in a month's time."

"Yes! For your spring wedding," Charlotte said with what Ophelia could tell was forced enthusiasm, but she appreciated her sister-in-law's attempt at lightening the mood. Though, the reminder of her postponed wedding stung more than she expected it to.

"Right," Ophelia replied before turning to Aria and resting her forehead against hers. "You rest up and grow a healthy niece for me."

Aria pulled back, raising her eyebrows. "Oh, a niece? Not a nephew?"

"Of course, a niece," Ophelia said, noting the dark circles under her sister's eyes which were made more noticeable against her pale cheeks. Her heart twisted in her chest for her sister, wishing she could do more to ease her sister's heartache though she felt as though she was drowning in her own. She urged a smile to her lips as she shifted her gaze to her father. "I'm sure Papa would love to spoil another little princess too, isn't that right?"

Alphonse smiled, though it didn't reach his eyes. "Niece or nephew does not matter. My grandchild will be spoiled regardless."

Aria's lips turned up, and her gaze grew distant. "Marius would love to spoil a little girl."

Ophelia wrapped her sister in another hug and offered her the only true words she could at that moment. "I love you, Ari."

"Love you, too, Elia."

Ophelia pulled back and turned to Nell and Charlotte. "Watch over her, will you?"

Nell's eyes softened, her and Charlotte's "Yes," and "Of course," blending together. Nell squeezed Ophelia's hand then wrapped her other arm around her in an embrace.

Ophelia's heart swelled yet ached all at once. Aria was her sister by blood, Charlotte her sister by marriage, but Nell was her sister by choice. For her to move so easily to Aria's side in her absence filled her with a relief she hadn't realized she needed.

She released Nell then stepped towards her father. Alphonse handed Gregor the torch he held as she approached.

"Are you sure you must do this?" he asked, placing his hands on her shoulders.

"Just say the word, and we bring you back inside, figure something else out," Gregor added from behind him.

She looked to Gregor then up into her father's eyes—familiar deep blue edged in gray, softened by the love and worry she knew warred within him.

"I know," she said, wrapping her arms around Alphonse's waist and laying her head to his chest. "But this is something I must do, and I must do it quickly. I can't let innocent people continue to die while I wait until it feels 'safe' to go."

Alphonse sighed. "I know." He pulled back and met her eyes again. "I love you, my girl. Come home soon."

She nodded, her throat working to swallow her emotions. "Of course, Papa. And perhaps this time we will actually hold a wedding upon my return."

Alphonse placed a kiss on her forehead before she stepped away.

"Protect our girl, Lord Barnham," Alphonse said. "This world would be a very dark place without her light."

Elliot nodded. "With my life, Your Majesty."

At that, Ophelia and Elliot mounted their horses and set off on a well-worn path through the wood, the night sky bleeding into a deep shade of navy as they rode away.

Chapter Nineteen

After a few minutes, Ophelia chanced a glance over her shoulder but found her view of the castle obscured by tree cover and darkness. Panic shot through her, and she whipped back around, taking a deep breath to calm the thrum in her chest.

This was the right thing to do, and no one knew what she was planning. No one saw her and Elliot leave. No one knew she was gone. No one was in the wood. No one was following them.

"Are you all right?" Elliot asked, breaking through the haze of Ophelia's anxiety.

Her head snapped in his direction. The sun was minutes away from cresting the horizon, but there was enough light for her to see the bend of concern in his brow.

No, she thought, but lingering on her fear would help nothing. She nodded and cleared her throat. "Where are we meeting our merchant hosts?" she asked.

Elliot's eyes narrowed, but he didn't push her. "Once we reach the main road it will only be about ten or so minutes to a junction in the road. We will meet our party there before taking the eastern route."

"I see. And what of the aliases we are to use around our fellow travelers?"

"I will be William Collins, and you will be my wife—" he paused, as though stung by the fact that his words weren't true, when they should have been in a matter of days. He cleared his throat, "—my wife Jane Collins."

Ophelia groaned. "Could you have thought up names that were any more boring than those?"

"Probably, if I tried *really* hard." Elliot chuckled. "The more boring and plain our names are, the less likely they will be remembered if anyone starts asking questions."

"Or, we could have incredibly fancy names that will be too difficult to say, in which case they wouldn't be remembered either."

"A compelling argument, but you and I must also be able to say our own names," he said, shaking his head with a smile. "Out of curiosity, though, what name would you prefer?"

"Hmm," Ophelia said. "I don't know. Perhaps Franklianna or Maximiliana or Guenevieve."

Elliot snorted. "Guenevieve?"

"I couldn't decide between Guenevere or Genevieve."

"Ah, yes. A common problem among the Marelian elite." Elliot smiled wide, the worry in his eyes replaced by laughter. "Then Lady Guenevieve Collins—"

"No, no," Ophelia said, holding up a hand. "Collins is also much too plain."

"Of course, it is. What family name did you have in mind, then, esteemed lady Guenevieve?"

A giggle slipped from Ophelia's throat. *What a fool this man made her.*

"Let's see," Ophelia said, making a dramatic display of thinking. "Guenevieve…Hershbergersonton."

They both erupted in laughter, disturbing a flock of birds from a nearby tree.

"I applaud your creativity," Elliot replied with a laugh as the two of them turned onto the main road from the path in the wood, the sun now peeking over the horizon, "but I must insist we stick with William and Jane Collins."

"And insult the proud Hershbergersontons? The family won't hear of it. You will make a social pariah of us both."

"Perhaps," Elliot replied, his expression growing wistful, "but our love is strong and will carry us through."

Ophelia rolled her eyes, and they both laughed. "You're no fun."

Elliot raised his eyebrows. "Oh, I'm plenty of fun," he said with a wink.

Ophelia felt a flush run down her body. *Well, he had her there.*

"Then the plain, unexotic Collinses we will be," she sighed.

They fell into light conversation as they rode up the road, discussing how the idea for traveling with a merchant caravan was George's. "George and his father have worked extensively with these merchants for years and assured me they are trustworthy."

A handful of minutes later, several horses and three covered, wooden carriages came into view. They were sturdy structures, not the rickety wagons she'd seen hay salesmen wheel around the square. The sides of each carriage held a window with ornately carved shutters. As they approached, she recognized the patterns as the geometric designs that she had first seen in Ravenhold in the market at Aria's wedding. She'd bought Elliot's necklace from a carriage similar to these, actually.

The group they would be traveling with seemed to be a good size from what Ophelia could tell. She counted ten men milling about, packing and loading various sized crates onto the carriages. Another four finely, yet practically, dressed men stood off to the side chatting as they monitored the loading of the carriages. She spotted the mercenaries slowly circulating the camp, maintaining sharp eyes along the tree line and the road. There were five that she could plainly see but wasn't sure if there were others off somewhere hidden.

As they approached, one of the finely-dressed men walked forward to meet them. He was a shorter man, with a thick black mustache crowding his upper lip. He wore a knee-length, long-sleeved burgundy tunic embroidered with golden thread along the collar and hem, and a burgundy, velvet hat with an impractically large, black feather. Bushy, black curls peeked out from underneath. Ophelia was surprised to see he wore riding leathers and boots, telling her he would be riding horseback with them and not in a carriage as she would have expected. But what Ophelia found most interesting about the man was the double wrap belt he and the other merchants behind him wore around their waists. *Merchants wearing belts meant to hold sword scabbards?*

Ophelia knew traveling from city to city and country to country wasn't entirely safe, but wasn't that why the mercenaries were hired? Were most merchants trained to wield weapons, and she was simply ignorant to this fact?

Before she had time to puzzle it out, the man reached them.

"You must be Lord George's friends, the Collinses," the man said, perching his hands on his hips, a broad smile lifting the sides of his mustache. There was a hint of a lilt to his voice, but only a hint. Ophelia could tell Balmorean was his first language, but the only indication in his accent were the deeper *r* sounds and heavy consonants she'd come to associate with the language.

"Are you Domenicio?" Elliot asked as he dismounted his horse. Ophelia took Elliot's cue and dismounted Blaze at the same time.

The man removed his hat, placing it across his chest, and bowed with a flourish. "At your service, My Lord and Lady. But please, call me Dom."

Elliot held his horse's reins in one hand and shook Dom's hand with the other. "Very well. I'm William, and this is my wife, Jane," he said, gesturing towards Ophelia. She nodded her head in greeting.

"Ah, yes, the newlyweds," Dom said, clapping his hands together and cocking his head to the side. "A pleasure to meet you both." He turned on his heel and led them into camp, hooking his thumbs into his belt. "No worries, dears, we all sleep like the dead around here, so no need to worry about staying quiet," he said, tossing a wink over his shoulder.

Ophelia's cheeks flushed as the rest of the loading party laughed and whistled. She looked over to Elliot and found him staring at her, a smirk adorning his face. She scowled at him.

"You'll have to forgive him," one of the other merchants said as he walked up. "Old Dom doesn't spend much time in civilized company." He was a lanky man wearing riding leathers and a long-sleeved, black linen shirt. His blond hair was fastened at the nape of his neck and flowed to what looked like the middle of his back from where Ophelia was standing. The same double wrap belt adorned his waist, and a silver pendant and chain hung around his neck.

Dom slipped off his hat and swatted the man across the chest with it, not being able to reach any higher. "You should be whipped for calling me 'old,' Brosey."

The man chuckled, stepping forward to shake Elliot's hand, his pale green eyes shining with mirth. "Name's Ambrose." He bowed his head toward Ophelia. "It's a pleasure to have you both journey with us."

Two members of the crew came over and took Elliot and Ophelia's horses' reins as the other two merchants stepped forward to introduce themselves. Ophelia felt instant relief when she saw they were both women. They introduced themselves as Naora and Sarada, two sisters who grew up with Dom and knew him like a brother.

Apparently, there wasn't much for them in their small mountain village in northern Balmorea, and when Dom headed south to make his fortune in furs, the girls followed him. Over the years, as opportunities grew and business expanded, fur trade became fine linen and silk trade. "And we haven't looked back since," Naora said, her accent similar to Dom's yet lighter, airier.

They both wore long, lavish velvet dresses with slits up to their hips, to make riding more feasible, and riding leathers and boots underneath. Naora was the older sister, with auburn hair falling down her back in tight ringlets. Sarada stood even with Naora and had the same curls as her sister, but hers were a deep shade of brown instead of auburn, and both of them shared the same long lashes and stormy blue eyes.

As the merchants chatted, Ophelia felt Elliot's gaze on her. She looked up and found his eyes locked on her, a gentle smile spreading across his face. It pulled the same smile from her, and she pressed into his side, resting her forehead to his shoulder. His arm looped around her waist, and he pressed his lips to the top of her head.

"Aw," Sarada said with raised brows as she looked at her sister. Naora matched her sister's expression and placed a light hand to Ophelia's shoulder. "Dom was right. You won't have to worry about being quiet," she said, looking between them both before walking away.

"Yes, and please do be sure to name the child you conceive on this trip after one of us. That would be lovely!" Sarada added with a wink as she followed behind her sister.

Ophelia felt her cheeks burn as she buried her face into Elliot's chest. "Is everyone under the assumption that we are going to be spending every night of this trip fucking like rabbits?"

Elliot's responding chuckle rumbled through her, and she felt the stubble of his beard along her cheek as he lowered his mouth to her ear.

"Apparently, so, but," he said, his voice low and smooth as he raised his hand to push her hair over her shoulder, "you did such a good job being quiet the other day, I'm sure it's no matter."

Her eyes widened, and she snapped her head up to meet his gaze.

Elliot bit his lip to hold in his laugh, and amusement flashed in his eyes. Her shoulders slumped, and she shook her head, holding in her own grin. "You are the worst," she said, losing her hold on her expression and letting the smile slip through.

He leaned down again. "I'd never dream of putting you in a situation you find uncomfortable." He pressed a kiss to her temple, and her nervousness eased back. "Oh, no. We've had to make some concessions in the past, but moving forward, when you're with me, I don't want your mind worried about who might see or hear." He brushed his nose along her jaw. "I want you hot and eager, every nerve, every sense trained only on me." He nipped the sensitive skin of her earlobe, and she sucked in a gasp. "I want you begging for me to send you into bliss, to fill you in every delicious way I can." She was breathless, heat pooling low in her stomach at the images his words conjured, and she clutched at the front of his tunic to steady herself. His voice dropped to a whisper. "And those pretty sounds you make when I have you under me?" He gently brushed his lips along her neck. "Those are for *my* ears only. No one else's." His grip on her hip tightened possessively, and desire tore through her.

"All right, love birds. We get it—you're mad for each other," Dom yelled across the camp, and light laughter scattered among the crew. "Peel yourselves apart and get over here."

Elliot pulled away, heat and want hooding his eyes.

Ophelia cleared her throat and tucked her hair behind her ear. "Right," she said with a nod.

Elliot released a dark chuckle before taking her hand and drawing her toward the gathering caravan.

CHAPTER TWENTY

GEORGE FOUND HIMSELF IN THE CASTLE DUN-
geon several hours later as the interview he was transcribing
with Lucias shifted into an interrogation. The man in question
wasn't an assassin but had definitely been discovered feeding
information from inside the castle to any bidder with the
highest price.

Before the attack on Ophelia, Alphonse and Gregor
had begun an investigation of the castle staff in hopes of
uncovering the assassin before they made their move. They'd
only begun organizing the hiring documents when Ophelia
was attacked, but the king and crown prince decided to
move forward with the investigation—a decision George
and Elliot had agreed with. He and Elliot had been assigned
duties to assist in the investigation, but since Elliot was now
trotting off to Balmorea with Ophelia, George was doing the
work both of them were meant to share.

It wasn't all bad. Now that they had a list of employees to

go through, George's main responsibility was transcribing all information discussed and revealed during these interviews. This one was only the second interview that had taken a turn into what Lord Lucias referred to as 'advanced interview techniques.' The man was currently passed out, and Lucias was wiping blood from one of his knives, allowing George's mind to wander toward more pleasant things to escape the gruesome sight before him. As of late, all of his pleasant thoughts seemed to center around one woman in particular, and that was no different now.

A groan pulled George from his daydreams as the man tied to the chair before him began surfacing to consciousness. A sigh pried itself from between George's lips, and he rubbed a hand along his jaw.

Lucias chuckled in response. "I'm not thinking there's much more he can tell us," the king's second asserted. "We'll finish with him and call it a day."

George nodded and opened his notebook to the last page he wrote on. He was ready to be done with this, his mind now occupied with thoughts of the fierce and beautiful woman who could hardly stand him. He'd seen her this morning when they all saw Ophelia and Elliot off, and she'd seemed well—as best he could tell in the pre-dawn light. But he knew the morning had likely been hard for her. It hadn't been the easiest for him either, but she'd rushed off with Aria and Charlotte once Ophelia and Elliot had disappeared from view, and he hadn't been able to speak with her.

A restlessness churned inside him at not knowing how Nell was doing. He knew she was doing everything she could to be strong, diving headfirst into duty to stave off the heartache. But no matter how busy she stayed or how sturdy she kept her composure, he could see how she was but a whisper of her true self. The fire that usually burned in her eyes had dimmed. The ease with which she'd smiled and laughed all those months ago during Ophelia and Elliot's hunt in the wood was absent from her. Cracks veined through her tough exterior, and he didn't know how much longer she could put herself through all of this before finally shattering completely.

He worried his bottom lip, determined to seek her out once he was done here. She'd likely be with Aria, depending on the time of day. Was it nearing midday, or had they missed lunch?

Another agonizing hour passed before Lucias deemed their work complete for the day. George left his notebook with Lucias for him to review with Alphonse and Gregor later that day, and was then dismissed.

George needed to change before he went to find Nell. The dungeon had smelled of mildew and piss, and he was sure some of it still clung to his clothing. He hurried up the stairs leading from the dungeon, finally allowing himself to take a lungful of air once he reached the top where the scent of misery no longer lingered. He began to make his way toward his chambers when a commotion near the castle entrance had him skidding to a halt.

A strange assortment of mages and maids huddled around three finely dressed women—or, at least, he assumed they'd have been finely dressed if their appearances hadn't seemed so travel-worn. Tangled hair fell from what had probably once been neat plaits and buns. The frayed hems of their ornate dresses were caked in dirt, the skirts torn in places, and any exposed skin held angry scratches.

When the women's faces came into view, a curse flew from George's mouth and he rushed toward them.

It was Aria's ladies. Lady Collete led the group, Ladies Philippa and Evandra close behind. Nell and Charlotte were with them. Evandra's arm was slung over Nell's shoulder while Charlotte had an arm around Philippa's shoulders. It was madness, each voice indecipherable over the other in the din. *Had they fucking walked all the way here from Balmorea?*

As though she'd heard his thoughts, Collete's eyes found George, and determination quickened her stride. She pushed past a pair of maids and continued towards him. Her eyes seemed dazed, distant, as though she were barely aware of where she was. "Lord George. Princess Aria, where is she?"

"We already told you, she's in her chambers, Lady Collete," Nell cut in, her voice gentle, yet stern.

"R-Right. We must go to her at once," Collete responded, her tone expressionless, as though the only thought her mind could produce and decipher was getting to Aria and nothing else. She was falling to panic and needed to lay down. She needed to go see Master Gaius in his study.

But before he could voice anything, Evandra's eyes met his and something akin to relief flickered across her face. "George!" she cried before throwing her arms around his shoulders. He stumbled backward, catching her around the waist before she could fall to the ground, and she clung to him, burying her face into his neck and sobbing.

"Vandra," he murmured, brows drawn together. "What happened?" He looked to Nell for answers once he steadied himself on his feet, but her gaze quickly flicked to Phillippa before their eyes could meet, and Evandra answered before he could ask again.

"We fled. The prince helped us escape, but it was such an ordeal! They had to smuggle us out, then we had to run. I tripped and hurt my ankle, but we couldn't stop!" She began to sob again, and he smoothed slow circles along her back, trying his best to calm her as his eyes roved over the expanding party.

He wasn't sure how accurate Evandra's account was, but if the state in which the three ladies arrived at the castle was any indication, their journey back to Sigova was no stroll through the gardens.

"How did you all get here?"

She pulled back to meet his gaze. Her grey eyes were bloodshot and watery, so different from the last time he'd held her gaze—when they'd been heavy with desire and bright with pleasure. That had been before the tournament. Months ago. Months that might as well have been a lifetime ago for all the desire he didn't feel as the memory of their last time together flew through his mind.

Her hands slid to his shoulders and clenched his tunic, but he didn't find desire in her eyes.

He found fear.

"Sandro was one of the prince's Shadows who helped us escape. He said the king reasoned that since Aria was gone and he couldn't simply send us back to Maraleon, there was no use for us. He got paranoid and held us in his dungeons so our presence without Aria wouldn't raise suspicions. He didn't want us sending missives or doing anything that might call undue attention to him, either. Prince Marius came with Sandro to free us. He said the king had made plans to have us 'taken care of' the following day to 'tie up loose ends.'" Her face crumpled, and her hands tightened on his tunic.

"Fuck, Vandra. How did you all escape? You said something about the prince?"

She nodded, taking a deep, steadying breath. "He had his Shadows smuggle us out in the middle of the night with some shipment or other. It was dark and cramped, and we only had passage to a certain point. After which, we had to get out and walk. But then we saw the king's Vidaar coming up the path, and we had to run before they spotted us. That's when I fell." She shifted on her good foot as if to emphasize her injury. "We finally made it to the border where some mages from the temple in Sigova were waiting for us. We made it to the city just this afternoon and came right to the castle."

George let out a breath and pulled her into his chest.

"I'm so sorry, Vandra. You never should have gone through any of that." He rested his chin atop her head, and she burrowed into his chest. "You all are safe now."

The words tasted sour on his tongue in the wake of Ophelia's attack, but he hoped they were true. As far as any imminent threat from the king of Balmorea was concerned, anyway. Evandra began to cry again at his words, whether in sadness or relief, he wasn't sure, so he simply held her in his embrace and let her cry, offering what small comfort he could after everything she'd just endured.

More maids shuffled toward their group, adding to the din of empty questions and unhelpful answers. Master Gaius was there now, apparently having arrived while he was speaking with Evandra, and the mage, Miss Lyla, and Charlotte were currently struggling to convince Collete that the three ladies needed to go to his study to have their wounds tended to. She frantically shook her head, insisting she go straight to

Aria. Nell had a crying Phillippa in her arms and was trying to take in everything as a whole as well, likely coming to the same conclusion as him that the situation was growing more unruly and chaotic by the second.

Without another thought, Nell handed Phillippa off to a maid, stuck two fingers in her mouth, and whistled so loudly he was sure they'd find hunting dogs from Nedorra on their doorstep come morning. The chatter of voices ceased immediately, and all eyes fell to Nell, waiting for her command.

There she is, George thought, pride swelling in his chest.

She didn't hesitate, and he watched on, dumbstruck, as she singled out maids and guards, and assigned them tasks or sent them back to their usual duties. She ordered the mages to return to the temple across the city and sent a guard to alert the king of what was happening.

In a matter of minutes, Nell had stepped in and swept order through the chaos, leaving the corridor cleared and quiet with not one person nosily idling where they weren't needed.

Nell then turned to Collete, her tone brooking no argument. "You, Phillippa, and Evandra will go with Master Gaius and Miss Lyla so they can tend to your injuries—"

"But Aria—"

"Is just fine. I will bring her to you all in Master Gaius's study." Nell gave the lady a reassuring smile. "She will be very eager to see you, but you all need to be taken care of first."

Collete nodded, the haze still clouding her stare, but she followed Nell's instructions, taking Charlotte's arm and following Lyla and Master Gaius down the corridor. The maid with Phillippa followed behind them.

When Nell turned to face him, he didn't even try to hide the smile he knew spread wide across his mouth. But when her eyes landed on him, and she took in the sight of him holding Evandra close as she cried into his chest, she stiffened. He watched as the openness and resoluteness in her expression hardened into something inscrutable and guarded, and his smile fell from his lips.

No, no, no! Fuck!

"Lord George, Lady Evandra needs to go with the others to Master Gaius's study," she said stiffly, her face a mask of indifference, and his heart sank.

"No—Nell, I—"

"*Lady* Nell," she corrected, sharp enough to cut glass yet wooden, revealing nothing of her emotions. "Her ankle is injured. She can't walk and will need help."

He nodded absently, taken aback by the flatness of her tone. He couldn't stand the sound of it—couldn't stand to have her level those beautiful, golden-brown eyes on him with such coldness. He'd take all the annoyed eyerolls and all the venom her sharp tongue could spit, but he couldn't stand to watch as Nell's light dimmed right before him, knowing he'd been the cause of it. It filled his chest with a hollow ache, and panic rose within him.

His eyes darted across the space in search of someone he could enlist to take Evandra so he could remedy this. He needed to talk to Nell and explain this before he became the next item on her list of heartaches that she worked herself ragged to avoid facing.

But as he looked around, no one remained in the corridor, all having gone off to complete the tasks Nell had assigned them, and his panic flared into desperation.

His eyes settled back on Nell. "What about you? Could you help me take—"

"I need to go get Her Highness," she replied curtly, striding quickly past him and Evandra. "And you seem to have everything handled here just fine."

"Nell—"

"Take her to Gaius's study, Lord George," she said with an air of finality before disappearing around the corner, leaving him alone in the corridor, holding the wrong woman, and wishing he'd stayed in the dungeons a few minutes longer.

Chapter Twenty One

As soon as word of her ladies had fallen from Nell's lips, Aria bolted for Gaius's study. Nell knew it was the love Aria held for her ladies that quickened her steps and etched the worry across her brow—the princess's own experiences with Raygon's cruelty likely supplying her mind with all manner of terrible images of what she might find when she arrived at Gaius's study.

All three ladies had made it to the mage's study, Evandra included, and were being examined or treated by either Gaius, Lyla, or one of the Temple mages that had elected to help instead of returning with the others. A cursory glance around the study told Nell that George hadn't stayed around, and she'd never felt more relieved.

Her heart sank to her stomach at the memory of how tenderly George had held and spoken to Evandra in the corridor. There had been such intimate familiarity between them, and it told Nell everything she needed to know about who Evandra had once been for George, and perhaps still was. She'd known George had partaken in dalliances—several and frequently, if rumors were to be believed—but she hadn't realized he'd dared venture so close to the crown. It was behavior more foolish than Elliot's had been at the Fall Tournament Archery Event last year, if she had any say in the matter.

Which she didn't.

Nell knew she'd let herself grow too comfortable around George. She knew opening herself to him was a folly of the most reckless kind. She'd known his proclivities and had been careful of them at first, but after so long, after all that they'd been through together, and all the kindness and sweet words, she thought she'd seen more in him.

The humiliation of being strung along so easily was what cut her so deeply. The heart will always look for what it wants to see, and when it doesn't find what it seeks easily, it reaches and stretches and embellishes that which it does find. And embellishments truly must have been all Nell had found among George's actions these past days, because the moment a more beautiful, desirable, and willing woman stumbled within his reach, he'd taken her right back into his arms without sparing Nell another thought. She'd merely been a diversion for him until one truly worth desiring came along.

Heartache was one thing, but she'd known George would do something like this and she let her lovesick heart hope for more anyway. He had fooled her, and she had only herself to blame.

No matter. She would keep busy and stay distracted, and the heartache would pass soon enough.

Chatter among Aria and her ladies pulled Nell from her thoughts, and she stepped further into the room to join them. The ladies' injuries weren't severe. Aside from some scrapes, bruises, and Evandra's sprained ankle, all three would make a quick recovery. Lord Lucias stopped by Gaius's study on behalf of the king and made Aria and her ladies aware that their old rooms had been prepared and would be ready for them after dinner. And once Gaius had finally finished his examinations and treated their injuries, Aria and her ladies took dinner in her chambers. And Nell joined them.

Dinner was nice enough, even after Collete, Phillipa, and Evandra explained all that had happened after Aria left Balmorea. There were tears, but then there were laughs, and Nell hadn't seen Aria so happy since her unexpected arrival. There was a light in her eyes again, even if they didn't shine as they used to. It's not that Nell hadn't tried to bring cheer to Aria in the short time that she'd served her, but, if the liveliness of the women around the table was any indication, being surrounded by those one loved most in the world is sometimes the only way to bring healing to the brokenness within that one cannot reach by themselves.

And as Nell sat around the table, among women she'd known most of her life yet had never felt more distant from, a heavy loneliness sank deep into her bones.

After another hour or so, each of the ladies, including Nell, excused themselves for the night. Since the three ladies were weary and still recovering, Nell went to call for the maids to clear away their dinner dishes. Tomorrow, she likely wouldn't need to do such things. Would Collete bring Aria her tea in the morning and would Phillippa help her dress as they had before? Would Evandra make arrangements for an outing or meet with Master Gaius and Miss Lyla about Aria's care? There were many more hands now, and it made the work light. Nell promised Ophelia that she would watch over her sister, and she intended to fulfill her word. She'd simply have to do so more indirectly.

Voices around the corner of the corridor that led to her chambers drew Nell's attention and had her slowing her stride.

"It's been a long day, and I just want to go to sleep," George said, weariness at the edges of his voice.

"Come now. It's been an age since we've seen each other, and I've missed you terribly," Evandra replied, her voice woven with seduction.

Nell felt the color drain from her face, and she pressed her back against the wall. A lame attempt to hide herself, but she'd seen them together once already that day. She wasn't sure she would survive the humiliation of having to face them again so soon, especially after having to feign indifference throughout the evening's dinner with Evandra.

But she didn't want to listen to this play out either.

She wasn't naïve enough to think Evandra wouldn't end up in George's bed—she just didn't think she'd have to play audience to it, or that it would happen so soon. Evandra had been exhausted mere hours ago and couldn't walk without help. Though, it's not like she needed a healed ankle to get what Nell assumed she was seeking at George's door.

George huffed a laugh. "I'm sure you've been managing just fine on your own, Vandra." Nell heard the smile in his voice, her mind easily conjuring a picture of the exact tug of his lips to one side and the glint of playfulness in his eyes that accompanied it—and she hated herself for it.

"Perhaps," Evandra said, a hint of hesitance in her voice. "It's just…after everything today. I don't want to be alone tonight." Her voice had softened, sadness lacing itself through her tone. How quickly she switched from seductress to a frightened woman in need of comfort. Nell rolled her eyes.

"Well, if it's company you seek, then you should stay with Her Highness," George replied, and Nell's brows shot down over her eyes. *She should what?*

"The princess's company is not the type I desire tonight." Evandra's voice was sharper—that was *not* the answer the lady was hoping for, nor was it the answer Nell expected of him.

"Are you so sure?" George replied, the playfulness returning to his voice. His impish grin materialized in her mind again, one that included a blond brow raising over his left eye and a slight cock of his head. "Perhaps the princess keeps better company than me and you simply haven't explored the possibility yet—"

"George," Evandra whined. "This is tiresome. Are you truly not going to invite me in?" Nell chanced a glance around the corner, hoping to garner some understanding of the situation herself. She couldn't see Evandra's face, but she saw George casually leaning against the door frame, arms crossed over his chest with his legs crossed at the ankles. The grin she'd seen so clearly in her mind was falling as his face took on a more hesitant expression. He pushed off the door frame and stood to his full height, dropping one arm to his side as he raked a hand through his dirty blond hair.

He heaved a tired sigh. "No, Evandra, I'm not. As I said. I'm simply tired and want to go to sleep."

She stepped into his space and slowly ran a delicate hand from his chest down his abdomen. "You know I can help you fall asleep," she said, so lowly that Nell almost hadn't heard her.

George hardly reacted besides a slight tug of his lips to one side that she knew was meant to portray amusement, but his eyes were too stern, his jaw too tense. Nell didn't think she'd ever seen George show any negative emotion about anything. She'd always known him to be unflappable. George was the one who found a way to make some sort of flirty quip to ease the tension of a situation. He would be the one to mention an embarrassing fact about someone at a dinner or capitalize on any opportunity to slide some sort of lewd play on words into a conversation. It irritated others, but never him, even when his same sordid behavior was tossed right back at him.

But that's what George was: clearly irritated. Why, though? Was it because he was losing his grip on his restraint? Why was he even trying to restrain himself at all?

George gently took the hand Evandra had skirting along the waistband of his pants and placed it at her side. "I'm aware of how helpful you can be," he replied, his expression inscrutable, "but I do not need, nor want, your help tonight." The words *another night, perhaps* were left unsaid, hovering between them.

"Very well," Evandra conceded. "Will you at least walk me back to my chambers, then?" George's eyes dropped to her feet, to where Evandra was clearly favoring her uninjured ankle, and Nell rolled her eyes. Gaius would have used magic to heal Evandra's ankle, so she was really laying it on thick.

Evandra winced. "I hadn't expected I would be walking back to my chambers after this, and now that I am, I'm not sure I'll be able to make it all the way back without assistance."

George pushed off the door frame and closed the door behind him, offering Evandra his arm. Evandra looked down to his elbow then back up to his face, her hands crumpling the skirts of her dress.

"It's just—my ankle—it's rather painful to walk on."

Nell saw the lady duck her head sheepishly, and she rolled her eyes again.

George heaved a sigh then, and either because he truly believed she was still injured or maybe because he still held some fondness for whatever used to be between them, he opened his arms, and Evandra eagerly stepped into them. She looped her hands around his neck before he leaned down and scooped her up.

"Thank you, George," she said before kissing his cheek.

He tensed then murmured something to her that Nell couldn't hear.

"All right," Evandra responded with a flirty giggle, and George made his way toward her chambers.

Nell's chest tightened as she watched George's retreating back race down the corridor toward Evandra's chambers, disappointment weighing heavily on her. She hadn't realized that, in the span of their conversation, she'd allowed the hope desperately fighting to stay rooted in her heart to bloom once again. George disappeared around a corner, and heartache stole the breath from her lungs for the second time that day.

Nell pushed off the wall and rounded the corner, walking the short distance to her chambers and shoving through the door before the tears began to spill over her cheeks.

Chapter Twenty Two

OPHELIA AND ELLIOT'S FIRST DAY OF TRAVEL WAS uneventful and seemed to pass by in a blink.

Domenicio organized their caravan in such a way that the two of them would travel in the middle of the group between the company's two carriages for easy cover should they be attacked.

The cover was meant to be for the unarmed members of the crew and Elliot and Ophelia. When Dom explained this plan, Elliot and Ophelia glanced at each other, knowing they shared the same thought: Elliot had his sword, and Ophelia had her bow. Neither of them would simply hide and hope for the best if they were attacked.

As for the rest of the caravan, Domenicio and Naora would ride at the front while Ambrose and Sarada took up the rear. Two mercenaries would ride directly in front of Dom and Naora, two more would ride behind Ambrose and Sarada, and the fifth would ride in the middle, just in front of Elliot and Ophelia. They weren't a very friendly bunch, the mercenaries, but they were attentive and took their job seriously.

At some point early on in their journey, the crew broke out into songs to pass the time. One of the men pulled a lute from one of the carriages and played melodies as the others sang. Another set a beat by drumming on one of the wooden crates being hauled by one of the carriages. The rest clapped and belted the words, some more poorly than others, but no comments of ridicule were made. There were simply smiles and laughter. It was casual and simple and noisy and the most fun Elliot had had in as long as he could remember. From what Elliot could tell, everyone in the crew knew every song—aside from the mercenaries—and not one of them stayed quiet as they traveled. It was so refreshing and different.

One song would end, a few beats would pass, and the next would begin. The merriment chased away hunger and thirst and the unease that had simmered in Elliot's chest since Aria arrived at the castle.

They must have sung the same ten songs for hours, because at one point in their journey, Elliot looked over and Ophelia was singing along with them, not missing a single lyric, and a wide smile on her lips. His heart flipped when their gazes met, laughter and happiness alight in her pale blue eyes, and he couldn't help but return her smile.

Once the sun began to set, and the shadows on the ground grew long, the caravan stopped. Dom barked at the crew to shut up and set up camp, and everyone did as they were told. Ophelia and Elliot did the same, removing their bed rolls and the other items they would need for the night and handing off their horses to be fed, watered, and unsaddled with the others.

Ophelia fastened her dagger holsters to her thighs then went with Naora and Sarada to tend to their needs. Elliot watched them leave, his stomach clenching when they slipped out of eyesight. As much as it went against every instinct in Elliot to let Ophelia leave camp without him, he stood by the confidence that George had in these merchants' trustworthiness. *George wouldn't have set this up if we couldn't trust them.*

While he waited for Ophelia to return, Elliot's eyes roved around the forming camp to find a place for them to settle. He chose a spot near the fire. It would mean that more crew buffered them from the camp's edge, and Ophelia would be closer to warmth. Despite how the crew had teased the two of them about not needing to *stay quiet*, Elliot was more worried about Ophelia's comfort and safety than anything else at the moment. Though the reality of having her all to himself, without the anxiousness of anyone bursting in and vehemently voicing their disapproval or taking what they saw to the king, did not escape him.

More than once while thinking about this trip, and for the one day they had been traveling, Elliot's mind ran wild; stolen moments would be too easy to come by—a luxury they'd never had before. The thought thrilled him, and blood started rushing south. He snapped his eyes shut and breathed deeply, willing his focus to return to setting up their bedrolls.

Less than an hour later, the sun disappeared behind the horizon, a fire was made and blazing with heat, and several rabbits were being skinned and prepared for roasting.

Ophelia sat down next to him on their bedrolls holding two cups. She handed one to him and took a drink from her own as Elliot wrapped a blanket around her shoulders and folded her into his side.

"Apparently, Dom is keen on the mead from a specific pub in Sigova and stocks several kegs of it for his returning trips," she said, taking another sip. "He poured me a cup and told me to give you this one."

Elliot smiled and took a sip from the drink she handed him. It was sweet with a small burn at the back end. "How fortunate we are for his generosity," he said.

"I agree." A pleased, closed-mouth smile tugged at her lips. She extended her cup forward and tapped it to his in cheers.

He exhaled, then turned his head into her and took a deep breath before placing a kiss into her hair. Their first day of travel went as smoothly as possible. It was over, and they were *safe*.

He repeated the words but still felt the twinge of unease in his stomach.

He was pulled from his thoughts by a hand sliding along his thigh. Ophelia's. He met her eyes and saw her brows bent in concern. "Are you all right?"

He nodded, releasing another exhale and hoping it might help dispel the knot in his gut. "We are in the safest company we could be in given our circumstances, but traveling out in the open like this...I—" He frowned and shook his head, dropping his eyes to her hand. "It's harder to protect you." The image of her on the floor in her chambers covered in blood flashed before him, and he flinched, squeezing his eyes shut.

She set her cup aside and framed his cheek with her palm, placing her forehead to his. "I know," she whispered, her thumb sweeping along his cheek. She brushed her lips across his, lightly, gently. The contact settled him somewhat, the tension in his muscles easing. He brushed his lips against hers again, pressing firmer when a slew of whistles erupted from around the fire, and they jumped apart, startled from the suddenness of it.

"Look at those two!"

"And they say true love is dead!"

"I'm moving my shit across camp!"

Laughter rumbled around them as Ophelia and Elliot both gave amused smiles.

Ambrose ambled up to the fire, cup of mead in hand, and sat across from them. Naora followed closely behind, eyeing Elliot as sat.

"So, Lord William," she said, a smirk on her lips. "We hadn't heard from Lord George in quite some time before he came to us to set up this little excursion for you. I found it… *interesting* to see he did not come with you and Lady Jane to see you off on your trip."

Elliot narrowed his gaze. "No, I'm afraid Lord George was held up tending to his duties at Hargrave with the Duke and Lord Barnham," Elliot said, taking another sip to try and appear unaffected by her question. Did she suspect them? Elliot felt Ophelia lean closer into him. "Do you have anything I need to pass on to him when we return?"

Naora sat up straighter and waved him off. "Oh, no. I just—"

"She was miffed she didn't get a chance to fuck him before we left," Dom cut in without ceremony as he sat on the other side of Ambrose. Ophelia snorted into her cup, and Elliot's eyes grew wide, a delayed laugh bursting from his lips.

"What the fuck, Dom," Naora sneered, snapping her head toward the merchant. "Can I not inquire about a mutual friend of ours?"

Dom just chuckled in reply.

"You and that silver tongue of yours, Dom," Sarada said with an eyeroll as she lowered herself next to her sister.

Dom shrugged. "No need to sugarcoat the truth. Better out with it and move on."

"Your insight into how one navigates polite society is inspired," Ambrose said with a huffed laugh.

"We haven't been to Sigova in months," Naora hissed. "And when Lord George only approached you about this trip and nothing else on behalf of the duke or his father, you didn't find it odd?"

"You only think it's odd because when he does come to talk business with us, he normally talks about a different kind of business with you, and this time he didn't," Dom said.

"Because that's not *normally* how he conducts his business with us!" she said with exasperation. "Ever."

Interesting.

Elliot interjected, clearing his throat. "And how long have you all been doing *business* through Lord George?"

Dom took a drink from his cup then rested his forearms over his knees. "Damn, how many years has it been now, Brosey?" he asked with a frown that wrinkled his forehead.

Ambrose pursed his lips. "We've worked with the earl and duke long before the lordling came of age. He began working as an intermediary between us a bit before he started at Hargrave with the Marxleys, though. What's that, seven years?"

It was eight, but Elliot didn't correct him, more concerned with this secret dalliance that George had kept from him.

He and George had enjoyed their fair share of female company when they were younger, even with girls much below their rank, but he'd never felt the need to keep any of it from George. The fact that George *had* kept this from him made him uneasy.

"Did you know George had some sort of relationship with her?" Ophelia whispered. Her raised eyebrows and mystified eyes told him she was as surprised by this revelation as he was.

"No. I didn't." Elliot glanced back at the others and was relieved to see they had taken over the conversation, having forgotten them for the moment. "He's never told me about her. And George and I share everything with each other. We grew up together like brothers."

Ophelia raised her eyebrows. "Perhaps he was afraid of your judgement regarding how he spent his free time?" she asked.

Elliot huffed a laugh and took a drink from his cup. "Trust me when I say he knew there would be no judgement of the sort from me."

"Ah, because it was common for both of you to frequent the lower town in search of female company."

"Right—" He cut himself off and pressed his lips together. The word sank like lead in his stomach. They'd never discussed his previous lovers before, not that they were of any consequence to him now, but it was only natural that Ophelia would at least be curious. He blinked several times, trying to ground himself and finding himself taken aback for the second time in one sitting.

He turned back to Ophelia, mouth poised to speak, when he noticed the wide grin spreading across her face. His brows bent in confusion, and she leaned in, her lips brushing the shell of his ear.

"Well, no wonder you know exactly how to use that tongue of yours." Her voice was low and breathy.

Elliot's cock twitched, and a flush crept up his neck. He opened his mouth to reply, but words evaded him.

She released a flirtatious giggle. "You should see your face right now." She took another sip from her cup with a smirk then returned her attention to the others. Elliot took a long swig of his drink and did the same.

Ambrose nodded his head to Elliot. "How is George, though? Like Naora said, we didn't get the chance to catch up with him."

Elliot cleared his throat. "He's well. From what I've heard, he and Lord Barnham spend much of their time at the castle due to Lord Barnham's betrothal to the princess."

Ambrose nodded, murmurs and nods of understanding echoing around the fire; Elliot's response seemed sufficient to explain George's absence. Though, Naora still seemed rather put out.

Ophelia leaned in again. "If George had needed to leave the castle for business and return later, he wouldn't have run into any issues," she said.

Elliot's brows dipped. "What do you mean?"

"I'm saying that if he had *wanted* to leave the castle to meet up with them or to share some friendly company, he would have been able to go and return without any problem."

She set her empty cup down and looped her arm through his. "I think something is keeping his attention at the castle. Or rather, *someone*—and I don't mean you, as lovely as you are."

Elliot smiled as the pieces connected in his mind. "George and Nell do spend a significant amount of time together due to the nature of their positions with us." His face hardened in mock disdain. "But, *surely*, they would merely be waiting on us. Standing by for our every beck and call."

Ophelia matched his expression and nodded. "Oh, certainly. And we are sure to work them to the bone when we aren't in need of them."

They laughed and returned to the conversation around the fire. Elliot pulled Ophelia to sit between his legs, and she leaned back into him, humming in contentment.

He loved this. The casual affection, the closeness. Their hushed flirtatious comments and easy conversation. Ophelia took a deep breath and relaxed into him, and it filled him with an overwhelming sense of rightness.

Elliot wrapped his arms tightly around her shoulders, buried his nose into the crook of her neck, and inhaled deeply.

One day down. Four more to go.

Chapter Twenty Three

GEORGE KNEW. WITHOUT A SHADOW OF A DOUBT. that Nell was avoiding him. Trying to find her the past few days had been like trying to catch mist with his bare hands. He'd seen flashes of her—a wisp of copper ducking into the kitchens or rounding a corner—only to find empty space when he had followed after her.

They had never gone this long without crossing paths before, even with their roles at the castle being different from what they normally were, and he hadn't realized how much he'd grown accustomed to her presence—nor how suffocated he now felt in the castle without it. George reasoned she might be spending more of her time with Aria and her ladies and that this was likely the main reason they hadn't crossed paths because George was doing his best to avoid Aria and her ladies. Or rather, he was avoiding Evandra.

Evandra had been stung, to say the least, by his rejection the other evening when she'd come to his room asking to stay the night. He'd told her no but wasn't enough of an asshole to make an injured woman hobble back to her own chambers, so, he had helped her back to her room if only to finally get her out of his doorway. He had thought he'd been decidedly clear when he'd said, "I'll take you to your door and no more, Vandra," as he had carried her through the corridor.

But her laughed, "All right," had apparently not been an understanding of his intentions but disbelief in his resolve, because once he had set her down, wished her good night, and began to walk away, her shrieked, "Are you fucking *serious?*" had rung so sharply through the corridor that it could have sliced diamond.

George supposed her assumption hadn't been unfounded. Half a year ago, he never would have turned away a willing woman. Especially not one that had come conveniently to his door. All of that changed, though, the first time he'd made Nell blush. Making her cheeks turn that pretty shade of pink had become an obsession, but at some point, things had shifted for him—had grown into something more than enjoying simple flirtations. Soon, he found himself wanting to make her smile and hear her laugh. Something in his chest settled into place when she was happy—when *he* made her happy. Oh, he still loved watching the flush rise to her cheeks—he didn't think that much would ever change—but the closer he grew to her, the more she made him want in ways he'd never wanted before.

He wanted all her laughs, wishing he could bottle them up and save them for times like this—when his loneliness clawed at him so deeply—so he could drink himself into a stupor on the sound alone.

He wanted to taste the smiles off her lips and wanted to catalogue every shade of golden brown that shone in her eyes. He wanted all of her eye rolls and sharp quips. He wanted her casual touches and kisses. He wanted to know her dreams and wishes so that he could be the one to give them to her. He wanted to be the one she felt safe to fall apart with and the one she wanted by her side to help weave herself back together. He wanted any and every piece of her that she would give him, and he'd treasure each one no matter how great or small.

And as the list of things Nell made him want grew longer and longer, the more abhorrent the idea of a casual tryst with her had become.

Fuck, when had that happened? When and how had she burrowed so deeply into his flippant, feckless heart? He'd felt a hint of it that morning Elliot and Ophelia told them of their plans to travel to Balmorea, had known then that what he felt for her was more than a simple, passing fancy. But to be so consumed by her that the thought of being intimate with anyone else turned his stomach sour? That the thought of *her* being intimate with someone else sparked a jealousy so hot within him he felt it sear across his bones? The possibility that she could be seeking comfort in the arms of another right now simply because she thought his were already full loomed over him like an executioner's blade.

George knew his image wasn't spotless. He knew Nell wasn't naïve to the things that were likely said about him throughout the castle, but did she truly think the affection he held for her was so fickle? Or did she doubt his feelings for her entirely?

The memory of how she'd looked at him when her eyes found Evandra in his arms taunted him. The sadness that had eclipsed her honey-brown eyes before flashing into that mask of indifference, her clipped tone, and the absence of her from his life the past five days all gnawed at his insides. The restlessness had him up before the sun, the determination to find her burning beneath his feet.

He quickly threw on some clothes and boots and rushed out the door as he buckled his sword to his belt. He decided he'd head to the kitchens first and wait for her to come for Aria's tea, but it was Lady Collete who arrived instead. He lingered a short time longer to see if perhaps she would come for her own tea and breakfast, but the morning stretched on, and he soon had to leave and report to Lord Lucias to continue with their interviews.

George couldn't concentrate, his mind fogging up or wandering so often that Lord Lucias began losing his patience with him for how many times he had to pull his attention back to the present. Thankfully, nothing of consequence was revealed in their interviews that day, and George left promising to be more attentive for their next round of interviews.

The moment he stepped out of the audience hall, he bolted through the castle to begin his search anew for Nell. There were only so many places she could be. It was late afternoon, and the weather was nice, judging by the light slanting in through the windows in the corridor. So, he'd begin in the courtyard. If she wasn't there, he'd try the stables next.

George rounded a corner, then pushed through the courtyard doors. Stepping into the gardens, his eyes slid over the space, looking for Aria and her ladies, and he found them meandering through one of the many winding pathways through the gardens.

Aria seemed to be doing better. Her eyes were brighter, and she smiled more, though it didn't escape him how sadness always seemed to linger in the corners of her mouth, keeping her lips from turning all the way up. It seemed to rim her ocean blue eyes and stifle the brightness fighting to shine through. It was good to see her up and about, though. The fresh air was good for her, and for the baby.

George's eyes slid from Aria to her ladies, but he didn't find Nell among them. He worried his bottom lip between his teeth and began turning on his heel to head for the stables when his gaze snagged on a familiar figure standing on the other side of the yard where the king's forces would train—a figure he would know upside down, in the dark, during a storm. She had a knife in each hand, and her eyes were trained on a target several yards in front of her. His lips twitched as the image of the exact furrow of her brow and purse of her lip came together in his mind.

He approached her, ensuring he made plenty of noise to alert her of his presence lest he end up sprawled out on his ass with a knife to his throat. Though the thought of having Nell straddling his lap wasn't a terrible one. The closer he got to her, the lighter his chest felt, and his smile spread wider across his lips. He wasn't sure how happy she would be to see him, but once she threw her blades down and turned to see who was walking toward her, honey-brown eyes leveling on him, relief flooded his chest.

Half of her hair was pulled back and braided down the back of her head while the rest of her coppery-brown waves fell loosely over her shoulders. He couldn't read her expression but felt it was a good sign that he found no outright disdain painted across her brow.

She quickly plucked two more blades from a nearby stone bench and returned her focus to the target. "What do you want?" she asked before launching one of the blades at the target. It landed just to the right of the inner ring, and George raised his brows.

"I didn't know you were so adept with throwing knives," he said, stepping to her side as she aimed and threw her second knife, again favoring the right side of the target.

She shrugged and turned to pick up the last two knives on the bench. "It was the only weapon my brothers were able to get away with teaching me to wield."

George nodded. "A lady of many talents." He faced her, hands clasped behind his back and a small smile tilting his lips, as she held her focus to the target once again.

"You didn't answer my question," she said before throwing her final knife.

George's eyebrows rose. "Hmm?"

She rolled her eyes.

"What do you want?" she repeated as she made her way toward the targets to retrieve her knives.

George sidled alongside her and shoved his hands into his pockets. "I fear I've upset you," he replied.

The tensing of her shoulders was the only indication she'd been affected in any way by George's statement.

"I'm not sure what brought you to that conclusion, but I assure you, I'm fine," she said while plucking each knife from the target.

He frowned and pulled a hand from his pocket, shoving it through his hair and tugging at the ends. "You've been avoiding me," he offered, and her hands stilled a moment before she tugged free the last three knives from the target.

She turned on her heel and walked back toward the shooting line. "It's not uncommon for our duties to keep us in different areas of the castle. The fact that we haven't crossed paths doesn't mean I've orchestrated it to be so."

"Perhaps." He picked up his pace then rounded to cut her off and face her. "But I saw your face when you saw me helping Evandra," he said, careful to keep all teasing from his tone.

Her jaw clenched, and her eyes flicked up to his with annoyance. "You flatter yourself," she bit out, and her fierce beauty momentarily stole his breath. Even on the verge of rage, she was stunning. Or perhaps she was especially so *because* of the unbridled emotion she allowed to flash across her face. It was raw and real, and though it may be prickly, it was still a piece of her.

The tension between them hung thick, and he knew she had to feel this draw between them, too. He saw how he affected her in the pulse fluttering in her neck and the quiet hitches of her breath each time he drew near to her. He saw it in the way her pupils dilated, even now, as her anger simmered in the brown depths of her irises.

She wouldn't address his accusation further, though, and, he realized, it was because doing so would be admitting how much it upset her to see him with Evandra, and that would leave her more exposed than she was yet willing to be with him. The idea that she didn't feel safe enough to be honest with him tightened his chest. "Fine," he conceded. "Then, if you insist it's not me that's upset you, what has?"

She shifted from one foot to the other, and her gaze flicked over his shoulder before dropping to her hands.

He glanced to where her eyes had traveled and found Aria and her ladies settled on a larger patch of grass across the courtyard, sprawled out and staring up at the sky.

He swung his gaze back to Nell as she pushed past him. "Did something happen with the princess?" he asked, following her.

Nell shook her head, her forehead creasing as she set all but two of the knives down on the stone bench. "No. Things are much better for the princess now that her ladies are back."

She faced the target again, and George dared a step forward, gently taking hold of her wrist. "Then what's wrong, Sweetheart?" he asked, trying to infuse as much gentleness into his words as he could muster, running his thumb across the back of her hand.

She shut her eyes and took in a steadying breath before releasing it, as though she were gathering her courage to respond.

He wanted to run his hands up and down her arms, wanted to encourage her and reassure her that she could speak freely with him, that he wanted to help her. But he held himself back, settling for the small comfort of the simple touch at her wrist.

When she finally opened her eyes with a sniff, she immediately ducked her head. "I feel useless," she said so low that he almost hadn't heard her.

Anger flared through him. "Useless?" he asked, rage heavier in his tone than he'd intended. "You haven't been useless a day in your life, Nell."

"I wasn't there when Ophelia was attacked, and if I had been, I couldn't have done anything, anyway! I would have just gotten in the way." Her face crumpled before she sucked in a breath, steeling her expression. "I failed her, plain and simple, George." George opened his mouth to refute her statements, but she kept going. "Now Ophelia's gone off to Balmorea, leaving me to look after Aria," she said, gesturing to the ladies beyond them. "I promised that I would watch over her, but now, with her ladies having returned, there is no place for me at Aria's side, and I'm simply left here, idle. And if I stay idle, I become trapped inside the whirlwind of my own mind with no way of keeping at bay the thoughts of all the terrible things that could have happened and how, if they had, I wouldn't have been able to do anything to protect one of the people I love most in the world!" Her knuckles whitened, and she sucked down breath after breath, dropping her head forward and closing her eyes to steady herself.

The knot in George's chest tightened, her pain and regret ringing in harmony with his own. He stepped forward and placed his hands on her shoulders. "Nell, look at me."

She swallowed, then lifted her head to meet his gaze.

"The princess's attack was not your fault. There was nothing you could have done to sto—"

"That's what I'm saying, George!" she said, dropping the knives and tossing her arms up in frustration. "Useless!"

"No," George said, shaking his head. "No. I will tell you the same thing I told Lord Barnham. The ones who hold all blame for what happened are Raygon and his fucking Reapers."

"Doing something would have been better than nothing," she whispered, dropping her eyes to the ground.

He placed his index finger under her chin, forcing her eyes to meet his. They were glassy with frustrated tears, and the knot in his chest grew impossibly tighter. "You did not fail Ophelia, because you wouldn't have been able to fight off a mage-assassin. Lord Barnham was there and hadn't been able to fight off Trella—do you hold him as responsible for the attack as you hold yourself?"

George felt the flex of Nell's jaw under his fingers, and he saw how she fought against the tears threatening to fall down her cheeks. She finally shook her head in response.

"And what about me?" he asked, dropping his hand to his side. "I wasn't there either. By your reasoning, I am responsible as well." He took a step closer, tucking a strand of her hair behind her ear. "If making me culpable will ease the unbearable burden you've placed upon yourself, by all means, Sweetheart, cast the blame on me. I will gladly shoulder it, if that is what will see you free of it."

She sucked in a breath and blinked, causing a single tear to roll down her cheek. He swiped it away with his thumb a moment before she pulled herself from his hold and pressed the heels of her palms to her eyes. She turned away and sniffed, picking up the knives from the ground and pretending to check for any damage they may have received after she tossed them down.

George clenched his fists at his sides. He knew in his gut that she hadn't been all right. His heart swelled and shattered all at once at the pain and regret he saw shadowed in her eyes. He didn't doubt her strength but knew better than to assume anyone, even this brave, beautiful woman before him, could process and heal from all that she'd been through alone. That's what she'd been trying to do, and it had been eating at her from within.

A fierce protectiveness washed over him. He needed to help her like he needed air in his lungs. He needed to comfort her, distract her—needed to keep her close and make sure she wasn't being shredded to pieces by her own maddening thoughts. But she'd never allow him to spend so much time with her without a proper reason—

The idea formed and was past his lips before his mind was given the chance to consider it.

"Train with me," he said.

She straightened and turned to face him, a crease between her brows. "What?"

He stepped toward her, a smile lifting his lips a touch to one side. "Let me train you."

She leveled him with an incredulous look, and he crossed his arms over his chest.

"I'm serious. If one of your great regrets is not having more skill in a fight, I can help you. Otherwise, I fear you will remain trapped in your whirlwind, and," he quirked his lips up into a half smirk, "you are much less fun when you have too much on your mind," he finished, hoping a shift in mood would help cut through some of her sadness.

Irritation flashed in her eyes. "And how terrible it would be for poor Lord George if he grew bored."

He beamed. "There she is."

She betrayed no reaction, but George didn't miss the light dusting of pink that bloomed across her cheeks. "Is that a yes, then?"

Her eyes darted from him to Aria and her ladies then back to him, and determination washed over her features. She gave him a sharp nod.

The knot in his chest loosened. "Good," he said. "I still have to meet up with Lord Lucias each morning, so we will need to train beforehand." He clapped her on the shoulder once then turned on his heel. "Get your beauty sleep, Sweetheart. We begin at dawn."

CHAPTER TWENTY FOUR

OPHELIA FOUND THEIR JOURNEY TO BALMOREA much more enjoyable than she anticipated. She'd made this same trip in autumn for Aria's wedding and had hated it, even traveling in a carriage with all the luxuries afforded a royal princess. One wouldn't think that traveling with less could improve the experience, yet somehow it did.

Sleeping was more uncomfortable, and despite being an experienced rider, she was sore after an entire day on horseback, but the atmosphere and liveliness of their company was making the hours pass by quickly. And even if they did sleep on flat pallets atop the lumpy ground and under itchy wool blankets, waking up each morning in Elliot's arms made the discomforts worthwhile.

After Elliot's comments about how he and George had sought female company in the lower town together when they were younger, Ophelia's curiosity had been piqued. She knew he'd led a life before meeting her and that, based on their intimate moments together, he had experience that he'd seemed worried would make her feel uncomfortable or possibly angry. So, she simply asked him about it.

"Are you upset?" he asked her after answering all of her questions, running a thumb over the back of her hand with a crease between his brows.

She gave him a small smile and pulled his hand to her lips, pressing a kiss to his palm. "Knowing there are a handful of women out there who have tasted you and, at one point, knew how to make you melt does twinge a bit," she replied honestly. "But if they don't have any place in your heart, then they need not have any place in my mind."

Elliot visibly relaxed at her words and lifted his head to press his lips to her forehead. "Some women may have captured my attention in the past, but none of them came anywhere close to capturing my soul as you have." He rested his forehead against hers. "You are my one, Elia. There's only you."

Their next few days on the road were almost identical to the first. Music and singing during the day as they traveled, and stories and teasing around the fire while they ate their meager meals of trail rations and small game at night.

Under the stars each night was their only true time alone—as alone as they could get in a campsite surrounded by merchants and crewmen.

It was those nights—pressed snugly together and wrapped in the other's arms—where they first found sleep without lingering on the terrible things that had happened to them. They spoke of superficial things, silly things, things that might seem insignificant when set against the canvas of someone's life, but were, in fact, the treasured details that intertwine and come together to form the grander, unique portrait of who the person truly is.

Each night, they laid facing each other on their pallets, talking, laughing, and teasing each other with a comfort and ease they hadn't known since the days they spent in the stables before Aria's wedding. So much so that a handful of crew members had to tell them to quiet down on more than one occasion.

"Dom," Elliot whisper-shouted, "I thought you said your men sleep like the dead."

Dom groaned and rolled over to face him. "Moaning is easier to fall asleep to than the incessant twitter of giggles, My Lord," he grunted before rolling back over.

Ophelia slapped her hand over her mouth to keep the laugh from launching out of her throat. Elliot's reaction was much the same. "Noted."

That night, Ophelia fell asleep with Elliot's hand curled around her waist, her hand pressed against his warm skin under his shirt, her face buried in his chest, and cheeks aching from laughter.

The morning of their fourth day of travel, Elliot woke Ophelia up with a much-needed hot cup of tea—the previous night had been frigid. They hadn't completely descended the Southern Lupos Pass by sunset the previous day and had had to sleep another night in the mountains, albeit lower down.

She eagerly sipped from her mug, ignoring the singe to her tongue as she luxuriated in the tea's warmth as it spread through her body and loosened her sleep-heavy limbs.

After allowing herself a moment to wake up, she took another swig from her mug before heading to the woods to relieve herself. Thankfully, there was no wind, but that didn't mean the cold air would be forgiving against the bare skin of her ass. She went as quickly as she could then returned to camp to pack her things, wanting to get moving toward some much milder weather as soon as possible.

She hurriedly finished the rest of her tea along with some bread and cheese as she packed, Elliot doing the same. The sun was peeking just above the horizon, causing the sky to bruise over in dark blues and purples. By the time the top of the sun crested the treetops, the camp was packed, and their group was on the move.

Deciding to ride through their midday break, dried meat, cheese, and skins of wine were passed around to hold everyone over until they reached the wooded foothills of the Lupos in Balmorea. It seemed no one was eager to stay any longer in the mountains than necessary.

Ophelia slumped in her saddle and let out a sigh of relief when Dom finally shouted for the group to stop for a break. As she dismounted Blaze, her eyes followed the winding path they'd just descended until it bent around the mountain side.

The mountain itself stretched and climbed into the clouds. It almost seemed to be leaning away from them, as though it was trying to pull itself as far from the southern country as possible. As though it felt the unnatural, repellant force across the land as well. Ophelia turned back to Blaze as an ominous chill sent her skin pebbling into gooseflesh despite the stillness of the air. She rolled her shoulders then divided up some of their trail rations as Elliot walked the horses to the nearby river to water them.

They rested maybe an hour before climbing back up on their mounts and heading east through the wood toward the Vast Plains.

The group rode in silence with only the sound of a few quiet conversations interspersed throughout their small caravan. A burst of laughter would crop up here or there, but the relative silence seemed odd after passing most of their travel with music and singing. Ophelia attributed it to the exhaustion of the journey—after three and a half days of travel, she certainly wasn't up for singing either.

Blaze's ears twitched forward, and he nickered. A moment later, Dom began whistling one of the tunes the crew had bellowed several times over the past few days. Ambrose perked up and joined in, seamlessly followed by two other crewmen down the line. Those on horseback began shifting out of formation, making light conversation as they moved into defensive positions.

Alarm rang in Ophelia's mind, and her head swung to Elliot, who was guiding his horse closer to hers. He leaned in, the concern flashing in his eyes belying his calm expression. "They're preparing for an attack," he said quietly.

Ophelia sucked in a gasp as Elliot took her hand, pressing it to his lips, she realized, to cover his mouth as he spoke. "School your expression," he whispered, and she instantly lifted her lips in a small smile as though Elliot was flirting with her—or, at least, she hoped that's what it looked like. "When they attack, run inside the middle carriage," he whispered as he lowered her hand.

Her brows bent before she remembered to hold her façade. She dipped her chin coquettishly and leaned toward Elliot. "And hide while you all defend the poor *damsel*? I think not."

His nostrils flared as he glanced around casually then leaned into her space again. "You will need cover to knock your arrows and find your marks."

Oh. That made more sense.

Still playing her part, she cocked her head to the side with a smile. "Right."

Elliot was an experienced fighter and had led hundreds of men in battle. His knowledge would be her best chance of making it out of this alive.

But what about him?

She squeezed his hand. "What will you do?" she asked, but he didn't have time to answer before an arrow flew, landing in the side of the carriage in front of her. Either it was a warning shot, or their attackers had a terrible archer among their ranks.

At that, brush and fallen leaves rustled as men in threadbare clothes armed with hunting knives and the occasional sword descended upon their group from the left and right. Another arrow launched from the wood, but she didn't see where it landed—she had to *move.*

Ophelia slipped off Blaze then pulled out her bow and unstrapped her quiver from her bow sheath. She grabbed her shooting gear from a pocket in her saddlebag then dashed toward the carriage. She threw open the back hatch, tossed her weapons inside, slid in, then closed it.

Sunlight filtered through the ornate carvings in the window shutters, giving her just enough light to see around her. She took a breath then shoved some crates out of the way to make room for herself.

The fight clamored on just beyond the carriage walls, and Ophelia did her best to ignore it along with the pounding of her heart as she strung her bow. She slid her gear on, quickly knocked an arrow, and tossed open the window shutter. She took cover just beside the window and assessed the scene before her.

It had only been a handful of minutes since the attack began, but the entire area was in a frenzy. Blurs of men fought hand to hand, metal clanged, and unintelligible shouts rang out around her. She spotted a body face-down maybe twenty feet away from her, and it sent her stomach roiling. She slumped to the side of the carriage and shook the feeling from her mind—Elliot and the others didn't have the time for her to work through this. She steadied her breathing then looked out the window for a mark.

An arrow hissed passed the carriage, and Ophelia's head snapped to the place it soared from. She wasn't sure if the shot was meant for her, but she followed the arrow's path into the wood and found the shooter. She drew her arrow, took aim, but hesitated. The man at whom she aimed her arrow was a member of mankind, part of her realm. The Essence within her writhed in her chest at the thought of felling him.

She thought quickly, shifting her aim, then loosed, willing the arrow to meet its mark. A faint purple mist fluttered before her but dissipated before her arrow landed, scoring right through the archer's draw hand.

Her eyes darted from side to side as she pulled another arrow from her quiver and knocked it. She naturally found Elliot right away and raked her gaze over him to make sure he was all right. His sword was drawn, and he was fighting a tall, thin man armed with a sword that was much too short for his stature. He was quick with it but clumsy, overswinging and falling off balance, or making to strike but coming up short of his target. Within three swipes of the man's sword, Ophelia could tell how helplessly untrained he was.

Elliot was shouting something at the man, but he wasn't responding. The man simply kept swinging and slicing, murderous intent painted across his face.

Another man with a knife through his chest crashed into Elliot, knocking him to his back. The man shoved the body out of the way then moved to bring his sword down on Elliot. Ophelia saw her opening. She drew her bow, aimed, and loosed, visualizing the arrow meeting its mark. Another mist of purple released, and the arrow landed in the man's shoulder, causing him to lose focus and stumble back, dropping his weapon.

Ophelia pulled in a deep breath, then restrung her bow, and searched for her next mark.

Elliot's head snapped back toward the direction the arrow came from and met Ophelia's eyes. She was already knocking her next arrow. They gave each other a quick nod before he jumped to his feet and bolted toward the closest crew member.

Sarada was holding her own in a standoff with two men—a fact that nearly stopped Elliot in his tracks.

She was a merchant. Wasn't that why Dom had hired the mercenaries—for experienced fighters to help protect their cargo? The younger sister wielded twin short swords with the fluid grace of a dancer. Every footstep was placed with precision, every spin pulling her out of reach of her enemy's blows only to add momentum to her counter strikes. She moved like lightning.

Who *was* she? Did all of them fight like this? He didn't have time to riddle it out before Sarada kicked out, sending one of the men flying towards him.

"You handle that one, Collins," she shouted. "I loosened him up for you. Figured you could use an easy one."

Elliot dodged a slice from his opponent. "How thoughtful of you," he yelled back as he blocked two more strikes from the man then knocked the dagger from his hand. The man blanched but didn't back down. He lunged forward to tackle Elliot to the ground. Elliot swung, slicing across the man's chest from below. Blood sprayed, and his opponent collapsed to the ground.

Nausea turned Elliot's stomach. Battles always began this way. The first few deaths were always the worst. Those were the faces that cemented themselves in the mind before the adrenaline kicked in and all the subsequent faces blurred.

He needed to seal his mind fast. Allowing it to wander would stall his blade, and hesitation meant death for him. In battle, it was either them or him, regardless of who the man before him left at home or what hopes and dreams the man laying at Sarada's feet died with.

He and Sarada fought back-to-back now as three men armed with little more than steak knives closed in on them. Sarada didn't wait for them to attack and lunged forward, Elliot following her lead. The fight was over before it began. The three men gasped and shuddered as they fell to the ground then gave the world their last breaths mere moments later.

Elliot and Sarada's eyes met. Remorse and pity shadowed her face. Much the same was happening around them as well—fight after fight between enemies so unmatched that they ended with little effort. It almost didn't seem real.

Could this be a distraction orchestrated to throw them off from the actual attack?

Dom must have been thinking the same thing as he, Ambrose, and a few others canvased the site and further into the wood, blood and gore staining their fine clothes.

They returned with no sign of anything more than their attackers' meager camp.

And that was it.

"These men were commoners," Elliot said gravely as he approached Dom. Ophelia slid out of the back of the carriage and sidled up next to him. "I doubt any of them had ever been called to arms for the king, much less the lords they served under."

"And they were fighting us with butcher knives and pitchforks," Naora added, sadness coloring her words.

"A few of them were properly armed," Ambrose said, "likely the leaders of this group." He sighed, guilt creasing his forehead. "They took Tyren and Kane before Sergo and I got to them." He ducked his head, and Dom clapped him on the shoulder. "I'll deliver the news to their families once we arrive in Ravenhold."

"I'm going with you," Dom said, leaving no room for argument.

A handful of moments passed in silence before Ophelia asked, "Why would they do this, then? Launch this sort of attack? Did they not expect us to defend ourselves?"

Dom turned to face her. "I'm sure they knew we would put up a fight, My Lady, but not all the travelers through these parts come as prepared as us." He, too, let out a deep sigh. "As I'm sure you'll see, much of our beloved Balmorea has been wrung from its people. And when people have nothing, and are treated like nothing, risks like this," he gestured to the carnage around them, "aren't truly risks at all."

Ambrose nodded. "Desperate men do desperate things."

Elliot felt Ophelia stiffen next to him, and he placed an arm around her shoulders, pulling her into his side. She leaned into him.

A heartbeat or two passed, then Dom was shouting out orders, organizing a small healing station out of one of the carriages and tasking those who weren't injured with gathering the bodies to be burned.

Elliot faced Ophelia and shock lifted his brows. Rage flashed violet across her eyes as she trembled in his arms, struggling to contain herself.

"This is unforgivable," Ophelia whispered. "The blood of these men, these *boys,* stains Raygon's hands, and he will answer for his treatment of my realm. I will cleave his hands from his wrists if that is what it will take to free these people from his crushing grip."

She pulled herself from his arms and made her way to the healing station—not as Ophelia, but as mankind's steward and protector.

The wrath of the Vilicus of Mankind had been awakened—Earth and Sea protect whoever stood against her.

Chapter Twenty Five

By the time all of the bodies had been gathered, the sun had begun making its descent. Sixteen total had died in the ambush, including the two from the merchant group. Nine had been injured but would survive.

The bodies of their Balmorean attackers were gathered on a few meager pyres and burned while several of the crew members dug graves for their two fallen friends. The smell of burning flesh mingled with the scents of freshly turned dirt and blood. It was a smell Ophelia recognized from the battle in the valley: the smell of death.

The four merchants, their crewmen, and the mercenaries stood around the two graves, the bodies of Tyren and Kane already lowered inside.

Ambrose stood at the head of the graves, holding a simple gold ring and a brown leather bracelet with three brass beads in his hand. Naora must have noticed Ophelia's stare lingering on the items because she leaned in and whispered,

"The ring will be returned to Kane's wife, and the bracelet will be returned to Tyren's family."

Ophelia's heart sank with the confirmation of what she had already surmised about the items, but curiosity had her asking, "Are the three brass beads on Tyren's bracelet significant?"

Naora gave a sad smile and nodded. "One for his mother, one for his father, and one for his little sister."

Ophelia peered down into the graves at the shells of the young men she never got to know. What were their dreams? What made them laugh? What did they hold most precious in the world? Her heart twisted in her chest for two souls from her realm taken so needlessly. Taken with so few seasons lived.

Then she raised her eyes, her gaze falling on the pyres of burning bodies thirty feet away. Bodies that represented suffering, desperation, and loss.

Flames engulfing her chambers and Trella's lifeless eyes flashed in her vision, and she flinched, snapping her eyes shut. Her heart pounded against her ribs as she worked to steady her breaths, but the images wouldn't fade.

Elliot must have sensed her disquiet, because he drew her to his chest— her back to his front—wrapped his arms around her waist, and pressed his lips to her neck. "I'm here," he whispered, "I've got you." She clutched his arms and leaned into him.

It wasn't just the memories clawing at her, though. The Essence within her ached, clenching her chest so tightly she felt as though it would crack open, spilling her sadness and pain to the soil in the only form of offering of penance she could give.

This was what she had come to fight for—for those whose voices were deemed too unimportant to hear and became unwitting victims because of it.

They deserved better than this.

Heavy silence hovered over the group as each member of the crew scooped up fistfuls of dirt and tossed them onto the bodies. Dom was the last to throw in his fistfuls and gave a final word of departure.

Drola toh elgo shabi frosha, gian reneli sharil, shabi kin elgo shabi frosha gian wenoli.

Then everyone said the final phrase as one.

Bravekin toh karian karil renek zudovi valigo kin toh strelgo.

From the soil and wind, we are born, and to the soil and wind we return. May the lives lived be found nourishing to the earth.

It was twilight by the time the crew finished burying Kane and Tyren's bodies. Dom and Ambrose made the decision to carry on a bit farther before stopping for the day, finding it unsettling to set up camp near burning corpses and the graves of their friends.

After an hour, before they lost all light entirely, the group stopped and set up camp. The horses were taken to a nearby stream to be watered while the others set up a fire and began preparing a stew for dinner.

The air of grief began to lighten around the fire as everyone ate, sharing stories and fond memories of Tyren and Kane. As Ophelia sat down to eat, someone was telling a story of one time when Kane had tried to impress his now wife.

"Kane hadn't shot a day in his life, but Darla had mentioned how impressed she'd been when she'd seen some hunters shoot fowl right out of the sky," a man named Sergo said. "So, Kane went and grabbed his uncle's bow—his uncle being at least two heads taller and about four stone heavier than him at the time—knocking an arrow and saying he could land it in a tree forty feet across the property." Snickers and light laughs were heard among the men who knew where the story was going while others smiled as they listened. "The string bean could barely pull the bow string to his shoulder, so when he loosed, not only did the arrow go no more than three feet, the string smacked his bow arm. He pulled his arm back from the shock of it then smacked himself in the face with the bow!"

Laughter burst from around the fire. Belly laughs and wide smiles. A few spewed drinks. "Poor fool ended up with a black eye, a bruised arm, and enough humiliation to last a lifetime!"

Another man piped up, "Never tried to learn the bow after that either! Always stuck with a blade!"

The story plucked at Ophelia's memory, and she realized she'd never retrieved her shooting equipment from the carriage she shot from during the ambush.

She quietly excused herself and went to the back of the carriage, opening the hatch to let herself in. With very little light from the moon, she struggled to see anything, rooting around in the dark unsuccessfully. She finally climbed in and set her hand down on one of the crates to push herself forward.

The lid slipped off the top of the crate, and she jolted forward, her hand dropping inside. A gasp flew from her lips when her hand slid across its contents.

Metal. Sharp metal.

She carefully grasped one of the items—a blade by the feel of it— and took it from the crate, stepping out of the carriage to get a better view of it in the moonlight. It was a dagger. And judging by the number of blades she felt in the crate, it was one of many.

She looked back inside the carriage and frowned, setting the blade down in the crate and making to open another. This one was longer and set against the length of the carriage. She propped open the lid and, with her eyes having somewhat adjusted to the darkness, could see it contained spools of several different colors and types of fabric. But when she jostled the top layer, the clank of metal came from underneath. This one held swords.

"Find what you were looking for, My Lady?" someone asked. Ophelia started and dropped the lid back in place, swinging around to see Ambrose leaning against the side of the cart.

"I—I just came back to get my bow from earlier and—"

"And the lid of the crate just jumped into your hands?" His face was unreadable, but there was none of the usual amusement in his tone that she was used to hearing.

"Not exactly. No," she answered. At that moment, Elliot walked up next to Ambrose.

"Everything all right back here?" His tone was casual, but Ophelia saw the nervous tick of his jaw.

"Ah, Mr. Collins. It seems your wife was doing some exploring." Ambrose clapped him on the shoulder.

Elliot frowned. "Exploring?"

"I stumbled upon crates of blades while looking for my shooting gear—"

"You were nosing about in things you have no business nosing about in," Ambrose countered.

Ophelia ignored him and drew her own conclusion. "You all are smuggling weapons from Maraleon into Balmorea," she said, deciding candor would be the best way to address the situation.

Elliot clenched his jaw, his eyes snapping to Ambrose. "I suppose that explains why all of them are so proficient in fighting." Ophelia climbed out of the carriage and stood next to Elliot.

"Aye," Dom said, walking up from the other side of the carriage. "That would explain it. And we'll be expecting you two to keep what you've seen here to yourselves, lest His Majesty get word that a member of the Marelian royal family has snuck into the country right under his nose."

Ophelia's stomach dropped, and she was sure her face had gone pale. Elliot frowned and met Dom's eyes. "What are you talking about?"

Dom rolled his eyes, and Ambrose crossed his arms with a huff. "We've been working with George for nearly ten years. We know who he works with and who he works *for*. We agreed to this little arrangement for his friend and his friend's wife, but as soon as you two rode up, we knew exactly who you were, Lord Barnham."

Elliot opened his mouth to say something then closed it.

"And all the talk of Sigova is centered around the princess and her lord's delayed wedding. So, when Barnham showed up with a 'wife,' we knew who you were too, Your Highness, even without your bright red hair."

Dom huffed a laugh. "And if we weren't certain about

who you were, your skill with a bow during the ambush was confirmation enough."

Ophelia stepped into Elliot who wrapped his arm around her waist and pulled her close. Her heart flailed in her chest, and she bit the inside of her lip.

George had set up this arrangement for her and Elliot with these particular merchants because he'd worked extensively with them for years and trusted them. And since they now knew the nature of George's relationship with Naora, there was no way he wasn't aware they were smugglers.

Ophelia could hardly believe it, but the fact was right before them: George was helping smuggle Marelian weapons into Balmorea—weapons which were likely forged by the smiths that made his father's region wealthy.

George's discretion about his relationship with Naora made a bit more sense now, but this was bad.

Dom said they'd been working with George for nearly ten years, even longer with his father, but to what end?

Ophelia glanced over to Elliot. She could see the wheels of his mind turning with this revelation as well and wondered how he felt about all of it. This was something else they had discovered George was keeping from Elliot. His head dipped, and she saw the flash of hurt pass over his face before he steeled his expression and returned his gaze to Dom and Ambrose.

Dom's face suddenly lightened, and he barked a laugh, slapping Ambrose's chest with the back of his hand. "You see their faces, Brosey?"

Ambrose smiled and let out a stiff chuckle. "You'd think they'd have seen a ghost."

Dom raised his hands, palm out, to the sides of his heads and shook them saying, "Ooooooh," as though pretending to be a ghost, but Ophelia didn't miss the hint of hostility that flared in his eyes.

Ophelia and Elliot didn't laugh. "We weren't looking for anything, and we aren't going to tell anyone," Ophelia said.

"We're simply trying to travel without drawing attention to ourselves," Elliot added. "This is a misunderstanding."

Dom narrowed his eyes at the two of them. "And why *are* you traveling to Balmorea? Tensions are rather high between our countries right now. This hardly seems like the best time for a visit to the jade mines."

Ophelia and Elliot exchanged looks. Of course, they'd be suspicious of them now. She needed to tread carefully.

She looked back to Dom and Ambrose and released a breath. "I have heard there is…trouble in Balmorea," she answered. Dom and Ambrose shifted uneasily on their feet but didn't say anything. She pressed on. "I assume that trouble is what has prompted you to smuggle weapons into your country, to arm your people."

The two merchants glanced at each other before Dom said, "Good people are being over-taxed and then having their land and homes confiscated when they can't pay. Or, if they have sons of age, they are conscripted into the king's forces to pay off their family's debt." His eyes darkened. "The soldiers often take what they want from the women, too, before stealing anything left of value from the home and leaving."

Ophelia tensed, and Elliot's grip tightened around her waist.

Ambrose's jaw worked, his amber eyes boiling with rage. "A spectacle to show their neighbors what happens to traitors who don't pay their king what he is owed."

"Has this behavior been reported to the king?" Ophelia cut in, her own rage taking the place of her manners.

Rage flared in Ambrose's eyes. "What kind of a question is that?" he asked aghast. "Of course, it's been reported! Each and every time, and the king does *nothing* to reprimand his men or compensate the families."

Dom placed a bracing hand to Ambrose's chest. Ambrose swatted him away and stepped back, turning around a few steps to calm himself.

"It's happened to Ambrose, hasn't it? To his family." Elliot surmised.

Dom nodded. "To his sister and brother-in-law. His nephew was conscripted two autumns ago. He was fifteen."

Ophelia's eyes widened. Was Ambrose's nephew in the valley? If he was conscripted two autumns ago, he would be seventeen, barely a man. The thought made Ophelia tremble with rage.

"Then there are the disappearances," Dom went on. "They're worse in the east but are becoming more and more common in central Balmorea and even into the Plains."

"And you think Raygon is responsible for these disappearances?" Elliot asked.

Dom shrugged. "He at least knows about them and, again, does nothing."

"And you've borne witness to what all of this is doing to our people," Ambrose said, stepping back into their conversation and gesturing back down the path they came from, to the ambush of desperate men.

"There's been no confirmation it's the king," Dom said, "but with all the other terrible things he does, kidnapping hardly seems something he would be averse to."

Ophelia was inclined to agree. She knew her sister likely would be as well.

"Each time, it's the same," Ambrose said. "The disappearances always happen during the full moon. Once night falls, a strange fog spreads throughout the village. Those unlucky enough to become trapped in it say their limbs grow so weak they can't move. Some fall unconscious from the weariness the fog brings. Those who don't lose consciousness say they see strange things."

"Monsters in black hoods with skin like ash steal away those too weak to fight against the sleep caused by the fog. They are dragged off and never seen again," Ambrose finished.

Ophelia felt the blood drain from her face, and her eyes snapped to Elliot. His eyes bored into hers in return, and she knew he was thinking the same thing.

"The people call it the Silent Reaping," Dom said. "There are never any screams or cries, and every full moon—as unfailing as the coming and going of the harvest—friends, neighbors, and relatives are taken away as though they were nothing more than bushels of wheat."

Ambrose eyed the two of them. "But what does any of this have to do with your traveling to Balmorea in secret?"

Ophelia looked to Elliot. He took her hand and squeezed, giving her a reassuring nod. She returned her gaze to the two merchants. "Did you all hear what happened in the Central Valley? During the battle between our countries?"

The two men narrowed their eyes. "The three nations fought, then the fighting was stopped by a powerful mage with purple magic. At least, that's what the rumors say," Dom said. "What was it they called her? The purple sorceress? The purple—"

"The Violet Mage," Elliot offered.

Dom snapped his fingers. "That was it."

"Get to the point, please," Ambrose said through a tired sigh.

Ophelia ignored him. "It was me." She held out her hands, palms up, and visualized her bow, arrows, and shooting gear floating into her hands. A purple mist drifted from her palms, encircling her shooting gear as it all stacked itself neatly in her waiting hands. Ambrose and Dom yielded a step back, and their eyes widened. "I go by another name as well, though, and that name is the reason behind my power." She carefully set her shooting gear to the ground at her feet.

"And what name would that be?" Dom asked warily.

"Vilicus of Mankind," she said. Confusion bent both of their brows in a way that turned up the corners of Ophelia's lips. "I know it's unheard of," she said, holding her hands up as if in surrender, "but it's true. I am mankind's steward, and I am coming to Balmorea to help her people."

Ophelia's declaration was met with silence. Not a pensive silence, but a tense, uncomfortable one. Ophelia held her breath as Dom and Ambrose stood beside each other with arms crossed over their chests and eyes narrowed on her.

Finally, Ambrose shifted his weight from one foot to the other and said, "I say this with as much respect as I could possibly muster at this moment, Your Highness, but that sounds like the craziest load of bullshit I've ever heard."

Ophelia sighed and clenched her jaw in annoyance. "King Raygon didn't believe me either."

"Are you here to kill the king, Your Highness?" Dom asked, eyes still narrowed.

Ophelia's eyebrows shot up at his candor. "That is not my intention." It was an option—one she felt would be the easiest and quickest way to solve many of the Raygon-centered issues that seemed to be cropping up. Her role as Vilicus of Mankind, however, complicated the use of murder as a means of resolving problems.

Her brow bent with the realization that she was strongly considering taking someone's life when only a matter of days ago she had questioned who she even was after justifiably killing someone to save her own life. She didn't have the time to consider this, though, so she pushed those thoughts to the back of her mind and continued. "The Vilicus, Pyotr, has made me aware of strange magic in the far east of Balmorea. It is poisoning the land, but his magic can do nothing to nullify it. I'm traveling to investigate the spell and find a way to break it."

More silence.

Ambrose looked to Dom, having already given his thoughts on Ophelia's explanation. Ophelia held Dom's gaze as his eyes bore into hers. There was no hostility in his stare, only acute consideration. Ophelia felt him look straight through her, as though he could see directly into her heart and was picking through its contents, weighing what he found against his trust.

After several minutes, he finally spoke. "You said you are here to help our people," he began. "How does this strange magic affect our people?"

"You mentioned disappearances occurring every full moon." Dom nodded, he and Ambrose both standing a bit straighter as they listened. "The spell I am looking to break is massive, and it was cast with a forbidden type of magic that gains its power through the use of a person's lifeforce—or through the use of many people's lifeforces, in this case. What I mean is this: I believe the people who are taken during these Silent Reapings are being killed, and their blood is being used to sustain this terrible spell."

Dom looked toward the sky and let out a curse in Balmorean that Ophelia didn't recognize, and Ambrose shook his head in disbelief. Dom returned his focus to Ophelia and Elliot and ran a hand down his face. "This does sound like madness." Ophelia's heart sank, but before she could protest, he continued. "However, I know George, and he has spoken of you many times, Lord Barnham—of your fairness and loyalty." He turned to Ophelia. "I don't know anything about you, Your Highness, but I trust that George wouldn't have set up this arrangement with people who he didn't consider trustworthy. I don't know what your thoughts are on our little operation, nor do I seek your approval. But if George trusts you all, and you all say you won't betray us, then I will extend my trust to you as well."

Relief washed over Ophelia. Even if Dom didn't seem to believe anything Ophelia had said about being Vilicus or trying to bring down the Aegis in the east, he did offer his discretion regarding their travel plans and their identities, and that would be enough.

"Likewise," Elliot said as he extended his arm to Dominicio. "I trust George with my life. If he trusts you, I will as well." The merchant grasped Elliot's hand with his own in agreement. "Thank you."

Dom nodded. "May our secret undertakings help those we both seek to defend."

Chapter Twenty Six

NELL KNEW A FAIR BIT ABOUT FIGHTING. HER four older brothers, all experienced fighters in the king's forces, made sure she could properly fend off any questionable men who might approach her before she left for court. She didn't know everything, but one thing she was painfully certain of was the fact that one could train with a blade or a bow or their fists at times of day other than the absolute ass crack of dawn.

Nell pointed this out to George, making him aware of all the other hours of the day that were also suitable for training. But George insisted that morning was best, arguing that the early hour was when the body was at its freshest and most nimble. He also noted how, at such an early time, before everyone in the castle began to bustle around, Aria would still be asleep and wouldn't be in need of her ladies quite yet. And though Nell no longer felt the princess truly needed her anymore—what with the recent return of her ladies—she still wanted to watch over Aria as she had promised Ophelia she would.

So, Nell reluctantly complied.

George's logic may have made sense, but she couldn't help but feel that some snide part of him was simply trying to punish her for avoiding him all week—a suspicion that was all but confirmed the next morning when she was greeted in the courtyard at sunrise by a beaming George, his green eyes alight with amusement. "I half-expected you not to show."

Nell leveled him with an irritated glare as she neared. "And why's that?" she asked, crossing her arms over her chest. He was standing in nearly the exact same place they'd conversed the day before, with wooden swords and daggers of varying sizes laying scattered on or propped against a stone bench behind him. He was wearing a midnight blue tunic and nondescript beige breeches with brown boots and had no business looking as handsome as he did at such an early hour.

He shrugged. "Part of me wondered if you only agreed to this arrangement simply to get rid of me so you could resume your very adept circumvention of my presence."

It's too early for this bullshit.

Nell closed her eyes and began massaging her temples. "The sun hasn't even risen yet, and you are already using words with more than three syllables. What is *wrong* with you?"

George's chuckle rumbled through the space between them. "I've always been a morning person."

"What fantastic news for me," she said wryly, and his smile grew wicked.

"Oh, Sweetheart, it really could be."

Heat crept into her cheeks at his insinuation, and she did her best to cover it up with an eye roll.

"If you are going to ply me with vague sexual advances this early in the morning, please at least have the decency to bring coffee with you."

He barked a laugh, a broad smile stretching across his face, and the sight made her heart leap.

"Coffee, is it?" he asked, a curious smile lining his lips. "Not tea? I didn't think there was anyone in all of Maraleon, aside from my mother, who shared my preference for liquid life."

Nell's lips slid into a small smile. "Liquid life, indeed. Ophelia can't stand the smell, so I have to enjoy my cup before I come to her chambers in the morning."

George tsked. "Such a shame, but I'll try to remember to bring coffee tomorrow in case the urge to ply you with more vague sexual advances overcomes me," he said with a chuckle before rubbing his hands together conspiratorially. "Now, where would you like to begin? Or rather, which weapon are you wanting to train—at least, I assume you want to train with a weapon." Curiosity lit his eyes. "Though, from what I saw yesterday, I don't think there is much I need to teach you in the way of wielding knives."

She shrugged. "I have four older brothers who weren't keen on sending me to court defenseless."

"Wise men," George commented, his light green gaze trained on hers, as if to encourage her to go on; she hadn't answered his question. The intensity of his gaze had her shifting on her feet.

"I do know my way around a knife. I feel rather confident I could hold my own in close range," she began but hesitated.

George nodded, leaning forward. "But?"

She searched his eyes for any sign of amusement, anticipating a ribbing or off-handed comment from him, but neither came. He simply gazed at her openly, waiting for her response.

Nell swallowed. "My father was very adamant that I not train with a blade. My brothers only managed to train me with knives and daggers because they're easier to conceal in hand-to-hand training." She waved her hands absently in front of her. "Self-defense against armed opponents and all that."

A knowing smile turned up the edges of George's mouth, as though he already knew what she was going to say before the words left her lips.

"So, I was never able to train with a sword."

George's eyes sparked. "And you would like to remedy that."

"I would," she replied with a nod.

George's expression sobered a fraction. "Sword training is difficult, and becoming a proficient fighter does not happen quickly."

Her nostrils flared. "I'm under no illusions that this will be easy, George."

His eyes crinkled at the edges with a smile before he turned toward the bench and picked up one of the wooden swords leaning against it. "Very well, then," he replied, closing the distance between them and handing her the sword. "Let's start with some drills, shall we?"

Two hours later, Nell sat slumped on the stone bench, her arms hanging uselessly at her sides while her wooden sword lay next to her in the grass. She glared at the offending object as if to shame it for what it put her through. How couldsomething so innocuous cause such suffering?

And that is exactly what Nell was doing right now—suffering.

The first hour had been spent learning different stances and motions then drilling them over and over and over with George correcting her form periodically.

She had kept expecting him to be more patronizing or to inject his flirty comments throughout their time together, but he never had. In fact, the moment she had taken the sword in her hands, all traces of amusement had stripped from his face. His tone had been stern but never cruel. His touches, when correcting her grip or arm position, had never lingered, though she had always felt them afterward like a brand on her skin. It had all heated her blood more than it should have, this serious, commanding side of George, and glimpses of what it might be like for him to use that same tone with her in much different ways, of what it might feel like for his touches to linger in much different places, had caused her to lose her footing more times than she'd ever admit.

This was a side of George she never would have considered possible given the carefree flirt he painted himself to be. And that's what all of it was, she realized—a false portrait. The innuendos and irreverent attitude were all a façade for him to hide behind. But what he was hiding from, she couldn't quite riddle out.

"You did well today," George said, shaking Nell from her thoughts.

She looked up to find him walking toward her, a small smile on his face and a waterskin in hand. His green eyes shone with warmth, something akin to pride flickering among the flecks of gold.

He sat down next to her and handed her the skin, but when she went to reach for it, the only thing that lifted was her hand. She scowled down at her arms, as though doing so might will them into compliance, but she had no such luck, and she inwardly groaned at how difficult this was going to make the rest of her day.

She lifted her eyes to his and sighed. "Will it be like this every time?" she asked.

His brows bent as he lowered the waterskin. "Like what?"

A flush of embarrassment ran up her neck. *This was pathetic.* "My arms feel as though they are being weighed down by stones," she said, and her frown deepened. "And now that I think about it, I'm not sure I'd be able to grip the skin in my hands either."

George barked a laugh and patted her on the knee. "No, it won't always be like this," he replied, turning to face her on the bench. "Make sure you try to move your arms—roll your shoulders, stretch them—or you'll go stiff. Drink a lot of water, and stop to see Master Gaius before you head to your chambers to clean up for the day. He will have something to help ease the soreness."

She nodded in reply and was about to stand when George slid closer to her, lifting her chin with his index finger and pressing the opening of the waterskin to her lips.

"Here," he said, his voice low and gentle, smoothing over her skin like silk.

Surprise skittered through her, and she sucked in a sharp breath before opening her mouth to allow the light flow of water to pass between her lips. His finger remained under her chin, using it to hold her head in place as she drank. His thumb brushed lightly along her jaw, and her skin warmed under his touch. Her heartbeat quickened as his gaze rose to meet hers.

She longed to reach out and return his touch, to see how he might react the moment her fingers met his skin, but her useless arms kept her from indulging. It was probably better that she didn't anyway.

After a few refreshing gulps of water, she lifted her chin from his hold to push the waterskin from her lips, signaling that she was done. He pulled it back and corked it, freezing when her tongue darted out to swipe up any water left behind on her lips. His pupils dilated, and he clenched his jaw before clearing his throat. "Right, well," he said, standing and retrieving her discarded sword from the grass. "I think we can start you on the striking post tomorrow."

"Thank you," she said, the words falling from her lips before she realized what she was doing. "For this. For training me."

A small smile turned his lips up, and he offered his hand to help her up. With effort, she raised her hand enough to take his and stood before him. His face softened, and he lifted her fingers to his lips, pressing a light kiss to her knuckles, never dropping her gaze. "It's no problem at all."

He lowered her hand, squeezing once before letting go. "Stop to see Master Gaius," he reminded her before making his way toward the small armory in the corner of the yard. "And I'll see you bright and early tomorrow," he tossed over his shoulder as a wide grin splayed across his face.

Nell's heart leapt in her chest, and she nodded, unable to keep a smile from spreading across her lips in return.

Chapter Twenty Seven

OPHELIA REMAINED UNDER HER BLANKETS A FEW moments longer, staring up at the sky as it began to bleed red and orange. Her thoughts lingered on what the day should have held for her, but wouldn't, and disappointment settled heavily in her chest.

Because of the attack, their group had lost half a day of travel. So, when everyone had woken up laying on the hard, lumpy ground with the scent of horse shit in the air instead of on the comfortable beds of the inn they should have been staying in, the irritability that had begun charging the air of the camp was understandable.

She finally sat up and began to pack up her things, wondering what Elliot was thinking.

A few conversations could be heard here and there about what to strap where and how to repack a certain bag, but, for the most part, everyone was quiet as they worked to tear down the small camp. Packing up everything lasted longer than normal, but they were on their way soon enough.

By early evening, the walls of Ravenhold came into view. Whoops and whistles scattered throughout their group as they approached, and Ophelia released a sigh of relief.

What she wouldn't give for a hot meal and a warm bath.

She looked over to Elliot who met her gaze with a relieved smile. Their journey was halfway done.

Ophelia and Elliot entered as part of Dominicio's merchant group then said their goodbyes as they parted ways.

"I hope the rest of your journey is much less exciting than what you endured with us," Dom said as he shook Elliot's hand.

Elliot huffed out a laugh and gave a tired smile. "I hope so, too."

"Thank you for allowing us to travel with you, Dominicio. I can only hope our paths can cross again one day under much different circumstances," Ophelia said.

Dom nodded. "As do I. Take care, you two." Then he rode off to rejoin his crew.

As they watched his retreating form, Ophelia realized she hadn't thought as far as accommodations in Ravenhold for when they arrived.

"Now what?" she asked.

"I asked Ambrose last night what inn he suggested for our stay. He said there are several in the city that would suit us fine but suggested we stick to ones on the outskirts," he leaned in, "ideally as far from the castle as possible, given our circumstances."

Ophelia nodded and smiled. "Lead the way, then, *husband*."

Elliot's eyes flashed at the word *husband*, but the heat faded all too quickly. A sad smile tugged across his lips as he turned his focus forward and led their horses a few blocks down the main road.

They passed several buildings that Ophelia assumed were homes or businesses—small square structures of brick and stone with thatched roofs lined the cobbled street. Vendors hung halfway out of propped open, shuttered windows, shouting what they had to offer for those passing by. Men and women alike shuffled on either side of the road, some stopping to chat with neighbors while others hustled by to quickly get to their destination.

Ophelia followed Elliot for several blocks before they turned down a street off to the left. The road dead-ended into a wide, two-story stone building. Several large windows lined the first floor of the main building, giving a clear view of the tavern inside. Just above, smaller windows lined the second floor, where, Ophelia assumed, the rented rooms were. The entrance, a black wooden door with a brass handle, was situated in the middle of the building, nestled between two windows. Hanging above it was a large sign that read: *The Wolf's Den.*

Ophelia raised her eyebrows as trepidation rippled through her. "What a cozy name," she mused.

Elliot laughed. "I said the same thing when Ambrose told me of it, but he assured me it's a relatively tame tavern that rents out rooms. He said they mostly serve traveling merchants, like him and Dom, and other members of nobility who travel for this reason or that." He took her hand and squeezed it reassuringly. "We will rest up comfortably before continuing our journey."

Ophelia nodded and continued down the road with Elliot.

As they strode closer, a tall wooden building just beyond the tavern came into view. Its wide wooden doors were propped open; the stalls, hay bales, and bridles inside easily identified the structure as a stable. Ophelia and Elliot approached with their horses and handed them over to the stablemaster who met them at the entrance. They unloaded what items they would need for their stay from their saddlebags then headed into the tavern.

The moment they stepped inside, the smell of warm stew and ale wafted over them. Their stomachs growled in unison.

Two rows of long tables and benches were situated in the center of the room with an aisle separating them. A few smaller tables and chairs were placed around the edges of the room for smaller parties. Four large, iron candelabras hung from chains in the ceiling, but with the midday sunlight shining through the windows, there was no need for them to be lit.

Ophelia's eyes landed on the bar that ran along the back of the space. The head of a snarling black wolf hung on the wall behind it. A wooden placard etched with the words *The Wolf's Den* in Balmorean hung underneath.

A short woman with blonde hair bound in two braids and expertly holding three steins of ale in one hand and a bowl of stew in the other, shouted at them to find a seat, saying she would be with them shortly.

They did as they were told, sitting at one of the smaller tables near the entrance by one of the windows. As soon as they sat down, both of them released a deep breath and slouched in their seats. They both gave a small laugh at their identical reactions, and Elliot reached over to take Ophelia's hand, bringing her fingers to his mouth in a gentle kiss.

Ophelia felt the exhaustion and soreness down to her bones and just wanted to plop into a plushy bed and sleep for days, but after almost a full week of trail rations, her body demanded hearty sustenance before rest. As her eyes canvased Elliot's face, she noted the dark circles beneath his eyes, affirming he felt the same way. Or, perhaps, something else was weighing him down as well.

The barmaid soon made her way over to serve Elliot and Ophelia. After taking their orders, she disappeared behind the door to the right of the bar, reappearing soon after with wine, stew, and a fresh loaf of warm bread.

Elliot and Ophelia didn't speak much while they ate. Ophelia attributed their silence to the weariness from travel, but, admittedly, she found herself distracted. The stew was delicious, the bread warm and fluffy, but this wasn't the meal she was supposed to be eating with Elliot today. She finished her stew just before Elliot and stared absently out the window, thinking of all the ways the day should be different from what it was.

The barmaid returned, and Elliot spoke with her about setting up a reservation to stay in one of their rooms.

"Ah, perfect timing," the woman said as she stacked their lunch dishes. "We had a room open up this morning. We'll get you and your wife set up in room three." Ophelia's heart swelled at the word *wife*, then quickly deflated. "If you would come with me, My Lord, to make the arrangements, you, My Lady, can go ahead and take your things to the room." She gestured to the stairs. "Up the stairs, last door all the way to the left." She turned on her heel and made her way to the bar.

Ophelia grabbed her things and stood up, and Elliot did the same. He leaned down and pressed a kiss to her forehead. "I'll see you upstairs shortly."

Ophelia gave him a small smile and nodded before he turned and followed after the barmaid.

She followed him with her eyes for a few moments longer, then headed for their room, the word *wife* a taunting echo in her mind as she climbed the stairs.

Chapter Twenty Eight

Ophelia walked through the door to their room, set her bag down off to the side, and sighed. She toed off her boots then canvased the room to take stock of their accommodations.

The room was small and simple but had everything they needed. Ophelia was relieved to find a copper tub off in the corner near the door in case they wanted to call for a bath. An ewer and washbasin sat in the middle of a dining table in the corner of the room with two hand towels draped over the back of one of the chairs for freshening up. Her eyes slid over the small hearth that sat cold near the middle of the room, across from the bed—their *one* bed.

Ophelia's heart jumped.

She wasn't quite sure why the thought of sharing a bed with Elliot would cause such a reaction from her. She'd slept next to Elliot before—had done much more than sleep with Elliot in a bed, too. Earth and sea, they had just spent five and a half days traveling and sleeping next to each other each night. Elliot had held her while she slept in her bed after the battle with Pyotr, and again for several nights after Trella's assassination attempt.

But *this* felt different for some reason.

Ophelia walked over to the table to wash as she unraveled her braid, pouring water into the basin as she sifted through her thoughts.

Here, there wouldn't need to be any sneaking around or fear of igniting her father's anger. They didn't have to watch the time to ensure Elliot left at an appropriate hour.

Sure, all of that was true, but as Ophelia took in their private room with their shared bed, what made her heart swell the most was the easiness of it all. Being in this simple room, with its relatively simple provisions, all felt so normal. They could simply *be.* Just as any other married couple could.

No one even considered they might need another bed. They traveled as 'husband and wife' and were, thus, given a room for a husband and wife without question. They wouldn't have to dodge any doubts or have to make up any excuses. They wouldn't have to anticipate if or when someone would come to their door. Privacy was expected and given. In fact, privacy was what they were paying for.

Ophelia's cheeks warmed as she thought about falling asleep pressed against Elliot's bare chest, waking up to his lips on her neck, his warm fingers smoothing across her sensitive skin.

She splashed her face with water from the basin to cool down. It was just a bed. She was giving this entirely too much thought.

After drying her face with one of the hand towels, she dipped the towel in the water and began freshening up as much as the meager basin would allow before they could call for a bath.

The door opened behind her, and the light thud of boots entered the room. Ophelia glanced over her shoulder as Elliot closed the door and set down the rest of their belongings. He set the lock on the door then toed off his boots.

Her heart began to pound, and she shook her head to clear her mind. She was being ridiculous. They were both exhausted—that's why her mind was tangled up like this.

Elliot's hands slid around her waist, startling her from her thoughts—she hadn't heard him walk across the room. The warmth of his chest radiated against her back. He dipped his head, his lips barely skirting the shell of her ear. "How are you finding everything?" he asked gently, his breath fanning across her neck.

Ophelia's skin heated. "Adequate," she replied. "It's simple, but I'm quite content with what we have."

Elliot chuckled as he gathered her hair in one hand and pushed it over the opposite shoulder. He pressed his lips to the crook of her neck. "I'm content as well, Elia." His voice was silk against her skin. "After five and a half days on the road, surrounded by sweaty men and sleeping on stone, I finally have you to myself."

She sucked in a sharp breath—maybe he *was* thinking as she was.

"Do you have any idea the agony of not being able to touch you while you lay right next to me? All night? Every night?" he asked, his lips skirting down her shoulder as his fingers slid up and down her arms. The fabric of her doublet was suddenly too tight, too stifling.

She tipped her head back against his shoulder and sighed. "Yes. Yes, I do." Ophelia turned in his arms to face him, finding a smirk on his face as she placed her palms on his chest.

"Do you, now?" he asked, sliding his hands around her waist, pulling her closer. He leaned down, brushing his lips across her cheek. "Did your mind conjure up images of my writhing, naked body as mine did yours every night before falling asleep?" His hands slid up her back and began slowly loosening the laces of her riding doublet. "Did you have to slip away every morning to...*relieve* your desire as well?"

She swallowed, her chest rising and falling to keep pace with her quickened pulse. "No," she whispered as her doublet slipped from her shoulders and fell to the ground at her feet. She unfastened the belt around his waist, and slid her arms under his tunic, finding his skin warm against her fingers. His stomach twitched with his sharp inhale, and she smiled. "I imagined the feel of your tongue on my skin, and the sounds you make when I satisfy you." She pulled his tunic over his head and discarded it on the floor. Her eyes snagged on the amber pendant she had given him, resting between the muscles of his chest, and she took it between her fingers, a small smile lifting her lips as she smoothed her thumb over the engraved sun. "I'd say it was a bit unfair, actually."

"What was?" he asked breathlessly before kissing his way down her neck. Her breath hitched, and her eyes fell shut as his tongue swiped across her pulse, his lips turning up at the sound. "What was unfair, Elia?" His hands scrunched up the fabric of her linen shirt.

"You at least found release while I rode for days, *aching.*"

A rumble resounded from his chest as his fingers bit into her thighs. "A true inequity if I've ever heard of one."

"Certainly so," she breathed, raising up on her toes to whisper in his ear. "Whatever will you do to right such a wrong?"

He chuckled softly as he lifted her shirt up and over her head. "I have a few ideas."

His mouth came down on hers before her shirt hit the floor. Ophelia's fingers raked through his hair, and his hands slid up her back, pressing her against his chest. His skin felt warm against her sensitive breasts. He smelled of the outdoors mixed with hints of amber and sweat, but he tasted like home.

Elliot backed her into the foot of the bed and gently pushed her down, placing gentle kisses down her stomach, swirling his tongue as he unfastened the laces of her pants. What felt like a moment later, her riding pants were gone, and she lay on the bed bare before him.

She sucked in a breath when she realized this was the first time she'd been completely naked with him, and nervousness clamped down on her chest.

His heated gaze raked over her, shattering her lingering doubt like crystal against stone.

Elliot lowered himself over her body, starting to push her further onto the bed, when she pulled away, pressing a hand to his chest. "Wait."

She felt his heart pounding under her palm before he pulled back and met her gaze, a small bend in his brow. She gave him a small smile for reassurance as she dragged her hand down his chest, his abdomen, down the light dusting of hair to the laces of his pants and tugged. "Fair is fair," she said against his lips.

His eyes darkened, and he gave her a crooked grin, the dimple on one side peeking out to tease her. He pushed up and stood at the foot of the bed, his eyes never breaking from hers. She sat up on her elbows and watched him as his hands deftly untied the front of his pants and pushed them down his legs.

Ophelia's skin flushed as she took him in. He had the build of a man who did not simply wear a sword on his hip for ceremony. Every inch of him exuded strength and was cut by discipline, and the look that hooded his eyes told her he would use every ounce of that strength to protect her, to love her, to consume her.

He was stunning.

And he did not shy away from letting her see just how much he desired her.

She dragged her teeth over her bottom lip as her gaze slid down his body, pushing up to her knees when her eyes came to the thick length of him. Her heart jumped, and she felt a flush run up her neck.

"You look so pretty when you blush like that for me," he murmured, lightly grazing a knuckle along her heated skin.

A shiver ran down her body, his words causing her nipples to pebble and sending heat rushing low in her stomach. She inched closer to him, wanting to take this moment for herself before he took charge. She placed her hands on his chest over the amber pendant, the connection to him anchoring her, and something inside her unwound, relaxed.

Her fingers traced along his shoulders then his collar bones. She slid her hands down the familiar path of his chest and abdomen, her lips following behind with open mouthed kisses. His breathing quickened as she moved farther, swirling her tongue below his navel and lightly sliding a finger up the underside of his length. He huffed out a breath and shivered.

She pulled back and rose up to her knees to fully see him, following her gaze with her hands, taking her time to learn every part of him still unknown to her. His throat worked on a swallow, and his hands clenched and unclenched at his sides as though he were struggling not to touch her. Her chest warmed when she realized that's exactly what he was doing. He was giving her this time to grow comfortable with his body without the pressure of any demands or expectations, and her heart swelled.

She looked up to see his face and found him watching her. If ever a color was needed to represent desire, it would be the shade of molten hazel that stared back at her. Her breath hitched at the sight, and familiar, delicious tension tightened low in her stomach.

"Was it my hand you imagined working you as you relieved yourself each morning?" she asked, gingerly wrapping her fingers around him. His jaw ticked, and he sucked in a quick breath through his nose as she slid her hand up and back down the length of him.

"No," he ground out. "I pictured you spread wide before me, moaning and begging for more. I imagined my fingers tangled in your hair and you clenching around me, back arched, as I took you from behind," he panted as her strokes grew rougher. "I imagined your beautiful lips around my cock, sucking me so hard I saw stars."

The heat in her stomach liquified, a flush burning through her at the images his words coaxed, and she dropped level with his hips. "Like this?" she asked, then took his cock into her mouth.

He released a sharp breath as his head fell back on a groaned, "*Fuck, yes, Ophelia.*"

A flash of heat burst in her core at the decadent way her name rolled off his tongue. He gently pushed his hips forward then drew back, showing her what he wanted. She followed his lead, eagerly sliding her mouth down the length of him then pulling back up.

"Use your tongue, too," he said, his voice breathless as he threaded his fingers through her hair.

She wasn't quite sure what he meant but let instinct guide her, rolling her tongue along the underside of his shaft. His hand in her hair tightened as a stuttered moan fell from his lips. "Yes. *Fuck.* Just like that."

She moved slowly at first, acclimating to him, listening for what made him lose his breath, for what pulled more of those satisfying sounds from his lips.

His thumb gently caressed her neck in silent encouragement, and it emboldened her, urging her to hollow her cheeks and suck him deeper. His hips jerked forward on a ragged moan, and satisfaction scored through her even as he hit the back of her throat and tears pricked her eyes.

Ophelia grew desperate for his release; the need to have him completely unraveled by her tongue consumed her. She worked him faster, moving up and down his length with quick, unpracticed movements. She swirled her tongue around the tip of him and added her hand in, squeezing as she traveled back down. Elliot's grip in her hair grew punishing as heady groans fell from his lips, and all of it sent liquid heat pooling between her legs.

She chanced a look up at him, and the sight turned her skin molten.

His eyes were closed, his brow slightly bent, and his lips were parted in ecstasy. His breaths turned to ragged pants, and his hips flexed in time with her movements. He was beautiful like this, undone and unrepentantly lost in her.

She moaned her approval, and he tensed in her mouth before suddenly dropping to his knees on the mattress and taking her face in his hands.

"Enough," he said, his voice deep and rough as he pulled her mouth to his. He kissed her frantically, as though she would slip through his fingers if he slowed. He set loose his pent-up desire, and she did the same, claiming his mouth with a wild desperation she hadn't known laid within her until his lips met hers.

He pushed her back into the bed, inching her towards the middle as he kissed her. His hungry mouth traveled down her jaw, nipping at her pulse point and dragging his teeth down her neck. She sucked in a gasp. "You're so beautiful, Elia," he whispered against her throat. "So. Fucking. Beautiful."

She felt the adoration in his voice pour over her. She felt it in every kiss he pressed to her body, in every breath that flitted across her skin—a warm summer rain to soothe the sting in her heart.

She felt it like the sharp edge of a knife—that these stolen moments were the only ones they could share together. That her life would never be free of danger or death, and it terrified her to consider that she might lose him, that he would be another casualty to her destiny.

The thought stole the breath from her lungs, and she clutched him closer, weaving her fingers into his hair as his mouth continued down her chest. His fingers played over one of her nipples while his tongue flicked over the other. Her hands tightened in his hair on a gasp, and he released a groan, closing his lips over the tip of her breast and sucking. A soft moan drifted from her mouth, and she tossed her head back, arching into him, seeking more—needing more. She needed the comfort of his body against hers. She needed the connection with him, the tangling of his heart with hers.

Elliot kissed his way down the valley of her breasts to the other side, yet it still took her by surprise the moment his tongue flicked her nipple, still shocked her with quick jolts of pleasure.

He lifted his head. "Do you know what today is, Elia?" he asked, his lips brushing against the skin of her breast.

Her eyes snapped shut. Of course, she knew what today was. It was the source of her heartache, the song of anguish that taunted her happiness.

She let out a breath. "Yes."

"What is today, then?"

"The day you and I were to be wed," she whispered as pressure began to build behind her eyes.

He hummed as he pressed more kisses down her stomach. "That's right."

This day and this night were supposed to be theirs. It was supposed to be about the commitment they would make to each other. A day where they were to profess their love unabashedly before those closest to them. A day of celebration.

Instead, they were here—at an inn in Balmorea, seeking answers to questions that others had been killed for asking.

"It was supposed to be our day, our night," she said quietly.

Elliot stopped and crawled up her body. "I won't give today up, Elia," he said, raising a hand to rest against her cheek. "You're right. This was supposed to be our day, and I still intend to make it ours." He lowered his forehead to hers and sighed. "Let's forget about all that is beyond that door and take the rest of this day and this night for ourselves. Simply you and me." He pulled back to meet her eyes.

She met his gaze and nodded, an errant tear rolling down her cheek. "Just you and me," she said.

He brushed his nose along hers. "Always," he whispered. Her heart tightened at the conviction in his words—at the promise they held.

"Always," she agreed before he took her lips in a slow, tender kiss. It was a kiss filled with longing and promise. It was not rushed or desperate, but slow and languid. She parted her lips for him, and his tongue swept into her mouth, sliding along hers, and his gentleness pulled a light moan from her throat.

Elliot stiffened at the sound, and something seemed to snap within him. He dropped his hips against hers, pinning her to the bed and deepened their kiss. The hard length of him pressed against her center, and another moan fell from her lips when he ground himself against her. She wrapped her arms around his neck and canted her hips upwards, moving with him.

But it wasn't enough.

The next moment, Elliot pulled away and began making his way down her body again. His kisses were not slow, and they were not sweet. They were rough and hungry.

He took Ophelia's breasts in each hand and traced his

thumbs over the peaked tips—every brush of his fingers, every swirl of his tongue, every scrape of his teeth pulling breathy sighs and gasps from her lungs. He set her ablaze, squirming with need underneath him.

He nipped at her hip bone. "Patience," he said with a smirk before settling himself between her thighs. She let her legs fall open, trembling with anticipation, and he chuckled against her thigh, brushing his lips along the sensitive skin. "So eager."

She mewled with frustration until he finally lowered his lips to the crease of her thigh and licked down toward her core. Her back bowed off the bed with a soft moan as he repeated the action on the other side.

Slowly, he kissed and licked his way toward her center, his breath sending shivers up her spine. Delicious tension continued to swirl tight within her, and she ran her fingers through his hair, trying to maneuver him to where she needed him. He chuckled again, then licked a line straight through her aching flesh. Her head fell back on a moan, and he groaned his approval.

"So fucking *sweet*," he murmured then licked her again.

She was wound so tight that it wouldn't take much for her to snap. She clutched his hair again as her hips writhed, seeking the touch she so desperately needed.

Elliot hummed, seeming satisfied with her reaction, when he finally ran his tongue across her sensitive bundle of nerves.

She cried out and held his head in place as his tongue flicked and swirled. Her cries turned into moans. "*Yes. Right there*," she whimpered as she rode his tongue, her movements growing more and more frenzied as she drew closer to the edge.

He dipped two fingers inside of her and curled, shooting pleasure through every limb of her body. Words escaped her, all awareness narrowing to the places his tongue and fingers worked her, to the riot of sensations skittering through her. Then his lips fastened over her sensitive nerves, and he sucked. She ignited, crying out as bliss so blinding and intense consumed her.

Elliot held her steady, gently guiding her through each crest of pleasure until she stilled and rested limply before him.

Elliot pressed soft kisses to the inside of her thighs as he smoothed slow circles along her hips. Her breathing slowed along with her heart, and once her mind finally cleared, she opened her eyes and slowly pushed up to her elbows. Her eyes met Elliot's, and her breath caught at the sight of him. His hair was mussed, and his eyes were wild. He gave her a wicked grin before nipping at her inner thigh, and desire pulsed through her again, hot and demanding.

Ophelia reached for him, and he slid effortlessly up her body, cradling a hand behind her neck, and pulling her to his mouth. She wrapped her arms around him as his body settled over hers, and groaned when his hips bore down on hers—at the faint traces of amber on his skin, the taste of her desire on his tongue.

"I need you," she whimpered against his lips. "Elliot, please."

He kissed her again, groaning at her words. "Anything," he rasped as he aligned himself to her entrance. "I'm yours." He met her gaze and pressed into her.

Ophelia gasped, and Elliot released a jagged breath into her neck as she enclosed around him. His lips fell to her skin, and he began peppering her throat with soft kisses.

He was heartbreakingly gentle, taking care to fill the moment with love and tenderness. Her heart clenched, emotion clogging the back of her throat as she tightened her arms around his neck and pulled him closer.

She lifted her hips to meet his, and he groaned as he sank further into her. He rested his forehead to hers, giving another tentative thrust of his hips, and she moaned softly against his mouth.

Ophelia framed his face with her hands and ran her thumb across his glossy lower lip, her heart swelling with so much love for him that she felt close to bursting. "I love you," she said.

He brought his lips to hers and rolled his hips. Her lips parted on a gasp, and his tongue swept inside. He began to move again, and she sighed, hands sliding into his hair and clutching the strands between her fingers. His movements quickened, and she moved with him, tension beginning to churn and rise within her again.

He suddenly sat back and withdrew, flipping her to her stomach on the bed. He slid a hand under her hips and lifted her to her knees, and she tensed with uncertainty. He paused, smoothing his hands along her hips before lowering over her, licking and kissing a path up her spine to her shoulder blades then farther.

His hands rested next to hers once he reached her nape. "Do you trust me?" he asked as his hard cock slid along her entrance, her body now trembling with anticipation.

"Yes," she replied.

He dropped a kiss to her shoulder as he aligned himself then thrusted into her.

She clutched the bed linens, a moan tumbling from her at the fullness she felt, at the depth he reached.

"*Fuck,*" he murmured, clamping a hand onto her hip as he thrust into her again. He didn't ease into her this time, and she didn't want him to. She wanted everything with him. Every sensation, every word, every breath and moan, every rough and gentle push of his hips—she wanted all of it.

In her next breath, Elliot wrapped an arm around her chest and pulled her up, pressing her back against his chest and framing her throat with one hand while his other bit into her hip. And he never stopped moving.

It stole her breath.

She reached behind her, placing her hand to the back of his neck and pulling his face down to kiss her. Their lips crashed together as they moved against each other in the frenzy of the moment. His hand at her hip slid down her stomach to where they were joined, a finger playing across the most sensitive part of her. She cried out into his mouth as the pleasure shot through her, and she rocked against his hand and into his hips.

His deft touch, the feel of his body moving against and inside hers, was all too much yet not enough. Her grip tightened in his hair as the pressure within her built, and her movements grew frantic.

"I love you, Ophelia," he panted against her mouth, and her release crashed over her, Elliot catching her deep moan with his kiss.

He lightened his touch as he eased her through the fringes of pleasure with long, slow strokes and deep, drugging kisses. But he didn't stop. He slid his hand back to her hip to steady her and began thrusting faster and sharper. His open mouth dropped to her shoulder, his panted breaths feathering across her back as he tumbled toward his release. "Perfect," he murmured against her skin. "You feel so fucking *perfect*, Elia."

She clutched the arm at her hip and the hand at her throat, her nails digging into his skin. She dropped her head back against his shoulder and moaned, rolling into him and gasping his name as delicious aftershocks rippled through her. He responded with a deep moan of his own before toppling over the edge. He clutched her to his chest as the waves crashed over him, his groan of pleasure dancing over her skin.

When his hips finally began to slow, his hold on her loosened, and Ophelia slumped against him. Elliot sat back on his heels, propping her against his chest in his lap, and simply held her.

She tilted her head to the side as he pressed his lips into the crook of her neck and lightly dragged his fingers up and down her side. She felt his heart pounding against her sweat-slicked back, and a content smile slid across her lips.

"Are you all right?" he asked, brushing his lips along her neck.

She hummed and turned her head to face his. "Very much so," she replied, her voice heavy with satisfaction.

Elliot pressed a kiss to her cheek then gently laid her on the bed. He reached for one of the towels draped over a chair by the table and wiped them both clean before tossing it to the floor and laying down so that he was facing her. She scooted herself closer to him and rested her palm against his chest. His heart still thrummed quickly under her fingers.

Elliot pulled the blanket on the bed over them both then took a deep breath and kissed her forehead. "I love you," he whispered against her skin. "It doesn't feel like enough. The words seem too simple, too plain for what I feel for you."

Warmth filled her chest, his words resonating with what her heart held as well. She tilted her head back, pressing a soft kiss to his chin.

"I know exactly what you mean," she whispered before pressing another soft kiss to his chest and nestling further into his warmth.

CHAPTER Twenty Nine

OPHELIA FELT HERSELF EASE FROM SLEEP TO light strokes along her spine. She took a deep inhale, catching the scent of the outdoors against salty skin with faint notes of amber lingering beneath. She released her breath in a relaxed sigh and nestled further into Elliot's chest, gently pressing her lips to his skin.

She felt his hum of contentment vibrate through his chest against her lips as he kissed the top of her head, his fingers continuing their slow, gentle glide up and down her back. "Are you awake?" he asked her quietly.

"No," she groaned, tilting her head up to see his face. "But I could probably be persuaded." A smile tipped her lips up. His face was still lazy with sleep, but his eyes were bright as they met hers. He dropped his head and brushed his nose across her cheek before pressing his lips to hers. His hand on her back slid up and into her hair, and a shiver ran down her body.

It was a sweet kiss—slow and gentle with no expectations. A kiss meant to be enjoyed, savored. She smiled into it then pulled back. "Is it morning?" she asked, noting how the sun was beginning to filter through the thin curtains.

"It appears to be," he replied with a yawn. "I've heard a bit of shuffling about downstairs, but I think it's still early yet."

Ophelia frowned. "I don't remember it being all that late when we came up to the room last night."

"It wasn't," he chuckled. "Six days of poor sleep on the road will weaken the body and turn even the humblest of beds into a divine place of respite."

Apparently so. They hadn't even gotten a chance to call for a bath before the exhaustion overtook them.

Elliot laid his head back onto his pillow as he ran his fingers through her brown strands. It still caught her off guard to see her hair in such a different shade. She scrunched her nose when Elliot's fingers snagged on a tangle, and he winced. "Sorry."

She chuckled. "It's all right," she said as she pulled his hand from her hair. "It's the burden ladies with long hair must bear." She sat up in the bed and pulled all of her hair to one side. Elliot propped himself up on his elbow, and his eyes glittered as the sheets fell from her body. He rested his free hand on her thigh as she began combing her fingers through the knots. "I think we could do with baths, though."

His eyes flashed, and a feral grin spread along his lips. "I couldn't agree more."

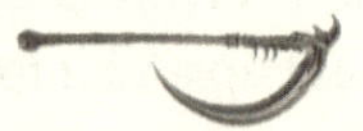

Shortly after, Elliot peeled himself from the bed and threw on his shirt, pants, and boots and left to call for breakfast and water for the bath. Once he left, Ophelia slid from under the warm sheets and dug out a shirt and some pants from her pack then slid them on before the inn staff began scurrying in and out of the room with pails of water for the tub.

While she waited, she walked over to the window, opened the curtains, and peered through the grimy glass down to the streets below.

The sun peeked over the horizon, the beginning traces of oranges and pinks starting to lighten the sky. Only a few people milled about in the street at such an early hour, shuffling to grab provisions for the day or heading out to begin their day's work.

Her gaze drifted farther off, landing on the castle across the city. The outer walls stood so high that, even from a distance, only the top half of the castle was visible. Ophelia hadn't noticed how menacing it looked the last time she'd visited Ravenhold.

The castle was built with stone black as pitch and held round towers at the four corners of the inner building. The towers stretched high into the air like lances in the hands of a knight ready to strike down anyone foolish enough to meander too close.

The massive structure sat in such stark contrast to the sandstone buildings that made up the rest of the city. It was beautiful and terrifying and didn't seem to happily watch over its citizens like the castle in Sigova.

No, this castle shadowed the town, watching its people—not out of fondness, but out of malicious suspicion. As though its duty was to ferret out traitors meandering the streets, it loomed over the city with the same oppression as the king who ruled inside its walls.

Ophelia shuddered as the memory Aria shared with her of her time in the castle dungeon flashed through her mind.

Thankfully, the door to the room opened, and Ophelia was pulled from her thoughts. Her chest loosened as she turned away from the window.

Elliot stepped inside, balancing a tray of food in one hand and holding a tea kettle in the other. He was followed by a flurry of women with pails of steaming water who were chattering away in quick Balmorean as they walked in. Elliot set the tray of food and tea down before joining her by the window.

He rested a hand on her hip and leaned against the windowsill as he gazed through the glass. "Anything exciting happen?"

She gave him a small smile and leaned into him, wrapping her arms around his waist. "No. Just a few people getting an early start to their day."

He slid his hand in soothing circles along her back as he met her eyes. "You seemed troubled a moment ago," he said, brow bending with concern.

She gave a small nod then laid her head against his chest. "The castle caught my attention and reminded me of Ari and everything she went through," she said quietly to prevent the maids from overhearing.

He hummed in understanding. "I see."

They stood by the window in silence a few moments more before Elliot tugged her toward the table to eat while the maids went for another trip of fetching water. While they waited, Ophelia suggested Elliot bathe first since she wasn't sure how much henna might end up washing out of her hair and didn't want him to have to bathe in it.

"You just want to watch me take a bath, you depraved woman," he teased as he dipped a piece of bread into his porridge and tossed it into his mouth.

Ophelia dropped her spoon in her bowl and placed a hand over her heart in feigned offense. "You and your accusations. Have you no shame at all, Lord Barnham?" she asked. "Though, watching you lather yourself down with soap while I sip my tea doesn't sound like a terrible time."

Elliot's eyes heated as a laugh burst from him. His dimples winked at her. "Well, I wouldn't want to disappoint my lady, now, would I?"

They laughed as a knock came at the door. Elliot stood up and let in the last group of maids.

Once they were finished filling the tub, the maids filed out, leaving behind two towels, a bar of soap, and a ceramic bottle of what Ophelia assumed was shampoo, in a chair next to the tub.

Elliot closed the door, set the lock, then began tugging off his shirt before he'd even turned around to face her. A blush warmed her cheeks. "Well, not wasting any time, then, are we?" she asked, trying to mask how affected she was by simply seeing him shirtless...with his hair mussed and tousled from pulling his shirt over his head...and the ripple of muscles along his strong body as he walked across the room.

When she finally met his eye, she noticed the smug grin on his face and scowled at him. He chuckled. "As much as I am pleased to have you ogle me, I actually am looking forward to being clean."

"I wasn't ogling," she replied too quickly.

He winked at her. "Of course, not." He toed off his boots at the side of the tub and began unfastening the ties of his pants.

Ophelia dropped her eyes to her teacup, suddenly very interested in its contents, as her cheeks flamed. She inwardly rolled her eyes at herself and took a sip of her tea. This man had stripped bare before her—had been *inside* of her—less than half a day ago, and she was blushing as he casually undressed to take a bath? She lifted her eyes back to Elliot as he pushed his pants down his legs, seemingly unaware of what he was doing to her.

Elliot turned to toss his pants to the side, and Ophelia was gifted a perfect view of his ass. She imagined what it would feel like to sink her fingers into it, to feel his muscles flex each time he thrust inside of her. What it would feel like to pull him closer so he could rock further into her. Heat swept over her body, and her core pulsed with desire.

Elliot stepped into the tub and groaned as he sank into the hot water, submerging himself fully. The sound was indecent, dragging her memory to the moment last night when he had sunk into her and that same noise had vibrated through her chest.

Ophelia stared openly when he came back up, releasing a contented sigh. She blinked away the haze that had fallen over her and shifted to cross her legs as Elliot reached for the bottle on the chair by the tub. Uncorking it, he poured a small amount of the shampoo into his hand and made quick work of washing his hair before slipping under the water again.

Ophelia's attention was locked on Elliot's form under the surface as she sipped from her cup. When he came up, he wiped his face with his hands then smoothed his hair back before closing his eyes, leaning against the back of the tub, and resting his head against the edge. Water dripped from his newly formed beard and slid down the long column of his neck, down his chest. She imagined following the path with her tongue.

As if he could feel her eyes on him, Elliot rolled his head to the side and cracked an eye open to look at her. He grinned. "And how is the lady enjoying the show?"

She let out a nervous laugh as she took another sip of her tea. "It's a bit too early to tell, I think," she said, feigning indifference even as she fidgeted in her seat from the tension tightening low in her stomach.

Elliot tracked the movement, cocking a brow and leaning forward. "Hmm. There must be something in particular the lady must want to see, then." He grabbed the soap from the chair, dipped it in the water, and began to lather it in his hands.

She shrugged. "Not really," she said, unable to keep the tremor from her voice.

His grin widened. "Well, then," he said as he pushed up to his knees in the tub.

Ophelia held her breath as she tracked every inch of his body rising above the water, only releasing it once he stopped, the water line achingly low across his hips. She raked her gaze over him as he began rubbing soap across his chest, over his shoulders, down his arms. She felt her heartbeat kick up as his hands slowly roved back across his chest then down his abdomen. He brushed a few circles over his taut stomach before sliding his hand further down, disappearing under the surface. Her heart stuttered when the muscles in his forearm flexed as he palmed himself.

Ophelia set her teacup down and leaned forward in her chair, biting her bottom lip as she watched his hand move under the water. "You keep looking at me like that, and neither of us are going to end up clean before this water goes cold." His voice was deep and gravelly, his tone shooting desire straight to her core, and she bit back a groan.

"I'm just supervising to ensure everything is properly washed."

Elliot's grin melted into a crooked smirk as he stroked himself again. "Proper washing is *very* important," he agreed. "You should come here for a closer look just to be sure I'm doing it right. My hands can get rather clumsy."

Ophelia huffed out a laugh and stood up, walking the few steps to the tub and leaning over to rest her palms on the side. She could feel his breaths brush across her cheeks.

Her eyes fell to his mouth as she said, "You and I both know your hands could never be described as clumsy."

CHAPTER THIRTY

SHE WOULD BE THE DEATH OF HIM.

Her voice was silk and sex, and as her words melted across his lips, his cock twitched in his hand.

Elliot had started this little game to tease her while he enjoyed his first warm bath in days. But she had completely turned the tables on him with every look from her hooded eyes, melting his resolve into a miserable puddle every time her cheeks bloomed that pretty shade of pink.

She placed a hand to his chest and gently pushed him down into the water, rinsing the soap from his body. She knelt by the tub and ran her hand down his torso as he sank deeper into the tub. Her fingers traced the sensitive skin below his navel then back up his chest as he sat up. His heart pounded with anticipation.

Once he sat up completely, Ophelia wrapped her arms around his shoulders, running one hand through his hair as she lowered her mouth to his ear. "Would you like help washing your back?" She asked, her lips brushing against the shell of his ear.

"What a fine idea," he said, turning his head to face her and handing her the soap.

She smiled coyly. "I'm full of good ideas," she said, plucking the soap from his hand.

That makes two of us, he thought as Ophelia moved to the back of the tub.

Elliot pushed himself to his knees again, giving Ophelia the full expanse of his back. He braced his hands on the sides of the tub and waited.

A handful of moments later, her hands rested against his shoulder blades and a shiver ran down his spine. He dipped his chin and closed his eyes, letting himself enjoy this simple touch from her.

She smoothed her hands in slow circles across his shoulders and down his spine to his lower back. She repeated the motions once more then gently tugged on his shoulders, silently telling him to dip into the water to rinse. He lowered himself back, dipping into the water to his neck, then sat up.

As soon as he came up from the water, Ophelia slid her hands over his shoulders and down his chest. Then farther. His eyes fluttered closed, and he sucked in a breath the moment her hand closed around his rigid cock. "Like you said," her voice was husky in his ear, "we must make sure *this* is properly cleaned."

"No truer statement has been uttered this day," he ground out as she stroked him once, twice. He bucked his hips and groaned before turning his head to face her and roughly took her mouth with his.

He ran his fingers through her hair, finding the base of her neck to pull her closer. She was just as eager for him, parting her lips and sweeping her tongue inside his mouth as she stroked him faster.

He moaned into her mouth as the pressure at the base of his spine built and built. He thrust himself into her hand, causing water to splash over the sides of the tub.

He couldn't take much more, but there was no way he would find his pleasure before she did.

He pulled away and pushed himself back up to his knees, facing her. Taking her face in his hands, he brought her lips back to his, almost pulling her in the tub with the force of it. She easily balanced herself on the edge of the tub and clenched one hand in his hair while the other sank into his shoulder. He groaned into her mouth then suddenly pulled back.

"Join me," he said before pressing his lips to hers again. He couldn't keep his mouth off of her. He needed to feel her, to taste her, to follow that pretty flush up her neck with his tongue.

"But the henna—"

"Fuck the henna," Elliot interrupted as he tugged at the waistband of her pants. "We can wash your hair last if you like, but I will burst into flames if I have to wait another moment to feel your skin against mine."

She huffed out a breath and nodded before he kissed her again, bunching up the sides of her shirt and tugging it over her head. He kissed her as his hands slid up her hips and settled at her ribcage, his thumbs playing along the underside of her breasts.

She pulled back to stand and slid her pants down her legs, stepping out of them quickly. Elliot stood, doing absolutely nothing to hide his desire for her, and held out his hand to help her in the tub.

His eyes roved over her as she carefully stepped in. He would never get enough of her, of seeing her like this, of having her in his arms. The way his hands molded perfectly to every dip and curve of her body, the way she shivered with pleasure under his touch, the way he made her melt with his hands and mouth and cock completely undid him. Only a lifetime would be enough. Yet he knew in that moment, as his heart swelled at her loveliness and his body ached with desire for her, a lifetime would still be too short.

The world felt bright and whole with her. She was where his heart called home. She settled him and made him hope for dangerous things, things that couldn't be guaranteed, like happiness and a peaceful life.

You are my solace.

The words rang through him as his eyes dragged up her thighs, then up her stomach to her full breasts. He lingered a moment, aching to take each one into his palms and pull those beautiful sighs from her lip. But he waited. Continuing to take her in, his gaze slid up her neck, then to her eyes—to the ice blue irises that darkened around the edges as they took him in as well.

She ran her hands up his arms and looped them around his neck, twirling her fingers in the strands of his hair as she pressed her body against his. A content smile spread across her lips.

You are my solace, his heart sang.

Warmth flooded his chest, and the easy expression on her face, combined with the hunger heating her eyes, stole his breath.

She loved him. She wanted him. She was his.

His hand slid up her back as he placed a soft kiss on her lips.

As much as he wanted to wrap her legs around his hips and thrust inside of her, they both still needed to bathe—a fact he was rather impressed with himself for remembering and prioritizing.

He indulged himself in a small taste of her before sitting himself in the water and tugging her down to sit between his legs.

He would wash her, ease her aching muscles, and make her feel clean. Then they could make the water filthy.

He pulled her back against his chest and wrapped his arms around her, pressing his lips into the crook of her neck. He sighed, and she hummed her contentment.

"This is much better than that rickety old chair," Ophelia said as she ran her fingers over his arms settled across her waist.

"Much better," he replied, nipping her earlobe. She giggled as he rooted around the tub for the bar of soap he dropped, finally finding it near his feet. He pulled it from the water and began to lather his hands with soap. "Let me bathe you," he whispered in her ear.

She nodded. "All right."

He pushed her forward slightly and draped her hair over one of her shoulders, setting the soap down on the chair by the tub. She leaned forward farther, giving him access to her back. He began at the top of her shoulders, rubbing soothing circles as he slid his hands down her back and applying pressure with his thumbs to soothe her muscles. She let out a groan, and the sound went straight to his dick.

"I didn't realize how sore I was."

"Six days on a horse will do that to you," he said, doing his best to keep his tone light and his hands steady.

"Mm, I guess you're right," she replied.

His hands slid up to her shoulders again, and he pulled her back to rinse off the soap. She rested back against his chest, and he grabbed the soap again, lathering more in his hands.

"And you tried to claim your hands were clumsy," she teased.

He pressed a kiss to her temple and smiled. "I may have exaggerated a bit." She chuckled in response.

Elliot set the soap down and slid his hands across the top of her chest, lightly tracing along her collar bones with his fingertips. She let her head fall back to his shoulder on a sigh.

He gently pushed her up to her knees, following behind her, then looped an arm around her waist to steady her. He dropped his mouth to her neck and dragged his lips and tongue along the sensitive skin as his hands gently spread soap over her stomach, over her hips, and up her sides.

She reached a hand back, like she had when they had made love last night, and ran her fingers through his hair. He hummed at her touch.

He smoothed the suds over her stomach again before finally sliding up to her breasts, taking one in each hand and circling her nipples with his thumb. A shiver ran through her before she relaxed into him. "Again," she said. Her heady voice sent heat coursing through his body.

"If that's what the lady wants," he said against her skin.

"It is." He heard the smile in her voice.

He did as she wished, sliding his hands over her breasts once more and taking the tips between his fingers and lightly pinching. Ophelia arched into his palms and let out a breathy moan that instantly tightened his balls.

She clutched his hair and pulled his head up, angling it so she could bring his mouth to hers. Their kiss was all tongues and hot breath. Elliot squeezed her breasts, circling her nipples with his fingertips. The action caused her to squirm, dragging her ass along his rigid length.

"*Fuck*, Elia," he ground out, hips bucking against her.

Earth and sea, she ruined him.

She didn't relent in her conquest of his mouth, her tongue sliding farther, deepening their kiss. He dropped a hand to her hip while the other slid in slow, lazy circles from her breasts, to her stomach, then below her navel. She pulled away from his lips and pressed her forehead to the side of his neck, her fingers still clutched in his damp hair.

Elliot took in the sight of her heaving chest as her lungs worked to keep pace with her speeding heart. He felt the squirm of her hips against his body and under his hand. She was absolutely stunning. His hand descended farther but paused just before her apex, brushing his fingers close but not touching.

"You are cruel, Elliot Marxley," she whined, and the sound of his name as it spilled from her lips—a breathy song soaked in desire—was the most fucking beautiful sound he'd ever heard in his life.

He squeezed her hip then slid his hand to cup her breast. "Tell me what you want," he said, gently pinching her nipple.

She whimpered, and he dropped the hand at her apex to the inside of her thigh, lightly dragging it up, up, up. Her hips continued to writhe. "I want you to touch me," she whispered.

"With *pleasure*." He cupped her sex with his hand and rubbed. If she needed to be washed, he'd be sure she'd never take another bath without thinking of his hands again.

She released a breathy moan as he traced his fingers over her swollen lips, then sunk a finger inside of her slick heat.

"*Fuck*," he groaned into her neck, drawing out the word. She was *soaked* for him.

He withdrew his finger from her, sliding it up to her sensitive nerves and beginning to circle and rub.

"*Earth and Sea*," she groaned as her hands flew to the sides of the tub to brace herself.

She canted her hips, changing the placement of his finger, and blessed him with another sweet cry of pleasure.

"That's right," he said into her ear. "Take what you need from me, Elia."

She moved against him faster, light, breathy moans floating into the air as she chased her release.

She was so close.

He slid a finger back inside of her and pressed the heel of his palm against her apex. She sucked in a gasp and continued to ride his hand.

"*Yes*," she moaned.

Fuck, he loved her like this—supple with need for him and so fucking gorgeous. Just for him. *Only* for him.

As she moved against him, his own pleasure rose, and he pulled his hips back before he spilled into the water. A whine of protest came from her at the loss of contact.

"Elliot," she said, and fuck if that didn't almost send him over the edge too. Her voice— his name as it fell from her lips—was velvet on his skin.

"Say it again," he groaned into her shoulder, willing his hand to move faster, press harder, so he could listen and feel as she fell into bliss.

"Elliot," she whispered, but she stopped moving.

Panic snaked through him, and he withdrew his hand. "What's wrong?"

She turned to face him and smiled. "Nothing." She placed her hands on his chest, over his amber pendant, and leaned up to kiss him. "Lose yourself with me," she whispered against his lips, dropping a hand and wrapping it around his length.

He let out a sharp breath and was easily swayed. "Where do you want me?"

She pushed away and stood, holding out her hand to him to help him up. He stood in front of her, his hands falling to rest on her hips, but she stepped out of his hold with a grin, playfulness gleaming in her eyes. Turning, she bent over and braced her hands on the side of the tub. "Here," she said, arching her back as she looked at him over her shoulder.

He met her gaze, and grinned back at her, running his teeth over his bottom lip. His eyes dropped to her ass and raked over her body as he laid a palm to the base of her back and slowly slid it up her spine. "An excellent idea," he said. "But might I suggest a slight change?"

Her brows bent, but he was already stepping out of the tub, reaching for her hand to tug her out as well. The cool air sent goose flesh rising on his damp skin. She stumbled out with a laugh, and he pulled her face to his to taste it off her lips. He took no time to be gentle and pressed his tongue between her lips with a hunger she reciprocated.

Earth and Sea, being able to kiss her like this—however he wanted, whenever he wanted—was absolutely, fucking *decadent*.

He dropped his mouth to her neck and dragged his lips and tongue down the smooth column until she was panting and breathless.

"Elliot," she begged, that high, breathy sound making his cock twitch.

He quickly pulled away and turned her, gently pushing her shoulders over the side of the tub. She caught his meaning and braced her hands on the edge, widening her stance.

He stepped close behind her and leaned over her back, resting a hand beside hers on the edge of the tub, then brushed a kiss to her shoulder. "I figured you might want clean water for washing your hair afterward," he said.

She huffed out a laugh as he aligned his cock to her entrance, peppering kisses across her shoulders as he coated himself in her slickness. She hummed, rocking her hips back and seeking more friction. A breath later, he pushed into her, and a moan fell from each of their lips.

Elliot wrapped his other arm around her waist and pulled her closer as he began to move. And just as Ophelia said, they lost themselves in each other.

Chapter Thirty One

Ophelia wanted to stay in their rented room forever, waking up wrapped in Elliot's arms with the scent of amber and clean skin encompassing her and his warm lips pressing to her skin. She would never forget this time with him. Her heart swelled as she tethered the sweet memories to her soul. The memories of their declarations and promises. The memories of his silken voice as they bound themselves to each other in ways no grand ceremony ever could. It eased the weight of sadness and grief that seemed to shadow them wherever they went.

It was so tempting to stay nestled, safe and loved, against Elliot's chest and simply let the world pass them by. To shove off the responsibility that came with her power and throw it clean over the cliffs of western Maraleon.

Her mind lingered on the possibilities that lay in those thoughts before it circled to a darker realm, bringing her to the memory of every crack of the whip against Aria's back and reminding her of the screams and rivers of blood from her dream with Pyotr, of the faces of those desperate Balmorean men that ambushed them on the road.

Her thoughts reinforced why she was there, of what she was there to fight against, and it was enough to sober her fantasies of an easy, burden-free life. And the more her thoughts lingered, the more restless she grew. She did not want to linger in the city where her sister was bloodied and bruised without cause—the city where the man who attempted to kill her called home.

Once the sun's rays began to brighten the room, Elliot and Ophelia peeled themselves out of bed and dressed for the day. Their plan was to gather supplies in the city for the remainder of their trip, then head east in the coming days. There were still logistics to hammer out, though. Would they travel with a group again? What would their story be? Would it be safe for the two of them to travel alone to the Aegis? Would it seem too strange for a young, newlywed couple to travel east where monsters and unknown dangers were thought to lurk?

The questions flew through her mind one after the other like an assault of arrows. Elliot seemed to sense the conflict within her because he brushed his hands in soothing strokes up and down her arms as he leaned down to meet her eyes. "Don't burden your mind with troubles that have yet to come, Elia." He pressed a gentle kiss to her forehead. "We will discuss the details tonight when we get back. For now, we're simply browsing the market to see what Ravenhold has to offer in the way of provisions for us."

She gave him a small smile and nodded before pulling the hood of her cloak over her head and leaving the room ahead of him.

With the fog of travel exhaustion gone, Ophelia saw the market clearer than when they first arrived. The vendors were not as finely dressed as those she remembered near the castle, and their wares, though sturdy and useful, were cruder in fashion, not crafted with the same smooth, refined edges and ornate patterns she remembered. There were no figurines of jade or quartz here, only practical items and sturdy clothes that would last at the cost of their appearance.

It was quieter than the evening when they had first arrived two days ago. Now, shops were just beginning their day. Shuttered windows were being propped open, and stands were being assembled. The smells of freshly-dyed cloth, burning coal from the smithy down the road, and roasted meat wafted toward her on a light breeze. Ophelia's stomach growled in response.

They both chuckled. "We're looking for a place to get some dried meat for the trip anyway," Elliot said. "I bet that," he pointed across the street at a sandstone building with meat spinning on a spit out front, "would be a good place to grab some breakfast and inquire about their stock."

Ophelia looped her arm through his then pulled him toward the stall with a wide smile. "Two birds, one stone, then. Let's go."

Elliot was pleased by all they were able to find in the market, despite its humble trappings. The food stand he and Ophelia first stopped at for some semblance of a breakfast turned out to have the dried meat they needed as well as some ingredients for preserving and seasoning.

After another hour or so of meandering throughout the market, they had acquired some decent wine, bread and cheese, some nut and seed mixes, dried fruit, and some feed to supplement their horses' grazing.

Their excursion to the market had been successful, but being so out in the open with Ophelia with nothing to disguise her except her dyed hair and a hooded cloak set Elliot on edge. This market wasn't as crowded as the market in the lower city of Sigova, but there were enough people to have his eyes constantly scanning the street as they walked.

They had told no one of their plans. They had left the castle through the wood and under the cover of the dim light of morning. If their absence had been noticed by now, which he was sure it had, no one would have suspected they'd come this way. Yet there was still a niggling at the back of his mind telling him they weren't safe. Dom and Ambrose had recognized him and Ophelia and said nothing, so who's to say someone at the tavern or a stranger passing by hadn't recognized her and reported back to the king?

He hated not knowing who was an enemy and who wasn't without having a more secure place to retreat to should danger spring up, and the anxiety of that sat heavy on his chest. He took stock of each person they passed and scanned the windows of each sandstone building along the road they walked searching for anyone who might seem a bit too interested in their presence. It was maddening—this unsettling anxiousness bleeding into fear.

Elliot and Ophelia were making their way up the road back toward the tavern when they noticed a crowd forming in a nearby square. A group of musicians just beyond the growing mass of people was setting up to play on a rickety platform.

On stage, there was a gangly man with floppy hair and a charming smile holding a lute. A woman with an annoyed frown and obsidian hair that fell in waves down her back stood beside him with a tambourine in hand, and on her other side, a man with a dour expression and silver hair pulled back from his face sat balancing a gemshorn on his knee.

The lutist seemed to be the only one happy to be there, if the expressions of the other two musicians were any indication. It was as if the lutist were the youngest sibling, forcing his older brother and sister to put on a show with him, and they begrudgingly agreed to it in order to spare themselves a thrashing from their parents. Elliot's lips quirked up at the thought.

A moment later, the three musicians came to life. With every beat and note that reverberated into the air, each musician fell into their own rapture as they played, and the lutist began to sing. It was a fast tune with witty lyrics that widened Elliot's earlier grin into a smile.

Making sure not to lose himself in the performance, Elliot wrapped his arm around Ophelia's waist and pulled her to his side to keep her close.

A few beats later, the crowd multiplied as spectators rushed forward with their partners and began dancing to the music.

Ophelia looked to Elliot, her squinty-eyed smile alight with joy. His heart melted into a puddle, and the strain on his chest eased.

"Let's dance!" she said as she dropped the goods they'd just purchased, took his hand, and pulled him into the crowd.

"Ophelia! Wait—" but it was too late. Her hand clamped around his before she skipped forward to the beat of the music. She glanced back at him, and the sense of freedom and happiness that shone from her stole his breath. He etched the moment into his memory, tucking it deep into his heart so he would never forget it.

You are my solace.

A shock of panic brought him back to himself as he realized how many people surrounded them. He hadn't had time to assess the square before Ophelia launched them toward the music, and the crowd had only grown.

"Ophelia! Stop!" he shouted, but she couldn't hear him over the music and laughter and the raucous singing.

The closer they drew toward the group of people dancing in front of the stage, the denser the crowd became. Onlookers pressed in around them, the confined space and the warmth of the sunny day causing his hands to sweat, and he felt his grip on Ophelia's hand begin to slip. She must have felt it, too, because she readjusted her hold on his hand and squeezed tighter without looking back.

The next moment, he couldn't see her, her body hidden behind the throng of people she pulled him through. Only the persistent tug of her hand told him she was still there.

Elliot's heart thrashed beneath his ribcage—there were too many people, he couldn't see her, and the crowd was too dense. He tried shouting her name again, but she didn't seem to hear him because she didn't stop.

Some dancers spun into the crowd, and a domino line of people fell to the ground, taking him with them, and Ophelia's hand slipped from his.

Another surge of panic had him shoving off the men on

top of him and scrambling to his feet, ignoring their shouts of protest. Elliot didn't give a fuck. His breaths grew ragged as he peered over the heads of those around him, desperately searching for Ophelia's familiar hooded frame.

He found her twirling among a group of women dancing in front of the platform that skirted the edge of the crowd. Her smile seemed tight but soon grew wide as her familiar laugh reached him. Elliot's chest loosened a fraction as he pushed past the onlookers to reach her.

Ophelia followed the lead of the other dancers, switching partners, and spinning and swaying with the rise and fall of the melody. Another burst of her laughter hit the air, her smile widening across her cheeks, and it stole his breath. He can't remember the last time she'd smiled so fully, so uninhibited.

He needed to reach her and take her in his arms, needed to pull her close and sway with her to the music. He needed to taste that smile on her lips.

He'd nearly reached the break in the crowd when a group of men slammed into him, one tackling another, and taking Elliot to the ground with them. One rolled off of him and scrambled atop the other, forcing his opponent into a headlock and yelling unintelligible, angry Balmorean to him. Something about his woman and keeping his hands to himself.

Elliot cursed but quickly jumped to his feet and turned to scan the dancers for Ophelia once more. His eyes hopped from person to person, but she never came into view.

She wasn't among them.

He shifted his eyes to the edges of the crowd where he'd last seen her, then into the mass of bodies itself, but she wasn't there.

Elliot shouted her name and shoved through the crowd, but he never heard her voice shouting his name in return. Panic seized him.

This wasn't happening.

This couldn't *be happening.*

He couldn't breathe. The air around him was too hot, too stifling, and his chest clamped in on itself again.

He spun in place, hoping and praying to anything that would listen that he would find her before the panic took all clarity from him.

He pushed through the crowd, making his way back to where they had stood before the musicians began assembling, but all he found were the discarded items they'd purchased earlier that day.

He shoved his hands into his hair as he struggled for breath, eyes continuing to dart frantically across the square.

Had anyone from the palace been here?

Were there Reapers hidden among the square that he hadn't noticed?

Who knew they were here?

He ran through the square, searching every alleyway, every nearby storefront, every passing cart, but she was nowhere to be found.

By the time the sun hung high in the sky, the musicians had finished their performance, and the crowd began to disperse. Elliot held one last hope that, as the square emptied, Ophelia might find her bearings and find her way back to him. Perhaps both of them had been frantically running about the square searching for the other and simply never crossed paths.

But as the last of the audience faded from view, the sounds of laughter and music fading from the square and the bustle of the market taking its place, Elliot's meager hopes burned to ash. Fear, stark and cold, swallowed him as the truth of the situation sank into his bones.

Ophelia was gone.

A pair of bulky arms encircled Ophelia's waist and pulled her so tightly to their chest that the wind was sucked from her lungs.

Fear sent her heart racing as she was pulled backward and out of the crowd. She sucked in a breath then launched a shrill cry into the air, but it was cut short by gloved hand clamping over her mouth. Her captor muttered a curse in Balmorean as he swept them into a shadowed alcove.

The last thing she remembered was her eyes and mouth being covered and gagged before a blow to her temple sent her into unconsciousness.

She awoke in a cold, dark cell with her arms chained above her head. The bite of the manacles at her wrists and the painful ache in her shoulders told her she'd been dangling from her restraints for a long while.

As she opened her eyes, her vision swam and her skull pounded, the pain blurring her vision and making her surroundings dip and sway. A wave of nausea crashed over her.

Ophelia took several deep breaths, willing her stomach to settle and her vision to clear.

Once her eyes acclimated to the dim light and the room stilled, the details of her cell settled into focus. Unease slithered down her spine as she took in the familiar, dank stone floor and walls. The only light in the space shone through a small, barred window at the top of one of the walls, the dim, orange glow filtering through being the only indication that dusk had fallen.

A grating chuckle sounded beyond the bars before her, and as Ophelia turned her gaze forward, she found herself staring into the face of the man she hated most in the three realms.

"Hello, *Madam Vilicus*," Raygon crooned, a malicious smile curving his lips as he leaned closer to the bars of her cell. "Welcome to The Black Keep."

Chapter Thirty Two

Fury, raw and fervid, coursed through Ophelia.

The phantom pain of every lash her sister took in this dungeon stung her back. Every scream and cry of loved ones lost to the Silent Reaping echoed in her ears. The lifeless faces of every slain man and boy from the caravan's fight in the wood flashed through her mind. And just as the flames had consumed the corpses of those desperate men, Ophelia's anger burned through her, leaving no piece of her untouched.

"*Raygon,*" she all but snarled, lunging toward the bars of her cell. Pain lanced through her shoulders and up her arms as her restraints yanked her back. She swallowed the cry that rose to her throat.

"That is *Your Majesty* to you," a voice hissed from the king's side. Ophelia's eyes fell to the obscured figure standing beside the king in the shadows. The hood of her brown robes was pulled low to cover her face, but the ashen gray hands fisted at her sides were unmistakable.

It seemed Raygon liked to keep his little pets close by.

Raygon clicked his tongue disapprovingly. "Now, now, Kira. That is no way to speak to our guest."

Ophelia huffed a laugh, tilting her head to peer up at her chains. "If this is how you treat your guests, I must say that your hospitality leaves much to be desired, *Your Majesty.*"

Raygon cocked his head to the side and gave her a derisive smile. "One can never take too many precautions."

"We should kill her now and be done with it," Kira said, curling her lip into a sneer.

Ophelia rolled her eyes. "What a novel idea, Kira. While we're at it, perhaps we could also light some candles, sing some haunting melodies, and make a ritual of bathing in my blood."

The Reaper took a step forward, but Raygon raised a hand to stop her. The same grating chuckle from before rumbled from his throat, scraping across her skin with its sharp talons. "There is something to be said of your creativity, *Madam Vilicus*," he replied, disdain heavy in his tone, "but there are much more…productive ways to spill your blood than for tawdry rituals."

Ophelia reared back. "What is *that* supposed to mean?"

A cruel smile slowly spread across Raygon's lips.

"You will find out soon enough." He patted the bars and stepped back. "For now, rest up. You have quite a trip ahead of you, and I want to ensure you have regained your strength."

Ophelia narrowed her eyes at him. A trip? She filed away the thought for later and glanced back up toward her chains.

"How kind of you to put such thought and care into my comfort."

Raygon placed a hand over his chest. "Isn't it?" He stepped away from the bars. "Do enjoy your stay, Madam Vilicus, as short as it may be," he said as he turned on his heel and made for the exit, his Reaper throwing Ophelia a feral smile as she followed him out.

Once the door to the dungeon clanged shut, the tension eased a bit from her body, only to be replaced by crippling uncertainty. Her blood pounded faster as question after question flew through her mind.

How did Raygon know she was in Ravenhold?

How had he found her?

Did Dom or Ambrose betray them?

Where was Raygon planning to take her on this 'trip?'

How would she let Elliot know where—

Her heart stuttered—*Elliot.*

A choked sob forced itself from her throat. Where was he now? Was he looking for her? Would he report her missing?

No, no, he couldn't do that. They weren't in Balmorea legally and were trying to draw as little attention to themselves as possible.

She gasped when the realization hit her: if Raygon knew she was here, he must also know of Elliot. He wasn't safe.

Had they taken him too?

She had to get out of there.

Ophelia flung her gaze up to the manacles chaining her arms above her head. In the fading light, she could hardly make out their shape around her wrists, but that shouldn't matter.

She held her eyes to the manacles and pictured them unlocking and releasing her.

Nothing.

She shook the chains above her, as though the sudden jolt would set the shackles to rights and they would open under her power as they should.

Again, she visualized the manacles releasing her, and again they held; the tug of power she usually felt with the release of magic was starkly absent from within her.

She closed her eyes, drawing into herself to find Conexus's playful warmth, to feel the hum of her connection to magic, but she couldn't. It was as though her Conexus, her connection to the energy of the world, was bound and placed just out of reach. And in its place yawned an aching hollowness.

She called to it, but it didn't answer.

She gasped at the loss, and her eyes burned, feeling as though part of her very soul had been ripped from her being—part of her she hadn't realized made her whole until its absence gaped within her.

Fresh panic sent her heart thrashing against her ribcage, her sobs tearing free from her chest. How was this happening? This shouldn't be possible. *How could this be possible?*

Her breaths grew unsteady as she fought to suck in air. Her head grew light, and the tumult of endless questions and possibilities and unknowns dizzied her mind further.

This was her fault. She had been too reckless and careless. And now, because of her flippancy, she was trapped in the clutches of a man who wanted her dead and put the life of the one most dear to her in danger of the same fate. She couldn't lose him. He could not become another casualty of her title. She'd never forgive herself if anything happened to him. This was not his burden to bear; these were not his consequences to face. Yet, he might very well have to pay the price for them anyway. His life was hers to protect just as much as hers was his, and she was failing.

She never should have led Elliot into that crowd.

She never should have given the musicians in the square any ounce of her attention. She and Elliot had just finished gathering everything they needed for their trip and had no reason to linger. She should have pulled Elliot right back to the inn where they would have spent the rest of the afternoon laughing and joking as they packed. They would have had dinner then tumbled into bed together and made love until they were too sated and limp to move.

Her eyes burned, and her cheeks were wet with tears by the time her mind finally fell silent, leaving her dangling from the ceiling in a cold cell, exhausted and empty.

The sun finally set. The entire prison chamber fell completely dark, and Ophelia had no idea what to do.

Chapter Thirty Three

O PHELIA HADN'T REALIZED SHE'D FALLEN ASLEEP until the click of a lock and the groan of worn hinges shook her into consciousness. Her head snapped up, eyes flitting along the bars to find whoever lurked in the dark.

The light of a small candle flame came into view, illuminating the visitor's face. Ophelia's eyes widened.

"Mariu— Your Highness," Ophelia said, trepidation skittered through her. She hadn't expected anyone besides Raygon or more of his Reapers. Was this a trick?

From what Ophelia had seen from Aria's memories, Marius appeared to be an ally, but that was weeks ago. Earth and Sea only know the methods Raygon may have used to bend Marius to his will. Had his allegiance changed?

"Marius is fine," he replied, the smallest hint of a Balmorean accent mingled in his words. His throat worked on a swallow as he surveyed Ophelia's condition. "This is exactly how he imprisoned Aria."

"I know," Ophelia replied, her trepidation easing at the pain sweeping over his features. His eyes went distant, and Ophelia knew his mind had taken him back to the last memories he had of this cell—his wife, dangling by her wrists from the ceiling, bloodied, bruised, and broken.

"She is well," Ophelia offered. "The moment she fell into my arms, we rushed to heal her. No trace of her time in this cell is visible anywhere on her body. I made sure of it."

Marius gave a small nod as he released a rattled breath. "A—And the baby...?"

"Healthy and well from what our physician can tell. That was the report before I left, anyway. But Aria is well looked after and resting. You can cast away your worries."

Marius shook his head. "That won't be possible as long as she's away from me." He paused for a moment, placing his free hand on the bars and leaning forward. "What are you doing here? Aria was meant to warn you of the threat against your life. Did she not tell you of the Reapers?"

Was the sacrifice I made in sending her to you for nothing? went unsaid, but she heard it in the clipped tone of his last sentence.

"She did." Ophelia let her head fall back on a sigh. "I even got the chance to meet one."

Marius's eyes went wide. "You *what*?"

"Oh, yes." Ophelia gave a wry laugh. "She wasted no time in acting on Raygon's orders."

"Was Aria hurt?"

Ophelia pulled her gaze back to Marius. "Not at all. Trella was completely focused on me."

Marius held her gaze, seeming to consider his next words carefully. "I'm assuming that, since you are alive—"

"The Reaper is dead," Ophelia said. "I—I killed her."

The images flashed through her mind unbidden—*Ivory handles in her hands. The scrape of blade against bone, the give of tearing flesh. Blood pooling on the charred, stone floor.*

A shudder danced down Ophelia's spine.

A beat of silence.

"I'm sorry you had to do that," he said, setting down the candle and pulling a ring of keys from his belt. Ophelia nodded and shifted on her feet as she watched him search for a specific key on the ring. "What is your purpose here, then, Your Highness?"

"Just Ophelia."

He met her eyes and gave a small nod. "Very well." His hands stilled while he waited for her reply.

Ophelia took a deep breath then explained everything, starting with what Pyotr had shared with her about the barrier in her dream, how it was distorting the balance of the land, and how she and Gaius deduced that Blood Magic was used to create it.

"You and Aria learned that the Reapers are versed in Blood Magic and that they report directly to the king," Ophelia said.

Marius nodded. "So, the king is responsible for the barrier." He found the key he was searching for and moved to unlock the cell.

"That is what we believe, but this then raised the question: how is the barrier being sustained?" Ophelia paused then went on. "Have you also heard of the disappearances?"

Marius inserted the key, but it wouldn't turn. Marius's brown bent. "You will need to be more specific. Disappearances are no odd occurrence at court."

Ophelia grimaced at the casual air with which Marius said that statement. *How terrible it must be to live here.*

Marius pulled the key out and tried another. It didn't turn either.

"The merchants we traveled with told us of something the people are referring to as 'the Silent Reaping.' Each full moon, people are taken from villages in the east in the night by hooded, gray-skinned monsters prowling in a fog. There are no screams or signs of struggle. But in the morning, there are always people missing."

Marius froze, all the information piecing together in his mind in the next moment. He cursed. "The king is killing his own people to sustain the fucking barrier." He rubbed a palm down his face, a muscle feathering in his jaw.

"I've come to the same conclusion. Do you have any idea why he would go to such lengths to sustain a barrier so large?"

"Because he's psychotic." Marius spat as he wore a path in front of her cell, keys forgotten in the lock.

After several minutes he finally said, "Nothing comes to mind as to why he would have the need for such a barrier, but my lack of knowledge is not unusual—I'm not made privy to any of the goings on in the king's inner court."

Ophelia nodded, then silence passed between them, both lost in their thoughts. Her mind whirling back to the events of the past day—back to thoughts of Elliot—and her heart clenched, panic sucking a gasp from her throat. "Elliot!" Her head shot up. "Marius, my betrothed. He's traveling with me. If the king knew where to find me—he could—he might—Elliot's in danger!" Fear wracked her body, her chest heaving to suck in breath. "I have to go to him! He can't stay there!"

"Shh," Marius said, returning to the cell door and holding his hands up in a placating gesture. "You must stay quiet or curious ears will catch me down here."

Ophelia took a deep breath as she swallowed down a sob. "Please, it cannot wait. We must go tonight—now!" She made to step forward but was jerked back by her restraints.

"We will get him, Ophelia. I promise." Marius returned to the keys in the lock, continuing his attempt to open her cell with the few keys that remained. His brow creased as key after key failed to unlock it.

"Did you not grab the right set of keys?" Ophelia asked, agitation lining her voice. *Elliot. They had to get to Elliot.*

"I'm positive these are the keys for these cells." He held up the ring of keys with his index finger. "I don't understand how none of them are working."

Panic flared in her chest. "What do you mean?"

"I mean there's something wrong. The keys won't unlock the cell." Marius knelt down, lifting the candle to inspect the lock. He ran his fingers over the mechanism, and his jaw tightened. "Fuck."

Ophelia's breaths sawed through her chest. "What's the matter?"

Marius stood and ran a hand through his hair. "There's blood on the lock." He narrowed his gaze at her, the wheels of his mind turning with his thoughts. "Why haven't you freed yourself yet? With your magic?"

Ophelia glanced up at her shackles. "I tried, but it wouldn't work." She swallowed. "And I can't feel my magic within me. It's like it's…" *gone.* But she couldn't bring herself to speak the words.

Marius nodded slowly. "I wonder if the blood on the lock has anything to do with that cut along your cheek," he said.

Ophelia's brows knit together—she didn't feel the sting of a cut on her face, the pain in her shoulders and wrists outweighing any other affliction she'd received. "What are you saying? You think—?"

Her eyes widened the moment she understood. "Blood Magic. He had his Reaper use my blood to lock the cell."

"It would explain why the keys wouldn't work," he replied, nodding toward her shackles. "And probably why you can't release yourself from those shackles."

Ophelia tilted her head back to see them, but it was too dark to discern any blood or markings or whatever it might take to use someone's blood to imprison them. Her eyes burned from the frustration.

Imprisoned. Trapped.

Her heart lurched, panic again clawing its way up her throat.

I have to get out. I have to get to Elliot. "Very well," she said, her voice cracking at the lump clogging her throat. She closed her eyes and took a deep breath, sucking down her despair. She had to think. "Releasing me will have to wait. Right now, you need to find Elliot and get him somewhere safe."

Marius frowned and crossed his arms over his chest. "Where can I find him?"

"We have a room at The Wolf's Den. It's a tavern in the north part of the city. Do you know it?"

Marius gave a curt nod, a small sneer curling his lips. "That's likely how you were discovered. As of rather recently, I no longer have eyes in that tavern. I have no doubt someone let word slip of some mysterious Marelian travelers passing through and made off with heavier pockets because of it."

Ophelia clenched her jaw. *Had Ambrose set them up?*

She huffed out a sigh. "What's done is done. Just please hurry and find him. Let him know I'm all right, and try to reassure him that this wasn't his fault."

Marius's eyes softened. "We will find him and get him somewhere safe."

"Where?"

"We'll take him to The Jade Raven. It's a tavern in the eastern part of the city, as far from the castle as we could get," he replied. "It's mine. My shadows run it, and I have people in and out of there frequently. If anything so much as smells suspicious, I hear about it. You and Elliot will be safe there once all of this," he gestured to the bars, "gets sorted."

"You're sure it's safe?"

"Were there a safer place, I would take him there."

"Swear it to me," she said, her words sharper than she'd intended. "Swear that you will get him there, whether we can get me out of here or not."

Marius met her eyes. "I swear it, Ophelia. We will find him and take him to safety."

Ophelia held his gaze and something loosened inside of her. She knew it was a promise he couldn't guarantee—there were too many moving parts at play, too many variables to consider to be able to make such a guarantee. But she knew Marius would do all he could. She recognized the fire in his eyes—it was the same fire he'd looked at Aria with all those weeks ago when he did what was needed to keep her safe.

Ophelia nodded and gave Marius a description of Elliot and the location of their room in the tavern if he couldn't be spotted downstairs.

"What if he doesn't believe I am who I say I am or that I come on your behalf?"

Ophelia chewed her lip as she thought of something only she and Elliot would know. The back of her eyes burned as the words came to the forefront of her mind. "Tell him, 'More than there are drops of water in the sea.' If he finishes with, 'or grains of sand on the beach,' then he knows."

Marius nodded, repeating the phrase once more before taking the candle and sliding out of the dungeons, the faint tinkle of keys drifting in his wake.

Chapter Thirty Four

Hours had passed—the nearly full moon well on its journey across the inky night sky—and Ophelia had not returned. If she'd simply been lost, she would have found her way back to The Wolf's Den by now, and as more time passed without her return, Elliot became more and more certain her disappearance had not been an accident. If she was safe, wherever she was, she would have contacted him by now, right?

Elliot barely registered the din around him as he sat alone at his table, gazing out the tavern window as he nursed his ale; too many questions rattled around in his mind for his focus to fall anywhere else.

Who'd taken her?
Why had they taken her?
Where were they?
What was happening to her?
Was she hurt?

Had someone found them out? If so, how? And by who?

His first thoughts went to Dominicio and Ambrose, but they would be giving themselves up if they had given up Elliot and Ophelia. The merchants could have given them the name of a seedy tavern, but that didn't add up knowing their background and history with George. Even if the merchants hadn't liked them, which Elliot didn't feel was the case, they were at least smart enough to not jeopardize their businesses dealings—both legal and illegal alike.

Kidnapping was, unfortunately, quite common in large cities like Ravenhold. And foreigners, who were usually unfamiliar with the language and lacked contacts where they stayed, were easier to victimize and control. They would be taken to be enslaved in one way or another and had little recourse to free themselves.

Other victims could be ransomed, if the kidnapper knew the value of the person they'd taken. This could be the case if whoever took her knew who she truly was.

But Ophelia's magic would have been more than enough for her to free herself from any captors, no matter how formidable they may be. She commanded the elements—the lifeforce of the very earth itself, for fuck's sake! There wasn't *anyone* who could hold her captive.

Unless the Reapers got to her.

They would kill her without a doubt. But the things they would do to her before they did so in the name of vengeance for their fallen sister...

Nausea turned his stomach, and he pushed away his ale.

Ravenhold was Raygon's city. There was no doubt the man had eyes and ears everywhere. Plucking one unknown woman from a crowded square would be a small feat for him with the resources at his disposal.

Elliot pressed the heels of his palms to his eyes. The more he let his mind wind and twist over what could have happened to her, the more he knew he was simply dancing around the truth, not wanting to admit what he knew in his bones was true. His instincts told him Raygon had her, and no matter how much he tried to convince himself otherwise with logic and other plausible possibilities, he couldn't shake the feeling.

He'd been a fool to go along with this idiotic plan—to think the precautions they'd taken would be enough to escape the king's notice.

Alphonse had been right.

Protect our girl, Lord Barnham.

Elliot's chest tightened as Alphonse's words taunted him. First the Reaper in Sigova, and now this.

He should have fought harder to keep Ophelia at home. He should have done more to keep her from pursuing this journey into Balmorea. She would have hated him for it, but she would be safe.

Fuck. How did this happen?

"Now don't you paint a solemn picture in such a lively place," a man's voice said from across the table *in Leonese.*

Elliot's head shot up, his hand flying to the dagger on his belt, as the stranger sank into the chair across from him.

There was nothing remarkable about the way the man was dressed—a leather, hooded jacket over a black tunic with black pants and boots. Elliot didn't note any visible weapons, but that didn't mean the man wasn't armed. The man's hood was pulled over his head, but Elliot made out the face of a young man with long black hair who seemed to be close in age to himself. Stern brown eyes met his across the table.

Silver rings adorned several of his calloused, nail-chipped fingers, but one ring stood out among the others. It was a polished, black signet ring with a raven intricately engraved in its center in gold. Elliot wasn't familiar with the symbol. Most noble families in Balmorea chose a wolf in some way, shape, or form as the animal to represent their house, not a raven.

Before Elliot could riddle anything out, the man said, "We don't have much time. I've sent a few of my people to liven up the bar, but that will only last so long."

Elliot's brows bent together as he took another sip of his ale, his eyes glancing to the bar where a raucous drinking game was stirring up interest. "Who are you?" he asked the stranger.

"I know where Ophelia is."

The noise of the tavern went silent against the sound of blood rushing in Elliot's ears. "*Who. The fuck. Are you?*" he ground out through clenched teeth.

"I am not your enemy, Elliot," the man said, holding his hands up in a placating gesture. "I did not take her, but I know who did and where she is. She asked me to take you somewhere safe. I will explain everything once we get there."

Elliot scoffed, shaking his head. "I'm not going anywhere with you." He took another pull from his ale. This city had already fucked him over once. He wouldn't let it happen again.

The man's nostrils flared, and he let out an exasperated breath. "She said to tell you: more than there are drops of water in the sea."

Elliot stilled, and the air left his lungs. Relief flooded his chest as his heart simultaneously went wild against his ribs. *Alive. She was alive.* He wanted to go to her, to touch her, hold her. With only a few words, the man before him had made Ophelia feel so close, her words for him still lingering in the air between him and this stranger.

The man's intense gaze locked with Elliot's. "Do you know it?"

Elliot nodded, his lungs working to take in steady breaths against his frantic heartbeat.

"Then you know the rest as well."

Elliot squeezed his eyes shut, the memory of the first time he'd muttered those words to Ophelia flashed in his mind. The lust-filled haze that enshrouded them after their heated kiss in the stables. The feel of her ragged breaths fanning along his neck. Her shy smile. It was the first time she'd told him she loved him.

His heart ached, but it finally steadied, allowing him to take in his first full breath since Ophelia's hand had slipped from his earlier in the square. "Or grains of sand on the beach."

The man gave a curt nod then leaned in. "We will get up and shake hands. I will wish you good night, and you will walk upstairs to your room. I will finish this," he frowned down at his tankard, "*delicious* ale then meet you in your room. Pack up all of your things while you wait for me. We're getting you out of this place *tonight*."

Chapter Thirty Five

Fifteen minutes passed before the stranger found his way to Elliot and Ophelia's room. Elliot was shoving his and Ophelia's belongings into any pack of theirs with enough room to hold them, giving no care as to what was whose or which bag something went into.

Her scent still clung to her discarded shirt, to the riding doublet he'd all but torn off of her the two days before. He squeezed his eyes shut at the anguish that flooded him.

Alive. She's alive, he reminded himself as he crammed her clothes into the pack set before him.

"Almost done?" the man asked as he collected the last items from the floor and tossed them next to Elliot onto the bed.

Elliot looked up and swept his gaze over the space, heart aching with the weight of the sweet memories he and Ophelia had shared there in such a short time. He swallowed then took a steadying breath. "Yeah, just a few more things."

He swiped the bar of soap off the chair by the tub, the memory of Ophelia shivering under his touch as he smoothed its suds along her warm skin burst through to the front of his mind. He gritted his teeth and shoved the image away as he bunched the soap into the last few items of clothing on the bed and wedged it between two bottles of wine he'd purchased with Ophelia earlier that day.

Had that truly only been a few hours ago?

Elliot tied the bag closed then slung it over his shoulder. He fastened his sword to his belt then bent down to pick up another ruck sack. "That's everything I think."

The man nodded then grabbed the rest of Elliot and Ophelia's belongings and made his way toward the door. "I've set up another distraction down in the tavern so we can slip out unnoticed. Follow me and keep quiet."

The two men stepped out of the room and silently closed the door. The man then turned left, heading away from the stairs down to the tavern.

Elliot stole one last look over his shoulder at the door to the simple room that, even if only for one night, had been more of a haven to him than his own chambers at Hargrave, then he turned and followed the man toward the end of the hall.

It was at that moment, when his eyes landed on Ophelia's pack slung over the shoulder of a complete stranger, that the uncertainty of the situation hit him. Elliot had no idea who this man was. The man had known those private words only he and Ophelia shared, but Elliot hadn't considered, before now, how the man had gotten the words from her. Had she given them up willingly, or had they been forced from her?

Elliot knew better than to trust the man completely—who knew where he was taking him or what he would find there—but desperation had Elliot driving those thoughts away and clinging to even the thinnest thread of hope that the man striding before him would lead him to Ophelia.

Elliot brushed his palm over the hilt of his sword for the reassurance that he wasn't helpless. He may not have any idea what he was walking into, but he'd be prepared to fight himself out if need be.

With renewed resolve, Elliot followed behind the stranger on silent feet, the only detectable sounds being those coming from behind the doors of the lodgings they passed. The creak of a bed and moans from one, loud grating of snores from another, shouts and laughter from a third.

Once they made it to the end of the hallway, the man led Elliot down the lone staircase that, if the heat and sounds of clattering plates were any indication, led to the kitchens.

The stranger slowed his descent, stopping before the final three steps. He leaned against the wall and met Elliot's eye, silently telling him to do the same. Elliot did so, and then they waited. For what, Elliot wasn't sure, but the man seemed to focus, leaning as close to the kitchen entrance as he could to glean what was happening.

After several minutes, shouts and crashes from beyond the kitchen filtered through to them. Within seconds, the shouts grew louder amid the shatter of glass and the distinct thuds and thumps of a brawl.

The kitchen staff grew frenzied as a deep voice from within shouted for all staff to rush to the front to help temper the chaos. A shuffle of quick footsteps responded followed by the slam of a door, and the kitchen went quiet.

"Let's go," the stranger said, then bolted into the kitchen, Elliot close behind him.

Warm, humid air wafted over his face as Elliot and the stranger rushed through the abandoned kitchen passing pots of various boiling liquids and discarded knives atop blocks of half-cut vegetables. A roasting pig sat abandoned on a spit over flames in a charred brick hearth, and a partially-plucked chicken lay sprawled across a tabletop near a door that Elliot assumed led into the tavern.

Opposite the door to the tavern, on the back wall of the kitchen, stood another door with a window with a direct line of sight to the stables. The stranger cut smoothly toward the back door and pushed through, holding it open for Elliot then closing it behind them with a quiet *snick*.

"Follow close behind me," the man whispered. "And stay in the shadows."

Elliot followed suit, making his way across the property with the stranger. The man moved like a wraith, making no noise as he swept across the tavern's property. Not the snap of a twig under a boot nor the kick of an errant rock across the barren ground was heard as the two men made their way toward the stables.

Once they reached the side of the stables, the two men huddled against the wall in the shadows and waited. Elliot couldn't see inside but heard the voices of two men casually chatting. *Stablehands*, he thought, but the stranger didn't move to step inside.

Elliot grew restless as time stretched on, and still, they didn't move when the stablehands bid each other goodnight and one walked from the stable toward the street. Once he was out of sight, three sharp whistles came from within, and the stranger bolted inside.

The stable was dimly lit, a few lamps placed periodically

throughout to allow a groom to tend to basic tasks. A different man, dressed in similar black attire as the man leading Elliot but with long, blond hair pulled into a knot at the back of his head, met them in the middle, holding the reins of two horses. He released one horse and clasped the stranger's hand and forearm in greeting. "We have maybe ten minutes until the night groom arrives," the new man said, gesturing to the stableman who just left. "I told him I would be here waiting for you for a while and would watch over things until the next groom arrives."

The stranger nodded, taking the reins of his black stallion, then turned to Elliot. "You need to saddle quickly. The idea is to be out of here without any eyes on us."

Elliot nodded. "Not a problem, but we will need Ophelia's horse as well." He walked over to his blue roan's stall and entered, giving Shade's mount a pat on the flank before nodding to the stall next to his. "He's the bay gelding next to mine."

The new stranger wasted no time entering Blaze's stall and quickly saddling him.

Five, maybe six, minutes later, the three men were trotting out the back entrance of the stable, Elliot leading Blaze beside him.

It was midnight by the time Elliot and the two other men arrived at an inn across the city. Situated on the outskirts in a part of town with even less finery than where they had just come from, there didn't appear to be much about The Jade Raven. But, Elliot supposed, that was likely the point.

Once their horses had been taken to the stables in the back, the stranger and his companion led Elliot into the inn. The building was smaller than The Wolf's Den and was situated between two other buildings of the same size. Its white paint was faded and chipped, the inn's sign a shade of green more reminiscent of a slimy pea soup than a vivid jade. Elliot's expectations for his new accommodations were low, which was fine—he'd sleep in a hole in the ground if it meant Ophelia was safe—but once they pushed through the tavern and into the rooms in the back, his shoulders slumped in relief.

It was no great luxury, but the room was spacious, the bed looked comfortable, and there was a connected bathing chamber. Elliot dropped his things to the floor and released a sigh, a wave of exhaustion suddenly flooding him.

"We'll speak in the morning," the stranger said, setting the items he carried at the foot of the bed. "Would you like me to have water delivered for you to wash?"

Elliot scrubbed a hand down his face then shook his head. "No, I'm spent for the night." He toed off his boots and set them by the door.

The stranger nodded. "Very well. Get some rest. I will have breakfast delivered to you in the morning, and then I will explain everything, just as I promised."

Elliot didn't say anything. He simply nodded then made his way over to the bed and sat on its edge.

The man was reaching to open the door when Elliot said, "Will you at least tell me who you are, if I don't get any other answers tonight?"

The man turned around and pulled his hood back, his sable hair stark against his pale skin, his sharp brown eyes boring into him. "I'm Marius. Ophelia is my sister-in-law."

Elliot balked. "You're the crown prince?" he asked, incredulity heavy in his tone. Yet even as he said it, the resemblance the man held to Raygon began to crystalize; the long, straight, raven-black hair, sharp nose, high cheekbones. Marius's eyes weren't cold and black like his father's, though, now that his expression wasn't guarded, he noticed how heavy they seemed—drawn down with sadness and weariness.

Marius gave Elliot a nod and a small smile. "Rest well, Elliot." Marius opened the door. "We have much to discuss in the morning."

Chapter Thirty Six

Once Marius left, Elliot saw to his needs then stood in the doorway of the washroom and stared blankly into the empty chamber, not quite sure what to do with himself. There were hints of Ophelia all throughout the room—her pack, crammed with clothes that smelled like her, the glimpse of ivory from the handles of the twin daggers he gifted her all those months ago peeking out the top, her bow and quiver of arrows laying next to his atop the table in the corner.

When he closed his eyes and narrowed his focus, he could detect faint notes of lavender in the air. Could feel the warmth of her body against his chest as his arms enclosed around her. Could hear her sleepy voice bid him goodnight.

But it wasn't her.

These were mere impressions of her—ripples of her that he desperately clung to lest the void of her presence swallow him whole.

And with every moment that lingered without her before him, his chest tightened. Invisible hands clamped around his lungs, preventing him from taking in a full breath, and his heart beat an uneven staccato.

The room spun, and stars danced in his periphery, causing him to crumple to the edge of the bed. He dropped his head into his hands and raked trembling fingers through his hair as he fought to suck in air. Painful sobs racked his chest, forcing breath into his lungs.

Her pack sat next to his ankle, as though she'd simply tossed it to the floor and seen to more interesting tasks before returning to unpack it. His eyes burned. She was everywhere and nowhere all at once, and it was shredding him apart from within.

It could have been minutes or hours before Elliot was finally able to take in a lungful of air. The painful tremors passed to make way for the hollowness following on its heels. Elliot listed to the side, his body's strength finally giving out.

He laid there, limp and unfeeling, and the only thoughts that made him want to see the next day instead of remaining suspended in the numbness was the reminder that Ophelia was still alive, and Marius said he had answers.

Elliot didn't remember crawling under the covers. It wasn't until he awoke to a knock at his door and a light, feminine voice announcing breakfast on the other side, that he realized he'd even fallen asleep.

Not that it had done him any good. Exhaustion had taken him into unconsciousness, but the tension never left his body. His back screamed as he pushed himself up, his joints and muscles groaning their own protest as he shifted to a seated position on the bed.

He was rubbing his eyes with the heels of his palms when another light knock came. He responded with a noncommittal "yes' in Balmorean which the girl must have taken as permission to enter, because the next moment, she was striding through the doorway and setting a tray of food down on the table in the corner, careful not to disturb the bows and quivers resting there.

His eyes widened at the open doorway. *Shit, the door was unlocked? All fucking night!*

Elliot let his head fall back on a frustrated sigh.

"Apologies for the disturbance, My Lord," she said in rushed Balmorean. Elliot dropped his head to meet her gaze only to find her rushing from the room, shoulders raised to her ears.

"Oh, no it's not—"

But she was already out of the room, pulling the door shut behind her.

He scrubbed a hand down his face. "Shit…" He'd have to have Marius apologize for him later—

Marius.

As though summoned by his thoughts, another knock came to the door. "Elliot? May I come in?" Marius asked in smooth Leonese.

"Yeah," he managed as he swung his feet over the side of the bed, cringing at the stiffness in his muscles.

Marius stepped through the door and closed it behind him before leveling his gaze on Elliot. "You look like you've seen better days."

Fuck if that wasn't the truth.

"You scared poor Jeanie out of her socks." Amusement quirked his mouth up to one side.

Elliot grimaced. "Please tell her I'm sorry. I wasn't vexed with her in the slightest."

Marius chuckled. "I know. I told her that was likely the case, but I'll be sure to send her your regrets."

Elliot nodded then pushed himself up to stand. "Where is she? Ophelia. You said you had information."

Marius gestured to the table where Elliot's breakfast was waiting for him. "I will answer all your questions while you eat."

Elliot sat down at the table shaking his head. "I'm not hungry."

Marius leveled him with another look then picked up a piece of toast and began to spread butter along its surface. "The king has her in his private cells." Marius's jaw feathered. "The same cells where he kept my wife."

Elliot's stomach sank. *He knew it.*

The man who'd sent an assassin to kill Ophelia in her own home now had her in the palm of his hand. Panic sent his heart into a frantic rhythm.

This couldn't be happening. This is exactly what he'd been afraid would happen. Hoping they could sneak through Ravenhold right under Raygon's nose while his eyes stayed focused on Sigova was a risk Elliot had begged Ophelia not to take for this very reason. She'd been so sure they would be safe. So certain nothing would happen. And he'd been right. The taste of vindication had never been more bitter.

He raked a hand through his hair, tugging unrelentingly at the strands. "He's going to kill her, Marius. He's already tried once! He won't risk the insult of failing twice." Elliot shot up from his chair, nervous energy pushing him to tread back and forth across the small space. "You got Aria out of there; you can get Ophelia out the same way."

Marius set down the toast and shook his head, turning in his seat to face Elliot. "I tried last night before I came to get you. Blood Magic was used to lock her cell, and I suspect to lock the manacles she's shackled with."

Elliot's hands curled into fists, his anxiousness boiling into anger. "So, that's it, then? We do nothing—"

"I did not say that," Marius interrupted, pushing to his feet and stepping into Elliot's space. He rested his hands atop Elliot's shoulders. "We just have to go about freeing her differently. As it is, Raygon isn't planning to kill her in the cells."

Elliot huffed a dry laugh. "Forgive me if that doesn't assuage my nerves."

Marius led Elliot back to his chair at the table and patted his shoulder. "I know, but it *does* mean we have time," he replied, pushing a plate with the buttered toast toward Elliot as they both sat down.

"What do you know?" Elliot asked before forcing himself to take a bite of the toast.

"One of my shadows reported that Raygon is planning to ship her out in a prisoner transport later this week."

"Where is the transport going?"

"To the mines, officially. But we've learned that when a prisoner transport destination is set for unspecified 'mines,' those prisoners never arrive at any mines, and they are never seen again."

Elliot frowned. "You've tracked these transports before, then?"

Marius nodded, replacing Elliot's empty plate with one loaded with eggs and sausage. "I've lost good people to 'the mines.'" His jaw worked. "We were too late to intercept the transport the first time. The next time, we lost track of it. The third time, we thought ahead and sent teams to each mine the king sends his prison laborers to. Not one prison transport arrived at any known mine in the Jade Mountains—jade, coal, or otherwise."

Elliot frowned as he grabbed his fork and speared a link of sausage. "So, he never actually sends prisoners to the mines."

"That's the thing—he does. The only prisoners that ever arrive at any mine are the ones designated to be taken to a specific one. The log will say 'Prisoner transport to Lake Lupos Jade Mine' or 'Central Coal' or 'Central Jade,'" Marius said. "But if there's no specified mine, the transport simply vanishes."

Elliot tapped his fork on his plate as the pieces of the mystery began connecting in his mind. "Do you remember the dates these unspecified mine transports traveled? Did they ship out at random times, or was there a pattern to them? Every third transport? Every other week? Every fourth week?"

Marius's brows knit together, and his eyes went distant as he thought. "I'd need to look back at our records." He returned his gaze to Elliot's. "What are you thinking?"

Elliot set down his fork and rested his elbows on the table. "It's just a theory, but it may be related to the reason Ophelia and I are here, and if it is, we absolutely must get ahead of this transport, and we cannot lose it."

Marius paused, his forehead creasing as though he was piecing something together. "Do you think this is linked to the strange barrier and the disappearances every full moon?"

"So, you know of the Aegis?"

A quick nod. "Only yesterday. Ophelia briefly explained to me why the two of you are here." Marius sighed, mumbling a curse under his breath in Balmorean before pushing to his feet and raking a hand through his hair. "Then he's not killing transports of prisoners at random."

Elliot shook his head. "We need to look at your records." Elliot stood and made his way to his pack, sifting through it for a clean shirt and pants. "I'm willing to bet the prisoner transports headed for 'the mines' all leave within a few days of each full moon. And if that's the case, then no, he's not killing transports of prisoners at random." Elliot closed his eyes and took a deep breath, hoping to slow his heart, to get ahead of the panic he already felt simmering under his skin. "He's sacrificing them to the Aegis right alongside the villagers he's kidnapping."

And if they fucked this up, Ophelia would be one of his next victims.

Chapter Thirty Seven

Within the hour, Marius and Elliot were gathered in a large room on the first floor of the inn with a handful of the prince's trusted Shadows. Hidden beyond a plain door behind the tavern kitchen, the space was rather ordinary considering who owned it—or who Elliot assumed owned it.

The room looked to be what Marius, or whoever ran the inn, used as an office. Along the back wall ran one wide window, veiled with a thick, forest green curtain, but a fire burning in the modest hearth set in one of the side walls and a few sconces throughout the room kept the space from feeling too dark. A long, wooden desk covered with scattered parchments and quills sat toward the back of the room in front of the window with a leather-cushioned chair behind it.

Three men and a woman occupied the remaining handful of mismatched chairs peppering the office, while Marius sat in the chair behind the desk. A cart with pitchers of ale and plates of bread, meat, and cheese rested undisturbed on the far end of the room. The space was quiet as each of the Shadows and Marius hunched over their respective stacks of prisoner transport records.

Working through each month, they cross-referenced the records with a lunar calendar Marius must have fished out from somewhere. Elliot paced back and forth before the hearth, too restless to sit, as his eyes traced over the same lines of information without truly reading them anymore—he'd found enough to confirm his theory.

After a while, one of the men, who Elliot recognized as the one who'd helped Marius sneak him out of The Wolf's Den the night before—Arwyn, Marius had called him earlier— tossed his stack of parchments on the desk with a curse in Balmorean. "Are we all seeing the same thing?"

Another man, with dark, short-cropped hair and several rings adorning his ears sighed and slouched in his chair. "One transport of prisoners a month headed for 'the mines' three days before each full moon?"

"I found one that left four days before," a redheaded man with a sparse beard chimed in. The three Balmoreans levelled him with irritated gazes, but the man only seemed to revel in the attention and waggled his eyebrows. "I have a very keen eye."

"Well spotted, Dax," Marius responded dryly without lifting his eyes from the document in his hands. Arwyn and the other man swatted Dax across the chest. Dax released a howl of protest, but Marius went on, completely unphased. "The frequency increased from once a quarter to once a month about a year ago, but the pattern goes back for *years*," he said, running a hand down his face.

The woman, who Elliot now saw had long black hair and sharp blue eyes, emerged from the shadows of the room and carefully laid her documents atop Marius's desk.

"Earth and Sea only know how long the wretch's been up to this," she added before propping herself on the armrest of the man with the earrings and casually draping her arm over his shoulders. She leaned into him, and he rested an arm across her legs, absently brushing his thumb along one of her knees. The casual display of affection made his heart ache for Ophelia.

Marius made a sound of agreement before turning his attention to Elliot. "Do you and Ophelia have any guesses as to how long this has been going on?"

Elliot's forehead wrinkled in thought as he shook his head. "No idea. Pyotr didn't mention anything to Ophelia about the Aegis being erected before he was sealed, though. And with his proclivity to rage over any and all atrocities of mankind, I doubt this would have been something he'd simply forgotten about."

Arwyn sighed. "So, it was conjured anywhere between the time Pyotr was sealed, eight hundred years ago, and—how far back do these records go? Twenty years?"

"Longer. These are just the ones Melina had time to copy in the short window of time she had in the archives," the man with the earrings answered, patting the woman's knee. "Does the time frame matter, though?"

"No, it doesn't," Marius said, standing from his chair. "What does matter is that the next transport for 'the mines' is scheduled to set out in three days' time, and we need to make sure we know exactly when it's leaving and what route it's taking."

"Any idea where we get that information?" Elliot asked.

Marius nodded to the man with the earrings. "Hayes and his brother run a tavern near the castle's north entrance." He shifted his gaze to the woman. "Melina's father is a cobbler, and his shop is on the east end of the castle. And Arwyn's brother is a clothier on the west end. We have eyes in each of these locations keeping tabs on the comings and goings at each entrance."

Elliot stepped toward the desk and dropped his papers atop it. "And we aren't worried about them taking the river south?"

Marius shook his head. "There aren't any mines to the south. If they were trying to make their prisoner transport look convincing, they would transport them using a route and means that people would expect."

"Hurry up and wait, then, as they say," Dax said as he leaned back in his chair and stretched his legs out before him, crossing them at the ankles.

Elliot ran a hand along his jaw, the rough hair of his beard catching him off guard. It probably looked a mess—not that the rest of him likely fared any better. He dropped his hand with a sigh as the office door flew open, and a familiar, dark mustache with a hat holding an impractically large feather protruding from the top strode into the room. A tall, blond man following close on his heels.

"Jeanie said you lot would be back here," Dominicio said by way of greeting. His eyes fell on Elliot standing next to Marius, and his face broke out in a grin. "Didn't think we'd be seeing the likes of you again, *Lord William*."

Elliot's lips turned up in a small smile as he reached out and took Dom's outstretched hand. "If only it were under better circumstances."

Ambrose sidled up behind Dom, a smile adorning his face as well. "Not too keen on The Wolf's Den?"

"The Wolf's Den was lost to us three weeks ago, you twat," Dax said from his chair.

"What? How?" Ambrose asked.

"Silvi was found out and disappeared. Turned up three days later in a ditch," Arwyn answered. "Marlo and Dain got spooked and jumped ship. The rest of our guys followed suit. Old Maddox had to fill the spots, but we couldn't get anyone to him in time. People we don't know were hired, and you can guess the rest."

"That doesn't make The Den lost to us."

"If it didn't before, it does now," Dax answered. "Poor Elliot's lady was snatched right after they arrived by whatever shady ilk the king has working for him."

Ambrose's and Dom's eyes widened. "No..."

"She's the reason I have you and Ambrose watching the castle, Dom," Marius responded.

Dom's gaze whipped to Elliot. "He has her?"

Elliot simply nodded. The reminder of whose grip Ophelia was in sent a bolt of panic through him.

"Fuck," Ambrose said under his breath, rubbing a hand over his mouth. Dom yanked his hat off and made his way to the forgotten cart of food and poured himself some ale. Ambrose ambled toward the hearth a few steps then turned right back to Elliot. "I never would have suggested The Den if I had known, Elliot. I swear to you."

Something in Elliot's chest loosened at Ambrose's words, at seeing something akin to grief lining his gaze. More than a kernel of doubt in the merchants had wedged itself into one of the fissures of Elliot's mind since Ophelia was taken, and he hadn't realized how much it festered until Ambrose's words freed it. "I know," Elliot said before his brows bent in confusion. "You and Dom are two of the business owners Marius has watching the castle?"

Ambrose nodded as Arwyn cut in, clapping the taller man on the shoulder. "Brosey's my brother—the clothier."

The pieces finally connected in Elliot's mind, and he raised a brow at Dom. "You two are Shadows?"

Dom raised his cup to Elliot before knocking back a swig. "Some of the first, if I remember correctly."

"And does His Serene Highness know of your other... financial ventures?"

The two merchants chuckled as Ambrose sidled up next to Elliot. "Who do you think we're smuggling for?"

Elliot's head spun. George and his father weren't just forging weapons for Balmoreans right under King Alphonse's nose—they were arming a rebellion headed by the fucking crown prince of Balmorea. "Does George know how deep into Balmorea your connections go?"

Dom waved him off. "We hold no secrets from the Earl and his son. Rest easy, Sir Lordling."

A pang of betrayal burst in Elliot's chest. What else didn't he know about his best friend?

"No worries, Elliot," Ambrose assured him as he took up one of the empty seats in front of the desk. "We figured out ways long ago to keep any trace of our business dealings with the Earl from getting anywhere they need not get."

He's never been up against Alphonse's countless sets of eyes before. If Alphonse got even a whiff of this and wanted answers—

Marius leaned over the desk, placing both palms on its surface. "As much as we love the pleasure of your company, gentlemen, why have you left your post in order to grace us with it?"

"It's not abandoned," Dom replied, setting his tankard down on the table before turning to face the prince. "Sarada and Naora are looking after the shop in our absence. But we come with word on the movements in the courtyard."

Marius gestured for him to continue.

"A big, ole prison wagon rolled through the gates before sun up this morning," he said, tearing up a piece of bread and tossing a chunk in his mouth. "Looks like they're starting to get things ready for their trip."

"Did you see Ophelia?" Elliot cut in.

"No, but if they plan on taking her away in that wagon, we'll be the first to know."

Elliot raked his hands through his hair and tugged at the strands, the familiar tightness clamping down on his chest again.

"Have you lot found what you were looking for with all of this?" Dom asked, gesturing toward the scattered documents on Marius's desk.

"Yes, and there's quite a lot more to it than we thought," Marius answered.

"And it isn't news that will make one light of heart," Arwyn added.

A grunt of agreement came from the three other Shadows in the office. Dom slid an empty seat near the desk and sat down as Ambrose leaned over his knees, resting his forearms on his thighs.

"Best get to telling us, then," Dom replied, shoving another piece of bread into his mouth. "We've got a rescue to plan."

Chapter Thirty Eight

Ophelia's palm laid flat against warm skin as gentle huffs of breath stirred her hair. A smile tipped up her lips as she inhaled deeply and pressed further into his chest. The scent of amber and clean skin enveloped her, and she pressed a kiss to his chest just above her palm.

A hum of contentment vibrated under her lips, and she tilted her head back to look into Elliot's face.

Blood ran from his broken nose down his chin, and his lip was split in two places. His eyes were purple and black and so swollen that not a sliver of hazel could be seen.

Ophelia gasped, springing up to sit over him on the bed. "Elliot!" Her hands flew to cup his cheeks, but she stopped just before she met his skin, afraid to touch him and make his injuries worse but desperate to comfort him. Her eyes burned. *What happened?*

She tried to run her fingers through his hair, but they snagged on dried blood tangling the strands together.

He groaned with the movement, and the sound shredded her heart. She pulled back, her eyes raking over the rest of him in search of more injuries, and what she found stole her breath.

His chest and torso were mottled in bursts of large, purple bruises. His arms were covered in slashes, the skin of his knuckles scraped and swollen. Dried blood and burns marred his palms.

A sob burst from her then. Her only comfort was the steady rise and fall of his chest.

A deep, grating chuckle from behind her sent a chill up her spine. The man's breath fanned across her cheek before he spoke. "Such power you supposedly possess, and yet, *this* happens," Raygon said in that crooning voice.

Ophelia turned her head, meeting his gaze. Rage, sorrow, and fear all scrambled within her, muddling her thoughts.

He grinned back at her. "You can't even protect yourself, Madam Vilicus." *Clanging chains and the slam of a cell door echoed in her mind. Phantom sores ached on her wrists.* "How proud you are to think you could protect *him*."

"No!" she shouted. She trembled where she sat but couldn't move. No chains or ropes bound her, but she couldn't swing her fists or kick out her feet. Her limbs remained unmoving, heavy as stone.

Raygon laughed, standing to his full height and stepping to the foot of the bed.

"*Ophelia!*" A voice called out to her. It was so faint that, for a moment, she thought that she'd imagined it, but she heard it again. "*Ophelia!*"

Her head shot from side to side, looking for the person calling to her, but the only people she saw were Raygon and two Reapers who now stood on either side of him, blood swords jutting from the palms of their hands.

Her eyes widened, and dread flooded her chest. "*No!*" She made to lean over Elliot to shield him, but her body wouldn't move.

She pictured the swords shattering to pieces, imagined the shards liquifying to harmless puddles, but nothing happened. She still couldn't use her magic.

"*Ophelia!*" The voice was louder now, familiar. But the person it belonged to was nowhere in sight.

One of the Reapers stepped away from Raygon and made her way toward Elliot's side of the bed. Panic burst in Ophelia's chest, her heart pounding frantically as she struggled to free herself from her invisible bindings. "*Don't touch him!*" she shrieked.

The Reaper stopped next to Elliot. She leaned down, clutched his hair, and pulled his head back, exposing the pale skin of his neck. Her heart fractured at the strangled cry he released.

"*Stop it! Let him go!*" The words tore from her throat. Blood rushed in her ears, and her vision narrowed; her only focus was on the Reaper's fist full of Elliot's hair, on the way his face contorted in pain.

And she still couldn't move.

Tears rolled down her cheeks. All she could do was scream and watch—utterly helpless and useless—as the woman before her killed Elliot. The man who held her heart—her whole world—was going to die, and there was nothing she could do.

The Reaper raised her palm above Elliot then turned her head to meet Ophelia's gaze. It was Trella's soulless, pitch-black eyes that stared back at her from under her hood. She cocked her head to the side, a malicious grin pulling across her face. "Call it *balance*."

A scream launched from Ophelia's chest as Trella's sword began to descend.

But it never pierced Elliot's skin.

Trella's hand halted mere inches above his throat. Blue mist encircled her wrist as she struggled against its hold, and what appeared to be a rope of water enclosed around the Reaper's throat. Trella's eyes widened as the water tightened around her neck. Her face grew red, her free hand clawing at the water digging into her throat until a sickening *snap* sounded, and the Reaper crumpled to the ground.

Ezra stood in Trella's place, and a relieved sob fell from Ophelia's lips.

He moved to sit on the bed beside her. "Ophelia, this is a dream. You must wake up."

Her brows bent together. "What?"

She looked down to Elliot, but he was no longer in the bed, the bedding and blankets still rumpled from where his body had lain. Her head snapped to the foot of the bed, but Raygon and the other Reaper were no longer there either. She closed her eyes and took three deep breaths before returning her gaze to Ezra. "A dream."

He nodded. "Simply a dream. That doesn't make it any less troubling," he said, taking her hands in his. "You can let your heart settle, Ophelia—Raygon does not have Elliot, and Elliot is not hurt."

Tears blurred her vision. "You can't know that."

His eyes softened. "Can't I?" He pulled a hand from hers and tapped her temple with his index finger. "We're all connected in here. Pyotr has followed your journey from Sigova and has kept an eye on Elliot in your…absence." A small smirk tipped up the side of his mouth. "The Vilicus is quite put out that you've been captured."

Ophelia huffed a laugh, rubbing her eyes with the heels of her palms. "I'm sure it's restored more of his hope in mankind."

"Perhaps not, but Marius delivered on his word—Elliot is safe."

Heady relief flooded her body, and she released a deep breath. *He's alive. He's safe—*

No. He wouldn't be safe, *they* wouldn't be safe, until both of them got out of this wretched city. Agitated energy had her rising from the bed and shoving a hand through her hair as she shifted on her feet. "I need to get out of here. Elliot and I need to get out of here. We need to leave the city as fast as we can."

"Yes, you do—"

The shock of ice water splashing into her face and down her body hauled Ophelia into consciousness. She sucked in jagged gasp, and pain from her shoulders and wrists hit her all at once. Bile rose to the back of her throat in response.

"You'll wake the whole damn castle screeching like that," a woman said from a few feet in front of her, her heavy Balmorean accent struggling against the Leonese she spat.

Ophelia shook her head to clear her watery vision and see who had, apparently, been sent to silence her, when the sound of melodic whispers and the writhing and clawing of horrid magic told her all she needed to know.

A moment later, the click of a lock sounded, and Ophelia dropped to the damp, stone floor of her cell. Pain radiated from her knees, her vision flashing white as she fell forward onto her hands. Her shackles bit into her wrists, and she immediately reached within for her magic, hoping desperately that the spell binding it had been severed with her release from the overhead chains. But as she searched, all she found was the same yawning emptiness she'd felt before, and she swallowed the curse that rose to her lips, despair causing her shoulders to sink.

She pushed herself up to stand, though, refusing to give this Reaper any indication that her spirit had fractured, nonetheless almost shattered, mere moments ago.

"You're coming with me," the Reaper said before placing a canvas sack over Ophelia's head. The woman clamped a hand around her arm then yanked her out of the cell.

It was still dark, from what Ophelia could tell. The only source of light she sensed through the canvas flickered just beyond her—*a torch, maybe?* Dawn must still be far off if her jailer still needed a torch to navigate the maze of corridors. Guessing at the time of day was a useless endeavor, but one Ophelia engaged in anyway in order to relieve her mind of the worries that clawed through it and the visions of Elliot's beaten and broken body, the sound of his cry of pain—

"Where are you taking me?" Ophelia asked, doing her best to make her voice sound bored.

"Getting you ready for your little trip, *Madam Vilicus.*"

Ophelia rolled her eyes. *So clever with their sarcasm, these Reapers.* "How specific and helpful," she responded flatly.

As she thought about it, she found it odd that Raygon hadn't killed her already. He hadn't seemed to have any particular purpose to keep her alive when he ordered her assassination. So, why the delay now? Why go through all the trouble of transporting her somewhere to kill her?

"...there are much more...productive ways to spill your blood than for meaningless, tawdry rituals."

Her stomach dropped as her mind flew through at least a dozen possibilities for what he could have meant by that, and none of them were good.

As they walked, she rolled her shoulders, and her body warmed, loosening her stiff muscles. But it also brought about greater awareness of the state she was in.

She was no longer hanging from the ceiling of a cell, but her shoulders still ached. The skin of her wrists was sore and achy. She couldn't see, but if she had to guess, she'd say the shackles had probably rubbed the skin so raw that it bled.

Her stomach felt as though it was turning in on itself from lack of food, and her throat was dry and sore, either from thirst or from screaming in her sleep—probably both. Dull pain bloomed from both of her knees with each step she took. Heavy discomfort low in her abdomen told her she didn't have long before her bladder burst.

With a stroke of luck, almost as though her jailer had read her mind and truly cared for her wellbeing, a door flung open, and the canvas sack was pulled from her head. The Reaper shoved Ophelia inside what seemed to be an empty closet save for a lone bucket, and barked at her to relieve herself quickly.

When the Reaper determined Ophelia had been given sufficient time to see to her needs, she clamped her hand around Ophelia's arm and pulled her from within. She replaced the canvas sack over Ophelia's head and resumed their journey down the corridor.

Ophelia couldn't tell whether the Reaper was taking her back the same way she was brought in, since she was unconscious the first time, but it felt like it was taking longer than it should have to get out of the dungeons. They couldn't be *that* far below ground if her cell had afforded a window.

She just wanted to lay down. To simply have a few moments to sprawl on the floor and let her muscles fall limp. A few moments where she could breathe and her mind could still and rest unplagued by the dangers that awaited her within and beyond these walls.

Finally, one last door swung open, and a gust of cool air hit Ophelia's body. She shuddered with the chill that skittered through her, her soaked shirt clinging to her skin and causing gooseflesh to raise on her arms.

Ophelia sighed. It wasn't too cold, but she wouldn't recommend the experience. At least she had the mild Balmorean winter working in her favor.

Gravel crunched under foot as she stepped over the threshold. Ophelia strained her mind to recall the memories Aria shared with her of her escape from Raygon's dungeons and briefly wondered if this was the same exit her sister had left through.

A handful of moments later, the canvas was ripped from Ophelia's head once more, and she found herself standing at the opening of an enclosed, wooden box carriage with small, barred windows on its sides—transport for prisoners.

Ophelia made a show of giving the cart a once over then gave the Reaper a wry smile. "Cozy."

The Reaper ignored her as she took out a knife and moved her grip to Ophelia's forearm. The knife sliced across

Ophelia's arm, pulling a hiss from between her teeth. She tried to pull away, but the Reaper's firm grip held. Ophelia gritted her teeth as the Reaper squeezed around the cut, forcing more blood to flow from the wound. The woman swiped up the blood from her arm with two fingers then shoved Ophelia in the cart.

Ophelia stumbled inside, falling to her hands and knees, the cut in her forearm stinging. She bit back a groan and shifted onto her ass, heaving a sigh as she examined the shallow cut on her arm. "They must not teach manners in Blood Magic school."

The Reaper narrowed her eyes on Ophelia but said nothing in reply as she closed the metal door to the cage. Ophelia kept her eyes on the Reaper as she scooted herself to the side of the cart. She leaned her back against it and slumped into a somewhat relaxed position.

The Reaper locked the door and began her song of whispers, weaving her magic with Ophelia's blood to keep her imprisoned and magicless. Ophelia let her head fall back against the bars and closed her eyes as the Reaper finished her spell, trying not to think about what 'meaningful way to spill her blood' Raygon had in mind for her.

Her downward spiral of thoughts was interrupted by the release of the loudest growl she'd ever heard from her stomach, and she winced, clenching her jaw against the hunger.

Something hit the side of her leg then fell to the floor of the cart with a light *thunk*. Ophelia opened her eyes and looked down at the offending object, finding what was probably the stalest, moldiest half-loaf of bread the entire country of Balmorea had to offer resting beside her hip.

She reached down and picked it up, raising it to the Reaper through the back window as the woman turned away from the prisoner wagon. "Cheers," she said, then bit into her meager meal.

Chapter Thirty Nine

Summer was always the best time for stargazing in Maraleon. The nights were warm but not stifling. Ophelia remembered how she and Nell would stay out longer on an evening ride and sprawl out in a meadow somewhere to stare up into the sky while their horses grazed. The last time she'd been able to get away for such an indulgence had been a few weeks before the fall tournament, when the nights, though still warm, began to carry with them chillier breezes and fewer singing insects.

That felt like an eternity ago—before any word of prophecies and Vilici had ever been uttered, and thoughts of having magic had only ever existed in childhood daydreams.

The song of singing insects didn't fill the quiet air here, though, and the breezes carried no late-summer chill. But the few stars she could see, that weren't washed out by the silvery light of the almost-full moon, were still bright, momentarily pulling her mind from the endless turmoil that filled her empty moments.

She rested against the side of the transport and stared into the sky through the small, barred opening above her head, finding a few familiar constellations and remembering the legends that gave them their names. Nell had been the one to teach her all of those. Ophelia's lips turned up at the memory of Nell with her nose pointed to the sky and a smile spread wide across her face as she told Ophelia story after story.

Ophelia's stomach knotted; would she ever see Nell again? Or her family? Would she ever get to meet her little niece or nephew? Was their brief farewell outside the kitchens at the back of the castle in Sigova the last time she would ever see some of the people she loved most in the world?

Would she ever see Elliot again?

And once her mind began to whirl, not even the stars could pull her thoughts away.

Not until a clamor of voices in jumbled Balmorean at the back of the wagon drew her attention.

Through the larger, barred opening in the back door, illuminated by the moonlight, Ophelia saw two Reapers approaching with a line of people behind them, all wearing the same canvas sacks over their heads that she'd had to endure earlier.

The jangling of their connected shackles grew louder as the group neared, quiet sobs becoming more distinct.

Ophelia met the gaze of the first Reaper as the woman approached the door at the back of the wagon. Black eyes met hers in what Ophelia could tell was a warning for her to not try anything. Ophelia simply gave her a flat look in return, holding up her wrists and shaking the shackles smeared with her blood and locked with magic. Not that the shackles were even needed at the moment; with the lack of sleep and food, Ophelia wasn't sure she'd even be able to push herself up from where she sat, much less fight her way through two Reapers to escape.

She rested her head against the side of the wagon again and returned her gaze to the sky, feeling more than hearing when the Reaper began her song of whispers to unlock the door.

A few moments later, the group of prisoners was shoved into the wagon one by one after being unlinked from their collective chain and having the canvas sacks ripped from their heads.

Ophelia studied them as they stumbled in. There were three men followed by two women, all barefoot and dressed in what appeared to be night clothes. The women's long, white night dresses held sodden hems while the men all wore loose pants and shirts that seemed to carry a fine layer of dirt and grime. A hint of smoke Ophelia hadn't caught before wafted in the air as they settled into the wagon. All of them appeared to have been ripped right from their beds, blindfolded, then made to walk the entire distance here—however far that had been.

Two of the men seemed close to Elliot's and George's ages while the other was older, appearing more weathered and graying. He walked bent over with a limp, but Ophelia soon realized it wasn't due to his age. All three of their faces bore scrapes and bruises telling of how they hadn't submitted easily to this fate, each of them wincing and grunting as they lowered themselves to sit in the wagon.

The two women followed behind the men. One looked about Ophelia's age with wide, innocent eyes, her nose and cheeks red from crying, strands of her dark hair falling from a messy braid. The other woman carried more marks of age with lines bracketing her mouth and gray-streaked, black hair that hung loosely around her shoulders. Pale blue eyes glanced over Ophelia before returning to the others.

The younger woman trembled as she curled herself into the side of the older of the young men, and rested her head on his shoulder. Silent tears rolled down her cheeks as he looped her through his shackled wrists and pulled her closer, pressing a kiss into her hair. Ophelia noted his scraped, bloody knuckles, glancing over to see the younger man's knuckles were in much the same shape. The older woman sat next to the older man, resting her head on his shoulder and folding one of her shackled hands into one of his.

Ophelia closed her eyes as the knot in her stomach tightened.

This was a family.

Why had Raygon imprisoned *a family*?

They didn't seem to be criminals; their faces were void of the hardness one would expect of those who made their living from hurting others. But if Ophelia had learned anything from the 'merchants' she'd traveled to Balmorea with, it was that appearances didn't always tell the whole story.

The door to the transport clanged shut, drawing Ophelia's attention away from the family before she could riddle anything else out about these newcomers. The Reaper at the back of the wagon wove her whisper-spell, raking a full-body shudder down Ophelia's spine as the woman worked.

A few moments later, she finished, then slid a shutter over the barred opening. The two other openings at the sides of the wagon were shuttered closed as well, leaving the prisoners in pitch darkness.

The carriage jolted forward, and Ophelia's stomach sank as the reality of her situation settled over her. Wherever they were going, her captors intended on killing her when they arrived.

Her mind drifted to Elliot, unconsciously seeking the comfort she found only in him, even if he wasn't with her. Where were he and Marius? Were they working on a way to free her? Did they even know she'd been moved?

Ophelia dropped her head back against the side of the transport and bit the inside of her lip. She hated this—this feeling of helplessness. All this power within her, and she had access to none of it.

Taking a deep breath, she began combing through ways to work through the obstacles in front of her to free herself and these people with her—which Reaper had the key? Where did she keep it? Would simply having the key be enough to open her shackles? How would breaks in travel be managed, if they took any at all?

The mages were likely armed. Maybe she could disarm one of them, then she and these people could overpower them? Not if they possessed the same power Trella had when they'd fought.

Ophelia's mind was lost in thought when she felt a soft kick against her foot and a whisper in Balmorean asking what her name was.

"I'm Ophelia," she managed, followed by a quick, "I don't Balmorean speak good."

A grunt sounded across from her, then another man replied in Leonese, "We no talk Leonese good. Will be fun time."

Her lips quirked up at that. All of them knew they were in a prisoner transport that was not headed to any cheery destination, yet one of them was making jokes.

She heard a remark in a chiding tone from the first man followed by a whiny, "What?" in Balmorean from the second, and a chuckle broke free from her chest. After that, an easy conversation began between them.

The man who had first asked her name was Evren. He was the oldest child in their family. The other young man was his younger brother, Lyall, the one who had cracked the joke. As Evren continued, Ophelia quickly worked out that his brother had greatly underexaggerated his proficiency in Leonese. Evren seamlessly introduced the rest of his family in Leonese—a skill he apparently acquired as their family's farm began expanding and trading at markets in Maraleon and Nedorra. The older man was their father, Allerick, and the older of the two women was their mother, Elowen, Allerick's wife. The younger woman Ophelia had seen clinging to Evren was his wife, Vanya, and they'd gotten married only two months earlier.

A pang shot through Ophelia's chest, the visceral understanding of what it was like to have the excitement of finally being able to start a life with the one you loved most in the world only to have it ripped from under you so suddenly still fresh and raw for her.

Yet that heartache had only been the beginning for their family.

Evren explained how they owned a farm on one of the larger plots of land a few miles beyond Ravenhold proper, and because their farm was so large, they were one of the few farms in the area that had been able to keep up with the heavy taxes Raygon had levied in the past few years. Until recently.

"We fell behind on payments after the recent conflict in Maraleon—much of our crop was seized to feed the forces, but the amount we were taxed was not adjusted to make up for our loss in profits." Ophelia heard the soft clink of shackles as Vanya burrowed further into Evren's embrace. "The Vidaar came to collect two days ago, I think it was. Naturally, we didn't have the amount they demanded."

Ophelia stiffened at that. "Raygon sent his *Vidaar* to collect a debt from a farming family?" The Vidaar were a highly trained unit of soldiers tasked with the protection of the king. They were brutally trained and just as brutally wielded; they were meant to be fierce and staunchly loyal protectors of the crown, not debt collectors.

Ophelia remembered what Dom had shared with her and Elliot about what happened to people who didn't pay when the king's men came to collect. He hadn't mentioned it was the fucking *Vidaar* that Raygon was sending. If Raygon was sending warriors most known for their brutality on mere debt collection missions, it's no wonder the people of Balmorea were arming themselves. Ophelia clenched her hands into fists, fury flaring hot within her.

"Yes," Evren replied. "We assume it's to send a message to those who witness the carnage." Dom and Ambrose had told her as much.

"Why are you here, then?" Ophelia asked, brows knitting together. "I've been told Raygon demands his debts, and if it can't be paid, he repossesses land or conscripts the young and able-bodied in the family…among other things."

To Ophelia's surprise it was Lyall who responded. "That is true. But we know before they come."

Evren continued, "Word has been spreading of what the king has been doing to the country's farmers. At first, groups started forming as a way to support other families should their land be taken. But the king's methods became more violent, and those support groups began to grow teeth."

He was talking about groups like Dom and Ambrose's.

"The people start to fight back," Lyall added.

"Yes," Evren agreed. "Those who couldn't pay were deemed treasonous, their inability to pay coming from greed and an unwillingness to give what the king was owed or whatever shit was being peddled. Collections grew more violent, and the atrocities committed by those sent in the name of the king grew more depraved." His voice grew tight, his words sharper.

Ophelia heard the light clink of shackles, faintly making out Vanya's hand smoothing back and forth across her husband's chest. He paused and took in a steadying breath, taking Vanya's hand and holding it to him, grounding him before he continued.

"A network of sorts formed from all of this, and when word of the next 'collection' is first whispered of, our countrymen come together to protect what they can."

Ophelia remembered Dom explaining what had happened to Ambrose's sister, his nephew. "Was one of your family taken?"

"No," Evren replied.

"We don't let them," Lyall added.

Ophelia's eyebrows shot to her hairline. "You refused the Vidaar?"

"Word reached us about the 'collection' the day before. We had little time for our family and village to prepare, but a man called the Wraith sent help. He coordinates a lot of the movement in the network, I believe. He sent a few men with weapons. They were the only ones close enough to make it on such short notice."

Marius. How long has he taken up this mantle? Did Aria know the extent of his actions within the kingdom?

"The day they came to collect, we told the Vidaar we didn't have the amount they came for. They dragged us out of our home to the center of our village and declared us traitors before our friends and neighbors. They announced that in order for us to pay our debt, our land would be claimed by the crown, and my brother and I would be sent to fight for the king."

"My father was brave. He never flinched when he told the Vidaar they could not have his farm nor his sons. For that, he was beaten as the rest of us were forced to our knees and made to watch while surrounded by Vidaar so that no one could interfere." Evren's voice began to shake then, venom coating his words. "Once they were satisfied that they'd made their point, they left him bloodied and bruised in the dirt and began hauling my brother and me away."

Ophelia held her breath as Evren went on to tell how he and Lyall had fought the guards' hold on them to reach their father, but once the Vidaar had turned their attention to his wife, Evren had gone into a rage. He and Lyall, along with the men Marius had sent and a few others from their village, had fought back and managed to kill the dozen Vidaar sent to their village that day. His voice grew louder, his words coming faster, almost panicked. "The moment I attacked the first Vidaar,

I knew we would never be able to return to the peaceful lives we lived before, but I didn't care. They were going to hurt her. We've all heard what the Vidaar do at their 'collections,' and I would not have it. No man would take pleasure from hurting her. I would not have her screams fill the square—"

A soft voice at his side gently shushed him, murmuring gentle words too low for Ophelia to understand. A stuttered breath left Evren's chest when Lyall continued.

"The king send more fighter. Only not Vidaar." He gestured with his chin toward the front of the wagon. "He send them. They come in the night and lock our doors and set our farm on fire."

Shock rippled through her, white hot rage following quickly on its heels. These were his *people*—people he was meant to lead and protect. Is that not what brought him to Sigova all those weeks ago, when word of Pyotr's imminent release was received? To protect his people?

And yet Raygon toyed with their lives. He got what he wanted from them then cut the strings from the marionette when it no longer served his purposes. How had he gotten away with this for so long? How was he keeping word of this hidden? Surely, her father knew nothing of this or else he wouldn't have entered into any sort of agreement with Raygon—especially not one that involved sending one of his daughters into such a place. Right?

Ophelia sucked in a deep breath to steady herself before saying, "But you all escaped."

"Barely," Evren said. "Lyall had brought the axe in from chopping wood that day and propped it by the hearth. Had it not been there for me to break down the back door with, I fear we would have been ash by morning."

"But when we run out of the house, they were wait for us," Lyall spat.

The Reapers. The only people in all of Balmorea worse than the Vidaar.

"They looked just like the ones who shoved us in here. Frail women in black cloaks," Evren explained. "They stood before us, then a strange mist filled the air. None of us remember the moments after that. We woke up inside a wagon the next morning in shackles."

"And now we are here—another wagon," Lyall added.

Silence hung between them a long while before Ophelia found her voice.

"I'm so sorry," was all she could manage. Anger and sadness lanced through her in a confusing mixture of fire and ice.

The weight of their story draped over her shoulders like a heavy cloak, and she suddenly found herself exhausted. Exhausted from travel, from lack of food and sleep. From the constant fear and worry. From the sadness and despair rolling off of these innocent people in towering waves, threatening to crash over her and pull her under too— to drown her in a pain that never should have been borne to this world.

Her people were suffering and dying, and she was stuck in a cage, weak and with her magic leashed.

"How are *you* come here, Ophelia?" Lyall asked, pulling Ophelia from her chagrin.

Ophelia sighed. Her mind was too overrun with everything the two brothers had just shared with her to mentally organize all the events that had brought her to this point.

She shifted where she sat, readjusting to a more comfortable position before resting her head against the side of the wagon and closing her eyes. "That is a rather long story, I'm afraid. And one that will have to wait until morning."

She heard an exasperated sigh and her words translated into mumbled Balmorean before letting sleep sweep her away.

Chapter Forty

THE LOUD CRASH OF THE DOOR BANGING OPEN shook Elliot from fitful sleep.

"Up, Elliot. We've no time to waste," Marius commanded as he strode into the room and ripped open the curtains, allowing the first rays of the sunrise to brighten the space. "Ophelia's transport left early."

His mind was still hazy from sleep, so it took a moment to register Marius's words, but once the pieces connected, a spike of panic had Elliot jolting up from the bed.

Fuck. It was barely daybreak. Her transport wasn't scheduled to depart for another day. He threw the bed linens from his legs and began pulling on the first items of clothing his hands could find. "How long ago did she leave?" he asked.

Marius shook his head. "Some time last night. A missive was delivered to my chambers while I was held up at a dinner the king was hosting for some of his nobles. I can't be sure when it was delivered, but I didn't read it until several hours later and wasn't able to quit the castle as quickly as I would have liked without calling attention to my movements." He grabbed Elliot's pack and began riffling through it, tossing out anything he seemingly deemed unnecessary.

Elliot straightened, and his blood boiled. "You couldn't send word sooner because you were afraid someone would notice you leaving?" he asked, his words slow and laced with ice.

Marius stilled, his jaw clenching as his gaze rose to meet Elliot's. "It is not so simple a matter as you make it sound."

Elliot huffed a humorless laugh. "Is that not the measure of it?" He carded a hand through his hair. "You were the one who said it was imperative we don't lose track of this transport lest it disappear and we can't find it in time! Ophelia's life is teetering over the edge of a cliff, but you couldn't come sooner because you were afraid of your *dad* catching you out of bed?"

Anger flared in Marius's eyes, and he threw Elliot's bag to the floor as he stalked towards him. "Believe me, I wish the reality of my circumstances at the castle could be explained away so simply, but it cannot." And since I do not have the time to lay out the precarious nature of my life at court for you, I will advise you to tread carefully with how you speak to me." Marius's glare pierced through Elliot, and he ceded a step to the prince. He stepped further into Elliot's space, almost nose-to-nose with him. "You are not the only one with someone precious to protect," he spat.

Elliot's arguments dried up in his throat as he considered Marius's words. He was well aware of the complexities of court life but hadn't thought they'd affect Marius in the ways the prince was alluding to. They certainly didn't affect Prince Gregor in the same way.

Elliot's jaw tightened, and he gave a curt nod. Marius held his stare a heartbeat longer before pacing away.

"The transport is several hours ahead of us. If we leave soon and find their trail quickly, I'm hopeful we can catch up to them by tomorrow," he explained, picking up Elliot's pack from the floor and throwing it at him.

Elliot caught the bag. There was no certainty in Marius's voice, and it only sharpened his anxiety into cold fear. He clamped his eyes shut and focused on another detail of the prince's statement. "We? Who all were you able to gather on such short notice?"

Marius made his way toward the exit. "Dax, Hayes, and Melina."

Shit. So few against who knew how many Reapers?

"Finish packing only your essentials, and be quick," Marius tossed over his shoulder before walking out the door. "We leave within the half hour."

Chapter Forty One

"How many more on the list?" Lord Lucias asked as the door closed behind their previous interviewee.

Twenty-four Balmoreans and seventeen Nedorrans had come under the employ of the castle as the three nations fortified the Central Valley this past winter in preparation for Pyotr's return. Lord Lucias and George had interviewed them all so far, having only encountered six traitors. Four were currently locked in the dungeons while the other two chose death over surrender.

George flipped to the front of his notebook where he'd taken down the list of names of Balmorean and Nedorra employees along with their positions.

"Only three more to go, My Lord," George replied as he snapped the book shut and leaned against the stone wall closest to the audience hall door. A knot of anxiety twisted inside of him—with Elliot gone and George not having any other formal position at court besides Elliot's second, once the interviews were concluded, he would no longer have a reason to remain at the castle…would no longer have a reason to be near Nell.

He shoved down the fierce longing that stole through him and focused his mind back to the present. There may only be three interviews left, but the woman who was walking into the room at the moment was the last one for the day. With any luck, this interview would finish quickly, and he'd have the rest of the afternoon and evening free. His mind had already begun to consider reasons he could give for seeking out Nell and spending time with her.

As the woman entered the room, she held her eyes to the ground with her head bowed and her hands clasped in front of her. She was wearing a plain, long-sleeved wool dress with an apron tied at her waist. Her hair was a mousy brown and was bound into two braids that ran down the back of her head and back. She was almost two heads shorter than George and quite thin, her complexion sallow. She reminded George of a sickly child.

George's forehead wrinkled, and he met Lucias's eyes, gesturing to his own face to indicate how pale she was.

Lucias gave a nod of agreement as he followed her into the room, then gestured to his eyes and pointed down. *She won't make eye contact.*

George narrowed his eyes. "Aida Rinald, correct?" George asked as Lucias walked across the room to the desk situated along a side wall. George flipped open his book and found her name on his list. She worked as a laundress.

"Yes, My Lord," she replied. Her words were soft yet seemed to strain her tongue, fighting against her thick Balmorean accent. George gestured for her to take a seat in the chair placed in the center of the room, and she complied, giving a slight nod before stiffly taking a seat. She sat with her back ramrod straight, resting her hands in her lap, one hand clasped over her wrist. Her feet were flat on the ground, her knees positioned directly above her ankles at a perfect right angle.

And she never raised her gaze.

There could be any number of reasons she wasn't raising her head. Expectations of women in Balmorea were much more rigid than in Maraleon, and this could be a behavior that has been expected of her back home.

Or she could be hiding something.

Trepidation skittered down George's spine. He looked to Lucias who met his gaze with a skeptical bend to his brow.

Sallow, ashen skin, eyes black as pitch, and the scythe tattoo were the three physical traits Aria and Ophelia had told them about for identifying a Reaper. The woman sitting before them had one of those traits, was likely ducking her head to hide the second, and, George suspected, was clutching her hand over her wrist to hide the third.

"Ms. Aida," Lucias began, "as you are aware, we are investigating a threat that has been made against the royal family from Balmorea." He paused, picking up a stack of papers and seemed to casually sift through their contents as he spoke. "And since you have recently joined our staff from the Balmorean retinue that left us all too recently, we would like to ask you some questions."

Aida nodded, and George flipped to the next blank page in his notebook to take notes as Lucias began to pepper Aida with questions. His questions ranged from asking her about where she was from and her family to how she came to travel with the king's forces into Maraleon and the type of work she did in the castle—all preliminary information they verified at the beginning of every interview.

She appeared to be forthcoming with her answers, though she was so soft-spoken that George had to move his chair closer to hear her responses. She never fidgeted, never bounced her knee. Her voice never wavered, and she never hesitated to speak. Her eyes never shifted, her face never rippled with any expression, and her breathing never escalated.

George closed his notebook, abandoning the task he'd neglected the past several minutes, and leaned over his knees, resting his forearms on his thighs. Lucias tracked the movement but continued with his questions, no doubt picking up on the same irregularities as George—even those completely innocent would show some signs of nervousness, but Aida sat so still that George wondered if she even drew breath.

"We have received word that these threats have been made by a radical sect of the Acolytes of Vindicta," Lucias began. "They call themselves Reapers. Have you heard of such an organization before?"

George raked over Aida's person for any sign, any tell, that she'd been alarmed by their knowledge of the secret rank of Acolytes, but she only shook her head.

"I know of the Acolytes, but have no knowledge of these Reapers," she answered.

"I see," Lucias replied, before angling his head and narrowing his eyes on her. "These Reapers are said to be an elite group of women assassins. Can you believe that, Lord George? *Women* assassins."

George was familiar with Lucias's strategies by now. He knew Lucias had all the questions he wanted to ask planned and ready in his mind. He knew the various strategies he invoked to get the interviewees to crack, which was how he knew to play along now.

He let a smirk tip up the side of his mouth and gave a derisive chuckle.

"The only time women can properly wield a blade is when preparing meals in the kitchen."

Lucias barked a laugh in reply. "Quite right, My Lord."

To her credit, Aida didn't so much as flinch.

Lucias continued. "We have also been made aware that these so-called assassins have a distinct appearance. Their skin appears almost ashen, and their pupils and irises are dark as night." He paused again, scrutinizing the woman for a reaction that she did not give.

"They also have a tattoo on the inside of their wrists," George added. "A red scythe, I believe it was."

"Yes, I do believe that is correct," Lucias replied before sneering at the knowledge. "Marked women. What a waste."

It was slight, but George saw Aida's grip tighten on her wrist. His and Lucias's gazes shot to each other then back to Aida. Lucias let a few more beats of silence pass before he asked, "Have you perhaps encountered any female under the employ of the castle meeting such a description?"

She shook her head. "No, My Lord."

Lucias set the papers he was holding down on the nearby desk then came to stand next to George, his stance wide and his arms crossed over his chest. The two men held their gazes to her and waited.

A thought formed in George's mind. "And what of the Aegis, Ms. Aida. Are you familiar with that?"

Her eyes shot to them in surprise, and George's stomach dropped at the bottomless pits of onyx that stared back at him.

Realizing her mistake, she immediately dropped her eyes and clutched her wrist even tighter. "No, My Lords. I've never heard of an Aegis."

Lucias stepped forward. "I'm afraid I will need to see your wrists, Ms. Aida."

She let go of her hand and slowly raised her downturned hands in front of her.

"Palms up."

The whispers began right before she flipped her palms up, exposing the blood red scythe on the inside of her right wrist.

Lucias jumped back but wasn't quick enough to avoid the slash across the forearm from the crimson dagger that shot up from Aida's upturned palm.

George was on his feet the next moment, sword in hand, watching in horror as Aida licked Lucias's blood from her blade and grinned. Her eyes narrowed on Lucias.

"You're mine."

She began her song of whispers again. George lunged toward Aida to disarm her when Lucias tackled him to the ground. George's sword clattered to the stone floor, and confusion skittered through him as he wrestled to break free from the hold of the king's second.

"Lucias! What are you doing?!" George shouted as Aida gave a shrill laugh beyond them.

"I said he was mine!"

The meaning of her words struck George like a blow to the chest—the cut on Lucias's arm, ingesting his blood.

Wild panic flared in Lucias's eyes as he pinned George to the ground, wrapping his hands around his neck and squeezing. George's heart kicked in his chest as his mind caught up to Lucias's quick actions, alarm bursting through him as his head grew light.

Lucias's grip continued to close around George's neck, but not with the speed nor the strength he knew the king's second commanded. Lucias's face reddened, and his body began to tremble with the effort of fighting against Aida's hold over him. George had seconds—a minute at most.

George swept his arms through Lucias's, wrapping his hands around the back of his neck and jerked his head down. Lucias fell into George's chest, the shift startling him enough to cause him to loosen his grip on George's neck. George took the opening and slid a forearm under Lucias's chin, the other to the back of his neck, and squeezed.

Lucias jolted in his arms, and George weaved his legs through Lucias's to keep him from thrashing or pulling away.

"You and I both know this won't kill you," George whispered, "but I'm sorry, anyway."

A handful of seconds later, Lucias went slack, and George rolled him off his body.

Aida's crazed laughter filled the space as he jumped to his feet and lunged for his sword.

"Clever, clever," she jeered as she approached him, the blade in her hand now stretched to the length of a sword. "But not clever enough." Her smile sent a chill down his spine, and she began another song of whispers as he lunged to attack.

"Guards!" George yelled as his blade clashed with Aida's. More crazed laughter poured from her as the doors slammed open and several guards rushed into the room. "Form a perimeter! Someone bind Lord Lucias's wound!"

Aida didn't let up. She came at him with blow after blow, singing her song of infuriating whispers, moving with a speed he hadn't expected. She lunged forward to stab him in the stomach, and he barely spun away, a tear in his tunic marking his close call.

Back and forth they struck and parried, traversing the length of the room. He drove his sword down, but she jumped back then lunged for him as soon as her feet found purchase on the stone floor. He blocked, throwing her off balance. Kicking out, his foot connected with her chest and sent her stumbling back and gasping for breath.

Now facing the opposite direction, George looked over his shoulder in horror as a rope of blood seemed to float from Lucias's arm, congealing into long spikes, like the ones Trella shot at Elliot and Ophelia. The spell stuttered with Aida's loss of breath but recovered a heartbeat later. George glanced down to Lucias's face and found it nearly leached of all color.

Fuck. She's going to bleed him dry.

"Bind. His. Wound!" he shouted again. One guard dodged a blood spike then dropped to the ground beside Lucias and began ripping fabric from his tunic.

George forced his focus back to Aida. *Disarm her. Don't let her cut you. Make her stop those infernal whispers.*

Her breaths came out in heavy pants now, and a sheen of sweat glistened on her forehead. Fighting a battle on two fronts was wearing on her.

Just a little longer.

George launched himself at her, raising his sword over his head and bringing it down upon her. She wasn't quick enough to evade the blow this time, but she was able to deflect it, albeit with much less resistance than before. He came at her again from the other side with another quick, powerful blow. Then again, and again.

Aida dodged and spun away from his strikes, but her speed was quickly diminishing. He backed her toward the guards now approaching the two fighters with drawn weapons. Shattered blood spikes peppered the ground, crunching underfoot as the guards drew nearer. One remained at Lucias's side, tying a bandage in place around his forearm.

A few heartbeats later, the guards came into Aida's view, and it pulled her focus from George for a moment.

It was long enough.

George struck, quickly disarming her before sweeping her feet from under her and taking her to the ground. He flipped her to her stomach and bound her hands behind her back, fastening her palms together. Two guards dropped on either side of him to help restrain her.

Aida let out another shrill laugh, and the sound grated against George's ears.

"It is no use, Little Lord," she said through breaks in her laughter. "He already has her and is going to make her pay for her treachery."

George's brows drew together.

"Who has whom?" he asked.

She sucked in another breath, and stuttered laughter fell from her lips. "It's so poetic!" she said. "He's taking her to the Aegis and is going to spill her blood to sustain that which her very presence threatens to destroy!"

George felt the blood drain from his face as she released another howl of laughter.

"*Who are you speaking of?*" he bellowed, terrified that he already knew the answer.

"The king has the princess," she sang. "The heretic who thinks herself an equal to the great Pyotr!"

George's eyes went wide, his heart thrashing to break free of his chest.

The king, the princess, the Aegis—Raygon had Ophelia.

George shot to his feet, shouting to send one guard for Gaius and another for the king.

"*Run,*" he growled, and they were out the door in his next breath.

George settled his attention back on Aida, kneeling next to her face. Her black eyes and wide, maniacal grin made his skin crawl and sent his hands trembling with rage.

"And what do you think your poor king can do?" she asked. "It is too late."

George clenched his jaw as he ripped a thick piece of fabric from his tunic.

"You've stopped your whispers," he noted, the chamber blessedly free of flying blood weapons, and her brow bent at his sudden change of subject. "Is that because your hands are bound? Or is your strength perhaps depleted?" He began to weave the fabric through his fingers as he spoke. "Or did you drain all the blood from the king's second and no longer have any ammunition to work with?" he asked coolly.

Her lips tipped up. "His heart still beats."

In her next breath, she began another whisper song, and the shattered pieces of blood spikes began to rattle along the stone.

So, she didn't require her palms to be free to wield.

He forced the fabric between her lips, effectively cutting off her song. "I don't think so," he said.

The rattling ceased, and Aida released a guttural scream into her gag as George tightened the fabric around the back of her head.

With the guards holding Aida and her song silenced, George rushed to Lucias and the guard tending to him.

"He's still alive," the guard said as George knelt before the king's second. The guard had bound Lucias's arm as instructed and had turned him to lay on his left side. A small pool of blood spread at Lucias's back where his arm had lain on the floor. A stain of blood began to bloom across the makeshift bandage on his arm. "He's still breathing, but it's faint."

George nodded. "He lost a lot of blood," George muttered as he scanned Lucias's face for signs of any other injury. Finding none, he sat back on his heels and sighed, parsing through the things Aida revealed through her madness and desperately hoping he'd interpreted her words incorrectly.

He worried his lower lip with his teeth, wondering how much time Ophelia had, and if he'd be able to get to her in time to stop whatever Raygon had set into motion. His mind flew to Nell, and he stiffened.

How the fuck was he going to tell Nell about this?

"Who is she, My Lord?" the guard asked, pulling George from his thoughts. "I've never seen fighting like that before."

George dropped his hand and cast a glance over to Aida. She was lying still on the floor where he left her, glaring at him.

"She's one of the reasons we were doing these interviews," George replied, swiveling his gaze back to Lucias. "And we found out much more from her than we anticipated."

Chapter Forty Two

GEORGE SAT IN THE KING'S STUDY. STARING blankly at the drink in his hands. It had helped the trembling to finally stop, but as he and Prince Gregor waited for the king's return, George found his mind suspended in a daze. With the immediate threat to his life gone, and with the flood of adrenaline in his veins diminished, George fought the exhaustion that threatened to suck him under with its promise of numb bliss.

His fight with Aida may not have been the deadliest fight he'd ever fought in, but he knew it would be one that would leave one of the darkest stains on his soul. He already felt the imprint of it. *She'd taken control of Lucias's body and used him like a puppet. She'd weaponized his blood.*

Once Gaius and the king had arrived at the audience hall, Lucias had been rushed to Gaius's study while George informed the king of everything that had occurred during Aida's interview.

Afterward, George was given time to wash and change out of his ripped and bloodstained tunic before reporting to the king's study. The trembling began as he worked to wash Lucias's blood from his hands. No matter how hard he scrubbed, he still felt a sticky layer of it on his skin. A pink tinge still clung to his fingers, as though the blood tainted by dark magic was trying to soak itself into his very being and take hold of him the way Aida had taken hold of Lucias. A coppery tang seemed to hover in the air around him, dragging his mind back to a tongue licking a blade and blood spikes forming in midair.

Gregor and Charlotte were already there when George had finally arrived at the king's study. Gregor had allowed him in, shoving a drink into his hand as he crossed the threshold, the two of them sitting with him in companionable silence.

George tossed the final dregs of his whiskey back as the doors to the king's study opened. He jumped to his feet as Alphonse entered and moved to stand behind the settee where he'd been sitting to allow Gregor and Charlotte to take his place. Aria followed her father into his study, and her ladies trailed in behind her. His eyes immediately landed on Nell as she entered the room, and his chest tightened with both the thrill of seeing her and the dread of what this news would do to her.

Aria took a seat on the settee across from Gregor and Charlotte, and her brow bent as her gaze bounced between her father and brother. After several heartbeats of a silence so tense George found it difficult to draw breath, Aria finally asked, "Papa, what's going on?"

Alphonse leaned back against the front of his desk with his arms crossed over his chest, one hand aimlessly stroking his beard.

"We found another Reaper," he replied, and Aria tensed.

"What?" she breathed. Collette placed a hand on Aria's shoulder, and the princess reached up and clung to it. Her other two ladies shuffled on their feet, but Nell stayed frozen in place.

George's eyes settled on her. She stood nearest him in line with Aria's ladies, and he edged the few feet remaining between them to stand beside her. She glanced at him, acknowledging his presence, then trained her eyes forward on the king.

His heart already ached for her, and a sense of helplessness wrapped itself around his throat. There was nothing he could do to protect her from what she was about to hear. There was no way for him to lessen the blow, no silver lining he could offer to give her some hope to cling to.

He reached for her hand and lightly brushed his thumb along the back, hoping she understood what he was trying to convey—that he was there, that she wouldn't be alone.

Alphonse nodded to Aria before shifting his gaze to George. "Lord George fought admirably at Lord Lucias's side, and thanks to his calm head and quick thinking, he was able to subdue her."

Nell sucked in a sharp breath as her hand clamped around George's. He gave her hand a reassuring squeeze before slowly brushing his fingers against her palm and twining their fingers together. She squeezed again once their hands locked into place, and something settled within him, her touch comforting him as much as he was hoping to comfort her.

Alphonse's jaw clenched, and his throat worked on a swallow. "She is in the dungeons now, but before her arrest, she revealed some disturbing information." He paused for several heartbeats, seeming to carefully choose his next words, and George felt every second of the silence like a boulder on his chest.

"The Reaper claimed that King Raygon discovered Ophelia in Balmorea and captured her."

Nell sucked in another breath and bit her lip to stay her emotion, but George heard the whimper she couldn't hold in as her grip on his hand turned vice-like.

"No! That can't be right!" Aria cried, her eyes widening in panic. "How did—Do we know if he truly has her?"

Alphonse shook his head. "We have no way to confirm if what she claims is true. She very well could be trying to bait us into making a rash move."

"Or she could simply be insane and wanted to have the last laugh before her execution," Gregor ground out.

The memory of Aida's shrill laugh resounded in George's mind, and he inadvertently clenched Nell's hand. His heart kicked in his chest as the echo of her laugh seemed to scrape against his skin. A shudder ran down his spine, and he rolled his shoulders and neck to rid himself of the sensation. Nell shot him a quick glance and began to brush her thumb along his knuckles. He stilled and took in a steadying breath, narrowing his focus to the soothing brush of her skin.

His heart slowed. His mind cleared. His breathing evened.

"He's going to kill her!" Aria shot up from the settee and strode toward her father. "That's what he's wanted from the start! When was she captured? We have to hurry. She slipped through his fingers once already; he won't delay if he truly has her in his grasp," she said, a sob escaping her chest. "If he hasn't killed her already."

Nell's hand began to tremble, and her breaths quickened, but she was careful to make no sound. She pressed her lips into a thin line and stayed rooted in place, her gaze holding steady on the king and Aria.

His heart fractured, and the urge to ease her worry had him turning to face her. "We suspect she is still alive based on something the Reaper alluded to," he said in a rushed whisper.

Nell's gaze snapped to him and his fractured heart shattered at the pain and fear melding within the honey brown of her eyes. She swallowed. "What did she say?"

George held her gaze. "She said Raygon plans to take her to the Aegis and will 'spill her blood to sustain that which her very presence threatens to destroy.'"

Nell's expression faltered, and she strained to rein in her hold on her composure. "That doesn't necessarily mean he intends to kill her though, right?"

George's stomach sank at the hopefulness in her tone, but he wouldn't lie to her or give her false hope. "Based on the fact that he's already tried to kill her once, we assume that is indeed what he intends to do."

"When?" she asked, her voice shaking.

George shook his head. "Aida made it sound like they wouldn't try to kill her until they made it to the Aegis, which is past the Far East River. So, if they're leaving from Ravenhold, maybe three, four days at most?"

Her eyes snapped shut, and an errant tear fell down her cheek. "We couldn't make it to Ravenhold in less than four."

George brushed the tear away with his thumb. "I know," he replied. "But I think—"

Aria's sobs drew their attention back to the king. "We have to go get her, Papa! We can't let him do this!" Alphonse's arms encircled Aria

Gregor shot to his feet. "I agree. It's an act of war to kill a member of another country's royal family."

The king nodded. "Our only obstacle is our lack of resources after the conflict in the valley. I think it's safe to say that Balmorea doesn't intend to pay their reparations, and without that, we won't be able to completely replace the munitions we lost. Then there is the matter of numbers." Alphonse smoothed slow circles along Aria's back but held his eyes to Gregor. "I don't need to remind you how many men we lost in the valley, nor do I need to remind you of the state in which we sent home many of those who did survive. Would it be wise to call on men so damaged so soon?"

Gregor crossed his arms and paced in front of the king's desk, biting a thumbnail as he thought.

Charlotte stood from the settee. "If we send out word to our forces regarding the threat to Ophelia's life, our men will rally to either save their princess or avenge her," she said.

Gregor nodded. "Especially after Balmorea's betrayal."

George agreed. The people of Maraleon hated Balmorea after the events of the valley. Word of Ophelia's capture would only bolster their animosity and spur them into action.

"Numbers, Gregor," Alphonse replied. "That will not be enough to march on Balmorea—they faced the least number of losses in the valley."

George pressed his lips into a thin line. He knew those called to arms in Balmorea had no love for their king and would hardly put up a fight. Gregor could lead an army of cooks over the Lupos and likely come out the other side of a conflict victorious, but saying as much would lead to too many questions George couldn't risk.

Gregor stopped in front of the king. "Nedorra," he responded. "King Stephan will ally with us. He believed Ophelia and saw what she did in the valley. He is no friend to Balmorea, either."

Alphonse's gaze went distant, and he nodded absently as he thought. He raised his eyes to Gregor. "Very well. Send word through the mirrors to Stephan's court to request an audience."

The mirrors.

He could get to Balmorea *today* if he traveled through the mirrors, but they were for temple and royal use only. Would the king grant him permission to travel through the mirrors so he could help rescue Ophelia? And if he did, were the temple mages on the other side trustworthy enough to keep his presence hidden?

"Raygon has Ophelia, *now*, Papa," Aria interjected, pulling George from his thoughts. She stepped back from Alphonse's embrace. "She cannot wait until we've amassed an army."

Alphonse and Gregor's jaws clenched simultaneously.

"You're right." The king's eyes bounced between his son and daughter. "Time is not on our side," he admitted, his voice soft, and more defeated than George had ever heard before.

Aria's face hardened with determination. "We have to try. We can't sit here and do *nothing*."

Gregor began to tread back and forth in front of the desk again. "It would take time to organize a specialized group to send."

"Your Majesty, if I may," George said with his head bowed. "I'll go."

All eyes snapped to George, and Nell stilled next to him.

"She's my princess and my lord's betrothed. And I have come to consider her a friend," he began. "I'm a trained fighter and have connections in Ravenhold through my father's business dealings. If allowed to use the temple mirror, I could get to the capital as early as this evening and begin tracking her down."

Aria looked to George then back to her father, and he saw the wheels turning in her calculating mind. "I know where Marius's network operates. I can send Lord George to the right people." She nodded, a small glimmer of hope lighting her eyes. "Marius likely already knows what's going on and is probably working out a plan to help her as we speak."

George had come to the same conclusions, but having Aria put voice to his thoughts lightened some of the weight from his chest.

The king frowned. "You won't be able to use the mirrors. You'll need someone of royal blood to pull you through, and this isn't exactly a state-sanctioned trip. Neither the crown prince nor I can be seen aiding your passage."

"I can help him through," Aria spoke up, and Alphonse's gaze sharpened.

"Absolutely not. You will not set foot in that country again until your safety is a guarantee."

"I would step through and pull Lord George with me. Then step right back through. It will take less than a minute—"

"*No*, Aria," Alphonse said, his tone brooking no argument. He clenched his fists and sucked in a deep, steadying breath, tamping down the rage George saw burning in his eyes, and he knew the king was remembering the state Aria had been in when she'd returned to them all those weeks ago.

After a few moments, the king released his breath and continued. "We also have no way of knowing which of the temple mages on the other side are loyal to the prince and would keep Lord George's presence hidden. Nor do we have the means to contact him and work out such an arrangement."

"What about the mages who helped you escape, Aria?" Charlotte suggested.

Aria nodded. "Sandro and Morgan! We could have Gaius ask for them and have him work with them to set up the arrangements for Lord George's discreet passage."

Gregor and Alphonse met each other's gaze.

"That could work," Gregor said.

Alphonse thought for a moment, then nodded to Gregor. "Very well. Take Gaius with you to the temple, so he can seek out these two mages while you request an audience with King Stephan."

Gregor nodded as he reached for Charlotte. She took his hand, and the two of them shot for the door.

George released his breath and felt a small weight lift from his shoulders. He might be able to get there in time to help after all.

The next moment, Nell stepped forward. "I'm going with him," she said, and George's heart stopped.

He whirled on her. "No, Nell—"

"Your Majesty, I may not be as skilled as Lord George with a weapon, but I can travel hard on horseback and am an asset out of doors should the need for either of those possibilities arise. And if history has revealed anything to us about the character of King Raygon, then we know that, when we do find the princess, she will likely not be in the best state." Her voice faltered, but she went on. "She will need someone to be there for her."

George felt the longing in her voice. After everything she'd faced in the wake of Ophelia's attack, Nell wouldn't let herself be set aside a moment longer.

He ran a hand down his face, cursing silently to himself. He had to convince her to stay, already knowing he wouldn't be able to.

George held his breath as the king's gaze flicked back and forth between him and Nell. He nodded at Nell before finally saying, "Very well. Begin making your preparations. You will leave as soon as we receive word from Master Gaius."

Panic burst in George's chest. Every instinct within him screamed to stop this, to keep Nell from danger. She couldn't go. She needed to stay here where she was safe and where he knew no one would kidnap and torture her. Blood rushed in George's ears as he gaped at her.

"Yes, Your Majesty," Nell replied, paying George no mind as she dropped into a curtsy and darted for the study doors.

George turned to the king to object, but Aria stepped between them.

"Let's go. We have much to discuss before you two leave," she said, looping her arm through George's and leading him out of the study after Nell.

Chapter Forty Three

Aria dragged George down the corridor, chattering almost as quickly as she stepped, relaying information to him about a district on the outskirts of Ravenhold where Marius operated and a tavern-inn called The Jade Raven that he used as a base of sorts. George nodded politely as Aria spoke, doing his best to pretend he didn't already know all of this information.

"When you arrive, ask the barmaid for Arwyn—he's Marius's second. He's a bit younger than Marius. Long, blond hair and a skilled fighter, but he's also learning a trade from his older brother. A clothier, I think it was?"

George nodded, a faint smile tugging his lips up. "My father does business with Arwyn's older brother Ambrose. I'm quite familiar with them—Ambrose is the one I negotiated passage for Ophelia and Elliot with."

Aria stopped short, amusement brightening her eyes before she narrowed them on him. "What are you and the

Earl doing connected to Marius's spy network?" A smile crept up the side of her mouth.

"Purchasing the finest silks Balmorea has to offer, of course," he replied, his smile widening a fraction before dropping. "We will head straight to The Jade Raven when we arrive. Thank you, Your Highness. You've likely saved us a lot of time."

Aria stepped back from his side and nodded. "Of course, Lord George. If I think of anything else, I will relay the information to you," she said, as her three ladies hurried down the corridor after her.

"Thank you." George sketched a small bow. "If you'll excuse me," he said then left her with her ladies to find Nell and begin getting everything in order for his journey.

His first thought was to head to his chambers to begin packing his bag. He'd need to make sure the king informs his father of his absence. He'd need coin for transport and his stay at The Jade Raven. *Their stay* at the Jade Raven, he reminded himself, and his heart rose to his throat. *She couldn't come.* The thought alone turned his stomach into knots.

George was standing in the doorway to her chambers, ready to knock on the door, when it flung open and Nell appeared on the other side, poised to head to her next destination and stopping just short of barreling into him. Despite the fear clamping down on his chest, the sight of her still sent his heart into a gallop.

She straightened then squared her shoulders. "Excuse me, Lord George, I have preparations to make before we leave and am in a hurry to do so," she said.

George's jaw clenched at the dismissal in her tone, and he stepped into her space. "May I have a word with you?"

She closed her chamber door and crossed her arms over her chest. "Not if it's to object to my coming with you to Balmorea, as I suspect it is."

George's eyes dropped to the floor, and she sighed. "Please move."

He pulled his gaze back to hers, desperation and fear sending his heart into a frenzy. *This must have been how Elliot felt when Ophelia told him of her plans to travel to the Aegis.* He immediately regretted the harsh tone he'd taken with his friend all those days ago.

"Reconsider this, Nell," he pleaded.

She stepped farther into his space, her head tilting back to meet his eyes, that familiar fire burning behind honey brown.

"No," she said with finality in her tone. "I will not. I have watched from the background and feasted on my own uselessness and loneliness long enough. I'm coming with you."

George released a shuddering breath. He raised his hands to hold her biceps. "Please," he said, swallowing down the fear clawing at his throat. "I don't think you are too delicate to make the journey or feel that you will be a burden to me. You are undeniably incredible, but everything that's happened just proves that Balmorea is not a safe place. And if Elliot, whose skill and ability have saved me on more occasions than I can count, was unable to protect—"

"George," Nell cut him off. "This is different. We present no threat to Balmorea. No one will be keeping an eye out for us. Perhaps you will be recognized because you were with Elliot during the valley conflict, but I won't. No one will be paying any mind to us in Balmorea, especially not to me."

George shook his head, releasing her arms. "You are not one that people pay no mind to, Nell. You can't step anywhere in this castle without every man—and woman—you pass taking notice."

She rolled her eyes, but George didn't miss the slight flush that rose to her cheeks. "I'm well-known here because of my connection to Princess Ophelia. No one in Ravenhold will glance twice at us. Neither of us are a threat to Raygon like he perceives Ophelia to be. No one knows who we are nor will they care—"

"*I* care about you," he said. "I know the dangers that lurk in Balmorea, which are more than you realize, and the thought of having you there with me terrifies me." His voice broke at the end.

Something flashed behind her eyes, and her gaze softened a moment before she replaced the steel in her gaze. "I think you might be embellishing this a bit, George," she said. "I've been to Balmorea too, remember? Out and about in the market with Ophelia—"

"With a guard, near the castle, under the protection of the king," he replied sharply.

"We will be in a part of the city under Prince Marius's protection, will we not? Isn't that what the princess said back in the king's study?"

"Yes, but that doesn't make everyone in the district an upstanding citizen." He shoved a hand through his hair and paced away. His blood roared in his ears. *Why was she being so stubborn?* "His base there will be safe, but there's a reason he operates in that area of the city. His movements are easily hidden against the backdrop of everything else that goes on there. There are good people there, yes, but—" he stopped and closed his eyes. He sucked in a deep breath, willing his heart and mind to slow.

He felt her step into his space. "But what, George?"

He released his breath and fixed his gaze to her, taking in the determined set of her brow and the sternness in her eyes. Her resolve wasn't weakening.

"They took every precaution and measure to keep the princess safe. Their identities were hidden, they didn't use official means of travel, they were both armed, and she was *still* taken, Nell." He raised his hands to her cheeks, needing to touch her, needing her to understand—to feel his desperation. "And just the *thought* of having you taken from me like Ophelia was taken from Elliot steals the fucking breath from my lungs."

Nell's expression gentled, and a hint of confusion flashed in her eyes.

"It does?" she whispered.

"Yes," he replied, his brow bending as he brushed his thumbs along her cheeks. Was that an actual question? How could she not know?

"I thought—" That sweet shade of pink brightened her cheeks, and she shook her head. "I saw you with Evandra—"

"*Evandra?*" He pulled back, eyes wide.

Her eyes dropped, and she pulled out of his hold.

His stomach knotted. *She still thought—*

He wrapped a hand around her waist and pulled her close. "No," he said, shaking his head as he slid his index finger under her chin and lifted her gaze back to his. "Evandra isn't the one who fills my every waking and sleeping thought." He brushed the backs of his fingers along her jaw then her cheek. "It's not Evandra's quiet strength that taught my heart how to beat." He leaned in and brushed the tip of his nose across hers, letting a playful smirk tilt his lips up to one side. "It's not Evandra's sharp tongue that heats my blood."

Her chest heaved with her quickened breaths. Her lips were so close to his. Her scent of honey and jasmine both sent his heart into a frenzy and calmed him. She melted away his anxiety only to make room for the desire quickly taking its place.

George's hand at her waist splayed across the small of her back, and he dropped his mouth to the shell of her ear. "That would be you, Sweetheart," he whispered.

A sigh fell from her lips, and she slid a hand up his arm to his chest, as if to steady herself. His other hand fell to her waist, and her body relaxed against his, molding itself to him. Awareness coursed through him of every place their bodies touched, of how perfectly she fit against him, setting him alight.

Her hand laid flat against his chest, and he knew she could feel his heart pounding against her palm, but he didn't shy from her touch. He welcomed it—let her see and feel the evidence of what he'd claimed with his words. Let her see what she did to him, and let what she finds scrub any doubt from her mind of what she meant to him.

She tentatively slid her palm up to the laces of his tunic, the friction of her hand leaving behind a path of delicious heat. Her fingers slipped past the hem to brush the skin along his collarbone. He sucked in a sharp breath at the contact, something like lightning bursting through him the moment her bare skin met his. He bit back a groan, not wanting to startle her, not wanting her to stop. It was such a small touch, but it made him ache for *more.*

He wanted her bare skin against his. Wanted to feel how soft her body was with his hands. Wanted to feel how warm she'd feel around his cock. He wanted to get lost in her and forget that there was anything else other than her and him.

Fuck, this was not how he meant for this conversation to go.

Her finger trailed back and forth along his collar bone, dipping to the hollow of his throat then skating on to the other side, turning his skin molten. Her touch grew bolder, and she pulled back slightly as she brushed her fingers up along the collar of his tunic to the side of his throat. His heart pounded in his chest, his pulse no doubt thrumming under her fingertips as she followed the column of his neck up to the hinge of his jaw and glided down the path to the corner of his mouth. Her eyes met his as she brushed her fingers over his bottom lip, and the heat radiating from her honey brown irises sent blood rushing straight to his cock.

He wanted to give in, to press her against the wall and kiss her until she forgot about Balmorea and assassins, until she forgot the heavy burdens they'd both placed upon themselves.

He clenched his jaw against the rush of desire, pulling his focus back to the reason he was standing before her.

He gently captured her hand in his then brought each of her fingers to his lips to press a light kiss to each one. He lowered her palm back to his chest, over his flailing heart.

"You are precious to me, Nell," he said, his tone low and gentle. "I just want to keep you safe—I *need* to keep you safe."

She peered up at him, understanding and tenderness shining in her gaze, and she gave him a small nod before raising her other hand to swipe a lock of hair from his face.

"Then do everything you can to keep me safe in Balmorea," she replied, and his stomach sank. He'd told Elliot almost the exact same thing, and look how that had turned out for him.

He closed his eyes with a sigh then nodded even as dread filled his chest. She would be coming with him to Balmorea. It would be fine. She would be fine. Everything would be fine.

She shifted in his hold and pitched up on her toes, surprising him by brushing a light kiss to his cheek before stepping past him and leaving him alone in the corridor.

Sandro and Morgan have not been seen in almost two weeks.

Gaius's solemn news from the temple clanged around in the din that was George's mind as he rushed to make preparations for his and Nell's departure in the morning. His mind wound incessantly around everything that could possibly go wrong while he and Nell were in Balmorea, around worries of Elliot and where he was and how he was doing, around the events of the afternoon with Aida and Nell.

There were too many risks, too many unknown outcomes hanging in the balance, and not knowing which would be the one they'd face strangled his already weary mind.

Packing and organizing everything they would need for an extended stay away from home offered a small reprieve, but when there was nothing left to do but rest, the anxiety within him would cause his chest to ache, or the scent of blood would jolt him awake.

George finally gave up on sleep when the echo of Aida's crazed laughter filled the quiet parts of his mind. It rang so clearly that he thought for a moment that she was in his room, standing over him at the side of his bed. He felt her grating peals of laughter scrape across his skin, and the sensation had his chest clenching in panic, cutting his breaths short.

He shot out of bed and threw on a new shirt and pants to chase away the feeling, but the vice clamping around his lungs was too tight to allow for even the smallest hope of rest.

He needed air.

George darted through the corridors, winding his way down two flights of stairs before finally bursting through the door into the courtyard gardens. He took a deep, steadying breath, and allowed his head to fall back as cool air filled his lungs. His gaze roved over the night sky before him, the countless stars slightly dimmed in the light of the waxing moon, and the tightness in his chest slackened a bit.

A familiar, rhythmic clacking of wood against wood tugged at his focus, and he swung his head in the direction of the sound, already knowing what it was before his eyes landed on the figure across the yard running through drills at the striking post.

His feet moved on their own in her direction, her pull on him inevitable, and the tightness in his chest lessened the closer he got to her. The focus of his thoughts shifted. It no longer lingered on the haunting memories from his fight with Aida, but on the memory of honey brown eyes filled with pain and fear. On the way Nell's hands trembled as she fought to tamp down every emotion he saw trying to flit across her beautiful face. She'd portrayed the picture of solemn strength that afternoon—even afterward when he'd followed her to her chambers and begged her to stay in Sigova, she betrayed nothing of how the news of Ophelia's capture was affecting her.

He knew her, though, and knew that, inside, she was crumbling.

The mere thought that she could be trying to wall herself off again and handle this alone had him quickening his steps to reach her.

As he drew nearer, he slowed his pace, giving her the chance to hear him coming so he wouldn't startle her. She wore her usual training garb—leather pants and a beige tunic with her scuffed brown boots—and he watched on as she struck the post, stepped back, then struck again. She placed each step precisely, carefully. She checked her posture and strike position, working methodically through each drill, just as he'd been teaching her every morning.

He stopped when about ten feet separated them and shoved his hands into his pockets.

"Nell," he called softly, and she stopped.

She glanced over her shoulder then lowered the wooden sword in her hands, before stepping back and setting it down in the grass. She straightened then turned to face him.

George held his breath as he took her in. His eyes locked with hers, and the sight of her nearly brought him to his knees. The moon cast her in silver light, giving her an almost aethereal glow. It softened her fair complexion, and George clenched his fists in his pockets against the urge to close what distance remained between them and brush his knuckles along her cheek.

She was stunning.

George let out a breath, the tightness in his chest finally releasing completely, and he took in his first lungful of air in hours.

"Couldn't sleep either?" he asked.

She shook her head. "I couldn't quiet my mind of worries."

He chanced a few steps forward, never dropping her gaze, when he noticed her puffy, red eyes, and his heart sank.

"You were crying," he noted, imbuing as much concern into his tone as he could.

She quickly ducked her head and wiped at her face with her hand, turning away to face the garden.

The urgency to take her in his arms and hold her to his chest overwhelmed him. She was shouldering too much on her own again. The feelings of helplessness, which he now shared with her, would tear her apart piece by piece—and he knew she would let it happen until she felt she'd paid proper penance for a transgression she didn't commit.

He tentatively stepped next to her, his eyes falling to the archery targets off to the far end of the courtyard, standing like sentinels keeping watch over Nell as she trained. It was quiet here, the only discernible sounds aside from Nell's wooden practice sword cracking against the striking post being the rustling of leaves across stone as they tumbled in the wind and the slow chirp of a few distant crickets.

Other than a few patches of camellias and primroses, most of the garden was dead, shriveled up by the cold of the winter months. Even still, shrouded in the moonlight, it felt like a place untouched by the cruelty of the world beyond the courtyard doors, and he understood why this was where Nell fled to when she felt troubled.

After several moments of silence, George chanced a glance at Nell then asked, "What keeps you from sleep tonight?"

Nell held her eyes to the garden. "I think you know," she said with a sniff, her voice wavering at the end.

"I imagine I do," he said. "But keeping it to yourself only makes the burden more stifling to bear. Let me bear it with you."

She took a deep breath before finally saying, "It's going to take us too long to get to Ravenhold. She will be long gone from the capital by then."

George turned to face her. "Maybe," he said. "But it will just be you and me traveling. We will be able to cover the distance more quickly. In favorable conditions, I think we have a good chance of making it there by the evening of our third day."

She shook her head. "That's still too late."

He stepped forward, finally giving in to the need to touch her, and took her hand. "Remember what Aria said: if Raygon found out she was in the capital, Marius had to have found out as well." He tugged her to face him. She obliged but kept her eyes trained on the ground. "I feel confident that he's doing whatever he can to help." His words echoed what they'd discussed in the king's study earlier that day.

Nell nodded. "I know, but," she paused, taking in a steadying breath. "Aria shared what she endured at Raygon's hand. And now that he has Ophelia, the fact that he hasn't killed her yet hasn't brought me any comfort because we don't know what terrible things he could be doing to her, or what state she will be in if we do find her."

She sucked in another deep breath, and the pain in her voice called to the answering anguish in him. He took a step towards her, opening his arms to her, and she stepped right into his embrace, wrapping her arms around his waist and resting her head to his chest.

He closed his arms around her and swallowed down the sigh of contentment trying to push its way up from his lungs. She felt so right in his arms, even if she was only there because she was hurting.

After a while, George finally leaned his head down and rested his cheek atop her head. "We'll find her, Nell. And we'll bring her and Elliot home."

She pulled back to meet his gaze.

"You can't know that," she said before taking in another breath and looking skyward—he realized—to hold back the tears that threatened to spill from her eyes.

"Oh, Sweetheart," he breathed, raising his index finger to her chin to gently pull her gaze down to his. She closed her eyes, and he took her face in his hand, gently brushing his thumb along her cheek. "Don't hide your tears from me."

She opened her eyes, and George's heart tripped. The utter devastation churning in her honey brown eyes tore his heart in two and stole his breath; he'd never seen grief hold such beauty.

Her face crumpled. And as though she'd finally been given the permission to be as broken on the outside as she felt within, Nell buried her face into George's chest and wept.

Nell was the first to arrive at the stables the next morning. She lit an oil lamp from the torch by the entrance then headed right to her horse's stall and got to work saddling her.

There would be no sendoff party for them like they'd done for Elliot and Ophelia when they left for Balmorea, and Nell preferred it that way. She and George would be able to get out on the road more quickly without a huddle of well-wishers in their way. Time was not on their side, and they couldn't waste what little of it they did have.

Soon after, George stepped through the door of the stables, a delectable smell following him inside.

"I promise not to use words with more than three syllables," he announced as he walked to Poppy's stall and handed Nell a steaming tankard of—

Her jaw dropped.

"Is this coffee?" she asked, eagerly taking the tankard from George and hazarding a careful sip of the hot liquid. A playful smile split George's face.

"Just want to make sure you are prepared for my vague sexual advances as we travel."

Nell spat out her coffee with a laugh, and George frowned.

"You're meant to drink it, not bathe poor Poppy in it," he teased, taking a sip from his own tankard.

Nell rolled her eyes, not missing the small quirk in George's lips. "You know, I really wasn't sure."

George tapped his cup to hers with a smile. "Always glad to help," he said before sidling down the row to begin saddling his horse.

She rolled her eyes again with a huffed laugh then took another sip before setting her tankard down to finish loading her horse. Her brows bent as she worked, not sure what to make of George's chipper demeanor. After the heavy day they'd had yesterday, and after their moments outside her chambers and on the training grounds, she hadn't been sure what to expect from George this morning. But arriving with coffee and spouting jokes hadn't been it.

And just the thought of you being taken from me like Ophelia was taken from Elliot steals the fucking breath from my lungs.

The intensity of his words still stunned her and made her heart flip. She knew he hadn't said them flippantly, yet he seemed so unbothered this morning. She bit the inside of her cheek. George was worried but didn't want her to see it.

"You ready to ride?" George called about twenty minutes later as he led his horse from his stall.

Nell sighed. "I haven't had enough coffee for your jokes yet, George."

George chuckled, levelling a crooked grin on her. "I was talking about mounting our horses and getting on the road, but if you had another type of riding in mind before we set out, Sweetheart, I wouldn't be opposed."

Nell's cheeks heated, and she inwardly kicked herself for playing right into his hand. "Earth and Sea, George, the sun isn't even up yet," she mumbled.

George's laughter floated to her from the stable entrance. "Finish your coffee, then meet me outside. We need to get going."

She knocked back the last dregs of her coffee and grabbed Poppy's reins. "Coming!"

George barked a laugh. "But, Lady Nell, the sun isn't even up yet."

Nell groaned at his response but couldn't help the smile that spread across her face as she shook her head and led Poppy out of the stables and into the chilly morning.

CHAPTER FORTY FOUR

OPHELIA SQUINTED AGAINST THE BRIGHT AFTER-
noon sunlight pouring into the Central Valley. She shielded
her eyes with her hand as she scanned the area, noting
how the meadow's usual lush pastureland had faded into a
brittle brown sward and how the branches of the bare trees
beyond stretched from their trunks like scraggly fingers.
The sky was clear, and the air held a slight chill that cooled
her skin, though it didn't reach her bones.

She closed her eyes as she inhaled deeply, the relief for
the reprieve from her living nightmare washing over her.
No tangle of fear or anxiousness twisted in her chest, and
no hunger gnawed at her stomach. Her lungs expanded
fully, and her muscles carried no ache.

She opened her eyes as she released her breath, and Mira
stood before her.

Silver hair framed her angular face, streaming over
her cloaked shoulders. Piercing blue eyes settled on her in

a patient, gentle gaze. And as though sensing the Essence within her steadying, Mira's lips tipped up into a warm smile. "Hello, Ophelia."

"Mira," Ophelia said, a smile spreading on her face as well. It was Mira, Ophelia realized, who was calming her. The Vilicus's soothing nature washed over her like the waves of the sea washing upon the shore, smoothing out her disquiet. "It's good to see you."

Mira closed the distance between them and embraced her. Surprise skittered through Ophelia before she returned the Sea Vilicus's embrace.

A moment later, Mira pulled back, resting her hands atop Ophelia's shoulders. "It is good to see you as well, though it seems we are meeting under unfavorable circumstances yet again."

The reminder of all that had happened shot a bolt of panic through her. "Ezra was able to reach you too, then?"

Mira shook her head. "It was Pyotr. We are keeping watch over your good man and his companions as closely as the balance will allow."

"Elliot's all right? He's safe?" She'd known Marius had gotten him out of the Wolf's Den, but any number of things could have happened to him between then and now.

Mira gave another nod. "They work to free you."

"They?"

"Yes," she said, her lips lilting up in a small smile. "He travels with a group."

A group? Was Marius helping him, then? Ophelia swallowed down the grateful sob that climbed her throat, taken aback momentarily by the realization that she hadn't been entirely certain they would try to come for her.

"And do you know where they're taking me, Mira?" she asked, hoping her suspicions were wrong.

Mira gave her a sad smile, having heard her thoughts through their connection. "East."

Ophelia's stomach dropped. A group of Reapers heading east during a full moon with a wagon of prisoners. Raygon's words rang in her mind.

There are much more...productive ways to spill your blood than for tawdry rituals.

Alarm rang through her, but she tamped it down, taking a deep breath and releasing it.

"Well," Ophelia said, "I came all this way to see the Aegis, right?" This wasn't how she'd wanted to get there, by any stretch of the imagination, but there wasn't anything she could do about that at the moment.

Mira winced. "Yes, but not in a cage. Not with your Conexus bound."

Ophelia's brow sank. "Is that what their magic is doing?"

Something akin to anger flashed in Mira's eyes. "Yes," she said. "They've taken your blood, and the Essence within it, and used it to clip your wings."

Ophelia sighed, rubbing her fingers across her brows. "Any ideas on how to release it?"

Mira's lip curled. "No. Pyotr and I have never encountered such vile magic before," she replied. "And just like with the Aegis, our magic won't have any effect on it."

"Why is that, do you think?"

Mira pursed her lips. "We think it has to do with the type of magic used to create it. The blood of man was used to erect it and to bind your magic. And since mankind is neither my nor Pyotr's realm…" She waved a hand around vaguely in front of her.

"Balance and boundaries," Ophelia replied, and Mira nodded. "Then I suppose I'm stuck in the shackles for now."

Mira's forehead creased. "The spell binding you is weaved in blood smeared on your shackles, remove it and you remove the binding. Then you should be able to use your magic to open the shackles."

Ophelia shook her head. "I doubt simply washing off the blood will do the trick. It's bound with Blood Magic. I likely need a blood mage to undo it."

Mira nodded. "You need magic to undo magic."

Ophelia released another sigh. "Know any blood mages up to the task?"

Mira's lip turned down in disgust. "Of course not. Why would I know any of those vile creatures?"

Ophelia huffed a laugh. "Right." Ophelia turned to face the mountains, crossing her arms over her chest. "What do I do, Mira?"

Mira stepped next to her and sighed. "I'm going to send a storm that will hopefully make travel move a bit slower for your captors." She shrugged. "Until those shackles are off, you won't have access to your magic, and if no blood mage will undo the spell on them, you will have to find a way to get them off."

It wasn't a solution, or even a next step to take, but it was all she could do—sit and wait and scheme.

Ophelia sighed. "Very well, then." She turned to face Mira. "Thank you—"

But Mira was no longer there.

A clap of thunder jolted Ophelia out of sleep. Judging by what she could make out of the startled expressions on the others' faces, they'd been jolted awake as well.

"And now it's raining?" Lyall whined from across her in Balmorean.

Ophelia wanted to explain to them that it was Mira who'd sent the storm to delay their journey, but the family hadn't been too receptive the previous day when she'd explained to them who she was and why Raygon had arrested her. Or rather, captured her.

She'd answered their questions as best she could without giving too much information, sharing with them a similar explanation to the one she and Elliot gave Ambrose and Dominicio mere days ago. She left out the parts about the Silent Reapings, and about how she believed Raygon was sacrificing his own people to sustain a magical barrier far in the east, but she did tell them she was in Balmorea investigating strange magic.

They'd peered back at her with wide, leery eyes, likely thinking her mad. And without her magic to prove her claims, she hadn't blamed them.

Mira's rain pelted the wagon as they continued on; the sound was more reminiscent of a shower of river pebbles than drops of water.

The storm never let up as they travelled, but Ophelia didn't feel like it was slowing them down all that much, if at all. Not that she could actually see how quickly they were moving with the shutters closed over the wagon's barred windows.

Ophelia worried her bottom lip. If the rain wasn't slowing them down, then they'd likely arrive at the Aegis sooner than she'd hoped, and Elliot and Marius might not be able to catch up to them. If they couldn't make it to her, she'd have to figure out a way to free herself and this innocent family on her own.

She needed her magic but knew there was absolutely nothing she could say or do that could convince the Reapers to unshackle her. She'd slipped through their hands once in Maraleon. They wouldn't risk underestimating her again.

Ophelia rested her head back against the wall of the wagon. Her stomach chose that moment to give an unearthly growl, and she winced. A loaf of stale bread had been tossed through the bars to them sometime the previous day, and they hadn't been given anything else since. She was almost frustrated that the shutters were closed because it kept them from being able to get any water to drink, though she didn't lament being dry and warm.

If they're taking us to our deaths, there isn't much reason to make sure we're well fed, the dark thought crept in, and not for the first time did Ophelia consider that the Reapers were intentionally keeping them weakened so they wouldn't have the strength to try to escape, or fight back against the fate intended for them.

The wagon jolted to an abrupt stop, and a flurry of curses rose from the front of the wagon. Ophelia would have thought it funny had she not been so relieved that Mira's storm had finally proven useful.

Ophelia heard mumbles from across the carriage, but the rain pelting against the wagon was too loud for her to hear what was being said.

"It sounds like the wagon is stuck," Evren finally said loud enough for her to hear.

She nodded, though, she doubted any of them could see her in the dark. "I think so. What else are they saying?"

Evren paused, seeming to listen to the chatter beyond the walls of the wagon, probably straining to hear what their captors were saying over the pounding rain.

"Something about being close enough to a village," he said.

Lyall groaned. "They are not making us walk in the rain, no?"

"It wouldn't surprise me," Ophelia mumbled, but uncertainty twisted in her gut. It didn't make sense for them to travel through a village, no matter how remote it was. Everything the Reapers did was covert—their very existence was one of Balmorea's most heavily-guarded secrets aside from the Aegis itself. If Raygon wanted to keep it that way, avoiding witnesses was a much easier and efficient way to do that than trying to mitigate rumors and gossip.

Evren shifted where he sat, his shackles clinking lightly with the movement. "They said the storm has delayed them too long. Tomorrow night is the last night of the full moon, and they still need a few more?" The upturn in his voice gave away his confusion. "A few more what?"

Ophelia blanched when he mentioned the full moon, and the pieces began to slide together in her mind: Reapers, remote village in the east, full moon.

Their captors weren't planning on passing through the village for supplies and a warm bed for the night.

They were going to the village to reap more sacrifices.

Chapter Forty Five

It had been at least a few hours since it had stopped raining, but the wagon hadn't moved. Why were they just sitting there? How much longer would they be cooped up here?

Dread hung in the stuffy air of the wagon, and Ophelia's chest tightened with anxious anticipation. She had until tomorrow night to figure out some way to get out of there or else all of them were going to die.

The slosh of muddy footfalls sounded from the front of the wagon to the back, drawing Ophelia's attention. The whispers began again, and Ophelia's stomach roiled, her painfully empty stomach only compounding the sensation.

The lock clicked and the doors swung wide, revealing six Reapers standing at the mouth of the wagon.

Ophelia frowned. There were more of them now, not just the two that had left Ravenhold with them. Is that why they'd waited so long? To meet up with the others?

Shit. She'd barely survived a fight against one Reaper, and that had been with her magic. Two Reapers hadn't seemed too daunting if she could've found a way to access her magic again, and even that had been incredibly optimistic. But six Reapers?

Hope drained from her heart like water from a cracked vase.

If she wouldn't be able to fight any of them off, the only chance their group might have of escaping was during the Silent Reaping while the Reapers were occupied with collecting their sacrifices. Her lip curled at the thought, and she doubted they would simply leave their prisoners unattended, but they would have better odds of being able to run with fewer Reapers guarding them.

Ophelia's stomach turned sour at the thought of running, and a sense of intense protectiveness coursed through her in protest. The people of this little village were part of her realm. She couldn't leave them at the mercy of the Reapers.

Maybe she could distract the Reapers so Evren and his family could run free, but would Allerick and Elowen be able to keep up with the others if given the chance to escape?

She didn't have time to think it through before she was tugged out of the wagon and her shackles were fastened to a chain linking all the prisoners together. A heartbeat later, the Reapers began dragging them forward in the direction the wagon was facing, simply leaving it behind.

Night had fallen, but the full moon shone brightly above them, illuminating the road well enough that the Reapers steered them into the cover of the trees lining the road. Two Reapers led from the front, riding the horses that had pulled the prison wagon, two took up the rear, and the last two traveled on either side of their miserable little line.

At least she was finally getting to stretch her legs after two days inside that infernal wagon. The late winter air was crisp and cool, and she drank it in; it was a welcome reprieve from the stale, humid air inside the wagon.

Ophelia sighed and let her eyes rove over her surroundings as they walked. She'd only seen this forest in her dream with Pyotr when he first showed her the Aegis all those weeks ago, and it seemed so different now, draped in darkness and moonlight.

She looked more closely into the wood, hoping to catch a glimpse of Elliot or Marius sidling parallel to their group and searching for an opening to snatch her away.

But all she could see was darkness, and all she heard were the footsteps of her and her fellow prisoners as they trudged through the foliage littering the tree line.

Mira told her in her dream that Elliot and Marius were working to rescue her. Had she been wrong? Had something happened to them? Had they even come for her at all? She worried her bottom lip as she thought, and their journey on foot seemed to stretch on and on. Her earlier relief at being able to stretch her legs began to fade as the ache in her thighs radiated down into her shins and ankles. The rain-soaked earth made it feel more like she was walking through sand than a forest in eastern Balmorea.

Ophelia was on the verge of collapse when the Reapers finally brought the group to a stop at the edge of a quaint village.

A few dozen cottages dotted the road while others squatted closer to the wood. Smoke drifted from several homes whose windows glowed with firelight, and lanterns lit the central path into the village to light the way for anyone wandering out past dark.

Ophelia let herself imagine what life might be like for those living in this sleepy little village when her attention was drawn back to her captors.

All but one of the Reapers were gathered into a group, distributing what looked like metal spheres about the size of an apple. Once each Reaper had a sphere, they quickly swept into the village.

All thought of her plan to find a way to free Evren and his family slipped from Ophelia's mind as the Reaper nearest her rolled her sphere along the main path into the village. The Reaper began singing her song of whispers as she followed after the sphere, and a mist floated from it as it rolled.

Ophelia's eyes widened as the mist thickened into a fog that began to spread over the ground, splitting off and diverging along the many footpaths worn into the dirt. The Reaper's whispers stopped, but the fog didn't. It climbed the walls of homes, dipped under cracked windows and slid through gaps in doorways. No place was left untouched by the fog as it sought and searched—as it *hunted*.

Ophelia expected to hear the sounds of panic the more the fog pervaded the meager dwellings. She waited for the villagers to pour out of their homes in a frenzy to escape the encroaching mist only to find they'd jumped from the frying pan into the fire.

But the screams and shouts never came.

No noise came from within the village or from the wood beyond. Silence hung over the place as though the haze had sucked all the sound from the air, leaving only the portrait of a sleepy, picturesque village carefully set against a blanket of fog.

Ophelia held her breath, transfixed as the mist began to billow and fill the empty spaces between the homes, rising higher and higher until, finally, the homes and outhouses and barns were enveloped entirely.

Everything was so still.

No breeze drifted through the boughs of the trees. No creaks rose from aged, wooden planks, and no squeaks sounded from doors swinging on rusted hinges. Life seemed to stand completely still.

After several agonizing minutes, Ophelia heard footfalls approaching them from within the village.

Four of the Reapers reappeared, each holding a body—a person. A collective gasp came from the group of prisoners, and a whimper of horror escaped Vanya. Ophelia felt the blood drain from her face.

Dom and Ambrose were right.

A sudden flash of rage burned through her, and she clenched her jaw against it. She knew the people held by each Reaper weren't dead, not yet, but they were the ones chosen by Raygon's beloved assassins to be some of the next ones to give their lives for his magical barrier. How could they do this? How could they choose their fellow countrymen—the citizens their king is supposed to serve and protect—for such a gruesome fate?

Ophelia stepped forward without another thought.

"Take them back! You have no right to do this!" she shouted, and every head snapped to her. "These people are innocent!"

Pain burst across her temple and her vision flashed white as her head flew to the side.

"*Quiet*," one of the Reapers hissed before shoving her back in line with the others. Ophelia raised a hand to her temple and winced. Blood came away on her fingers.

She looked up. "I thought there were more productive ways to spill my blood. Best not tell His Majesty you wasted any before even making it to the Aegis with your precious sacrifices."

The Reaper rounded on her, grabbing her by the neck and yanking her down to eye-level. Bottomless black eyes bore into her. "Who told you of the Aegis?" she hissed.

A venomous smirk tilted Ophelia's lips. "Pyotr sends his regards."

The Reaper's lip curled. "Enough!" she growled before shoving Ophelia back. The world spun, and Ophelia lost her balance, knocking into Lyall. He caught her and helped steady her on her feet.

"Thank you," she breathed before standing upright and taking a deep breath of the cool night air.

"Are you all right?" he asked, gesturing to the cut at her eyebrow. "You are hurt."

Ophelia nodded and waved him away. "I'm fine."

The Reaper who'd hit her barked an order to one of the others, but Ophelia didn't catch what she said.

Lyall never dropped his gaze from Ophelia. A deep crease formed between his brows, and she sensed he wasn't only worried about her injury.

"Those word you say. Before," he started. "What you mean 'sacrifices?'"

Before Ophelia could answer, one of the Reapers shoved a cloth in her mouth and tied it around the back of her head. She growled in frustration.

Fantastic.

A few minutes later, the fifth Reaper finally appeared, sitting atop a cart drawn by two horses. She came to a stop next to the group of prisoners, and they were herded into the back of the cart. A man in night clothes was already in the cart lying on his back. His eyes were closed, and he didn't have any injuries. He simply appeared to be asleep, and the sight prodded at something else Dom had shared with her when he told her of the Silent Reapings. The fog either made you fall unconscious or hallucinate, but in every case, it incapacitated those who encountered it.

The man was incapacitated. Alive, but only so he could be killed later.

Ophelia's nostrils flared as she climbed into the cart and sat down next to Lyall. Evren met her eyes across from her, his expression tense and stony.

"Sacrifices," he said, an echo of Lyall's same question from before. She closed her eyes and sighed. Her chest held such a weight, and she wished like never before that she could give him and his sweet family any other answer than the one that was true. *They deserved so much better than this.*

She opened her eyes and gave him a small nod.

Evren's hand tightened in Vanya's as she laid her head on his shoulder and started to cry. Vanya didn't need to speak Leonese to understand what Ophelia had confirmed to her husband, and the weight in her chest grew oppressively heavier.

Ophelia's attention was pulled to the back of the cart where the other four Reapers deposited the bodies they'd collected like sacks of potatoes, each one already bound with a pair of iron shackles.

She bit into her gag, anger reigniting in her veins only to be quelled by an overwhelming sense of helplessness. Her people were being led to the slaughter, and she was powerless to prevent it.

The cart jolted forward, and the group continued on their journey toward the Aegis. Two Reapers rode at the head of the cart while the remaining four split themselves among the two horses that had drawn their prison wagon from Ravenhold.

Ophelia watched as the village shrouded in eerie fog grew smaller and smaller behind them. When it disappeared from view, her eyes fell to the two men and three women that now joined their party. Who were they? What positions did they hold in the village? Did they have large families? Small families? Or were they, perhaps, just beginning to build their own families, like Evren and Vanya? Like her and Elliot?

She let her head fall back against the side of the cart as the pressure behind her eyes began to build. She was so tired. Tired of bearing the burden of dangerous secrets. Tired of bearing the deaths of innocent lives taken for a corrupt man's gain.

She wished Elliot was with her. She wished she was back home getting married and riding Blaze through the wood with Nell. Wished her sister hadn't been tortured and separated from the man she loved. She wished she could get out of these damn shackles and actually do something to help these people.

Ophelia closed her eyes to the stars above and wished so many things as her silent tears fell.

Chapter Forty Six

ELLIOT WAS SURPRISED TO FIND THAT. AFTER TWO whole days of chasing Ophelia's prison transport across eastern Balmorea, Dax had not run out of things to prattle on about.

Or complain about, in tonight's case.

"The son of a bitch swooped right in and snatched her from me while I went to take a piss!" Dax groused as the group sat around the fire after a meager dinner.

Hayes leveled Dax with a flat stare.

"I fucking swear it!" Dax protested. "I'd been sweet talking her all night, and she was giving me those 'fuck me' eyes." He motioned with two fingers between his and Hayes's eyes. "I was about to invite her up to my room—"

"But you had to take a piss," Hayes finished with an eye roll.

Dax was undeterred. "—but I had to take a piss! Very impolite to piss on someone when you're trying to gain carnal knowledge of them—absolutely kills the mood—"

"Earth and Sea, Dax, please tell me you don't know that

from experience," Melina groaned as she sat between Hayes's legs and leaned against his chest.

Dax balked, his hand flying to his chest. "You wound me with such an accusation, dear Melina."

A clap on the shoulder pulled Elliot from the conversation. "Lost in thought?" Marius asked as he took a seat on the ground next to Elliot.

"More often than not these days." He nodded toward the others. "Though Dax and his distinct variety of absurdity always seem to lighten the mood."

Marius laughed. "Depends on who you ask."

That seemed to be true. Dax's ramblings may have given his mind a reprieve from its worries, but Hayes and Melina hardly seemed as amused.

"We'll find her," Marius said with a confidence Elliot desperately wanted to believe. "We're getting close. We should catch up to them by tomorrow."

Elliot nodded his agreement. When their group first set out, they had a difficult time determining which route the transport had taken after leaving Ravenhold, which had delayed them. Blessedly, a heavy rainstorm had swept through the area ahead of them, and, with any luck, hopefully caused a delay for a prisoner transport as large as Ophelia's.

That's the hope he was clinging to, anyway.

"His hands were up her skirts, and his tongue was down her throat when I came back from the pisser, Hayes!" Dax bellowed, the tendons in his neck straining. "I'd hardly say I misunderstood what was happening between them!"

Melina's head fell back on a laugh as Hayes raised his hands in surrender, ducking his head to hide his smile. *Maybe they were amused after all.*

Marius let out a low whistle. "Still lamenting your blunder with Sadie the other night, are we, Dax?"

Dax leveled a finger at Marius. "None of that, Princeling! You know Brosey's the one in the wrong here."

Marius raised a brow. "Do I? I was under the impression that this was some sort of sport you and Ambrose played against each other."

Dax waggled his eyebrows. "A sport I excel at far more than Ambrose."

Everyone around the fire rolled their eyes.

"Only because Ambrose is actually productive with his life when he's not working for the prince," Hayes said, shaking his head.

"I have no time to take up such diversions as a *trade* like Ambrose," Dax argued. "My skills in stealthy reconnaissance and my prowess with a sword are more than enough to keep me productive at all times of day—not just in my free time." Dax winked, and groans rose around the campsite.

"Stop talking about your dick in polite conversation!" Melina said, tossing a rock at him.

Dax swatted away the rock, shit-eating grin firmly set on his face. "When you all find things more interesting to talk about than my dick, I will stop finding ways to insert it into our conversations."

Marius, Hayes, and Melina shoved, smacked, or kicked him, but all Dax did was cackle in response.

Elliot shook his head, and a laugh rumbled from his chest. He'd seen a glimpse of Marius's casual air with his Shadows when they'd all met in his office at The Jade Raven, but he hadn't expected *this* at all.

Marius met Elliot's gaze. "What? Never kicked someone for making too many dick jokes before?"

Elliot chuckled. "I have, just never with the crown prince of my country."

Marius tilted his head from side to side. "That's fair. I haven't met my brother-in-law, but Aria made him out to seem rather stuffy."

Elliot pressed his lips together to hold in his laugh at the expense of his future king. "That's one way to put it." Earth and Sea knew he couldn't imagine Prince Gregor ever making a dick joke. "I'm more curious to know how you came to be so un-stuffy," Elliot said. "Why create your Shadows? Why be the Wraith? Surely the king has his own spy network that will pass to you one day."

The amusement fell from Marius's expression, and the liveliness around the fire dimmed. Elliot thought he had crossed a line with one of his questions, but before he could backtrack with an apology, Marius replied.

"The king does have a spy network," he said with a nod, picking up a leaf from the ground and beginning to tear it into pieces, "but he does not see fit to teach me of its structure, who it involves, or how it functions, nor does he see fit to include me in meetings with his council or advise me on the inner workings of the court. And he refuses to give me any responsibilities of import."

"Really?" Elliot frowned. "Why?"

Marius shook his head with a mirthless laugh. "Perhaps he finds me lacking and doesn't trust me to make sound choices. Perhaps his thirst for power is so great that even the thought of surrendering the smallest fragment of it offends him." The prince released a weary sigh, tossing the shredded remains of the leaf into the fire. "He has not made his reasons known to me, and after years of asking to be included on matters of state—and after years of being turned away each time—I concluded that if I was going to understand the workings of my own country and its people, I would have to do so on my own."

Marius picked up another leaf to shred and continued. "I started working alone at first and soon discovered the state in which many of our people lived. I did what I could—when I could—for those in dire circumstances as a result of the crown's negligence. Word of what I was doing spread, and, eventually, Dom and Ambrose tracked me down to recruit me." A smile tipped his lips up. "They both almost shit themselves when they learned who I was."

Dax chuckled while Hayes and Melina gave small smiles.

"We began building up our ranks from there, and now, here we are." He held out a hand, gesturing to their small company.

"A merry band of traitors," Dax supplied.

Hayes raised a brow. "Revolutionaries."

"Something like that." Marius paused, taking a breath as he gazed into the flames. "When I ascend the throne, I want to know my people and their needs and concerns. I want to know the beating heart of my country and understand her from within and without. I see the disconnect between Raygon and the people, and it's caused needless hardship and pain." The prince's eyes, hardened with grim determination, rose to meet his. "I want to see Balmorea flourish, and I want to bring my wife home, but neither of those can happen so long as Raygon sits on the throne."

Silence hung heavily over their campsite. No remarks of dissent with the prince's words came from his Shadows, and Dax didn't seek to fill the space with a pithy comment. Marius's declaration had tightened the air like a bowstring.

If what he said was true, each person around this fire had suffered at Raygon's hand in some way or another—had watched as their friends and loved ones endured the same suffering. But Raygon's cruelty hadn't stopped at the Lupos. It seeped through the range, creeping all the way into the heart of Maraleon like the disease it was, and nearly took Ophelia's life. Aria's too.

No. Elliot held no love for the king of Balmorea, and he couldn't deny that his feelings and Marius's seemed to align.

Four sets of eyes stared at him as he took in everything Marius had said, and the stark understanding of just how entangled he and Ophelia had become in Balmorea's bloody secrets sank into his bones. He leaned back on his hands and released a heavy sigh. "Well, I suppose there will be no getting rid of you all after this," he said, and a chorus of hesitant chuckles rumbled around the fire.

Elliot sobered as he considered how Ophelia's plans fit into all of this, and he frowned. "Ophelia will want to help. Her duty is to steward mankind—to protect her realm from those like Raygon who pursue their own endeavors with no regard to those they harm along the way. She will want to deal with the Aegis first, but," he paused, pursing his lips in thought, "I suspect Raygon's abuse of his power and his obsession with protecting the Aegis aren't mutually exclusive issues, and I fear bringing down the barrier will resolve one problem only to inflame another."

A feral smile crept across Marius's face. "Then let's set it all ablaze."

Chapter Forty Seven

They were not as close to the Aegis as Ophelia had thought they were. When she woke up late the following morning, their group was still traveling. The terrain seemed similar to what she'd seen last night—dense forest lining a dirt road—but she struggled to grasp any details. Every time she lifted her head to look around, the world tilted and spun, likely from the strike to the head she took from one of the Reapers the night before. She was probably concussed.

The rest of her seemed to be falling apart as well. Her throat was dry and sore, her jaw ached from the protrusive gag in her mouth, and her stomach felt like it was going to cave in on itself from hunger.

She knew she needed to wake up, take stock of her surroundings, check in on the others—especially the new prisoners from the Reaping—but she couldn't muster the strength.

She thought she heard Evren's voice speaking to a few of the newer prisoners, and relief flooded her. It was probably better for Evren and Lyall to speak with them since her Balmorean wasn't very strong, but a pang of guilt pierced her. She was responsible for these people; she should be the one reassuring them, comforting them, figuring out a way to get them out of this.

In a minute, she told herself before resting her forehead to her knees. *Just another minute, and then I'll talk with them.*

When she next lifted her head, though, the sun was leaning toward twilight. Her gag had been removed but remained looped around her neck. She grabbed it between her fingers and frowned.

"It stupid," Lyall said, drawing her attention. "I take from your mouth for you can breathe."

She forced a smile in return. "Thank you."

Ophelia hadn't realized she'd fallen back asleep until the rush of a river roused her awake.

River?

The Far East River.

Every one of her senses sharpened. She sat up straight, ignoring the pounding in her head, and looked around. The sun was close to dipping below the horizon, and they were still surrounded by dense forest, but a riverbank and bridge had come into view.

Shit.

They were almost there—they were almost to the Aegis.

Seeing her reaction, Evren and Lyall also straightened, brows bent over their eyes.

"What is it?" Evren asked.

Ophelia met his gaze. "We're close."

The color drained from his face, and he pulled Vanya tighter into his side as Lyall shoved worried fingers through his hair.

"How much longer?" Evren asked.

Ophelia strained to remember how long it had taken her and Pyotr to walk to the Aegis from the river, but she couldn't tell for sure. Time flows so differently in dreams. She squinted her eyes toward the wood across the river. "Maybe half an hour once we cross the river?"

"Is this the Far East River?" Lyall asked, his eyes wide with fear.

Ophelia nodded.

Lyall's gaze snapped to Evren, and he muttered something in Balmorean that she didn't quite hear, but she did catch the word *plenekimalin*.

"They don't exist," she said. Lyall and Evren snapped their gazes to her. "The creatures—the *plenekimalin*. There are no monsters on the other side of the river."

The brothers frowned. "Have you been out here before?"
No? Yes?

"A good friend of mine has." Not a lie. Pyotr showed her what he'd seen when he'd found the Aegis, and he'd seen no beasts. "He said there's nothing over here. No game of any kind. No birds or insects. No monsters."

Lyall pursed his lips, and Evren gave her a sharp nod. They didn't believe her. In any other circumstance, Ophelia would think them smart to be cautious, but now their doubt just annoyed her. They believed her about the Aegis and the Reapers, but telling them that she had magic and that giant, winged, man-eating beasts don't exist was where they drew the line?

They crossed the bridge, and Ophelia winced in preparation for the repulsion. She knew it wouldn't hit right away but wasn't quite sure how far into the wood they'd need to travel before it did.

The Reapers stopped the cart just beyond the bridge on the eastern side of the river. One of the Reapers opened a pouch fastened at her belt and pulled out what looked like several circular, silver pendants with red crystals in the center. She looped one around her neck then distributed the rest of the medallions to the others. She hopped back up into the front of the cart, and they continued forward.

About five minutes later, Ophelia felt the uneasiness begin to churn in her chest. She clenched her fists and noticed that Vanya and Elowen's breathing had begun to quicken. Evren's eyes darted around them as though sensing danger, and Lyall clutched his stomach.

"Stop! Please, stop!" one of the new prisoners shouted in Balmorean. "We can't go this way!"

They were breathing raggedly, too. One of the women had begun crying, and both of the men clutched at their chests. The Reapers didn't acknowledge their pleas. *They must be used to the cries of discomfort from their victims.*

Her lip curled at the thought when she realized none of the Reapers seemed to be affected by their proximity to the Aegis. They looked straight ahead, almost bored.

That must be what the medallions were for.

The repulsion grew more intense the closer they traveled to the Aegis. Ophelia's heart thrashed, and her stomach churned. The throbbing in her head grew stronger and stronger until it exploded into the searing pain she remembered. She clutched her head in her hands and cried out at the pain. Sobs and screams began to ring out in the cart as Ophelia clawed through her memories to remember what Pyotr had told her to do the last time she experienced this.

Inhale. Hold. Exhale.

She focused on her breathing. She put the screams and cries of the others out of her mind. She set aside her own pain and discomfort and imagined the air filling her lungs then spilling from her lips.

She did it again and again—as many times as she needed before logic finally took control of her body back from its primal instincts.

Evren seemed to catch on because he quieted, then Lyall and Vanya did the same. Elowen struggled to calm, and a man and woman from among the villagers fell completely to panic. They were unreachable, completely consumed by their fear.

Several minutes later, they came to a stop, and Ophelia's stomach plummeted.

She was about to die.

The Reapers pulled the prisoners from the cart, one-by-one. It took two Reapers each to subdue the man and woman whose panic had exploded. They thrashed and flailed, screaming about how they all needed to run.

One of the Reapers pulled a dagger from her belt and sliced along each of their arms, before licking the blade clean.

Ophelia's eyes widened in horror, and several gasps sounded from behind her. This couldn't be—she didn't actually…

The Reaper began singing one of her whisper songs, and the man and woman stilled. They no longer thrashed or screamed or tried to run away, but the anguish still remained on their faces.

The Essence within Ophelia roared at the horrendous breach of will, and for the first time in days, her Conexus thrashed against its bonds in response. Tight relief flashed through her at the feeling of her magic, but it was like trying to take a full breath in a tight corset; she could sense her magic writhe within her, could brush the fingertips of her will against its edges, but couldn't take hold of it.

The Reapers connected the villagers to the chain connecting Ophelia with Evren and his family then pulled them further into the wood.

"Focus on your breathing," Ophelia reminded, and Evren relayed her message in Balmorean.

Ophelia's gaze didn't wander as they walked. She didn't need to look to know she would simply find an abandoned wood vacant of life. She held her eyes forward, searching for what she'd come all this way to lay her own eyes on.

The group walked another couple dozen paces before stepping past the tree line into a small clearing. Ophelia sucked in a breath as she took in the sight before her.

Twenty yards ahead of her, the clearing abruptly ended in a familiar, translucent, gray curtain that stretched high into the clouds. The Aegis looked just as it had in her dream, flowing and shimmering in a nonexistent breeze. And there was no sound, just like in her dream and the night before in the village—as though sound itself fled from the vile magic.

One by one, the Reapers removed the prisoners from the chain and fastened them to one of a dozen or so posts set into the ground in front of the barrier. Ophelia hadn't noticed the posts before, and when she slid her focus to them, her heart kicked in her chest.

They were, essentially, posts one would tie off a horse to, but much shorter…and covered in countless layers of dried blood.

How many people had died here? How many people spent their final breaths of life fastened to a wooden post like livestock?

The thought enraged the Essence within her, and she all but heard the Conexus snarling in her chest. The energy around her buzzed.

If any of the Reapers sensed the magic warring within and around her, they didn't seem to be concerned by it. The six of them shuffled back and forth between the prisoners and the posts, methodically unfastening their prisoners from the chain and quickly refastening them to the posts—motions that had become familiar and practiced, like a cook chopping an onion or a stablehand saddling a horse.

Ophelia was unfastened from the chain and dragged to her post. Her blood rushed in her ears, and her vision narrowed to the post before her. To the place where she would breathe her last breath. The post and the murky, gray barrier would be the last things she would see before her soul slipped beyond, and the realization turned her blood to ice. Her heart mourned the future she was denied. Her Essence lamented the realm she would abandon.

The Reapers began to sing their whispers, and Ophelia stiffened. She lifted her eyes and looked on either side of her, watching as the Reapers approached their first six sacrifices, daggers in hand.

One slid behind Ophelia, the Reaper's whispers grating across her skin like jagged nails, causing her stomach to roil.

Ophelia felt the Reaper's hands stretch around her. One sallow, bony hand gripped her jaw and tilted her head back, while the other raised a dagger to her neck.

Panic tore through her, and she jerked her chin from the Reaper's hold, kicking her head back as hard as she could.

Her skull didn't connect with anything, but pain like lightning shot through her head with the movement. Her knees weakened, and the Reaper took the opening to clutch Ophelia more tightly before yanking her head back.

The Reaper's whispers continued as a wet gurgle sounded at the post next to her, and she continued to buck against the Reaper's hold. This couldn't happen. She couldn't die here. She kicked her heel into the shin of the Reaper, but the woman didn't budge, only tightening her crushing grip on Ophelia and continuing with her whispers.

A whimper escaped Ophelia when she felt the sharp edge of a blade press into the skin at the side of her neck. She clamped her eyes shut and held her breath, anticipating the feel of the dagger breaking her skin, the pain lancing through her, the blood filling her lungs in the agonizing seconds before darkness claimed her.

The whispers stopped.

A heartbeat passed, then the grip on her jaw slackened, and the blade at her throat fell away. The Reaper hit the ground with a *thud,* but it was the spark in her chest that sent her staggering forward. A spark she feared, mere moments ago, she'd never feel engulfing her ever again.

The spark caught flame, and its warmth swelled, filling the yawning emptiness she'd grown so painfully familiar with.

The bonds around her connection to magic burst, and she gasped as her Conexus took back its rightful place within her, settling into a soothing hum beneath her ribs and mending her torn soul.

If you kill the spell's caster, the spell dies with them.

Ophelia's eyes widened before dropping to her shackles. Purple mist released around her as she guided the energy with her will.

A *clink* sounded, and the shackles fell from her wrists.

Chapter Forty Eight

Like a plume of smoke after an explosion, Conexus billowed within Ophelia, charging the air around her with magic. It sparked through her, filling every fissure of her being to overflowing.

She wiggled her fingers against the tiny pinpricks elicited by the returning flow of magic to her limbs and inhaled deeply. The shattered pieces of her soul finally knit back together, and she felt restored, whole, brought back to life.

Screams rang around her, pulling Ophelia back into the present. She whirled around and found chaos unfurling around her. Cries of fear and pain were stark against the backdrop of clanging metal and the eerie chanting of whisper songs.

Her eyes darted across the small clearing. One Reaper lay dead at her feet. The villager at the post next to her dangled by her shackled wrists, blood spilling down the front of her body from the slash across her throat.

Alarm flared through her before she tamped it down and refocused, adrenaline pulling her attention to the clearing where several men fought four Reapers.

A man with red hair wielding a battle axe fought a Reaper five paces in front of her. Marius and a woman fought back-to-back against two others.

Terrified screams pulled her eyes from the fighting to the Balmorean prisoners who stood helplessly chained to the remaining posts.

In her next breath, every shackle clicked open.

"Run to the tree line!" she shouted as she rushed down the line of posts. "Move! Go around the fighting!"

Evren yelled something in Balmorean then grabbed Vanya's hand and yanked her toward the trees. Lyall did the same with his mother, and Allerick followed swiftly behind, but two of the women from the village clung to each other in a heap on the ground. Shock carved their pale faces as they stared wide-eyed at the man who lay before them with a slit throat and unseeing eyes.

Not women—*girls*.

Ophelia knelt in front of them, grabbing their chins in her hand and pulling their faces up to hers. "Run! Move!"

The girls simply stared back at Ophelia, frozen in place. Before Ophelia could protest further, another one of the villagers, a man, ran up to the girls, shouting at them in rushed Balmorean. He clamped a hand around each of their arms, hauling them up to their feet and dragging them into the wood.

Ophelia spun to the fighting, and her heart stuttered when her sight fell on Elliot locked in a fight with one of the Reapers no more than twenty feet away from her. The red-haired man was still fighting, along with Marius and the woman, and a fifth man she hadn't seen before.

Her eyes jumped from group to group, the din of fighting and the blood rushing in her ears muddling her thoughts.

A shout of pain sprung from the redhead, and Ophelia's gaze snapped in his direction to see a blood dagger protruding from his shoulder. He fell to his knees, and the Reaper he was fighting bolted for the tree line, an arm banded across her stomach.

Ophelia ran to the man without another thought until a familiar voice called to her from across the small battlefield.

"Ophelia!"

Time slowed as she whirled toward his voice—the voice that had kept her anchored to her sanity the past few days. The voice that was sunlight at the end of a storm and the warmth of a hearth in the winter. It was whispered promises against heated skin and the peacefulness of home. Her heart took flight when her eyes found him the moment before a Reaper's blade slashed across his chest.

Ophelia screamed as Elliot staggered backward with a shout of pain. She ran towards him, fury lighting her veins as she watched his blood bloom across his tunic.

The Essence within her thrashed, demanding action. It prodded her will, urging her connection to the magic to ignite and eliminate the threat.

It took only a thought.

Purple mist pulsed around her as Ophelia clenched her hands into fists.

"*Enough!*" she shouted, and the remaining four Reapers froze in place.

Blades pierced flesh, blood poured, and the four bodies crumpled to the ground.

Marius and his fighters stood stunned, breaths sawing from their lungs in heavy pants as their minds struggled to comprehend what had just happened.

But all Ophelia saw was Elliot as he rushed toward her and engulfed her in his arms.

A choked sob launched from her throat as she wrapped her arms around him, pulled him close, and buried her nose in his neck. The nightmare she had of him in Raygon's dungeon flashed unbidden through her mind, and she flinched, pulling him closer. She clutched the back of his shirt and pressed her body into his.

Real, whole, alive.

Wetness seeping through her shirt had her drawing back. Her eyes fell to his injury, and she frantically pushed out of his hold.

"Your wound!" she cried, readying her hands over his chest to begin healing him.

In her next breath, his mouth was on hers, his fingers sliding into her hair to pull her back into him. His lips moved desperately against hers, claiming her mouth with such intensity that it lit her from within, and she met his intensity with abandon.

She melted into his kiss and clung to every hitch of his breath and every brush of his lips. From the familiar taste of him on her tongue, to the new scrape of his beard against her cheeks, every sensation solidified his presence to her, allowing the image of him in her heart to grow sharper, more vivid.

Real, alive, here.

This wasn't a dream or a fantasy. That was his heart pounding against her chest, and those were his breaths coasting across her lips. It was his warmth that seeped into her, and it was his body pressed so perfectly against hers.

Alive, alive, alive.

Mere minutes ago, she toed the edge of a blade, certain it would be what forever separated her from him—and she'd never been so thankful for being wrong.

Several moments passed before Ophelia returned to herself and remembered where she was and what had taken place. She pulled back and surveyed the area, taking in the blood and death surrounding them. Her eyes landed on the man across the clearing with the blood dagger in his shoulder, and her stomach dropped. The dagger hadn't liquified, meaning the Reaper who conjured it was still alive—the one who fled.

Fucking coward.

"Marius! One got away!" she shouted as she ran toward the redhead and dropped to her knees before him.

Marius shouted some commands in Balmorean, and a figure darted into the wood.

Ophelia's eyes caught on the silver pendant the wounded man wore around his neck. It was the same as the ones each of the Reapers placed around their necks before taking them the rest of the way to the Aegis. Her brows bent as she took it in her hand.

The circular, silver pendant spanned the breadth of her palm. An intricate border of engraved knots skirted the edge while the profile of a howling wolf was etched into the center. In place of the wolf's eye sat a blood red gem. She ran her thumb across the pendant, and when her skin connected with the gem, a wave of nausea rolled through her. Her eyes widened.

Was this a blood stone?

"Where did you get this?" she asked in Leonese, her mind still a bit too frazzled to attempt the question in Balmorean.

Thankfully, he understood her.

"Melina," he said in a thick accent, nodding toward the person who'd just darted into the wood. "It's a long story, but she got them for us."

Ophelia nodded then dropped the pendant and shifted her focus back to his shoulder.

Marius rushed up behind her, followed by Elliot and the other man in their group.

"What do you need us to do?" Marius asked.

Ophelia looked up to meet his gaze when she caught sight of the Balmorean villagers huddled together at the tree line.

"I will deal with his injury; you should go see to your people," she said, nodding to the villagers. "If I'm not mistaken, those are the very first people to ever survive a Silent Reaping. They're very scared, and being this close to the Aegis is likely still causing them distress. You should lead them farther away from it." Her gaze caught on the man and woman lying dead near the wooden posts, and a pang shot through her chest. "They will also want to see to their dead."

Marius nodded, then he and the other man stood and made their way toward the people gathered at the tree line. Ophelia returned her focus to the injured man.

"What's your name?" she asked him as she took in his injury.

"Dax," he said.

"Well, Dax. She landed high and wide," Ophelia said to him. "Looks like Lady Luck favored you today."

The man snorted. "The fuck she did. There's a fucking dagger sticking out of my shoulder if you hadn't noticed."

Ophelia's lips quirked upwards as her eyes roved over Dax's injury, working through a plan to dislodge the dagger and heal him. "That Reaper was undoubtedly aiming for your heart, and Reapers don't miss their targets." She flicked her eyes to his. "I'd call it luck that she did."

He shrugged his uninjured shoulder. "I'd say that speaks more to my agility as a fighter than to the influence of luck."

An exasperated sigh rose from Elliot, and Ophelia chuckled.

"Then we will drink to your agility once we leave this awful place." A smile spread across her face, and Elliot groaned beside her.

"Don't encourage him, Elia."

She slowly moved her palm to grip the handle of the dagger as Dax barked a laugh. "I need no encouragement! I—"

Ophelia wrenched the dagger from his shoulder and slammed her other palm to his wound. A flurry of colorful curses flew from Dax's lips as his blood seeped through her fingers. Elliot swiftly sat on Dax's legs to hold him down as purple mist poured from Ophelia's palms.

She held her focus to his wound, imagining the tissue knitting back together and picturing smooth, unmarred skin.

Dax writhed, crying out as the torn flesh tugged and pulled itself back together. The other man ran back to them, dropping to the ground behind Dax and wrapping himself around the man's arms and torso.

"Why does it fucking *burn*?!" Dax ground out.

Alarm rose inside Ophelia—it had never been painful for others when she'd healed them before.

What she wouldn't give for some of Gaius's wine right now.

"Almost done, Dax," the man said.

"Fuck you, Hayes!" Dax panted.

"Don't tempt me with a good time," Hayes drawled as he tightened his hold around Dax's arms.

Minutes passed before Ophelia finally pulled her hand from Dax's shoulder and sighed with relief.

"Done," she said as she wiped Dax's blood from her hands in the grass. Dax slumped against Hayes's chest. Sweat beaded along his brow, and he sucked in several deep breaths before raising his palm to Hayes's cheek and patting it twice.

"And here I thought Elliot and the princeling were spouting horse shit," he said. "She does have magic. And it's purple!"

Hayes released Dax then stood, reaching down to help him up, which he did with a groan. The next moment, Elliot had Ophelia back in his arms, pulling her as close as his injury would allow.

"And just like that, I'm completely forgotten, Hayes," Dax teased, yanking them from the moment. "I almost died a mere five minutes ago!"

Hayes rolled his eyes and ushered Dax toward the wood to join up with Marius and the rescued prisoners. "What, did you think she healed you because she wanted to stick her tongue down *your* throat?" Hayes tsked. "I knew you were stupid but—" Dax cut him off with a punch to the arm. He snapped back at Hayes with some sharp remark, but Ophelia didn't hear it over the thrumming of her heart. Relief crashed over her as she sank into the hazel depths of Elliot's eyes, and she took her first deep breath in days.

Elliot rested his forehead to Ophelia's and took a steadying breath, the vice that had been clamped around his heart loosening with each long pull of air he took and with each inch closer he drew her.

They'd gotten to her in time, he chanted in his mind, hoping that if he said it enough, his heart and mind would finally come to heel.

Their group may have arrived in time to intervene and save her, but only just.

Elliot had never knocked and shot an arrow faster than the moment he arrived at the clearing and saw a dagger poised at Ophelia's throat. Fear and anger had sharpened his focus and narrowed his vision. He'd aimed and loosed in one breath, not lingering for a second on how taking a life had never been so easy for him.

"We almost didn't make it in time," he whispered, snapping his eyes shut against the reality of his own words. "I thought I'd—" his breath caught on the words. He swallowed. "I thought I'd lost you."

She pulled back and cupped his face in her palms, piercing him with her ice blue eyes.

"You didn't," she replied.

"It was too close." He leaned down to kiss her again, needing the reassurance of her touch, needing to feel her warm lips against his, her soft curves against him. He slid his hands around her hips and tugged her flush against him, unable to stand any distance between them, but she resisted. Her gaze flicked down to his chest and worry painted her brow.

"It's really deep. Will you let me heal it now?"

She began raising her palms back to his chest when he took hold of her hands and shook his head.

"Not now. Yes, it's deep in some places, but I'm not in mortal danger. We'll worry about it later." He raised her hands to loop around his neck and drew her closer. "You were a moment from death less than an hour ago, and I just need to hold you right now."

The injury was painful, and would be a bitch to heal, but the pain was manageable and the fatigue from blood loss minimal. He probably had some lingering adrenaline pumping through him which helped in that regard, but healing him could wait. He needed a moment where he could simply be with her and finally catch his breath.

Understanding lit her eyes, and she nodded, though the bend in her brow didn't ease. She needed this too, he realized— to simply be near him, touch him, hold him, *feel* him.

He swept his hands around her waist and tugged her closer. She was careful not to press her chest against his injury and slid her palms to his cheeks. She ran her fingers through his beard, then down his neck and across his shoulders. The tension in her body seemed to ease with each passing moment, taking with it the tension in his body as well.

He stared down at her and took her in a moment longer before her sense of duty as Vilicus of Mankind pulled her from his hold. Earth and Sea, she was so beautiful. Even with a battered soul and a weary heart, her beauty stole his breath.

She stepped out of his arms and reached for his hand. Her worried gaze flicked to his wound as she slid her hands into his.

He gave her hand a reassuring squeeze. "I'm fine."

She nodded and took a deep breath before turning her attention to the Aegis with a frown. She stepped towards it, Elliot close behind her and holding tightly to her hand.

"What are you looking for?" he asked.

"I'm not sure," she replied before releasing his hand. She took another step towards the barrier and tilted her head to the side as she considered it.

A gasp slipped from Elliot's throat as white-hot agony tore through his torso, taking him to his hands and knees. He dropped his eyes to the source and found the point of a blood spike jutting from his chest just below his collar bone. His body quaked at the fresh wave of pain that washed over him, causing his lungs to spasm and a wave of nausea to roll through him.

This couldn't be happening.

He strained to lift his head to find Ophelia, his vision spotting at the edges as he scoured the area for her familiar form.

"Ophelia!" he rasped through labored breaths, and she whirled around at his distress.

The Reaper drove the spike further through his flesh, and searing pain eviscerated his right shoulder, his fingers growing numb and his arms trembling under his weight.

Ophelia's eyes blew wide as the Reaper's strides ate up the handful of steps between them.

She had *seconds*.

Step.

He shouted her name.

Step.

Her eyes met his, and his heart twisted at the sadness and resignation he found swimming in their ice blue depths with devastating clarity. *No, no, no—*

Step.

Elliot roared as he lurched toward her, the sight of her blurring against the answering pain radiating through his body. The Reaper crashed into Ophelia, sending them both careening headfirst into the Aegis.

"No!"

His voice evaporated against the sound of crunching bone as Ophelia and the Reaper disappeared through the barrier.

A choked sob escaped his throat before his body collapsed.

Then his vision went black.

ACKNOWLEDGEMENTS

I didn't think writing a second book would be so different from writing a first book, and, naturally, I was entirely wrong. I knew where I wanted this story to go and how I wanted it to end, but the words didn't flow like they did for *TVM*. Finding time to write with a full-time job and full-time family added to the struggle on top of life insisting on lifing really hard at me.

I began writing this book in the spring of 2022, right before I graduated with my master's degree and made a big career change. I then fell into a deep depression that, with the help and support of dear friends, family, and my doctor, finally began to fade toward the end of the summer. Then, a week before I started my new job, my father unexpectedly passed away.

Some great things did happen in 2022, but it was not a great time for me.

I trudged on, then in March 2023 my flash drive broke, causing me to lose 30,000 words that I'd fought so hard to write. I was so defeated and felt like the universe didn't want this book to happen. So, I let myself have a good mope, gave the universe the middle finger, and kept writing. I found early versions of a few chapters and scenes I'd shared with alpha readers and author friends but did end up having to rewrite several chapters—one of which was one of the most difficult scenes I'd ever written. It was arduous and exhausting and made me feel like I was walking backward on one of those moving sidewalks at the airport, but it happened, and I'm actually really proud of how it all turned out.

Writing took a back seat in 2023 when focus shifted to getting *The Violet Mage* published. I didn't dive back into drafting book 2 until 2024, then it took me the entire rest of the year to finish the story (see my first paragraph for more details on why it took so freaking long).

By the first week of January 2025, my first draft of *The Silent Reaping* was finally done, and I nearly wept with relief. So much of my heart went into this book over the three years it took me to finish it, and I'm so proud of how it turned out.

As always, though, I would never have been able to get TSR out into the world without the help and support of a few people who are dear to me.

Thank you to my beta readers Sarah, Michelle, Rae, Prerna, and Jennifer for taking the time to read through this story and help me make it better. Your honesty and enthusiasm were so encouraging and invaluable to me!

Thank you, Michelle, for all the writing meet ups, for brainstorming and hashing out ideas with me—for smiling and nodding as I chattered through all my thoughts at you. You deserve all the gold stars, and I'm so thankful for you.

Thank you, Kody, for being my backbone through all of this. From herding the girls away from the office so I could write in peace, to watching the girls at home so I could go somewhere else to write in peace. Through every stumbling block, heartache, and victory, you were at my back, believing in me. I'd never want to do any of this without you, and I love you so much it's disgusting.

And, finally, thank you, dear reader—especially if you made it this far. Thank you so much for picking up a book by an indie author, giving it a go, then hopping on this crazy train to join me for the ride. I'm so immensely thankful you are here and I desperately hope you love this next installment in Ophelia's journey. Thank you from the bottom of my highly caffeinated heart. Please don't hate me for that ending.

About the Author

L.R. POWELL is a Texas-native who's obsessed with fantasy and romance books and drinks entirely too much coffee. She lives with her family in the Houston area and works in education. When she isn't reading, writing, or working, you can find her chasing around her two small humans or catching up on her favorite anime or Star Wars shows with her husband.

CONNECT WITH L.R. POWELL

TikTok and Instagram - *@l.r.powell.author*
Website - *lrpowellbooks.com*

To get all the exciting news and bonus content first, sign up for L.R. Powell's newsletter at the QR code here!